THE
WIFE'S
HOUSE

ARIANNE RICHMONDE

THE
WIFE'S
HOUSE

bookouture

Published by Bookouture in 2020

An imprint of Storyfire Ltd.
Carmelite House
50 Victoria Embankment
London EC4Y 0DZ

www.bookouture.com

ISBN: 978-1-83888-951-7
eBook ISBN: 978-1-83888-950-0

For Betty Kramer, with so much love.

They always say if Big Sur wants you, it'll keep you.
If it doesn't, it'll spit you out.

Jeanne Crowley, ex-manager of Deetjen's Big Sur Inn

CHAPTER ONE

One was my lucky number. Until I became a widow.

It had been six months. Six months and three days of living alone without my husband. We were supposed to spend our whole lives together, but I had lost him like a pebble to a wave. The slow trickle of singlehood seeped inside my bones, soaking into my skin, bleeding into my organs, making my heart thud heavy and low. Pounding out the words:

Widow.

Widow.

Widow.

Standing on the sweeping bay below my house, I lifted my eyes to the horizon. Another smashing breaker brought the tide in closer. I tasted the ocean spray on my lips, and the mist fizzled with tiny diamonds as it spooled off the rolling surf. A pod of pelicans flew in neat couples and torpedoed into the water, their sword-like beaks vertical as they fished their prey. I envied them. Even they had mates.

With cold sand oozing between my toes, I turned my head and gazed up at my house upon the cliff, cleverly camouflaged and nearly a mile away.

My house. It sat majestic, yet low and discreet, melding organically into the rocky cliffside, its great glass walls reflecting the mother-of-pearl sky. Modern, and sleek, and almost invisible. The first time my husband showed me Cliffside, I was standing in this exact spot.

"You like it?" Juan had asked, pointing up at the cliffs.

"The view is stunning."

"I'm talking about the house up there," Juan said, laughing in a way that made you believe you were the only person he cared to be with, the only one. "That's why I love that house so much, because nobody even knows it's there till they *know*. You can't get houses like that around here anymore. They won't give planning permission; you can't even buy the land, however much money you have. It's in the middle of a national park. A one-off. Unique. It comes with four acres of private woods. See it?"

At first I thought he was pulling my leg. "I see those tall trees but not the house. Am I blind?"

"The roof's covered in lawn and it's hidden by cedars and redwoods. See?" He pointed, his slim finger an arrow to the spot. "You can catch a glimpse of the big stone pillar to the left. It's a once in a lifetime house; there are none like it in the world. Its name is Cliffside." He sighed and then looked at me, his eyes flickering with steely intent. Or perhaps it was amusement. "I'm going to get you that house, sweetheart," he said. "I promise."

As if by magic, the sun emerged from behind a wisp of a cloud, and the house's great glass walls shone brilliant in its wake. Golden streams of light glazed its honey-colored stone pillars, and a hawk flew overhead and then swooped down onto its grass roof, as if to train my eyes, to make me focus exactly where it desired me to look.

"Is it even for sale?" I asked.

"No, but watch me make an offer they can't refuse. I'll get you that house."

I smiled. "How do you know?"

"Because I do."

I didn't pry any further, having learned through enough stony silences that Juan liked to keep little secrets concerning business deals. Perhaps a client of his was selling and he'd get a great bargain. Juan was a master at negotiating.

In that moment I imagined myself at Cliffside's crown, sitting on one of its decks or patios, my shoulders proud, scanning the coastline, where waves are beaten every day to foamy froth on ragged rocks. Above the house, great oaks and redwoods reared up, standing tall between the Santa Lucia mountain range and the ocean, as if Cliffside were some splendid jewel glinting in the sun, held fast between these two great feats of nature.

"I'd do anything to live there," I said, giddy at the thought of owning such a place.

Juan looked at me hard for a second but then broke into a smile. "Anything?"

I didn't respond. But he was right to ask.

As I was about to set off back home, I heard that familiar hornet's nest hum, high in the sky, hovering maybe a hundred feet above me. There it was again. A drone. This coastline was famous; Big Sur was a magnet for travel bloggers, YouTubers, and Instagrammers, but this was the third time in the same week. The beach was empty, there were no hikers in the woods, at least none that I could see. So who was operating it? And from where? As I craned my neck and followed the drone with my eyes, it disappeared behind the trees, towards Highway One.

The sudden buzz of my cell phone made me jump. I whipped it out from my jacket pocket, and the rush of adrenaline, when I read the anonymous text, jolted me further out of my skin.

I'LL BE WATCHING YOU.

My pulse picked up. A coincidence that this text came seconds after I'd spotted the drone? No, that drone was spying on me. Spying on my house, my garden.

My woods.

I'd call the police. Could they trace an anonymous text? No, I'd get a pistol and shoot the drone down. Drive into Monterey, to the gun store. Buy something small and discreet. And yet I had no idea how to use a firearm. Where I came from, no law-abiding citizens had guns, unless they hunted pheasant or were members of a shooting club. And I needed to be careful. Since my husband's death, I'd been making foolish decisions. Buying stuff I didn't need, not being able to follow my instincts, losing and misplacing things, my brain scatty and unfocused. I couldn't rely on myself to do the right thing. It's a strange feeling when you can't trust your intuition anymore. I was a cat without whiskers, a black sky without stars.

I wanted to call Juan and ask his advice. That had happened a lot lately. I couldn't accept he was dead. Kept thinking he'd stride through the front door any moment. The man who had an answer to everything.

I stuck the phone back in my jacket pocket and tightened my pink silk scarf around my neck. I had read somewhere that pink makes people like you more, so I had taken to wearing a lot of pink since I'd been grieving. Every smile counted, every kind human connection, even from strangers.

As I began my hike back home, determination fueling my resolve to buy a gun and shoot that drone down, I spotted a lovely family with their baby on the beach—the baby in one of those carriers on her dad's back, giggling with joy. They would have hiked to get down here, as there was no access by car. Busy with their baby, they were definitely not the drone operators. My heart ached to see such happiness.

I could have had a family like that if it had all worked out.

I had considered going to visit my parents and friends back home in England, but I couldn't face them all feeling sorry for me. That soulful, big-eyed, "Are you all right" look. The look that isn't even accompanied by words but just says it all. Besides,

Big Sur was my home; I found it hard to imagine life back in Britain, even for just a visit. Who *wouldn't* want to live here, so at one with nature? It just might be the most stunning, unspoiled coastline in the world. California was home. I may not have lost my accent, but I was integrated here.

And Cliffside was my last link to Juan. I would never leave.

I would never leave my house.

CHAPTER TWO

I raced back, peeled off my hiking clothes, took a quick shower and changed into a pink cashmere sweater and some jeans and loafers. Got in my Land Rover and set off to Carmel-by-the-Sea, my local town, a good forty-five-minute drive along the winding Pacific Coast Highway.

People didn't live along this coast for convenience, that's for sure. Whole Foods was over an hour away. We residents learned to stock up our freezers and we all had generators, just in case. Living here wasn't for sissies, however much money you had. And now with my husband gone, I craved company. Neighbors were dotted here and there, but even along this fifty-mile stretch of coast, there weren't more than five hundred residents in all. Carmel was the nearest hub of activity—great for people-watching. Family-watching. Something I knew would calm my nerves before I braved it into the gun store in Monterey. Yet the idea of owning a weapon terrified me. Shouldn't I learn to shoot first? Under supervision? Or just get the damn thing? What if having a gun was more dangerous than not having one? If I didn't know what I was doing, someone could snatch it clean from my hands and use it against me. The drone operator, for instance. The thought of having a loaded weapon in my home made my stomach fold over. But if not loaded at all times, at all hours, what was the point of having one at all?

I never tired of this iconic coastal drive. On some days, if you stopped the car on one of the little layovers, you could spot so many sea lions or harbor seals on the beach below that you might mistake them for rocks. There were sea otters, sometimes, too, now a protected species, floating on their backs among dense beds of kelp.

The highway was still slick from yesterday's rain, with deep red earth squelching down the banks that flanked the road.

It had rained cats and dogs this autumn. It wasn't normal.

The canyons rose above me on my right, and to the left, the raw coastal wilderness of pines and redwoods, with the ocean beyond. Buzzing open the window, I let in the aroma of wild sage and tangy salt.

As I approached Carmel, my appreciation swelled. What a perfect American town. Clint Eastwood came to mind. Doris Day. Quaint boutiques tailored from pretty pastel Hansel and Gretel cottages. A picture postcard, this town seemed to me, with its endless art galleries set amongst perfect little streets fringed by wispy cypress trees. A veritable movie set.

Once I found parking, I installed myself in a discreet spot on the outside terrace of a corner café, ordered a club sandwich and Perrier, but then changed my mind and asked for a white wine. I checked the messages on my phone, hoping that somehow it was all in my head, that the next time I looked I'd realize it was my imagination, a trick of the eye. But no, it was still there, looming at me:

I'LL BE WATCHING YOU.

My stomach dipped.

The waiter reappeared. "Ma'am, would you like another wine? Your club sandwich will be right with you."

"Yes, please," I replied distractedly.

The waiter went away, and my attention was now caught by a couple in their late twenties. "Why didn't you pick up, then?"

the man was asking, fire in his eyes. The woman shrugged. I knew they'd be having sex later. A jealous man is a good thing. Not too jealous, though, but a touch possessive. It keeps the flame alight. My heart skittered with vicarious longing, wondering why I hadn't just stayed home with my melancholy view, wondering why I was punishing myself by watching other people's happy moments. Family moments.

Six months and three days without Juan.

The sun glided out from behind a cloud, and I was lit up out of the shadows, more so than I wished.

"Guess who?" a breathy voice said as a pair of sticky hot hands blindfolded my eyes, jolting me from my reverie. They smelled of stale cigarettes smoked on the sly.

Pippa. The last person I wanted to see.

"Hi, Pippa," I said, without even turning around.

She sat down opposite me, plunking her Prada handbag on the empty chair beside her. "Finally found a parking space," she said huskily. "Not easy with my bloody big new car, I can tell you."

I had to give it to her—despite a long-jawed face, Pippa was not unattractive. Glossy, almost black, shoulder-length hair, and chompy white teeth that always showed when she smiled. She smiled a lot. There was something homey about her. People tended to divulge their secrets to Pippa, without her even asking. She was Juan's best friend, from way back. I'd forgotten how they'd met.

"What a coincidence," I said, "to see you here."

"You've finally come out of your gilded cage." A wide grin crept across Pippa's face. "The bird hasn't got clipped wings after all. So now you're out and about, darling, why don't we have dinner sometime? Catch up."

"Maybe." I smiled at her, but my mind was still with the drone. I said, to make conversation, "So you bought a new car?"

"Yes, but I still keep the old Toyota in case of emergencies. You were *rash*, darling, to let go of Juan's lovely white Range Rover after he died. One needs a second car round here. And going around in that cranky old Land Rover of yours on these treacherous wet roads is a tad risqué, don't you think?"

"It's very reliable, actually. And I feel safer with gears than with an automatic on those hairpin bends."

Pippa's eyes glazed over for a moment, and before I could read into her odd expression (was she still in love with him?), she looked down and put her hand on mine and squeezed it.

"You're right," I said. "I should get a second car."

Being British like me, Pippa thought we were in some sort of cozy club. Just because she was Juan's friend didn't make her mine, but since his death she had made a huge effort to "look after" me. The fact I didn't reciprocate hadn't dampened her ardor. "We understand each other," she'd say, "we're from the same world." And I'd think, *No, Pippa, we are not from the same world. You have no idea who I am. No idea at all.*

Pippa worked as a freelance journalist—hard to keep at bay and dangerous to know. The last thing I needed was Pippa squeezing information out of me. She was clever; asked too many questions. I hadn't bargained on bumping into her today.

Rifling through her Prada bag and taking out some ChapStick, which she applied to her generous lips, she said, "How *are* you, darling?" Her eyes raked down my body with scrutiny. Pippa was always comparing other women's bodies to her own. She was probably envious that I'd lost a few pounds, or thought I was too scrawny and needed fattening up.

"I'm fine," I replied. "Doing great."

She gave me the "Poor you" look.

"Honestly, I'm doing really well," I said. "Can't mope around, got to get on with life, you know."

"It's been tough, hasn't it?"

"Yes," I admitted. "It has."

"You must be so lonely up there in that massive see-through house. Especially at night. Have you thought of selling?"

"No," I said flatly.

"What about getting a dog?"

I was almost tempted to tell Pippa about the drone and the text, but I laid my tongue gently between my front teeth and squeezed till it hurt, to stop myself blabbing information I'd regret later. "I can't, Pippa. I've told you before. Allergies, remember? I can't do dogs or cats, as much as I'd love to."

"What about a poodle, darling, or a Labradoodle or whatever they're called?"

"It's not about the fur type, it's the dander," I explained, my voice stonier than I wished.

"Don't you get scared living up on that cliff, all alone?"

"That's what my mother always asks me. But no, not really, although lately…" I halted the rest of my sentence.

"What? What were you going to say?"

"Just—well, I actually had in mind to buy a handgun today but then thought better of it. I'd need to learn how to shoot first, and the whole idea scares the crap out of me."

She laughed. "I know what you mean, darling. I did a couple of classes once, years ago. Thought it was fun, you know, the thrill of having the 'right to bear arms' and stuff. Even bought myself a little pocket Smith & Wesson. Then I regretted it. Kept meaning to take the gun back to the shop and get my money back, but I lost the receipt. So it just drives around with me in the car, sitting in the glove compartment. Actually, it's still in the old Toyota—I'm too scared to even touch it. English girls and guns don't really mix, do they, darling?"

"Not so much."

"Never did bring that pistol into the house, felt it might jinx things, you know, attract a burglar or something." Pippa made a pyramid with the tips of her fingers. Then she fastened her eyes on mine, her smile replaced all of a sudden by the sad, "Poor you" look again. "You can't get him off your mind, can you?"

My cheeks flushed, and I heard my own breathing, hot in my ears. "I'd rather not talk about Juan, if you don't mind."

"Course. Sorry."

It always annoyed me that Pippa felt she had carte blanche when it came to discussing Juan, simply because they had been old friends. Somewhere between the lines I read a different message: had they dated? He always denied it, but even if they were romantically involved, it didn't matter. Pippa thought he was the greatest thing since sliced bread and never held back letting me know her feelings. I bet she wondered what gorgeous Juan ever saw in plain little me.

We sat in silence. Just the bustle of people walking by, the clicking of expensive heels, the bark of a happy dog with its owners, another couple sickeningly in love. The woman had a newborn in her arms. The baby was wearing pink, the same blush-pink as my sweater. I followed them wistfully with my gaze and pushed back the lump in my throat.

"I bet you really pine for him," Pippa went on.

I stared at her. Why was she tormenting me? Why was she so fixated on the husband I'd lost?

I observed her with her long slim face. Smiling away. She was one of those people who always seemed jolly, although with her recent divorce I couldn't imagine she felt a hundred percent. The truth was, I knew very little about her. She lived in Carmel Highlands in a rather fancy house, which, she told me, would have to be sold and the money split two ways. Like me she was childless, but I had always got the impression that in her case, it was by choice. Her husband was in real estate, so must have made a lot, and I wondered why she wasn't getting the house as part of her alimony. But she had hinted at moving abroad and starting again. I hadn't pried, because I didn't want to get too close. Just because we were from the same country shouldn't be a prerequisite for being friends, so I always kept her at a distance. Strangely, as buddy-buddy as she and Juan had been in their twenties, she didn't seem to miss him much now.

"So you've been busy with plans for your hotel idea, have you?" she said, after I'd pointedly ignored her comment. "How's it all coming along?"

It wasn't a hotel, but a retreat. After Juan died, I came up with the idea. Something to stave off the loneliness. To keep me occupied. Even though he had traveled a lot, negotiating mergers and big real estate deals all over the world—his work as one of the country's top attorneys had been all-consuming—I didn't experience a feeling of solitude when he was away. We'd do video calls and he was just a text or email from my fingertips. After I lost him, I thought by hosting a retreat at Cliffside it would busy me, since I'd given up my job at Juan's firm when we'd moved here to California from New York. Perhaps it would make me feel better about not having children, too—the company, that feeling of human connection.

Cliffside wouldn't host just any old retreat. I'd invite interesting people to study yoga, eat healthy food, and take painting or poetry classes, all under one roof, with the backdrop of the ocean serving as inspiration. I had thought of adding an extension to the house in the same style. All the rooms would stay unique. None of that generic stuff you find in faceless, expensive hotels. Mine would be all bespoke furniture and sumptuous bed linen from France. Most of the stuff already in the house had been included in the sale, but I wanted to put my stamp on the place. I'd buy some of those double-thick bath towels that cost an arm and a leg.

I thought of that expression often, "Costs an arm and a leg." Juan had told me that in Spanish they say, "Costs a kidney," not an arm and a leg. Nice expression, either way, for describing something expensive.

If only he'd known.

"It's not going to be a hotel, exactly," I explained to Pippa. "More like a retreat. I've applied for the permits—there's all the renovation work to think about, adding bathrooms and stuff. But I'm, you know, reluctant to change things. A part of me wants to keep everything exactly as it is."

I didn't want to go into detail. Especially as I now questioned the whole thing anyway. Even if the guests were scintillating and I could cherry-pick the clients, I was wary of sharing my house with people who might not appreciate its uniqueness. Cliffside was too close to my heart.

"You should *sell*, darling," Pippa said. "I mean, that house must be worth a *fortune*. You'd never have to do a day's work in your life again. You could retire young. Not to mention that massive life insurance payout you got and the inheritance from Juan."

I flinched at the mention of the life insurance money. "I'm only thirty-seven! I like working, I like being busy. I've got a part-time job, actually, just three days a week, helping an elderly gentleman called Mr. Donner sort out his estate. He told me he doesn't want his assets gobbled up by Uncle Sam so needs a lawyer to put everything in order, in case he 'gets run over by a bus,' he says."

Pippa cocked her head. "Good for you getting a new job. Lucky that Juan had sorted his will out before he died, don't you think?"

Silence. I regretted bringing the subject of wills up.

But Pippa steered the conversation back to Juan again. "It's just that you could start afresh, darling, and do something completely new. Not have him haunting you."

Him? How dare she! I didn't even know why I was letting her sit at my table. "What are you saying, Pippa?"

"You could start dating again, darling. Start anew. Sam the contractor, for instance. He's very cute, don't you think?"

Her words were so shocking I was left speechless. I blinked away an unbidden tear then wiped the wet from my cheek with the mound of my hand. It was Pippa who had introduced me to this contractor. He had come to Cliffside on several occasions to discuss the extension. On too many occasions, for my liking. He had flirted and made me extremely uncomfortable. And then he wouldn't stop calling. Pushing me for an answer, to sign his contract, to "get to know each other over a good Bordeaux." I hated being a widow and living alone. Nobody had dared behave that way with me when Juan was around.

"Darling, you need to move on," Pippa whispered, her hand slipping over mine again as I clutched my empty wine glass.

The young waiter arrived with my food, smiled and said something about enjoying my meal. Probably an out-of-work actor who had strayed north from Los Angeles during the summer and somehow got stuck here, disillusion snapping at his young heels.

Pippa picked at one of my French fries, so I pushed the whole plate over in her direction. I felt nauseous at the thought of getting into a heavy conversation with her. She would press my buttons. I didn't trust her.

"You eat this, Pippa. I'm not hungry anymore." I pulled out a crisp one hundred-dollar bill from my wallet and stuck it under my wine glass. "I'm going home. Sorry, I just don't feel like baring my soul right now. Please give the waiter all the change for his tip." I got up, and before Pippa had a chance to protest, I had walked away.

CHAPTER THREE

It was that little baby all in baby-pink—in Carmel—that perfect couple's baby, with its big, watery blue eyes—that really got me falling into a spiral of despair over the next couple of weeks that followed. I'd agonized about that a lot lately. What color eyes our baby would have had. I pictured Juan's cerulean eyes edged with thick black lashes, which would sometimes make actual shadows on his cheeks. The sort of lashes only children have, although Juan's face was decidedly masculine, with his strong jawline and straight, almost aquiline nose. But then again, perhaps our baby might have had nondescript eyes like mine.

With one more year of trying we could have done it, surely? That was all I had asked. But, no, that chance was snatched away from me. It wasn't that I begrudged them—these lovely, perfect young couples with perfect babies dressed in blue or pink—but it was like having all your failures blown up on a giant neon billboard, lit up, on the corner of a building in Times Square, or Piccadilly Circus. In the olden days, I would have been labeled infertile or even "barren." Nobody said those words anymore, but I bet they felt them. Thought them secretly. Even if it was, in fact, Juan's fault we didn't have children.

I needed to wipe all these what ifs out of my head. The baby that never happened. Juan. My secret. The sadness. The shell of what I'd become.

Most of all, my secret.

*

I kicked off my shoes and padded upstairs to the bedroom: my sanctuary, where the beautiful ocean view could distract my thoughts. Set back only twelve or so feet from the bluff, the house's position made me feel like I was suspended in mid-air.

I sat cross-legged on my fluffy white rug—a gift Juan had brought me back from Mexico one time—and flipped open my laptop, bringing back to life old pages I'd bookmarked before his accident. Adoption agencies.

I stared at a little boy with melty blue eyes and dark hair—a dead ringer for a mini Juan, and I sighed in defeat. There was no way I'd ever go through with this, even if I hadn't felt like danger lurked around every corner. I wasn't the type to journey this alone. Being a single parent? A friend of mine was doing it back in England and was quietly miserable.

Deep down inside me, a little rage bubbled. I was alone, abandoned, just when I needed my husband most. And his lies and secrets sat like heartburn thick in my throat.

Juan had been trying to steer me away from the adoption idea. Said we had a chance of conceiving naturally. I knew that wasn't true. But I hadn't wanted to push him.

The helpless look in the little boy's eyes made me slam my laptop shut. My mind wandered back to the drone, the anonymous text, back to the gun dilemma. I never did make it to the gun store after I bumped into Pippa in Carmel, two weeks ago. I figured in the state I was in, it was dangerous for me to possess a weapon. Perhaps I'd been foolish, as now I sat alone, vulnerable, with no means to protect myself.

My hands shaking, I needed to calm my nerves. Crates of champagne were sitting in the basement, still waiting for our house-warming party—the party we never got round to throw-

ing. Juan and I had only been here a couple of weeks before his
accident. It had taken me a while to open up one of the crates of
Mumm, to finally admit the party was never going to happen, that
Juan was gone for good. We had enough of the stuff, and who else
was going to drink it besides me? I'd been stashing it for a rainy
day, and it had been—both figuratively and literally—pouring.

"So you know nothing about wine?" That was what Juan
had asked me on our first dinner date. I felt so uneducated, so
uncool. But he loved it. I think he saw himself as a sort of Henry
Higgins with me. The mousy-haired English girl he could teach
and mentor.

"I'm afraid not," I admitted, smoothing my boring corduroy
skirt over my knobbly knees and wishing I'd dressed more
flamboyantly for our first date. I wanted to tell him I was used
to drinking no more than half a pint of beer with my mates
down the pub, or at best, a vodka tonic, but I was too shy. Too
intimidated by his laser-blue eyes and flashing, fast-as-a-gunshot
smile. No man this handsome had ever paid me such attention.

"We've got all the time in the world," he'd said, "for you to
learn about wine."

All the time in the world. Well, he was wrong about that. I
could taste the bitter tang on my tongue now.

I slipped downstairs, emptied a bottle of Mumm into a big
old Thermos and set off for my daily hike down to the beach.

I wondered if the drone operator would be back. I hadn't seen
it since that day it coincided with the anonymous text, a couple
of weeks ago.

I laced my sneakers up tighter and surveyed the dramatic
seascape below. The rumpled ocean curled its waves on the rocky
coastline before it smoothed out to the beautiful, sweeping bay.

Reaching the shoreline half an hour later, I was a little breath-
less from my hasty walk. The twisty path wound itself beneath

Douglas firs and dipped through a redwood grove, in some places so steep and rocky I had to watch my step. Once on the beach, I needed to make sure I had enough time before the tide gushed in. Any later, and I'd be up to my knees; it would be a scramble to get back before being swept out to sea.

There was no sign of a drone on the walk down. What a relief. The backpack baby and her parents were nowhere to be seen, either. The beach looked eerily empty this afternoon, with the pearly mist bouncing off the waves like dry ice.

I took off my shoes to feel the sand beneath my feet, but it was glacially cold. At the eve of winter it was a little mad to go barefoot, but it made me feel alive. Feeling alive was something I no longer took for granted. I could never get enough of this restless foamy ocean. Never tire of its haunting, mystical beauty, the salty spray running along my skin, the hairs on my arms lifting with its chill. I needed to feel it: the sand between my toes, sucking at my heels with every slam of every ceaseless wave, reminding me that some things would never die. The tide. The rising of the moon. The sun setting in the west.

I heard a distant harbor seal bark and the sound of a guitar gliding on the wind. As I turned the bend in the bay, I spied—in the distance—a group of young people. Not children, not adults, and not even typical teenagers. I can't explain it; they had an ethereal quality about them, especially amidst the swirling mist, as if they were floating on air. I could make out two girls of almost equal height and a boy, quite a bit taller.

I pulled out my binoculars. The trio had the same faces: almost heart-shaped; one of the girls was a brunette, the other had cool, long blond hair, and the boy's was a shade somewhere between the two, half covering his face. The blonde with long hair was playing a guitar. Siblings? Maybe twentyish, maybe more. The guitar girl wore a dress—long—like a Laura Ashley design from the 1970s. Flowery and floaty. She looked like she'd stepped out of the movie set of *Picnic at Hanging Rock* or a vintage clothing shop. The other girl's hair was cut in a neat dark bob, hip and stylish. She was wearing a black catsuit. Exactly the sort of bohemian, arty types I had imagined as guests at my would-be retreat.

And here they were now, having a picnic, the girl strumming a guitar; it made me ache with longing.

I didn't want to stalk or seem like some sort of peeping Tom, so I spun my gaze around in a semicircle pretending, with my binoculars, to look at hawks circling above the pine trees. Occasionally, you might spot a California condor, and that was particularly thrilling considering the species had once been threatened. The wind whipped my hair across my face into my mouth, and the saltiness of the breeze took my breath away for an instant, causing me to gulp air.

Lowering my binoculars, I glanced behind me, up towards my house.

As I watched, I saw—I swear I saw—a figure, tinier than my thumbnail, dashing across Cliffside's garden. The facade of my house faced the ocean—the cliff a sheer drop below—but to the side stretched my lawn, and behind that several acres of woods, where maybe someone had broken through. How? I lifted the binoculars to my eyes again to make sure I wasn't imagining things (a big bird? a deer?) but got them all twisted up in my hair. When I focused again, whatever, whoever it was had vanished. The fear of being spied upon rose up inside me again, the notion I was alone without my husband. Vulnerable. Exposed. I hadn't realized how dependent I had become on Juan, how much I had grown to rely on him for even the smallest things. When we met he was my boss and somehow that had translated into our marriage, too. Being so in love, so smitten, I had lost myself to him, lost sight of my own strength, my core. Like Cliffside, I had become almost camouflaged and saw myself through him.

I pushed my salty hair from my eyes and refocused the binoculars in the direction of the picnickers, but they had left—just a dip in the sand where their tartan blanket had been.

Then I remembered that to quench my thirst I had drunk nearly a whole Thermos flask of champagne on the hike down.

Was the figure in my garden my imagination?

CHAPTER FOUR

Even before I unlocked the door of my house, I knew something was up. When I got inside, I sensed there had been a visitor. A whiff of something. Perfume? Men's cologne? A frisson shimmied up my spine, but I had Dutch courage from the champagne. If someone had it in their mind to kill me off or rape me, they would've done it by now. And there was no sign of a break-in. No smashed furniture or pictures flung from walls. Everything was exactly in its place. No, this person was after something else.

This person was playing with my mind.

Watching me, seeing if I'd slip up.

My heart plunged. How the hell did they—he, or she—get in here? The driveway gate had a code, which I had changed recently. I raced around in a frantic spin, into the kitchen then checked the sliding doors around the house. All locked. Windows too. This place was like Fort Knox, our security pretty state-of-the-art. Then I remembered. There was a key. For emergencies. In case I lost mine on the beach or something. I ran outside into the garden, to where the old tree stump was. A tree had died there, a eucalyptus I think, long before we came to the house. I stuck my trembling hand deep into its crevice, expecting a void, but it was still there: the key to the lower ground floor nestled in its ziplock bag, snug and hidden. I pulled the bag out. It was eye-crossingly stupid to have a key "hidden" like this, with drones and satellites and spyware everywhere these days. And strangers who might know more about you than you do yourself.

I shoved the little bag and its fragments of peaty earth into my pocket.

As for what else was buried on our property, I didn't even dare go near that deep part of the woods—I hadn't since Juan's accident, over six months ago. It was far enough away from the house, I'd managed to resist. Anyone could be watching. Had the drone caught sight of something? It was telling what subtleties you could see from above that you couldn't catch at eye level. What would a drone catch flying over my land? Would it spot the difference in the earth? The part dug up and covered again? No, that was ridiculous, of course it wouldn't with the camouflage of bushes and trees. But I'd been a fool not to get that gun. What if the drone returned?

I knew there had been a visitor. Just knew it. The cleaning lady, Mrs. Reed? No, she came on Mondays, Wednesdays, and Fridays. Had always worked those days at Cliffside, for years. She'd come as part and parcel with the sale of the house. Finding new people to work for you around here was no easy feat, especially in the colder months. Something about the woman and her shoe-button eyes intimidated me. She was brisk, efficient, and made me feel that by chatting with her I was wasting her time. So I didn't dare ask anything out of the ordinary from her, like cleaning the floor-to-ceiling windows, even though the window cleaner had never showed up. I tried to stay out of her way, not be here, or leave soon after she arrived. Mrs. Reed, of course, had her own key. Could she have come on her day off? Or what about Sam, the contractor? He knew this house inside out. But I certainly hadn't given him a key, and the other contractors who had done quotes had only come to Cliffside once. Unless Sam knew about the key's hiding place?

I sniffed the air again and smelled a heady whiff of… what was it, jasmine? I thought again of calling the police and telling them about the anonymous text and the drone, but instantly remembered what a crazy idea that would be. The last thing I needed was them firing questions at me. I sure as hell didn't want to open up *that* can of worms.

CHAPTER FIVE

Every day I half expected to see the drone again. But it didn't reappear. Or another menacing text message to pop up on my phone, but none came.

Hush, hush, I told my clattering mind. *Let sleeping dogs lie.*

The backpack baby and her parents didn't resurface on the beach over the next couple of days. Nor the young sibling trio. Perhaps they had just been on vacation like most people passing through Big Sur. Even in town, now that vacation season was well over, I saw fewer families and more boring, retired people—people with more money than they knew what to do with. And a lot of the fun people—the Brazilians over the hill, for instance—would usually stay away during wintertime and they certainly wouldn't come now, with the thunder and dangerous sloshy roads of late. Big Sur used to be home for so many artists and writers, like Jack Kerouac and Henry Miller, but these days few artists and writers could afford to live along this coast. Hence the retreat plan.

Pippa hadn't called, thank goodness. I guessed I'd iced her out somewhat. But I couldn't deny how lonely I felt.

On the days I wasn't working for Mr. Donner, I spent my time surfing the Internet for retreat ideas, as if on automatic pilot, knowing I'd never go through with it anyway. Everything revolved around good weather. Yoga, Pilates, painting courses. We had a lot of sunny days, too, the sky a crystal-cut blue, but never guaranteed. We had as many days of fog. People wouldn't want to be here in blustery, damp weather with mist rolling in from the ocean, sometimes so thick you couldn't see three feet in front of you. No, people on vacation want full-on sunshine and swimming pool weather, every single day. And the rain hadn't let up.

I thought about my own predicament. What would I do this Christmas, all alone?

A faint but insistent beep-beep of a vehicle in the distance interrupted my thoughts. Funny how the wind can carry sound if it's blowing in the right direction. I cursed in annoyance that the delivery people sometimes refused to make their way down my twisty, two-mile driveway and tended to leave bulky things atop or beside my mailbox by the road. Luckily, nothing had been stolen so far. I put on my raincoat and decided to go by foot to see if they had brought me something, but then changed my mind and drove up by car. Above me, I heard the familiar buzzing. The drone again? I leapt out of my Land Rover but could see nothing. Hear nothing. Just the sound of distant cars on Highway One and the far-off lapping of ocean waves.

On top of my mailbox was a long parcel. Curiosity overriding my nerves, I ripped it open immediately. Inside was a huge bouquet of flowers. Scarlet roses. Not a usual bouquet covered in transparent plastic, but chic, expensive, long-stemmed roses, tied with a silk ribbon to match. Like something out of a classic movie. It made me furious that these beautiful flowers could have dried up, that the delivery guy had just dumped them at the top of my driveway without sending me a text message, which is what Interflora would do, surely? I searched for the company's logo, so I could call and rail at them about bad customer service, but there was no logo, just the flowers. Then I saw a note attached.

I looked around to see if anyone was there—had I imagined the sound of the drone?—but the lane was quiet, just some rustling of the last, dead autumnal leaves sailing to the ground and the faint breath of briny wind. I pushed my hair away from my lips and eyes to see clearly what was written.

HERE.
LOOKING AT YOU.

My heart hammering, I could hardly breathe. I couldn't see the elegant roses.

All I could focus on was their thorns. And the color: the deepest darkest red.

The color of blood.

CHAPTER SIX

I called all the florists, Interflora. Everyone. Nobody admitted to sending the flowers. I spent hours googling, but was none the wiser. Who the hell had sent them? I stared at the note again, written in capital letters on thick, baby-blue card, probably in the handwriting of someone from the flower delivery company. But not being able to trace the source, it gave me no clue at all.

HERE.
LOOKING AT YOU.

I *was* being spied on, no doubt about it now.

My first instinct was to lock myself in the house, but I decided to check my land, furious, suddenly, that I couldn't just go out and buy a German shepherd or Doberman for protection. Should I call the police? And tell them what? I was sent expensive flowers with an enigmatic note? They'd laugh. And I didn't want them sniffing around. I would tell Mr. Donner though. Someone should know about this.

I grabbed my Thermos and marched out the door, full of bravado, willing myself not to be spooked.

Just after I passed through my garden at the top of my woods, I heard voices in the pines. They came and went, carried along by the husky wind like chattering birdsong and then floated towards me again. A man. Throaty laughter. Girls giggling. A tangle of happiness.

And then I saw them coming closer, and I stopped dead. It was them. The sibling trio I'd seen on the beach. How old were they? Early twenties? Very young anyway. Even more attractive than the binoculars had allowed me to believe when I'd spied on them picnicking. They were on my land. I shuddered. Coming from the direction of the beach, they would've had to climb over the bit of broken fence and clamber through huge aloe vera plants with their tenacious spikes. Brazen, considering the gun laws in this country. Considering I could be a pistol packer with the right to defend my property. I stood my ground, my Thermos and binoculars flung across my shoulder, my rain hat skew-whiff.

I wanted to confront them and ask them what the hell they were doing on my land, but the strangest words flew out of my mouth. "I'm bird-watching, and you?" Perhaps I said this because I didn't want them to know I lived here (woman alone, vulnerable). Or perhaps I was excusing myself and asserting myself all in one breath. Excusing myself for going around with a flask of champagne masquerading as coffee? Why did I even care what strangers thought? But I did. The fallout of being judged by someone was my Achilles' heel. That feeling could be ignited by the smallest thing. A look. A raised eyebrow. A sigh. A laugh. Being bullied at school—and don't get me started on my parents—had given me a dichotomized personality: touchy, chippy, insecure, eager-to-please. A person with a silently ticking, don't-push-me-too-far breaking point. Silly not to confront this trio considering they were standing on my land and should've been apologizing to *me*.

"They said it was going to be sunny," the boy said. "But they were wrong." He was strikingly handsome, with wide, greenish eyes and unkempt, sandy hair. He looked familiar, but then, he had that typical movie star aura about him, and I'd seen a dozen like him on TV. Usually in soap operas. The chiseled jaw, the perfect set of American teeth that somehow manages to be revealed even when someone isn't smiling. The worked-out physique. That's the USA for you. Perfection in a neat package. Especially in California.

"I love it when it's like this, though," the girl with long blond hair said. She was like a female version of the boy. Her jaw not as firm and her eyes a touch softer, but still the dazzling Aegean green. Then the other girl spoke—the brunette with the chic bob-cut. She was the smallest of them all, though something told me she was the other girl's twin. They were too alike not to be twins.

"Yeah, it's always like this, this time of year."

No apology. They all looked as if they belonged here.

"What direction are you headed?" I asked.

"Just up here."

I didn't say anything. In Britain, there are rights of way that often cut directly through someone's private land. Public footpaths, they're called. Footpaths that have been in place for centuries that no amount of influence or money can erase. Even Madonna had had public footpath issues on her property in England. Perhaps there was a walkway coming through here I didn't know about? Maybe the last owners had illegally put the fence up? I stood there awkwardly, not knowing whether to go down towards the beach or turn right around and go back home.

"We were kind of hoping to go and visit the house up there. Take a look around. Meet the owner."

"The house?" I echoed.

"The one that's all glass and stone. You the owner?" The boy nodded in the direction uphill, toward Cliffside.

I hesitated then answered, "Yes, that's my house up there." It clicked into place, why he looked familiar. The waiter at the restaurant where I'd met Pippa. He didn't seem to recognize me, though. With my mousy hair and indistinct features, I was used to going unnoticed.

"The most beautiful place in the whole wide world," the brunette said, and sighed. She was dressed all in black. Tight skinny jeans, black Doc Martens, and a black T-shirt. She wore a diamond stud in her nose.

"Yes, it's my house," I repeated.

"Lucky you," the blonde said, smiling at me. I remembered she was the one who played guitar. She wore a long flowery dress and a woolly green scarf the same color as her eyes. All three of them could have been in a rock band or a hit TV series they were so attractive, so charismatic.

"Yes, I'm very fortunate," I answered.

"That's so cool you're the new owner!" the boy said, grinning. "You going to invite us in?" He took a step closer. "You're British, right? I can tell from your accent. Invite us in for a cup of tea. Isn't that what you Brits do every afternoon? Drink tea and eat crumpets?"

I smiled a little. I loved hot toasted crumpets dripping with butter. I hadn't eaten any in years. The young man's familiarity amused me, but my hackles were raised. Who were these kids so interested in my house? They were disconcertingly sure of themselves, to the point of being pushy. I allowed my eyes to rove over him. Just for a few seconds. I didn't want to seem rude, but I had to protect myself. Had to weigh up the pros and cons of being friendly with total strangers. They seemed innocuous, but their confidence, especially the boy's, made me wary. Inviting three people I didn't know right into my house, all at once, might not be the smartest thing to do, despite their youth and friendly manner. But at the same time I was glad to have them around. The flower delivery, or rather, the note that came with it, was freaking me out.

"I was on my way to the beach, actually," I told them.

"Then we'll come with you. Unless you'd rather be alone."

"No, that's fine," I said, happy to have the company. I could check out the lay of the land with them by my side. See if some stranger was lurking in the woods. I strode ahead as three pairs of footsteps followed me, crunching on crispy dead leaves and pine needles. I stepped aside and let them catch up, but stumbled, and the girl—the shorter one—caught me by the elbow.

"Watch out, this part here's a little slippery. I fell flat on my face once."

I let her steady me. "It sounds like you come here often. Why haven't I seen you three around before?" I asked, not letting them know I'd spotted them picnicking on the beach a few days before.

"That house that's yours now?" the boy said. "That was *our* home. Our entire lives, up until you and your husband moved in, what, some seven months ago, that was our house."

I stopped walking, stunned, my heart in my throat. The urge to unscrew my Thermos and take a swig was overwhelming. "I'm sorry," I said. "I had no idea." Was he kidding me? Was this really true? My memories flurried over themselves as I tried to piece together details about the purchase of Cliffside that Juan had taken on solo.

Juan had told me it was a foreclosure, owned by the bank. I had always imagined that some billionaire hedge fund manager owned Cliffside, or some faceless somebody. But the idea of a *family*, of children being kicked out of their own childhood home, had never crossed my mind. I hadn't even asked Juan for details. I was so excited by the idea of owning such a dream house I hadn't thought to ask. I realized now I hadn't wanted to know.

"You're freaking her out, Dan," the blonde said. "I told you this was a dumb idea."

True, he *was* freaking me out. He knew all about who the buyers were—who we were. Who I was. The person responsible for taking their home from them.

"Sorry we bothered you like this," the brunette said. "We just wanted to see our house. Just felt homesick, you know. But we totally, totally understand why it isn't appropriate."

Dan looked down at his feet. "Sorry, my sisters are right, we shouldn't've come, shouldn't've laid all our shit on you. Hey, no hard feelings, give the house a hug from us. Psyched that Cliffside's in such great hands. You seem like a very cool person." He leapt over a rock then skipped at a brisk pace down the hill towards the bay. The girls followed.

I thought of the note, the roses. Inviting them in for a cup of tea wasn't such a bad idea. "Wait!" I called after them. "Listen, don't go! It's fine, really, I completely understand why you'd want to visit your old home. Please come back. Let's all go in for a cup of tea. No crumpets though. But I do have some biscuits. Cookies, I mean."

They all turned round at once. The girls, as if on cue, beamed at me. "Really?" they said simultaneously.

"Yes, really, you're welcome." Their faces were so friendly, and my curiosity, my empathy, and most of all, my yearning not to be alone, won me over.

CHAPTER SEVEN

We introduced ourselves. The girls told me their names were Jennifer and Kate. Kate was the brunette all dressed in black, her face a little wider, but otherwise they were uncannily alike.

"Twins?" I asked, as we approached the front door.

"Triplets," Dan said. He too was dressed in black, with a David Bowie T-shirt.

"Gosh, triplets! I've never met any triplets before. I saw some in a game show on TV once, and in newspapers, but have never *met* triplets—grown-up triplets—in the flesh." I unlocked the door to my house—their house too, once, as it turned out. I noticed my hand was shaking as I held the key. We all walked inside. My heart thrummed with anticipation and excitement. But an undercurrent of doubt tugged at me, too. "Triplets, that's quite something."

"Yeah, it sure is," Dan agreed, gazing at the ceiling and the skylights and scanning the entrance.

Cliffside was pretty much all open-plan, with a fireplace bang in the middle of the room. The vaulted ceilings high, light flooding in from everywhere. There was a long dining room table at one end and giant sofas sprawled out at the other. Windows everywhere. Or rather, walls of glass, only broken up by wide pillars of stone. The view a moving painting. I didn't need any art on the walls, although there were a couple of modern paintings that Juan had bought at auction, years ago, before the artist—with an unpronounceable name—became famous. It reminded me to start using the burglar alarm. I had a habit of leaving it switched off. It was one of those talking ones, which terrified me. A man's robot voice would say things like, "Side east door open." Just the voice alone was ominous. Watching. Waiting for a burglar. *Willing* a burglar, almost. So I kept it off. Not the most intelligent thing to do. I needed to switch it back on.

Cliffside didn't look like it had ever belonged to a regular family but something out of *Architectural Digest*. Modern, sleek—a homage to Bauhaus. It was definitely a "grown-up's" house. No frivolity. No frills. So different from the tiny, low-ceiling cottage I grew up in, with dated flowery cushions, peeling wallpaper, and old creaky plumbing that was constantly breaking down. Cliffside seemed to me the sort of house you only see in movies, not in real life. The sort of home that was perfect for a dashing, sexy man like Juan. But me? I couldn't believe my luck. First marrying Juan, then moving here.

Except, in the end, I'd missed out. Not having kids made all this space a little pointless. This house was meant to be shared, not lived in all alone by a grieving widow. I laid my Thermos sadly on the table, and watched the triplets with vicarious pleasure charging around so happily in my home. Not having children made me feel like an artist without a paintbrush, a nurse in an empty ward. The retreat plan was a poor, wishful substitute. Cliffside needed love to fill her great glass walls, not just company.

Cliffside's lack of triviality did suit my personality though. I was a grown-up before my time. I was never a giggler or show-off or a gossip at school. I wanted to be. I longed to emulate the other girls, the confident ones who made eyes at boys and discussed hair and makeup on weekends, and in long telephone conversations when they were supposed to be doing their homework. Not me. I was all about reading and studying, handing my papers in early, getting top grades, and helping my mother set the table.

A goody-goody.

A good girl who turned out not to be so good after all.

"So," Jennifer said. "Where's your husband?"

"Um, he's away on business." I didn't want them to know I lived here alone, or for them to have any excuse for prying into my private life or Juan's death. It was safer that way. I was already taking a big risk, but their faces were so trusting and their eyes kind. It would be fine, I told myself, to let them have a quick look around.

"Congratulations," Dan blurted out, shedding his bomber jacket and flinging it on a chair, "it all looks the same. So far, so good."

"Awesome!" Kate said, piling her jacket on top of Dan's. "Let's go and check out our bedrooms. Can we?" Before I had a chance to answer, all three were racing around the house, opening doors, drumming down the stairs to the lower ground floor. It led to spectacular views and the bottom half of the garden, before it dramatically dropped off in a vertigo-inducing cliff shielded by glass verandas.

I was taken aback by the ease with which the three made themselves at home, and although it slightly irked me, it was a relief to be amidst the bustle and noise, the feeling that Cliffside really was a family home. It brought the place alive.

Jennifer ran back into the living room. "Wow, you have no idea what a relief this is to us," she gushed, her eyes shining with gratitude.

"What do you mean?" I said. I finally took off my hat and hung it and the binoculars up by the door.

Kate shot up beside me, out of breath, almost crashing into me like an overgrown puppy. "This is so cool." She gave me a hug. I gingerly let her embrace me, not knowing where to put my hands. They hung limply, not touching her but hovering midway in the air. I realized it was the first real hug I'd had since Juan died. I could feel the girl's warmth. Her sweetness.

"What have I done right?" I asked perplexed, strangely thrilled.

Jennifer unraveled her woolly green scarf and chucked it on the growing pile. "It's not what you've done, it's what you *haven't* done."

Dan made his way toward the kitchen, hands deep in pockets, contemplative eyes appraising the smooth white walls, the whippet-gray slate floors. "Man, this is so, so great!"

"Nice to see your house again, then?" I said. I wandered to the kitchen, filled up the kettle with water, and set it on the stove. It was one of those haute cuisine, state-of-the-art chef stoves, with shiny silver rivulets and polished chrome set into deep, grayish-blue enamel. It must have cost a fortune—far too sophisticated for my basic cooking skills. Wasted on the likes of me. I tended to buy ready-made food from swanky delicatessens in town. Or frozen meals I could heat up. My mother was a terrible cook (tins of Heinz, fish fingers with frozen peas and ketchup, M&S only when we could afford it), and I'd picked up some lazy habits. I was a grazer, a snacker. Family packets of crisps. Marmite on toast. A secret vice all British girls have, especially ones who grow up in cash-strapped families like mine.

"You haven't screwed with the house. Haven't spoiled its integrity," Dan said. "We were kind of nervous the buyer would ruin everything."

My plans for the retreat loomed in my mind. The extra bathrooms, the extension. All new architectural plans. I just smiled wanly, hoping the triplets couldn't read my mind. Why did I care so much what these triplets thought? Perhaps because of their tactile presence? So three dimensional. Some people own a room when they walk into it, others are observers. The observer types, like me, are nourished by people like them. That's what had made me fall in love with Juan. He was my sustenance. My food. He was a human *being*, not just a human.

I had fed off him.

For the first time in ages, I felt relaxed, less tense than usual. Was it their company? Ironic that I was feeling more at home than ever in my own house. And the triplets had been here less than ten minutes.

"God, I missed this view from the kitchen!" Kate raved. "Seriously, have you ever seen a better view in your life? The ocean always changes into different blues, and the sunsets from here are to die for."

To die for. So true.

"Tea, anyone?" I offered.

"Sure." Dan and Kate spoke simultaneously. I guessed that happened a lot with twins or triplets. I often wondered what it would have been like to have a sibling myself. Would we have been as united? As close as this lot seemed to be?

I thought of Rupert.

Kate took out her phone and snapped a few photos. "I swear I could just look at this sunset all day. I mean..." she paused and laughed "... that's a dumb thing to say, because it doesn't last all day."

"Sunsets and sunrises never actually happen, Kate," Dan said. "But you know that of course."

She glared at him. "What are you talking about?"

"The sun never rises or sets. While the earth moves, the sun never moves at all. It's all a beautiful illusion."

I observed this boy's deep eyes set in such a thoughtful, intelligent face and remembered how much I missed clever conversation. Not small talk I could find anywhere, but bright, sharp conversation—things that made your brain tick a little. Stuff that made you contemplate. I fumbled around in the cupboard, wondering what sort of tea I should give them and which flavor I was in the mood for myself. After what Dan had just said, I decided they deserved a stylish tea. When Juan traveled for work he'd always bring me back fancy teas.

"When I was a little girl," I told them, "my friends' parents used to offer tea, you know, as they always do—no child in Britain is too young for a cup of tea. Coffee, that was for grown-ups, but tea? That's a drink for everyone. Anyway, they always asked me if I wanted China tea or Indian tea, and I had no idea what they were talking about." My little story thudded dull in my ears.

"So what did you tell them?" asked Dan, who was now sitting on my countertop, his black-sneakered foot bobbing up and down expectantly.

I shrugged. "I used to say—as all children do, I suppose—'I don't mind.'"

Dan laughed. A husky, throaty laugh. "I don't think I've ever said, 'I don't mind' in my life! Because I *do* mind. I mind about a lot of things, all the time."

"Even as a child? You had the confidence to speak up?"

"Sure. I wouldda said, 'Hey, please explain me the difference between China tea and Indian tea, 'cause I don't know.' By the way, what *is* the difference between China tea and Indian tea?"

I laughed. "Good question. It's the taste, I suppose. I'm wondering which you would all prefer. I happen to like Lapsang Souchong. It has a sort of smoky flavor. As you can tell by the name, it's Chinese. Or there's Earl Grey, a favorite of mine that's blended with bergamot oil. That's from India. Actually, you know what? Maybe it isn't from India at all. Silly that I don't even know."

"Google it," Jennifer suggested.

Kate looked down at her phone. "No reception. Cell phone reception sucks up here, remember?" Kate looked at me. "What's the Wi-Fi and password?"

I told them and warned, "But the reception for the Internet's also sketchy, it comes and goes."

"I'm not getting a connection either," Dan said. "Man, the Internet's so fucked up in this house. The *downside* of living on top of a cliff."

"Very funny. Don't mind my brother and his lame jokes," Kate groaned. "I'm not getting a connection, either. Jen?"

Jennifer swept her hand through her mane of honey hair. "I left my phone at home on purpose. I have a life, you guys, without a phone. Jeez, I wish we'd been born in the 70s, you know, when people actually communicated without technology."

I smiled. "I know how you feel, Jennifer."

"Call me Jen. Hey, why don't we look it up the old-fashioned way? You got a dictionary?" She had already got up and rushed off to the other end of the room, to my bookshelves, her long dress billowing behind her. I scrambled after her, almost tripping over myself. There was a certain "book" I did absolutely not want her to get her hands on.

"Manners, Jen," Kate called over. "I swear to God my sister's the rudest person in the universe."

"I am so not!" Jen fired back.

Kate's words hung in the air. It was true—not just Jen, but all of them behaved as if they'd known me forever, with their easy familiarity. How strange this must feel for them, I thought, to be visitors. I grabbed the dictionary from the bookshelf and handed it to Jen.

I observed her pretty face and the sweep of blond hair the wind had mussed up outside earlier as she browsed through the onion-thin pages. Then she looked up at me and grinned. Her eyes looked so trusting, the pupils large and deep. I had a knack for divining people's natures by their eyes. Was it Shakespeare who said that eyes were "windows to the soul"?

"And?" I said. "What does it say?"

Kate shook her head in disapproval. "*Jen*! You're so nosey."

"Kick us out if we're bugging you," Dan said.

For a second I wondered if these three had found the hidden key in the tree stump, opened the front door and then put it back again, but then I dismissed the idea. None of them carried that same jasmine scent, and they were too messy and clumsy, by the way they dumped their jackets around and traipsed clods of mud and dead leaves into the house. I would've seen breadcrumbs of their presence if they were the culprits. Besides, they had the confidence to simply knock at the door, barge their way in, as they had pretty much done now. But I wasn't complaining. No, I liked their lively company, despite their cockiness. My house had never felt so homey. So bustling and active.

"'Lapsang,'" Jen read out, "'is a specific Chinese tea grown on Wuyi Mountain, dried and processed near a pine fire that gives it its distinctly smoky flavor.' Hmm, think I'll pass. Tea tasting of smoke sounds gross."

"Read out what it says about Earl Grey," Dan said, but Jen had already snapped the book shut and was more interested in the whistling kettle on the stove.

I ambled over to the kitchen and took a large white teapot from the counter. I didn't have an electrical kettle for two reasons. Firstly, the stove was such a masterpiece of engineering I needed an excuse to use it daily. And secondly, with the occasional power cuts up here, the last thing I needed—or wanted—was to be stranded in the dark without at least a cup of tea. The teapot lived here on the counter permanently, never put away. You can take the girl out of England but you can't take England out of the girl. I poured in the boiling water, swilled it around then emptied it down the drain.

Jen's pale brows gathered with consternation. "What are you doing?"

"Warming the pot. It makes the tea taste better," I explained.

"You're so full of shit," Dan joked, grinning at me. I must have looked aghast, because he added, "Just kidding."

I raised my eyebrows in mock surprise, secretly enjoying his cheekiness. "Excuse me, young man, but you shouldn't speak to your elders that way." His intimacy was unnerving, yet charismatic at the same time. He had the same sort of confidence as Juan. Not taking "no" for an answer. Cocky. Self-assured. California boy. I couldn't help but be as charmed as I was disarmed.

"Speaking of elders, how old are you, anyway?' Dan asked.

I feigned an expression of shock. "Another thing a man should never ask a woman. A man should never ask a woman her age. It's bad manners. Did your mother never teach you any manners?"

The triplets all went silent and looked at each other, their radiant smiles instantly wiped out. Their delight smeared right off their faces because of what I'd said. Something very hurtful, obviously. Oops. Kate looked as if she was about to burst out crying.

"Just joking," I assured them, shoveling myself out of my grave. I didn't want them to leave, however inquisitive or cocky they were. "I didn't mean it, I'm sure your mum is a wonderful person. I was just joking."

"It's because of our mom we had to sell this house," Dan said solemnly.

I concentrated on reaching for a new tin of Harrods Earl Grey from the cupboard. "Oh."

"She has lung cancer," Kate said, in a monotone. "That's why we had to sell. We needed the money to pay for her treatment. Her medical insurance didn't even scratch the surface. It's been real tough."

My heart jumped right into my stomach. Why hadn't Juan known about this when he bought the house from them? "How *awful*," I said. "Where is she now?"

"In this special treatment center in Switzerland. She's stage four. It's real bad."

"How awful," I repeated dumbly. "So where are you all living now while she's away in Switzerland? You're in college, I assume?"

"We had to drop out," Jen said. "One more year to go, but there was no way. I mean, it wasn't just the fees; none of us could concentrate on our studies. I'm a musicology major, Kate and Dan chemistry majors. A shitload of studying. We got real behind. Taking a year off was, like, the smartest thing to do—till things get better."

Kate was playing with her hair, twisting it around her fingers. Nervous. Terrified. A tear ran down her cheek. "*If* things get better," she said in a trembly voice.

"Where are you all living?" I asked.

"On couches, with friends."

"*What*? You don't even have a home?" My heart pinched. These poor things without their mum, no real place to go, it was simply awful. I felt an instant need to help them somehow.

Dan cleared his throat, looked at the others again then spoke. "We'd do anything to have a real home again. We were in school when Mom got diagnosed. First she was in the hospital then she moved to an apartment, after she sold this house. There was no point getting something for all four of us, us being away at college and stuff, and besides, you know what rent costs around here? This is Big Sur, man, it's freakishly expensive. Then Mom had to go to Switzerland. We wanted to go, too, to be near her, but it's even more crazy expensive there—she's near Zurich—like impossible, unless you're a Swiss banker or something. So we got jobs round here."

I so ached for them all, being flung into such a hopeless situation, that I found myself awkwardly changing the subject. "You waited on my table the other day, didn't you?" I asked Dan. "The corner restaurant in Carmel?"

"Yeah, I work there. But I don't remember seeing you before today."

What Dan said didn't surprise me. My face is the forgettable kind. I've always been a wallflower, a listener, a blending-in-the-background type. Still, his comment chipped another little chink off my shoulder.

"You want to see a photo of our mom?" Jen said brightly. "I carry it with me everywhere. Brings me good luck." She grabbed her jacket from the pile on the chair and pulled out a faded green wallet, opened it up and showed me a dog-eared photo—one from a photo booth—of a beautiful blonde. Laughing. Carefree. Head tilted back.

"She's lovely," I said. "Looks identical to you all. She must've been very young when this was taken."

"When she was an exchange student in Paris," Kate said.

Tears welled in my eyes. They were losing their *mother*. Slowly. And they couldn't even be by her side. My mind was being pushed and pulled, contorting itself with varying emotions. Empathy. Guilt. Fear. Dread. The darkest sorrow. Guilt, most of all, for living in the house they'd lost through tragic circumstances. As if I were somehow responsible for everything.

"What about your dad?" I asked. "Can't he help out?"

Dan jumped off the countertop and moved over to the window. Rain clouds scudded across the horizon in thick purple swathes, racing preternaturally as if in a sped-up film. "Nope," he said to the view. "Mom's a widow."

My heart thumped with sympathy. "Oh, no, I'm so sorry."

Dan threw me a misty-eyed glance. "Our dad was a marine and died in the line of duty. We were just babies." He pulled something from beneath his T-shirt and held it to the window. The metal glinted in the light. A dog tag. I'd seen those in movies. "I wear this every day," Dan said. "He was a brave man. Wish I'd had the chance to know him."

"I'm so sorry," I said again, feeling embarrassed that I'd pushed this answer out of him. "Your dad made the ultimate sacrifice for his country. How brave. But so awful for you all to be left without a father."

The information hovered in the space between us. Wretched. Desolate. I didn't know how to react. Poor children. Practically orphans. Their mother with lung cancer, them homeless, with no ongoing financial or moral support. What was I supposed to do? All sorts of solutions and possibilities spun around my mind. But it was too much to digest. I'd just met these people. I needed a drink, but it was still only teatime. I got some cups and saucers out from the cupboard and some teaspoons.

"Excuse me," I said. "I'll be right back."

I slowly walked—forced myself not to run—to the lower ground floor where my wine cellar was. It wasn't a real wine cellar, more like a fridge, the temperature set perfectly. I grabbed a Chablis, because un-popping the cork of a champagne bottle would draw too much attention, even from down here. After what they'd told me about their mother, it might sound too celebratory.

I slipped into the bathroom that served one of the downstairs bedrooms, and once inside and out of earshot, glugged down half the bottle, hardly stopping to breathe. I let out a satisfied sigh. A new, dazy sort of confidence bloomed through my limbs—a buzzy buoyancy that paradoxically made me weighty and light all at once. I could deal with this! But then I felt instantly contrite. What was I doing?

I needed to stop. Needed to stop using alcohol as a means to numb my grief over losing Juan, to make things seem all right. Habits lock themselves into your system fast. And I was forming a habit that would soon spiral into addiction if I didn't watch out. Not me. Not who I was.

I wasn't an addict.

I gazed at my reflection in the mirror: two of me, just for a flash. But then my face settled, and I regarded just one rather sad human being with sad, dull eyes. With the flat of my hand—it was cool and calming—I wiped off streaks of mascara that had blurred into my under-eye bags, making them worse. I brushed my teeth, rinsed my mouth to mask the smell of wine.

Decisions, decisions! There was no choice but to make a *decision*. Start afresh.

Sometimes in life you are offered opportunities and gifts. But you can't dither. Dithering is the enemy of progress. Opportunity rarely knocks twice in a row. I, of all people, knew this. I had wanted kids forever. This was a sign. *There are no coincidences*! These three had been brought to me, not only to alleviate my loneliness, but as a way to open my heart, to share a part of myself.

"Yes!" I said to my reflection. "I will do this. I will *do* this!"

I rushed up the stairs, buoyed and dizzied by alcohol, excited with the rush that comes with a one hundred and eighty degree turn in your life.

"Guys," I called out to the three of them. "I have a proposal to make!" In my eagerness, one foot bashed itself into the other and made me tumble flat on my hands and on the side of my face before I reached the top of the stairs. I lay there in a lump, grateful the triplets couldn't see me. The searing pain in my ankle told me I'd twisted it. Not too badly, but enough to jolt me back to reality.

Normal people don't make hasty choices like this. These kids were not my problem. It was insane to think I could take on a trio of young adults and ask them to stay. Who was I to offer comfort when it wasn't my place? I didn't even know them. Didn't know anything about them. Not really. I had to be stronger than that. Keep that nagging loneliness that gnawed at me daily in check.

"Are you okay?" Jen asked, when she saw me limp into the kitchen.

"I just tripped over and twisted my ankle a bit, no damage done."

"Sit down, I'll get some ice. Better, frozen peas." Rummaging in the freezer, she hauled out a bag of frozen vegetables.

I sat down, cradling my ankle. I could feel my face flush with embarrassment, or was it the liquor flaming through my cheeks?

Jen took my ankle in her hands and curved the bag around the swelling. "This should help. Just hold it here for, like, twenty minutes."

I rolled down my sock and pressed the bag on my flesh. "Thanks so much."

They all looked at me, full of concern.

"I'll be fine, really. Honestly, don't worry."

"Let me get you some water," Kate said. "And you should take an aspirin or some kind of anti-inflammatory for that. You want me to get something from the bathroom?"

"I'm fine, really. I hope I can drive, that's all. My Land Rover's a stick shift and the clutch is rather stiff." The words "stick shift" felt like a tongue twister. I was drunker than I realized.

Dan offered, "Can we help in any way? You know, like do some shopping for you or something?"

"No, I'll be fine. Thanks anyway."

"By the way, what's your proposal?" he asked.

"I can't remember now," I lied.

Dan got up. "We should go, this is a bad time for you."

Jen's eyes misted. "Did we do something wrong?"

I clutched my stomach; I felt a nauseous rush gurgle inside me. "I'm not feeling very well, that's all."

"Oh," said Dan. "I get it." He looked down at my stomach. I was wearing a fluted blouse and baggy sweater, which made my tummy look puffed out. And although Pippa's scrutiny had told me I looked too thin when she saw me, I felt like I'd put on a bit of weight, nearly all of it around the middle and on my cheeks. Not fat, but bloated. Drink can do that.

Jen said, "You're *pregnant*? You didn't land on your stomach when you fell, did you?"

"No! No, don't worry, I just get nauseous sometimes."

"Morning sickness? Congratulations!" Kate said, and grinned. "Boy or girl?"

"I don't know yet," I answered back without thinking. And then added recklessly, "I'll find out with my next ultrasound." The lie sat thick on my tongue.

Another one for the repertoire.

CHAPTER EIGHT

The house quivered with silence after they'd left. As if it were judging me for my thoughts, my actions; as if it could crawl inside my mind and reach into every dark little crevice, into every corner. I had never felt spooked here, even since losing Juan, but the triplets' friendly chatter had inched itself into the walls; their laughter tinkled through the air.

I missed them already. They had been so friendly and caring. So *present*.

A sharp ringing pierced my reverie. I limped over to the landline, hoping it was one of them, but remembered I hadn't given them my phone number.

"Darling."

"Mum, hello, what a nice surprise."

"Nice surprise? It's Saturday, I always call on weekends." My mother was often quick to feel judged. A trait I'd picked up along the way.

"Yes, of course, I'd forgotten it was Saturday. I mean, I hadn't even been aware of it in the first place."

"Well, that's what happens when you mope around and don't make an effort to socialize. Most people make plans for the weekend, darling."

My mother had been at me to get out of the house more, to join associations, to stop being so solitary. Going to parties, she assured me, would help fix things. As if. As if I could simply shrug off my sadness with roomfuls of people feeling sorry for me. Or men I wasn't interested in coming on to me. It hunkers in deep, down inside you, grief does. Eats at your self-confidence. But Mum changed her tone and then asked sweetly, "How *are* you, darling?"

"Oh, you know. Getting by." I wasn't going to let her know I'd fallen flat on my face and twisted my ankle. *Clumsy girl.*

"Still no better?"

"Still so... broken-hearted."

"You need to get out more, meet new *friends.*"

"Actually I met some fun young people today. Early twenties, I suppose. A boy and two girls. Fraternal triplets."

"Oh, yes?"

"They're a real laugh. One of the girls plays guitar. Poor things' mother's ill and I felt sorry for them. Invited them over for tea. Met them out walking."

"Be careful, darling, with those long solitary walks of yours. You shouldn't go round picking up strangers, willy-nilly. Find some *proper* friends."

I knew what she meant by "proper" friends. She was worse than Pippa. Mum was hoping I'd start dating. She never did like Juan.

"You can't mope around forever, my love. Not good for you. What about coming *here* for a stint? It would be lovely to see you." *Nice English boy, someone of your "own kind."*

"Maybe. Maybe for Christmas."

"That would be wonderful. Just wonderful, darling. You could combine it with Rupert's birthday."

I closed my eyes and tried to suppress the little rage bubbling inside me that flared up every year. Rupert was my non-existent, older brother. Non-existent because I had never known him. He had died at thirteen months old of congenital heart disease. It was pitiful how my parents still stuck a candle on a cake for him and had dragged me (every year) into their "celebration of his short but sweet life." This year would have been his fortieth.

"I can't let Mr. Donner down," I told Mum. "Too much workload."

She changed the subject. "Cold there yet?" My mother never cared to hear about my work or career. As far as she was concerned a woman was nothing without a man. It didn't matter about the A-grades I'd earned relentlessly through school and university, my scholarships, the prizes I'd won over the years for Latin, my fascinating job as an attorney at Juan's law firm. Once, in one of her icy tempers, Mum had even called me her "terrible disappointment."

"You know it never gets that cold here," I said, carefully keeping the bitterness out of my voice. "But it's been raining a lot. Unusual for round here. Especially after last year's drought. And the mist. Sometimes I can't see two feet in front of me. But then we have loads of days with full sunshine. The lemon tree still seems happy. And the hibiscus is in full flower."

"It's not safe where you live, darling, along that nasty San Andreas fault line. The whole lot will split in two one day. Floods, fires, earthquakes, you're living in the most hazardous place in the world! What idiot thought of balancing a big glass house on a clifftop, I'll never know. Californians. Honestly. And you were foolish to even think of buying that house. Come home, darling, sell up, you know I'm right."

I didn't answer. *Stupid girl, you can't do anything right*, I could hear her thinking.

"It's dangerous, perched on that terrifying cliff like that. One day it'll get—"

"Washed into the sea." I finished her sentence. I'd heard this speech a thousand times before. "How's Dad?" I said, veering away from the lectures I'd heard so often.

"The same. It's a nasty disease, you know. Takes hold of one bit by bit. Before you know it, you're not the same person at all."

"But he still knows who you are?"

"Goes in roundabouts. But let's not talk about that, darling."

"I miss Juan, Mum. Life's so silent without him."

"Of course you do. It's only natural."

"It shouldn't have happened like it did."

"No, of course not. Life can be shocking sometimes. Look what happened to your father. Things can sneak up on you unawares."

"It was so unexpected. I just wasn't prepared."

"Course you weren't."

"I miss working with him, too."

"But that new job you told me about with that elderly man, what's his name, Mr. Donner, sounds all right."

"It's not the same, though. Still, it gets me out of the house, I suppose, and I do like him."

Silence. My mother felt—I was only too aware—that I should be back in England, and any discussion about any topic at all would end up leading in that one, cul-de-sac direction. I wasn't in the mood to explain why I could never go back.

"How are your bed and breakfast plans coming on?" She said this with a clipped voice. She always referred to it as a B & B. Never did catch on to my retreat idea.

"You think it's a good plan? I've suddenly had doubts."

"You know what I think."

"That I should come home?"

"Of course you should come home! Rattling around in that big transparent house of yours, all alone. In that remote place. Come back to where your *real* friends are. Where your family is! Your dad needs you."

"Dad didn't have a clue who I was last time I visited."

I heard her sigh, but she didn't reply. *Who I was? Whom I was?* I could picture her mouthing the words, correcting my grammar.

"I can't give up this beautiful house," I went on. "How many people get to live in a place like this? Not even one in a million. It's a dream home."

"There you go again. Materialistic things will not buy you happiness, believe you me! *Are* you happy, with those big glass doors and big glass walls, living like a tiny fish in an aquarium too big for you? You don't even have any curtains in that place. Up on that cliff, alone. Husband gone. Come home where you belong."

She didn't understand the magic of this place. Home to her was a cozy semi-detached with low ceilings, padded chintz curtains with matching armchairs, and wall-to-wall carpeting. And the TV always droning on in the background like a soundtrack. She even had the horse racing hammering away now, because that's what my father always watched on weekends. She is that sort of person. A slave to her man: likes what he likes, and agrees with everything, including every single one of his political beliefs, however bigoted or racist, however divisive. My dad hated the fact that Juan was half Mexican.

"I've got to go, Mum. I promised I'd meet… a friend. Speak next week?"

She sighed again, as if I tired her out. "Take care, darling. Think about what I've said. We miss you."

I hobbled into the kitchen, trying to keep the weight off my ankle. Unwashed teacups and plates were strewn about the countertop. The triplets had made themselves tea while I had been holed up in the bathroom with my wine. Half the teapot was filled with loose, soggy tealeaves. They'd even helped themselves to an extra packet of chocolate-chip cookies. I should've been irritated by their familiarity, but I was pleased they'd made themselves at home after my little disappearing act.

A chilling quiet rippled through the house. Their presence had made me so happy.

With their mess or without it—and even with their nosiness—I wanted the triplets back.

CHAPTER NINE

"You're like blotting paper." Juan's words floated with the sound of the wind, the rustle of trees, the bark of a distant seal, and the ever-crashing waves. Were his words a memory or a dream?

I tossed and turned, trying to get to sleep, but memories of Juan, especially around the time we first started dating, circled in my mind like an eagle hovering over its prey, homing in on me, forcing me to remember. Sleeping a full night was a luxury I hadn't known in the last six months. This new, sexless life made it hard for me to tune out or relax. Whatever our ups or downs, Juan had skills when it came to the bedroom. I'd had one boyfriend before him, and his only knack was making me numb, focusing on certain areas as if they were islands isolated from my body and nothing to do with my brain. I felt less than nothing. I was not alone. Women all over the world complain about men like that: blissfully unaware, only catering to their own needs. Not my Juan. Little Miss Librarian became a tigress between the sheets—I couldn't get enough of my husband.

Especially at night.

"Blotting paper?" I'd repeated back to him. "What a weird thing to say to me. What do you mean by *blotting* paper?"

"You soak up all my worries. I mean it in a good way, honey. When I'm with you I don't have a care in the world."

"Why blotting paper, though? Why not a sponge? Not that I like the idea of being a sponge either, but blotting paper sounds so... who uses blotting paper anymore anyway?"

"Sponges you have to squeeze out," he said, his husky voice a croaky whisper. "Blotting paper just sucks up all that ink, over and over again."

I laughed. Finally I got his sexual innuendo.

Awoken from my dream with my own laugh, I lay there now, my eyes staring into the thick velvet night. There was no moon, or if there was it was just a sliver, and the sky's clouds still swirled above the horizon, masking any possibility of light. Tiny stars scattered behind the blanket of clouds. Some people can't sleep without blinds or curtains. I can never sleep with them; they make me claustrophobic, I have to see the sky.

Blotting paper, I thought, has a limited lifespan. You throw it away when you're done.

CHAPTER TEN

As I drank my morning tea I thought about the triplets. That could have been me. Could've been me having triplets. If only. If only Juan and I had had children. Pippa and my mother wanted me to find a new man. But I didn't want a new man. I wanted what wasn't possible: my husband. Despite his betrayal, despite his lies.

Tires crunched on the driveway. I pricked up my ears like an alert dog. Was I imagining it? Had the gate not clicked shut? I needed to be more careful, under the circumstances, to protect myself, be on my guard.

A car door slammed. I cautiously got up and limped to the front door—my ankle was still really sore. I pressed my bruised eye up against the spy lens and saw a distorted Dan. A grinning face. He tried the door handle. It was locked. He buzzed the bell.

I opened the door. "Dan, what a surprise!"

"Hey," he said. "I won't come in. Just swung by to bring you some organic eggs from Joe Flynn's farm over the hill and thought we'd come and cook you dinner tonight. You know, figured you might need some help with your ankle and all." He held out a box of eggs and a posy of wild flowers.

"Oh, wow, that's so kind. Hand-picked flowers, how thoughtful." I stood there, still in my pajamas, cupping my mug of tea in one hand and taking the flowers with the other. It was only around nine a.m. Too early, surely, for a visit? My mother had always taught me never to call anyone before ten in the morning or after nine at night, especially on weekends, unless you knew their habits extremely well. Apart from being a beauty and having cancer, I had no idea what kind of person the triplets' mother was. I craned my neck around the door and caught a glimpse of Kate and Jen waiting in the car. It was a black pickup, with a dented fender and bashed all over. Marks of a young, inexperienced driver.

"You okay?" Dan lightly touched my eye with his hand. "Looks like a bad bruise."

"I'm fine, really. Gosh, you didn't have to go to all that trouble. These flowers... thank you *so* much."

"You're welcome. See you later then."

"By the way, was the gate not closed?" I asked.

"Wasn't clicked shut. The automatic arm must be broken or the electronics out."

"Really? It was working just fine before."

Dan smiled his lopsided smile. "I can fix it for you if you like. I'm pretty handy with a tool kit and security systems."

I must have looked dumb and blank, still groggy from sleep, still wondering how they drove right on in. But I wasn't going to pick holes and was happy that they all cared to be so friendly, especially after my indirect rejection—not following through on my proposal. It was wonderful to have new acquaintances, albeit a little overwhelming. Maybe I'd take Dan up on his offer to fix my gate and the video intercom?

"Let me give you some money for groceries." I turned to get my purse.

But Dan stopped me. "We'll take care of it, okay? Just enjoy your day, and we'll swing by around five. Dinner at seven, so don't be late."

"It's my house, why would I be late?" I said, realizing a beat too late I'd missed his joke. "I've got wine so no need to buy any," I said, then realized under the circumstances how bad that sounded.

"We don't drink, we'll bring juice. See you later," and then he added with a grin, "alligator."

He turned and strode back to the car. Kate and Jen smiled and waved, and then they all drove off, the wheels squealing a little when the car was out of sight. Their bright, excited faces filled me with happiness. It was great to know I wouldn't be eating alone this evening. And with my ankle so sore, I wasn't sure I could even drive my car anyway—the clutch was really stiff. The kitchen cupboard was practically bare—I was a lazy shopper. Dinner sounded great.

It occurred to me I should do a little research and check that the triplets and their mother were who they said they were: the ex-owners of this house. Why hadn't I done that last night? I hadn't even thought to check with Mrs. Reed, who had worked at Cliffside for years before Juan and I moved in. She would know. She'd know the whole family. Sometimes when things take you by surprise, your brain goes out of kilter—makes you forget to use your common sense. The triplets had certainly taken me by surprise. But something about them fascinated me so much I couldn't resist the possible risk involved. I wanted to be their friend.

I phoned Mrs. Reed and left a message, asking her to return my call. Curiosity nagging at me, I needed an immediate answer and, being a Sunday, the local real estate agents I found online were closed. I didn't have a clue who had sold Juan the house, as he'd been the one dealing with everything at the time. I now remembered being away in England. Anyway, buying Cliffside was his big surprise for me, so he'd kept his cards close to his chest. Juan was romantic that way; he loved springing gifts and surprises on me.

Rummaging through drawers, and with no reply from Mrs. Reed, I finally came across a phone number and an email address—on the back of a photo of Cliffside—that read: REAL ESTATE AGENT CLIFFSIDE. I phoned. No answer. So I tried my luck with an email, and wrote quite a long, detailed message. To my delight, I got a friendly reply a couple of hours later. The agent confirmed she had met the triplets when she came to value the property—they were the ones who had shown her around the house. She didn't know about the mother having cancer; but then some families are private about things like that. The agent's answer satisfied me. At least I knew I hadn't befriended a trio of weirdoes who were about to chop me up. Ha!

I poured myself another cup of tea and checked my emails. Streams of them awaited me, mostly from charities. Mosquito nets, elephants, unwanted pipelines, dog sanctuaries, whales, toxic waste, poisoned drinking water. Even personal messages from Leonardo DiCaprio and Robert Redford. I never had the heart to unsubscribe from these mailing lists so, as usual, I added my name to all the petitions and made some donations. Picked the ones that tugged at my heartstrings the most—training puppies for the blind, fixing children's cleft palates—which only made me feel guiltier for not ponying up for the others.

To cheer myself up, I clicked on Facebook, the great vacuum of time. But I quickly remembered, too, how it is an instant depression instigator. Either people posting about their illnesses and hospital visits, or the radiant grinners gleaming into camera lenses, showing everyone how thrilled they are with life. Lots of selfies and couple photos. Perfect children doing ballet or winning prizes. People hugging moms and dads and grandparents. Toothy smiles. Babies. *Families.* Families everywhere! Misty-eyed, I was about to slam my laptop shut, when a banner caught my attention: a neat oblong box edged in bright red, flashing brazenly in my right-hand column.

I'll Be Watching You.
Click Here to Learn More.

That ominous message again! I zeroed my cursor in on "Learn More," but by mistake I pressed an ad next to it, one for flat stomachs. It reloaded and then I got an ad for a pizza restaurant in Carmel. I frantically clicked over and over, to will the banner to come up again, but now all I was getting were ads for gyms. I slapped my computer shut.

Someone was watching all right.

Someone who knew too much.

CHAPTER ELEVEN

Dan, Kate, and Jen arrived on the dot of five, laden with groceries. I tried to slip a hundred-dollar bill in Dan's jeans pocket, but he dodged me, refusing to take it.

"This means so much to us," he said. "To be here with you, in our house again. How's the ankle?"

"A little better, the ice really helped."

"Did you take something for it?" Kate asked. "To help the swelling?"

"A couple of painkillers," I said.

We hung out in my open-plan kitchen. I hovered uneasily while they navigated their way around with perfect ease, chopping vegetables, chatting about old times and preparing the meal.

"You eat chicken, right?" Dan asked—and before I had a chance to reply—"'cause this isn't just any old chicken, but one from Joe Flynn's farm. Same place we got the eggs. All his animals run free and he feeds them right. No antibiotics, no hormone crap. They lead a good life."

"I've never been to that farm. Never heard about it before."

"Yeah, there are a lot of cool, secret places in Big Sur and around," said Jen. "Stick with us and we'll show you all our favorites. Places you won't find online."

The idea of hanging out like friends and having them share their secret places with me made my heart leap a little.

"It's so nice to be here," Kate said. "So cool to be home and chilling with you."

A buzz of warmth flowed through my veins. The triplets were the first real company I'd had since Juan died.

Dan placed the chicken into a large casserole dish and squeezed fresh lemon juice over it. I noted the roped muscles in his arms flexed with even the smallest movement. He was wearing a black T-shirt with a peace sign on it. "So where's your partner in crime?" he asked. "Your husband? The man who bargained down our mom with the deal of a lifetime."

I had a knife in my hand, awkwardly looking for something to do. "I'm so sorry, I had no idea he did that. I never would've—"

"We're *so* not blaming you," Jen cut in. "That's life. Please don't feel—"

"She knows," Dan interrupted. "She knows I'm fooling around."

I regarded his face—he was hard to read. When a man is handsome he gets away with things. I knew Dan must get away with all sorts. "So where's your girlfriend?" I asked, instantly wishing I hadn't been so nosey, but then heard myself say straight afterwards, "Anyone special?"

"Just friends with benefits." He winked at me.

"He gets all the benefits," said Kate. "The girls not so much. We don't like his attitude, do we, Jen?"

"No, he's on the verge of being a scumbag." Jen bared her teeth at him with an oversized, fake grimace.

"That is *so* not fair! You know I treat all women with respect. They know the deal upfront." Then he asked me, "Where do you keep the salt?"

I reached into the cupboard and brought down a box of Maldon sea salt.

"All *right*!" he exclaimed, punching the air. "You have great taste. You even know what kind of salt to buy, dude. You're so cool! Yet… you don't like to cook?"

"Oh, yes, I love cooking," I lied. Where did they get the notion I didn't cook? I moved decisively to the fridge and brought out a half-opened bottle of champagne. Kate monitored my move.

"You're going to *drink* that?"

"Yes, why not?"

"Even though you're *pregnant*?"

Blood roared to my cheeks. I had forgotten all about that one: my "pregnancy." The urge to dig myself out of my lie trembled on my lips, but the fib about the ultrasound had been too definite to deny. I should've been more vague. I'd need to whip up a miscarriage, or this make-believe baby could get to be a real bore. Then again, maybe this was an opportunity to stop drinking altogether. It was nice to know she cared enough to notice.

"You're right," I said. "I just wanted to taste it on my lips, but you're right, I shouldn't even *touch* alcohol. Not even one drop." I made a silly "Oops you caught me" face.

"Not even one drop," Jen repeated. "Unless you want a deformed baby with a big head." She surveyed me. A little smile tipped up the corners of her mouth as if she knew about my fib, and for the first time I noticed she possessed a chilly beauty, full of poise, not the all-bubbly persona I had first taken her for. Jen stood tall, her posture erect as if she carried a book on her head. The kind of confident, popular girl I had longed to be at school.

"I'll lay the table," I said, suddenly feeling as if Cliffside had nothing to do with me at all, and I was their guest. "And thank you, girls, for keeping me in check about the champagne."

Kate smiled. "It's because we care."

The subject changed, thank God, to solar power, and robots, and our future.

"Do you remember when that movie *Enemy of the State* came out?" I offered up. "No, of course you don't, you were all too young. I *think* that was the film. Actually, maybe it wasn't, you know, I can't remember. Well, the main guy—was it Will Smith?"

The triplets looked at me blankly. "Well, the Will Smith character was constantly being followed. The bad guys knew where he was twenty-four seven. It seemed so far-fetched and impossible. That was the first time we—the general public—got an inkling of how satellites watch your every move. How the government can keep tabs on you. It was startling. A real eye-opener. Of course, now it's not just the government, but anyone, any time. Thanks to Snowden, we know it's not just our paranoia."

I pictured the text. The note. The Facebook banner. I was the "anyone." *I* was the one being watched.

"A lot of stuff from movies has come true," said Kate. "Things we take for granted now. I see that when I watch movies from the eighties and before. Even *Star Trek*."

"Technology's moving, like, crazy fast," Dan joined in. "Faster than since the Industrial Revolution in Britain. But the masses aren't psychologically prepared yet for stuff that's already possible. Stuff that's already been invented, already out there."

Kate was rhythmically peeling potatoes. "It's not that we aren't ready, Dan, its 'cause they want to make more money, drip-feed us slowly with their crap. Milk the cash cow. Shove products in our faces we don't need."

"I know," I chimed in. "Facebook, for instance. Have you noticed how many ads there are? How specific? How do they know how to target the right person? Is there some way they know where individuals live?"

"Course," Dan said. "They know everything. How old you are. How much you earn. Your likes and dislikes. Where you live. What you buy. Your birthday. Why? 'Cause we've given them our data whether we meant to or not. It's easy for them to nail down their target demographic."

I filled a jug with water and ice and set it on the table. "Yes, but there's no way they could target one *individual* with their ads," I said.

"Course you can. All you have to do is create a custom audience with chosen email addresses. For the ad to serve, you need a list of, I think, at least thirty people. Let's say you wanted to target just me. You could add twenty-nine email addresses from people in New York, and me—then when you go to choose your audience for your ad set, you'd target only people located in California. Since all the other email addresses would be New York, I'd be the only person seeing your ad. Ensure that you choose an age range which includes my age, gender, and you can also use geographic micro-targeting, just to be extra sure."

My mind was spinning. *Micro*-targeting?

"Companies might want to target a specific address—a convention center, maybe," Dan went on. "*All* businesses use targeted ads. Even with all the publicity around Facebook recently, people have no idea just how powerful these tools are. Of course in most cases it's just about advertising, about selling products but as we know now politics has—"

"They love that people are sitting around Tweeting about the size of someone's ass," Jen interrupted, "or posting dumb selfies on Instagram or Snapchat so we get dumbed down. Then they can advertise shit to us that we don't need. They're doing their best to brainwash us so we forget about what's really important, like—"

"Hey," Kate said, "I do Snapchat, it's fun."

Jen gave Kate a withering look. "And the oil industry has a lot to answer for," Jen went on, "and our governments that want to keep us going round and round in this vicious circle of fossil fuel consumption. Look at the Swiss man—the psychiatrist—who flew across the world in a solar plane without stopping even once! Zero emissions! That should be on the first page of every news headline. Governments should be sponsoring all this cool technology, not private individuals. But it isn't in their interest to move forward, no, they want the status quo to stay right where it is. Keep having wars, keep selling armaments. It's all about the dollar. So fucking shortsighted."

Dan's knowledge about Facebook ads startled me. There was no way he was behind the Click-Here-To-Learn-More banner, or he certainly wouldn't be letting on he knew so much. But if he was so au fait with the ins and outs of how all this worked, who else knew? Was this stuff common knowledge? I guessed it was, and I was uninformed. These three weren't your average young adults, but clued-up. Intelligent. Frighteningly so. I hadn't had such animated discussion about things since Juan.

"You're right, Jen," said Dan, raking his hands through his thick mop of hair. "Take quantum computers, for instance. Google has a couple. Right now they cost over ten million dollars. These two computers? They've invented their own language between themselves. A language humans can't even begin to understand."

"A *language*?" I said. "That nobody can decipher?"

"The computers had no choice. Our language is too goddamn slow for them to express and communicate with each other fast enough. They think so quickly they need their own language! A quantum computer can calculate the outcome of thousands, no, millions of possibilities."

My mind swam off to my own possibilities, and the outcomes that could pursue me because of the bad choices I'd made recently. The various paths I could go down. I wondered what a quantum computer would advise me to do now.

Dan was marching around the room, pacing up and down, his hand pinching his chin in thought. "Computers are designed to work with the principle between one and zero. Any letter, any number, any word is coded like that. That's the binary way. Even a picture is coded between one and zero. We humans decided, at some point, that the binary way was the best method for computers to find solutions to problems. Quantum computers will be able to be creative, because they won't be limited."

Kate laughed and said to Dan, "Don't geek out on her, dude."

"No, this is interesting," I said. "Please go on."

"Quantum computers will open up a shitstorm of possibilities," Jen agreed. "Especially in the medical field. They could really help people. Help the environment too. Invent cures. Prevent disease."

Dan said, "No doubt about it, robots and computers will take over the world as we know it."

I pondered what he said. "What if all their knowledge and technology is used toward evil?" I asked.

Kate answered. "Evil for who? Evil's relative. 'Evil' people usually think they're working for some common good, so in essence, they're not evil."

I caught her eye and turned away.

"Our smartphones are going to seem so archaic soon," Jen said languidly, her eyes flicking to mine as if to check if I was on her side.

"Do any of you own a drone, by any chance?" I asked suddenly.

"Next paycheck, maybe," Dan said. "The one I have my eye on is pretty expensive."

Was it my imagination or did his gaze shine ice-green for a brief moment? Then the look on his face relaxed, a gentle crinkle framed his eyes, and he smiled his big Dan smile.

"Remember that drone that closed down Gatwick Airport?" I said. "How come nobody could find its operator?"

"You can fly a drone from anywhere," Dan explained. "In real time from the comfort of your chair at home. Via 4G or any mobile Internet or satellite phone. Like a military drone. As long as the geo-fencing's set up there's no way the drone can crash—"

"Geo-fencing? What's—"

"*Boring*!" Jen sang. "Can't we talk about something else? This conversation's getting majorly geeky. Let's talk about movies or books."

I wondered why Jen felt so uncomfortable. "I was reading a novel the other day," I told them, "and the protagonist, a police officer—our heroine—was texting and driving at the same time. The author lost me then. I couldn't root for her character after that. I stopped reading. I just couldn't accept a police officer texting and driving simultaneously. Is that very prim of me?"

"Not at all," Dan said. "When someone who represents the law's a hypocrite, it's hard to root for them."

I thought about my own profession as a lawyer. Representing the law, or at least an interpretation of the law, and how I'd not just broken my oath, but broken the law. I looked down at my feet and then stole a glance to see everyone's reaction to Dan's comment.

But nobody said anything. *Awkward.*

Kate silently arranged the potatoes and carrots in the casserole dish. Jen opened the fridge door and grabbed the half-drunk bottle of champagne and splashed some over the chicken. I wondered again if I'd be able to keep my hands off the booze over the course of the evening. I fished some napkins out of a drawer, linen ones that someone had given me and Juan for our wedding day, and laid them slowly on the table. I got out the crystal, too. Chunky, sparkly wine glasses—though none of us would be drinking wine—which chimed and echoed when you tapped them, and sprang prisms of rainbow light around the room. It was the golden hour. Sun streamed through the glass walls and doors. All yesterday's clouds and mist had dissipated. The ocean was calmer, lit up in a buttery yellow from the late afternoon rays. It had been a long time since I'd had guests at my table, and I wanted to impress them. Mrs. Reed had returned my call earlier and told me that although the triplets could be a handful, they were "good kids," and they certainly seemed to be. Treating me to this marvelous dinner, at their own expense, spoke volumes.

My eyes, straying around the room, reminded me that this house was bought with all the furnishings and fixtures in a real estate bargain that ousted a family from its home. The globe that hung above us, lighting up the breakfast bar. The sumptuous Italian sofas. Even the Persian rug splayed out across the floor, in all its softly woven, silken glory, almost as big as the room. It too had come as a package deal with this beautiful Big Sur property. None of this felt like mine at all. The whole lot was their inheritance, which had been sold from right under them.

I could only imagine the sheer desperation their mother must have felt to get in so much debt to fund her cancer treatment. The family had been cornered. I felt personally responsible somehow.

Dinner was delicious. The way the three of them had cooked it as a team and chatted with one another was like an ensemble dance and, although I thought wistfully about being their choreographer and being part of it all, I was just an onlooker, a member of the audience. But then things evened out. I had an old collection of DVDs, of films they'd never seen before, and the triplets were a little wowed. Finally, I had something of myself to offer them. We watched *Play Misty For Me*, and then *Rebecca*. Amazingly, none of them had seen either. Watching classic movies was something Juan and I did often. The best was going to the cinema, but we'd also stay home with a takeout sometimes and binge on Hitchcock or black and white oldies and goodies. *All About Eve*, *12 Angry Men*, *Citizen Kane*, *A Streetcar Named Desire*, and of course our beloved *Casablanca*. Those classics really meant something and with so much intrigue and heart. We'd recite our favorite lines to each other. He did great Bogart and Brando impersonations, and I surprised him with my breathy rendition of Marilyn's "Happy Birthday Mr. President." He teased me that I was his "dark horse." I often wished I had the confidence to go blond like Marilyn, wear high heels, be a sexy siren or femme fatale like Rita Hayworth, but Juan always insisted he liked me just the way I was. "My funny valentine," he'd call me. "My delicate English rose."

It was pleasurable to take on the role of "educator" myself for a change, passing down my knowledge of classic movies to the triplets. To be sharing again, to chat and discuss the plots, the characters and their motivations. That first evening with them—bright and animated—stretched into night. Long and vibrant and really entertaining. The first fun I'd had in over six months.

And I hadn't even had a drink.

CHAPTER TWELVE

It became a ritual a few times a week with the triplets. Long discussions about thought-provoking topics then dinner and a movie. Sometimes two films in a row. We even played charades, something I hadn't done since childhood. It was Jen's idea. We had to look up the rules. Movie, book, or TV. Only miming allowed, no words.

It was a Friday. I was flattered that these gorgeously attractive youngsters were choosing to spend their Friday with me. Even Dan, who was bound to have a string of eager beauties texting him at all hours, wanting to go out with him.

Kate stood before us, miming, manically pointing at her eye. We were all on the sofa, rapturously attentive to her every hilarious move, her wild gesticulations. No teammates. We weren't playing competitively. We were guessing a movie. Five words. Second word. It wasn't long before Jen leapt up and screamed:

"Eye. Honey, eye… *Honey, I Shrunk the Kids!*"

"Yay!" Kate shouted. "You got it!"

"Although, grammatically speaking, it should be, *Honey, I 'Shrank' the Kids,*" I chimed in, my mother's words spilling from my mouth. I shrugged. "That's Hollywood for you."

"Dudes, that one was way too easy," drawled Dan. "Next one should be really tough."

It turned out to be *2001: A Space Odyssey*. And it was a little harder. I was impressed the triplets knew about this iconic film. Or were they trying to impress me? I loved the idea that I had a positive influence on them.

"We didn't know about it," Jen told me. "It was you. You educated us, you told us we should watch it."

At those words my pride swelled. I felt like their big sister. Like part of a real family hanging out together.

Another evening we played Novelist. It was Dan's idea. It turned out he loved reading.

"So," he said. He had gathered up some pencils and pens from drawers and tabletops and was now ripping a sheet of writing paper into quarters. "We take it in turns to be the moderator. Let's say Jen's the moderator. She finds a book, from the library here, or going on Amazon and searching in the 'Look Inside This Book' feature. She just needs the first sentence. She can even give us the title of the book, or at least the genre. She writes that sentence down. Then we all write a fake but real-sounding sentence in the style of the genre, on our separate bits of paper. She mixes them up in a hat, reads them out, and we have to guess which one is the real one and which are the phony ones. It's a lot of fun."

I bit my lip. "I hope you don't pick sci-fi."

"I'll suck at romance," Dan said.

An Italian cookbook came next. I won the round and fooled them all with my first sentence. "The onion is at the center and heart of every Italian meal."

Dan won another round with, "She'd been dying slowly for ten hours." (Crime fiction.)

Jen's was: "The women filed past in a single line, steam rising from their bare, wretched backs." (A dystopian novel.)

Kate's: "Blackie sniffed the air." (A children's dog book.)

A few days later, a Monday, when everyone had a day off work (Kate worked as a hiking guide and Jen was a receptionist at one of the chic hotels nearby), the triplets suggested lunch. Then, on Wednesday it became lunch, a long walk on the beach, and a movie afterwards. I didn't need to graze around the kitchen or dig through the freezer for ready-made meals anymore. The three of them insisted on cooking (I paid for all the groceries), and with all the delicious leftovers, I enjoyed hearty meals for the week. They were so generous with me. Always bringing little gifts, or posies of wild flowers they'd picked themselves. These kids behaved like self-sufficient grown-ups, despite their circumstance. Unusual for young people these days, considering so many still live with their parents. Kate took to calling me twice a day. Telling me her troubles, which strangely never included her mother. Having the triplets around distracted me from my grief. And, more importantly, it made me feel needed, and being needed felt so good. I could give something of myself. It brought out the best in me.

As well as their wonderful company and the great rapport we were establishing, they proved themselves to be invaluable in practical ways. Dan was true to his word; he was a wiz with the tool kit and electrical stuff. He fixed the gate (connected it back to the alarm system), the broken part of the fence, adjusted the TV satellite, practically risked his life cleaning all the windows (suspended like Spider-Man on a harness) until they gleamed, and he even unclogged a bathroom drain. Kate, also, was fantastically helpful. Very strong and physically fit from her hiking, she thought nothing of lifting heavy objects—the weighty boxes of law books I still hadn't unpacked, for instance. She became invaluable to me, acting as my chauffeur (my ankle was still sore), and all sorts of other favors. With Kate—and Jen coming along for the ride—grocery shopping was no longer a lonely chore. I offered to pay the triplets for their time, but they refused. Their kindness touched my heart. Juan was gone, but this lot had become my sort of surrogate family. My life felt purposeful for the first time since his death. I was no longer agonizing about not having kids or beating myself up about my lack of courage to adopt a child as a single mother. I wasn't ready for such a huge step. The triplets were the perfect antidote: independent young adults, yet attached to me. They were like a gift.

Before I knew it, this lively trio was part and parcel of the house, and I was falling in love with each one of them. They had the entry code for the gate to come and go as they pleased. I had really begun to rely on them. But not just that, I valued their friendship, their company.

I was truly happy for the first time in ages. And, as if by total coincidence, I hadn't received any more anonymous texts. No drones, either. No Facebook banners. It was wonderful to have Dan, Kate and Jen come and go. The buzz of their presence, the warmth of their laughter. Jokes. Clever banter. Discussions. And I felt much safer no longer being alone. The triplets were almost like my protectors. Especially having brawny Dan around.

One afternoon, Sam, the contractor, came to visit. I had forgotten all about him and the whole retreat thing. The retreat was obsolete now—I had the triplets.

"Hey, stranger," he said, speaking through the video intercom. "It's me." I buzzed the gate open and went to meet him outside.

"Wow, looks like you've been working hard. The windows look great. See you oiled the front door—brings out the wood real nice." He got out of his pickup and stood tall and muscular, his razor eyes surveying the house and the new terracotta pots of hyacinths that flanked my front door. He raked his hand through his buzz-cut hair. He could have been military he looked so upright and well kempt.

Dan strolled up by my side. "How can we help you?" Dan said, shaking Sam's hand and introducing himself. The "we" made me feel good. I was glad Dan was here. I didn't want another pushy invitation from Sam to have a drink or discuss architectural plans.

"Just came by to see if you wanted—"

"All plans are off," I interrupted. "Can I get you a glass of water for the road?" I had never told the triplets about my retreat idea, and I wasn't about to explain now.

Sam took a step back, rebuffed. "No, I'm good, just thought I'd drop by."

"Thanks for the thought. Great to see you. I'm so sorry but—"

"It's okay, I'll be on my way." He smiled a polite but rejected smile, turned on his heel and got back into his car.

I smiled back, feeling a little mean but relieved. "Thanks for coming by, Sam," I called after him, trying to be nicer.

Kate strolled up beside me and Dan, wiped her dark bangs from her face and whistled. "A handsome admirer of yours?" she asked, after Sam had driven away.

"I don't think he'll be back," I said, and then it occurred to me. Was it Sam who'd sent the roses and the note? The text?

Having the triplets around was a definite plus.

Kate brought her laundry over one morning. It was funny how at first the three of them seemed so alike, particularly physically. But now their mannerisms, their facial expressions, the planes of their faces, and even the sparkle in their eyes were all as different from one another as summer is to winter. While Jen was willowy like a silver birch bending in the wind, Kate was grounded like a solid oak. It was these differences I grew to love. Jen wrote songs, and strummed away on her guitar. Kate loved to talk about politics and current affairs, Jen ecology. Kate was the practical one, Jen the dreamer. Kate and I could be silent together for long stretches of time without feeling we had to fill in the gaps. She was the sort of person I knew would save me from drowning. She called a spade a spade, chose her words carefully before she spoke.

"Why do you love this house so much?" she asked me as she stuffed the darks into the washing machine. She added soap powder and switched the button to ON. The old thing roared to life—even this had come with the house. Another reminder that made me feel more like a guardian than an owner of this property. But I was aware of a tinkle of a thrill by the silly fact that our clothes—Kate's and mine and Dan's and Jen's—were mingling together in a sort of dance inside the drum of the washing machine.

The family wash.

"Why do I love this house so much?" I pondered. I was surprised by her question. It was usually Jen who asked me stuff about myself. "Wouldn't anyone who had any taste, an appreciation for beauty, fall in love with Cliffside?"

Kate swept her hand through her dark bob and narrowed her sea-green eyes. "Yeah, I mean, of course it's an amazing house, but what is it in particular that makes it so very special to *you personally?*"

"Mainly because it's so open," I answered. I plucked a sheet from a pile of clean washing and totted up all the myriad reasons why this was the only place I'd ever want to live. "Help me fold this, Kate. Let me see, I love the rusticity of the landscape, that we're surrounded by such a sense of natural power, it—it makes me feel part of something big. Something so much bigger than myself. Something infinite. Maybe it sounds corny but, well, I feel closer to God, whatever, whoever God is."

"Don't you feel the woods closing in on you from behind sometimes, though? At night? When it's dark? I mean, there are no curtains, and when the lights are on anyone could, if they were—"

"We can always draw the blinds."

"But we never do, do we?" Kate said. We took a step towards each other in unison, touching hands as we folded the king-size sheet. I took the corners, matched them together and then we stepped back and shook out the wrinkles, before we stepped forward again.

"No, you're right," I said, concentrating on the folding. "We don't ever close the blinds, do we? And I didn't before you came, either. I can't bear feeling closed in. Can't bear the absence of light. Even when it's dark, you've got the stars and the moon, the light from the Milky Way."

It was true; the blinds were electric and could work as shutters against possible storms, but they were on the outside of the house, hidden behind stone, so I never even gave them a thought. Who wants to wake up in the morning enclosed in a box? Not me. I never pressed the button to draw them down. Ever. Now that the gate and fence were fixed, the only onlookers that could possibly get in were wild animals. Raccoons, skunks, wild turkeys, black-tailed deer, or maybe the occasional bobcat. Certainly nobody was going to crawl up from the side of the precipitous cliff below. Our only audience was the great ocean and the sky above, or condors gliding on an eddy of air. And, at the side of the house, the cathedral-like redwoods, pine trees, bays, and oaks. We were at one with nature. The wind would whisper through the canyons, through the forest, up from the ocean, as if it were talking to me.

"It's like being outside, really," I continued, now folding some T-shirts that I'd washed for Dan the day before. "I mean, when you're on a walk, you don't worry about being seen by invisible elements—the wind or the spray of the ocean. You blend in. You're part of nature. Am I talking nonsense?"

"No," Kate said, touching the diamond stud on her nose. "I totally get what you're saying."

It was the first time I'd had such a personal conversation with Kate. "I mean, this house is like an extension of outside, isn't it, Kate? You're simply *inside* nature, just a bit cozier, because you're protected by her glass walls. The house is part of the view, blending in organically with the woods and rocks. The interior's a shelter, I suppose, a sort of refuge. I feel safe here."

"I love the way you make Cliffside feminine." Kate threw her head back and laughed. I couldn't get over how like the photo of her mother she looked in that pose.

"Feminine?"

"You said *her* walls. Her glass walls."

"Did I?"

"Yeah, you did."

"Also," I went on, "there's another reason I love this place so much." I hesitated. Sharing traumas of my past was something I rarely did.

"Go on, you can tell me, I won't bite."

"I freak out in small spaces. When I was at primary school, I got locked in the art department cupboard by some classmates—"

"Class *mates*? You mean class *bullies*," Kate said. She pushed her dark bangs away from her eyes and paired a couple of socks together.

"I think the lead bully girl regretted it though." I didn't elaborate. Didn't let Kate in on the rest of the story, how I got my revenge with a pair of scissors. Chopped off pretty Emma Staunton's long, silky braid when she had her back turned. I had always dreamed of having a hairstyle like that. But my mother wouldn't let me have long hair, kept it pudding-bowl short—she cut it herself—because it was more practical, and she refused to pay for a hairdresser. The crunching sound—as I passed scissors through Emma Staunton's hair—was so satisfying after years of her taunting, her snickering. But sticking up for myself didn't pay off. I was punished severely. My mother wouldn't let me have any friends over for tea after that, and I was accused of being "unpredictably dangerous" by teachers. "Freaky Fingers" and "Edward Scissorhands" were added to my repertoire of nicknames by the mean girls. So when I arrived at my next school, a few years later, I devised a cleverer, more integral way of dealing with the bullies.

I folded a T-shirt of Dan's, my hand smoothing it into sharp, vertical creases. "That feeling of claustrophobia has never left me," I told Kate. "I hate elevators, public toilets, anywhere small and closed in. In New York, I always took the old-fashioned service elevators when I could—you know, the birdcage kind?—because there was air. And see? Notice how I've left the laundry door open? That's why I love Cliffside so much. The way it's exposed to the ocean makes me feel free. I never pull the blinds or close the door to my bedroom. I'd rather someone see me naked than draw the curtains, pull a blind, lock a door."

Kate thought about what I'd said for a beat. "Dan and Jen and I feel the same way about Cliffside. Our friends would get freaked out of their minds when they stayed over. Said they were being watched. Got spooked by the trees, said they moved, that their roots had legs and their branches arms. We just laughed at them."

"I'm so glad I'm able to share your old home with you three. To share Cliffside with like-minded souls. My mum also gets negative vibes from this place—says it's eerie. For me it's heaven on earth. I'd never ever want to leave Cliffside."

"Never, *ever*?" Kate lifted her gaze to mine almost as if her eyes—now a slatey-green—were searching for some change of heart.

"Never," I said emphatically. "Not as long as I live."

Silence. Kate looked down at the floor and chewed her lip. I almost felt as if I'd insulted her. I steered the conversation back to the architecture of the house. "The architect did a great job. Cliffside's as functional as it is beautiful. Although I have to say, I feel very claustrophobic in here with just that slit of a window, whose only purpose is to let in air, so I usually like to get things done as fast as possible or get Mrs. Reed to do the washing. In fact, I haven't been down here in ages."

"I love it down here," Kate said. "It used to be my secret bolt-hole. Dan used to hate it like crazy though. Never sets foot in here."

"Men hate doing washing, don't they?"

"It's not that." Kate's face flushed a little.

"What then?"

"When he was out of control, Mom used to lock him in here."

"Time out?"

"Yeah, but she was pretty harsh sometimes. You know, over-night and stuff. Sometimes she'd lock us all in the house. Once Dan tried to smash one of the glass doors with a hammer. He didn't get very far. They're totally smash proof."

I tried to picture the scene. A sort of *Mommie Dearest*? Or just an exhausted single mum trying to do her best? It was strange that this laundry room could be locked at all. Most houses didn't have locks on laundry room doors. Or even bedroom doors. But Cliffside had locks everywhere. I had gathered up the keys—two sets—and tied a different colored ribbon on each one, then stashed them all in two biscuit tins, one hidden in the garage, in a toolbox, and one in a kitchen cupboard, well out of the way. "It can't have been easy for her bringing up three children as a single parent, all three of you the same age," I said. "You must've been pretty wild at times."

"Dan could be a real pain in the ass, you know? He's better now but was a very dominant child. Jen and I had to learn how to stick up for ourselves, kick his ass once in a while."

"Well you're both strong and intelligent young women because of it," I pointed out, careful not to take sides. I thought of Dan and his latent temper and identified. In his case he needed a father figure. In mine, I had the opposite problem: an authoritarian, domineering tyrant. "My dad did things like force me to have ice cold showers in winter," I told Kate, "so I wouldn't be a 'sissy.' Or if I made him a cup of tea, he'd hurl it across the room if the milk-to-teabag ratio wasn't just so. I never played on weekends, just studied. He'd test me, and if I got any answers wrong he'd put the 'Princess Dummy' crown on my head. A plastic diamanté crown Mum had once bought me—I'd begged her for it—and he turned it into a mockery. If he'd been drinking, the belt might come out. He'd regret if afterwards, of course, and beg my forgiveness."

"Dude, he sounds like a total jerk!"

I realized I'd revealed way too much, but something about Kate made me want to share a part of myself with her. "He's got dementia now," I said. "And whatever he did, he's still my dad."

Kate looked at me uneasily, not knowing how to react. "You know who designed this house, don't you?" she said, changing the subject.

"An architect named Lee something-or-other," I answered. "He did an amazing job."

"She, *she* did an amazing job."

"Why did I always think Lee was a man? How ignorant of me! What else do you know about her? I'd love to know more. I googled that name once but found nothing."

"I promise I'll tell you everything. But I'm running real late for work. Get back to this later?"

Kate had me intrigued.

But not long after she left—just a matter of minutes actually—things shifted into a different gear, or rather, my paranoia raised its head again. I had told Kate I'd fluff and fold her clothes, and when I pulled them out of the dryer, I found some loose coins that she'd forgotten to take out of pockets, and sodden clumps of paper mashed together, stained blue from her jeans. They were the bits of paper from Novelist.

The blue reminded me of the note that came with the roses. Where *had* I left that note? I'd left it—hadn't I?—in the back pocket of my trousers, in my gray slacks? I went into my bedroom and found my trousers folded on a chair, ready to drop off at the cleaner's. Dan had offered to take them by on his way to work, but he'd forgotten, and they'd been sitting there for over a week. I emptied out the pockets then searched through other pockets of other clothing, just in case my memory was mixed up. But I found nothing. I rummaged in waste paper baskets, too (perhaps the cleaner had been careless?), but the rubbish had all been emptied, down to the last Q-tip.

No trace of the note.

Had someone taken it? No, I thought, I was being over suspicious, my mind acting like a dirty boot plunging into clear water, kicking up sludge.

CHAPTER THIRTEEN

A few days later, I braced myself to venture into the woods to check the spot. I had to do it, just had to.

But as I was on my way out, I heard a key turn in the front door. Mrs. Reed, no doubt. Her presence made my palms sweat. I had forgotten it was her day to clean.

"Good morning, Mrs. Trujillo," she said efficiently. She was dressed in deep mauve and armed with a bag full of things for the house. I had always left it to Mrs. Reed to stock up on cleaning products and decide the way Cliffside should be managed and organized. I was the newcomer—what did I know? Perhaps she had adored her previous boss, the beautiful, smiling blonde—the triplets' mother—and saw me as an interloper who had no place at Cliffside. Mrs. Reed's dark, ratty eyes held mine. I looked away nervously.

"Good morning, Mrs. Reed, thanks so much for coming. With all this rain of late it can't have been easy."

She brusquely shrugged off her coat and dumped the shopping bags on the floor with an exasperated thump. "Something bad will happen," she predicted. "This downpour will not let up. God's punishment, I guess."

I was about to say, "*Something bad HAS happened*," but I replied, "Well you've done well to get here, despite the weather." I had donned my raincoat and binoculars, the Thermos at my hip, my ankle feeling much better. I needed some fresh air. "I'm sorry, Mrs. Reed, I can't stay, as I was just on my way out." I slipped by her while she hung her coat on the rack. I smiled a vapid smile. I needed to get out of the house before I ended up wearing washing-up gloves and scrubbing toilets with her. That had happened before. Delegating had never been my strong point.

"See you in a bit," I mumbled. "And thanks again for making the effort to get here with the bad weather." I stepped forward and opened the front door. A gust of wind and rain whooshed in.

"You're going out for a *walk*, Mrs. Trujillo?" She raked me up and down, her eyes like claws, a subtle sneer masking her concern. "In this rain?"

I stopped in my tracks, closed the door, and turned my eyes away from her scrutiny, averting my gaze to the living room view. Raindrops slid down the glass walls of my house like tears. The sky was black, the ocean choppy, the air several degrees cooler.

With my head held high, I gathered some self-composure and answered, "You're right! I just wasn't thinking. Well, um, I have a lot of work to catch up on." I'd leave the visit to the dreaded spot in the woods for another day. In fact, better to leave it completely.

I wanted to chat to Mrs. Reed about the triplets, the history of Cliffside, their mother, but she was making me so edgy all I could think of was slinking away to the other end of the house. The sound of the rain patted at my nerves. I thought of the triplets again. Driving on Highway One in this unpredictable weather took skill. I knew how Dan drove. The idea of any of them having an accident filled me with dread. I was beginning to feel responsible for them.

"This is silly," I told Kate after dinner that evening. "Really silly. All this driving back and forth in the dark. I'd feel so much more comfortable, more at ease, if you all stayed overnight." I imagined how their mum would feel about them driving in the dark along these twisty roads, and knew that if I were their mother—and I couldn't help but put myself in her shoes—I'd be freaking out. "Knowing what the roads are like around here," I went on, "all those hairpin bends. I mean, look what happened to Juan." Oddly, the subject of Juan had not come up again, thus far. I had taken it for the triplets' discretion. Surely they must have known something? Maybe they had even asked Mrs. Reed about him. Now I regretted bringing him into the conversation. I'd really put my foot in it.

"Your husband?" Jen asked, not missing a beat.

No turning back now. "Yes," I said. I fidgeted with the collar of my blouse, fingers trembling slightly. I hoped they wouldn't notice, and I wondered if the shaking was because of being abstemious from drink or if I was just on edge lately.

"Why is your husband never here?" she quizzed.

I didn't say anything, but I knew I had to. Had to appease their curiosity. "He had an accident. On that nasty bend near Ragged Point. I don't like you all driving around in the dark. Why don't you stay the night?" I thought my invitation would steer them away from the topic of Juan, but I was wrong.

"You lost your husband in a car crash?"

I hesitated before nodding vaguely, wondering how much she knew. "I had the shock of my life."

"So that's why he hasn't been here all this time?" Dan said. "Like, almost seven months ago, right?"

I nodded. They knew a whole lot more than they'd let on. Were they simply trying to be discreet, keep my depression at bay by not bringing any of this up earlier? "It happened exactly seven months ago last week. Just after we moved in. I can't help counting the days." I held my head in my hands; a migraine was threatening to bloom.

"You must be so sad," said Jen, taking my hand.

I nodded again. "It turned my life upside down."

"But you told us when we first met you that your husband was away on business," Kate pointed out. "Why didn't you tell us the truth?"

My mouth felt like puffed up cotton wool. I shrugged, smiling weakly, trying to look calm. "It's easier that way, to just pretend it never happened. And I don't like strangers knowing I'm alone up here. Alone in this big house."

Kate put her hand on my knee. "Well, you're not alone now. You've got us. And *we're* not strangers."

I smiled.

"We can be your family now," Jen said sweetly.

CHAPTER FOURTEEN

It wasn't just the idea that the triplets were driving around in unreliable cars at all hours of the night that made me want them to stay. There was something else far more profound, almost palpable: I was beginning to feel I needed them. They filled the house with warmth, made it a real *home*. The family I had always wanted and never had. Laughter. Jokes. Even their shoes flung about, and dirty plates made Cliffside feel lived in as never before. The nonsense with losing the note that came with the roses… I brushed that aside. I'd been forgetful and my head scrambled since losing Juan.

I observed Dan now—he was always doing chores and favors for me—as he fixed a loose bolt on one of the sliding doors. His muscles in his forearms flexing, his eyebrows knitted in concentration locked beneath his tousle of hair, he smiled as he worked. I thought about his dead father's dog tag that he wore every day. It must have been tough for Dan as a boy growing up, not having a father figure. He looked up and caught me staring at him. I felt mortified for a second as if he could read my thoughts, but he just grinned, which made me avert my eyes.

"What?" he said. "What are you looking at?"

I shrugged my shoulders. "Nothing."

"Something's on your mind."

"No, really, just watching."

"Thinking I'm going to fuck up?"

"God, no, the opposite."

"It bugs me the way it's been rattling when it's windy. Just need to tighten it up a bit."

"I'm impressed, actually. I'm hopeless at handyman jobs. Can't even change a tire."

"Man, that sucks. Specially living round here where cell reception's so crap. You need to know that shit."

My ineptitude bubbled up inside me. "Just never got around to learning, that's all. Nobody ever showed me."

He winked at me. "Probably 'cause men always came to your rescue."

I had no clever retort so said nothing. He was right. Juan had always taken care of everything. And before Juan, my father.

Dan smiled. "Daddy's little girl?"

A burn of fury flared in my cheeks. My dad's voice purred "*That's right,*" in my ear—it did that a lot, his voice came out of nowhere, doling out advice, opinions, telling me how I needed him, how he'd "protect me" because "stupid weak girls can't think for themselves."

"I obviously need to give you a lesson," Dan said.

"A *lesson?*"

"Teach you how to change a tire."

"What? Now?"

"Yeah, why not? Now's as good a time as ever. You need to learn to be self-reliant. Something my mom taught my sisters."

"But I was living here all alone before you three turned up. I *have* been self-reliant."

"It's always a good thing for a woman to be able to get herself out of a bad situation, don't you think?"

"Well, I—"

"Come on, put something warmer on and we'll go outside. I'm going to teach you how to change a tire. You'll be glad I did."

I grabbed a jacket. Dan opened the door for me. How many twenty-year-olds open doors for women? Dan was always considerate. He'd also leave the last square of chocolate for me, thoughtful details like that. Accompanied by his broad smile, he made little gestures like passing me a cushion, or a throw to keep me warm when we were watching a movie, or handing me my e-reader, before even I realized I was in the mood to read. Sometimes he even suggested a book or author to me; he was surprisingly well read. I loved his taste in books. He was one step ahead of me and my needs. When Dan smiled, a little dimple popped to the right of his cheek. There'd be a wink or a nod, something to make me feel special. And it wasn't just Dan. The girls, too, could be so adorable. Braided my hair while we watched a film, or sometimes Jen would put makeup on me: blusher, eye shadow, even false eyelashes. She made me feel pretty, brought out my confidence. "There, you see?" she told me one evening. "You look gorgeous." She handed me a mirror. "See how the blue tones bring out the deep hazel of your eyes?"

The girls were organized, too. Always took care of loading and unloading the dishwasher and, since I'd had that chat with Kate in the laundry room, she and Jen did all my washing for me, to the point where I felt guilty. They'd been staying on friends' sofas, poor things, so I'd encouraged them to bring all their laundry here. The least I could do.

These three were like the family I'd always dreamed of. Jen had even written me a song.

"I still can't believe you don't know how to change a tire," Dan said.

We went outside. I trailed after him, remembering that somewhere, at some point in my life, I *had* learned to change a tire but had never done so since. Or perhaps I had just watched on helplessly all along, feigning interest as someone else did the dirty work. I never did like getting my hands messy.

"Don't look at me like that," Dan said. "I'm not letting you off so easy. We'll practice on my car."

It slightly annoyed me that he was bossing me around, but he was right, I should be able to change a tire. "That heavy old thing?" I grimaced.

"That's my point, you shouldn't feel intimidated by its size."

"Why not my Land Rover then?" Then I remembered I'd let Kate take it to do the grocery shopping.

Dan talked me patiently through the steps. Showed me the jack, the lug wrench (which surely wasn't called a lug wrench back home?), and where to place the jack, how to raise the car six inches off the ground, how to unscrew the lug nuts and remove the tire. How to put it back by lining up the rim with the lug bolts and tightening them by hand first, before lowering the car with the jack again—all this before you were even allowed to use the wrench. My hands were filthy, but I smiled away, determined to show Dan what a trooper I was.

"There we go, that wasn't so bad now, was it? Okay, so let's do it again," he said, an annoying grin stretched across his face, his strong jaw set in determination.

"What?"

"Change the tire again. Just to make sure this wasn't beginner's luck."

"I'll remember," I said. "I don't need to do it twice."

"You might not remember when you're in a panic and stranded in the rain late at night, with no reception on your phone. I worry about you. I want to know you'll be safe."

"Okay, point taken." My heart warmed to know he cared so much about me.

"This time I won't give any instruction, not a word, you'll do it on your own."

I surveyed his big, bashed-up car. The whole lot could come tumbling down on me. I wondered, for a flash of a second, if this was a crazy idea. "Please don't go," I pleaded. "Just in case."

"Just don't put any of your body parts under the car and you'll be fine," he said, reading my mind. "But I'll stand here and watch to make sure you're not doing anything dumb, don't worry."

I began the whole process again, asking myself how it came to be that dominant men had a hold over me—that I let them get away with "educating" me. My father. Juan. And now Dan. Whenever I thought I had broken free from one, I invited another into my life, the pattern repeating itself. Men advising what to do, even when they were trying to help me.

I stood there with the wieldy wrench in my filthy, oily hand. "You're so capable, Dan, you could get a really high-paying job. You could do anything if you put your mind to it."

"Don't change the subject, daddy's little girl," he teased.

I flinched at his new nickname for me. "Please stop calling me that!"

"Hit a nerve?"

"The joke's over," I snapped.

"Sorry, I was just kidding."

"My father happens to have dementia and is in a very bad way."

"Oh." Dan chewed his lip and looked at the ground. "So sorry, man, that's harsh."

"Just don't call me that silly nauseating nickname again, Dan, okay?" My eyes were pins, my gaze icy.

Dan took a step back, his hands up in surrender. But I could tell by the alarmed look on his face that he was scared of me.

CHAPTER FIFTEEN

Getting to know each of the triplets was like a study in anthropology. I couldn't decide which of the three I felt the most at ease with, who fascinated me the most. I was still unpeeling their layers, finding out what made each individual mind tick the way it did, what made each heart flounder, or race, or rejoice.

"You know, the other day," Kate began, "when we were talking about the architect who designed this house?"

Kate was driving me to Mr. Donner's, to work. My ankle was still playing up, and she was only too happy to act as my chauffeur. She'd drop me off, go to work herself, then pick me up, and we'd drive back to Cliffside.

"The architect?" I said. "Lee what's-her-name, the woman I had assumed was a man?"

Kate turned out of Cliffside's driveway. "A lot of people think that. Kind of sexist really."

"It's just the name Lee," I said. "It does sound like a man's name, you have to admit. Well, in England anyway, and let's face it, sexist or not, there are a lot more male architects than female. And to be fair, I do remember googling the architect when we bought the house and finding no information."

"That's because this house was the only building she ever designed. A bit like Harper Lee with *To Kill a Mockingbird*? That was before they forced her into being a two-time novelist, of course. I mean, she was a one-time deal for all those years. My mom was the same. Also named Lee."

"Your *mum*?"

Kate glanced at me then back at the road and said, "My mom's name is Lee le Sueur. She took my grandmother's last name. So you see why, with Mom being the architect of this house, Cliffside's part of our DNA."

This news left me speechless. A childhood home is a powerful enough force at the best of times, a place that forever remains part of your psyche—for better or worse—but a house designed and built by your *own mother*? This was a full-on magnet, a force so strong it would hold power over you for life. No wonder the triplets were drawn back here. Cliffside was the only home the triplets had ever known. I'd had a life—a shitty time at school, yes, but then university and Juan. A career. New York. Marriage. There was a big world out there, something the triplets hadn't really experienced yet. Cliffside was their cocoon. How could I, as owner of this house, deny them the loving embrace of their true home? Cliffside was too big for one person anyway. They'd been so helpful, especially Dan with all his fixing and window cleaning, and Kate, ferrying me about all over the place. They practically lived here anyway. I felt I owed them one.

"Kate," I said.

She kept her eyes on the road. It was raining again. "What is it? Everything okay?"

"Would you three like to move in with me?"

Her eyes misted. "Oh my *God*, are you serious?"

So the triplets all moved in the next day and commandeered their old bedrooms. At first Dan refused to accept, told me I was being way too generous and they'd be fine, but I insisted. It was my idea and my idea alone for them to live here full-time, to have their old rooms back, to ensconce themselves at Cliffside once again.

I admit, my decision was not out of pure generosity. I *wanted* them to live with me for selfish reasons.

"It's okay," I told Kate, as I walked with her down the hallway, carrying an armful of clothes. "I'll move out of my bedroom. It was Juan who wanted this as the master anyway. Really, take your old room back. Too many memories, I'll be glad for the change."

"*Really?* Are you *sure?*"

"Honestly. I want you to feel completely at home."

She hugged me. A great big bear hug. In that moment I felt I had absolutely made the right decision. "Thank you," she said. "You've been so amazing to us. We've told Mom all about you; she's so grateful, you can't imagine."

"What's life if you can't share it, right?"

"Right."

"You know, I think it would be a great idea if I had a chat with your mum. Let her know you're here. Let's set up a Skype call."

Kate shrugged and touched the stud on her nose. "Sure, why not?"

I was still waiting for one of them to bring up the "pregnancy," but nobody had. Had they forgotten? Or did they know I'd been lying? I made up my mind to nip it in the bud myself so as not to lose face or embarrass them.

"Anyway," I said. "I'm glad you're taking my old bedroom. The privacy of my new room will work better for me."

Kate smiled, her eyes twinkling, the dimple in her cheek showing me how thrilled she was to be invited to live here as family. "I get that. We're all a pretty noisy bunch, right? Please shut us up if we go too far." She took some of the weight from my arms. A coat dropped to the floor and I bent down to pick it up.

"It's not that," I said, my eyes cast down.

"What?"

"I just need time to rest a little, get my energy back."

"Oh, yeah, right... the *baby.*" Had she just put "baby" into quotation marks?

I nodded gravely. "But… I lost it."

"No!"

"Yes. I guess the writing was on the wall."

"The writing?" she echoed.

"I'd been feeling… not quite right," I said with a sad face.

"I'm *so* sorry."

Silence.

"Mom had a miscarriage once," Kate told me, saving me from more embarrassment.

I nodded in solidarity. After all, I'd had a miscarriage once, too, so I wasn't lying exactly, just extending the truth by several years. "There was a lot of blood," I elaborated.

"Jeez, did you go see a *doctor*? When did this shit happen?"

I thought about it for a beat. "A couple of days ago, when you were all at work. It happened in the middle of the day. Blood, but not crazy blood, you know. It was manageable. I mean like a heavy period, no more." To mask the shifty glint in my eyes I focused on the floor and hoped Kate would interpret it for sadness and drop the subject. Sharing intimate details like this felt too close to the bone.

"I am sooo sorry," she said again.

"When did your mum have a miscarriage?" I wondered if it had been before or after her cancer diagnosis.

"When I was little," said Kate. "We were all psyched about having a baby brother or sister, but it wasn't meant to be, I guess."

I felt a stab. I knew what it was like to lose a baby—at least, the beginnings of one. And my brother Rupert's death was something that had haunted me my entire life. It had shaped me, really. The daughter who had never lived up to her parents' expectations. The girl who should've been born a boy. The "disappointment."

"Your mum sounds like a very brave woman," I said. "Raising you on your own, battling with cancer, as she is now. She must be quite something," I said. "Very valiant. Very courageous."

It was Kate, now, who looked at the floor. "Battling, yeah."

"Maybe once you all get settled you can catch up with your studies," I suggested, changing the topic from her poor ill mother.

"Funny you say that, I was thinking the same thing! It's tough when you don't have your own space to study. Hard to even think straight."

"I know. But now you can. Like Virginia Woolf. *A Room of One's Own.* You *have* that now."

Kate took another of my dresses from my arms, and we continued our journey to my new room at the southern end of the house, to the swimming pool side. It was too cold to swim now, but there was a Jacuzzi, which I'd have all to myself. Or maybe not. Maybe the triplets would use it too. Wonderful on a starry night. This room was where my mother had stayed. I'd given her the most private bedroom in the house. I doubted she'd be back, though, now that Dad's dementia had taken hold. She hated Cliffside anyway.

"Why did you lie to us about being pregnant?" Kate asked, out of the blue.

My smile froze into a grimace. "What?"

"There's no way a pregnant woman would be taking so many painkillers. You know, for your ankle. Or drinking. I saw that empty bottle in your room, hidden under the bed."

I stared at her, not knowing whether to laugh or explode.

"It hurts when you don't tell us the truth," Kate said, biting her lip. "We need to feel trust."

A beat of silence. I didn't know how to reply. Luckily, after a minute or so, she changed the subject. "Were you a good student?" she asked.

"Yes, I—I—slogged hard."

She dumped the heavy load of hangers and dresses on the bed. "Did you go to college?"

"Yes. Yes, I did. I went to Exeter University. Studied Law."

"*Really?*" she said, her eyes wide with surprise. "I would've never guessed. I mean, don't get me wrong, you're smart and all, but—"

"I don't seem the type?"

"You're just… you don't… I can't imagine you fighting in a courtroom, that's all. You're too—"

"I wasn't an attorney, but a solicitor," I explained, still shamed by Kate catching me out with my pregnancy lie.

"A *solicitor?*"

I laughed nervously. "I know, it sounds dodgy, doesn't it? 'Soliciting,' as if my job is to stand on street corners in a miniskirt. I have no idea why it's called that in Britain."

"So what was… *is* your job, exactly? What the hell's a solicitor?"

"In the UK, there's a difference. You're either the type of lawyer who takes a bar exam and gets to argue in court—to prosecute or defend—or you're behind a desk negotiating contracts. I was the paper-pushing kind."

"You make it sound so, like, unglamorous."

"It's hard work, pushing papers around, believe you me. Let me know if you need anything, Kate. I'll have all my things out of your room by this evening."

"Hey, no rush." She looked around the bedroom, walked up to the sliding doors and gazed at the view beyond. She turned back again, her eyes scrutinizing every detail of the room. The limestone floors, the stone fireplace in the corner, the alcove leading to the cool Italian marble en suite bathroom with a massive walk-in shower and bathtub you could get lost in. "Love the way you've kept the room just the same, by the way," she said.

It was true. Apart from a few paintings we'd hung, and a rug or two, nothing about the house had changed at all. I never had been one for decoration or design, despite my grand ideas for the retreat. The retreat had been a fantasy, I realized now, nothing more. No, this was much better than a retreat. Having a ready-made family. These three had saved me from misery.

"By the way," I said to Kate, "I've been meaning to get extra keys cut for you all but keep forgetting. Remind me next time we go out."

"You're our lifesaver, you know that, right?" Kate said, her eyes misting over. "You're like a mom to us."

I smiled. In that moment I felt whole. She was so accepting of me, even with my fibs. These three were beginning to feel like my real family.

CHAPTER SIXTEEN

For the first couple of weeks after the triplets moved in, all went beautifully. They busied themselves at their jobs and I with mine, helping Mr. Donner sort out his estate. Just three days a week, it suited me perfectly. Trusts, mainly, for his children and grandchildren. He was being smart. A lot of people, including lawyers and even CEOs from Fortune 500 companies do not—extraordinarily enough—make a last will and testament. Perhaps it's an ego problem; because they're so wealthy they imagine they're invincible and will escape the inevitable. I had learned, through my profession as a lawyer, that rich and educated people can be dumb. As if their descendants are all going to sit nicely around a table, drinking sherry and discussing amicably how everything should be divided up fairly. And even those who do make airtight wills would roll in their graves if they knew how much discord and fighting goes on after they've passed away. The amount of families I had seen ripped apart from inheritance was staggering, and it didn't even matter how much money was at stake. People morph from being perfectly decent to lifelong enemies, even for the sake of a painting or a set of silverware. It is uncanny the amount of people who measure their late parents' love, not by memories or what they have done for them during their childhoods, but with material objects, postmortem.

Sad but true. And this is how I had earned a living while I worked at Davis & Trujillo, Juan and his partner's firm in New York, before we moved here. I had specialized in estates, inheritances, and mergers. It gave me insight into certain traits of human nature—how quickly love can turn to hate—and sometimes back again.

As fast as a hummingbird's wing.

My new life with Dan, Kate and Jen felt perfect. They were as helpful as ever. Kate now organized all the shopping and continued to drive me back and forth to work. In fact, I realized with shame that I had begun to rely on the triplets with abandon. To the point of wondering how I had ever managed without them.

But by week three of them moving in—sometime at the beginning of December—I became aware of whispers. They mingled with the winter mist, stole into the cries of barking seals, blended with the crashing surf.

Was I imagining things?

I was no longer drinking. Okay, that's a fib. I was drinking, just not so much. And although the triplets' presence replaced the hollow misery I felt after Juan's death, I still pined for him and had trouble getting to sleep. A good night's sleep was as hard to catch as the edge of a cloud. Sometimes I could snag it and ride its wave as I nodded off. Other times—most of the time, lately—it was like jump-starting a car. Just as I was swaying into bliss I'd get jerked by some outside force, like falling off a cliff. I'd often find myself sitting bolt upright in bed, awake and covered in sweat, going over and over what happened to him, and the part I had ultimately played. Why had he railroaded me into doing something so out of character? Why had I put my blinkers on? It had felt to me in that moment I had no choice, but we do have choices.

I had made mine.

As I lay awake each night, agonizing over my rash decision, the spot in the woods loomed like a bruise on my brain, garish and green, its purple intensity pressing on my migraine-tortured mind. It had brought on a new need for the odd sleeping pill—

over-the-counter ones, nothing too strong. Then I wondered if I'd been dreaming, imagining voices.

Overwhelmed with guilt and regret and sadness, my days became irregular. Naps here and there. I'd miss dinner sometimes, get up too late for breakfast. Go to work on automatic pilot, Kate dropping me off, picking me up. I'd notice myself drifting off sometimes when I got home, and although it was wonderful to have the triplets around, I felt alienated from everybody. But it was my own doing. Perhaps it was just latent grieving? Knowing I had company and so much help, I could finally let myself go, finally let myself mourn.

But one thing I hadn't expected was the intense paranoia that stalked my every step, my every thought.

It was midnight on a Friday when I knew the first whispers were real and I hadn't been imagining things. It was an unusually warm night. Or maybe I had been suffering from one of my unbearable, hallucinatory sweats? I had left the sliding door to my bedroom ajar, and I heard the triplets outside, on the patio above me. They were talking about me, no doubt about it. Indistinct snippets wafted down. I didn't catch it all.

"So she's basically saying he died in a car crash but—" It was Jen. The scraping of a chair blocked out the rest of the conversation.

Then five minutes later: "Disappearing? That is so fucking weird, man. Something's up." Dan.

More talking, but the whispers were so sparse and faint I couldn't hear a thing. A few minutes passed of muffled voices.

Then: "That would be the dumbest move of all," Dan whispered, "getting them involved. We don't want to get kicked out of here. Where would we live? We need to dig some more. Dig deep. And watch out for ourselves. Be really careful. We don't even know the woman. Not really. We don't know what she's capable of."

Dig deep. That was the last thing I needed. My blood ran cold.

After a small time lapse, I slipped my way upstairs barefoot, to see if I could catch more. But all I heard was Jen having a conversation with her mother. I could hear Jen smiling into the phone and imagined the animation in her eyes. She had a special voice when she parlayed with her mum. Switzerland was, what, eight hours ahead of California?

"We miss you sooo much. But, you know, things are cool here. What?" A pause. "Sure, we're studying again. I know, I know, we'll get back into the swing of it. What? Oh my *God*, that's such great news! Your oncologist sounds amazing. Sorry, when? Next week? Okay, we'll pray for good results. We'll pray real hard. Miss you, love you."

Her friendly chitchat made me wonder if I was being paranoid. Had I imagined those whispers? Were my sleeping pills playing tricks on my mind?

Or was my grave secret in grave danger?

CHAPTER SEVENTEEN

I couldn't resist. Something about the triplets' conversation got my mind ticking. My inner voice (very chatty as of late) was urging me, once again, to check the spot in the woods. "Dig deep." Yes, they'd been talking metaphorically, but those two words began to haunt me. Take me over.

Dig deep.

Dig deep.

The red roses flashed into my head. The text. The drone (that had miraculously not been around lately), Jen's constant questions, Kate's odd looks. She was a dichotomy, Jen was. Not as airy-fairy as I'd once presumed. I'd catch her rifling through drawers, "Just looking for a pen," or "Have you seen my phone?" or "I think my earring fell out," or nosing about the garage or the guest room. I'd put everything in the safe, out of her reach, just in case. Changed the code to a combination I wouldn't forget.

Just the week before, I'd spotted her rootling around the garden shed. In the dark.

"What are you doing?" I quizzed.

She looked guilty in the way only the guilty do and spun some tale about wanting to surprise me with planting a magnolia tree in my name. Told me how she felt competitive with Kate because Kate was my "favorite." I eyed her warily, but then she pulled out a piece of paper from her pocket and sang me a new song, a cappella. She'd written it especially for me. My heart melted a little and I berated myself for being so suspicious.

But my suspicions were back. I knew I should fight the urge to go to the woods, but I needed to see with my own eyes, see that the earth hadn't been disturbed. I couldn't lie still, couldn't sleep after hearing their whispers last night. Had they found something? Had they snooped around the grounds? They had offered to cut up logs from fallen tree trunks and branches and tidy the forest floor. I explained that creatures and other trees thrived on rotting matter, and I made the triplets promise to leave it well alone. That the detritus, the decomposition of leaves, wood, bark and stems was an integral part of the forest's ecosystem. For the biodiversity of flora and fauna. God forbid the triplets should start raking around.

I hadn't been near the dreaded spot for over seven months. Too paranoid about those electronic eyes and ears. Didn't want to be caught with my hand in the cookie jar. They could put spyware just about anywhere. Up close and personal, too. In trees, with infrared cameras, like they do for nature documentaries to spot leopards at night.

I'd played it safe so far. But things were taking an unexpected turn, and I couldn't control my impulse.

It was just after dawn. An early fog had rolled in, hanging over the bluff, mingling with the salty air. I could taste its whiteness on my tongue. It was only after I'd been walking awhile that I realized I was barefoot. This was the kind of thing that was happening to me lately. Scatty thoughts. Not thinking things through. My mind whirring with too many ideas and problems and solutions, through lack of sleep and bouts of melancholy. Why hadn't I put shoes on? Especially with my dodgy ankle still playing up.

I padded from the garden towards the woods, crushing the peaty piney earth beneath my feet, twigs scrapping at my heels, poking through the gaps between my toes. Starlings tweeted in pine branches overhead, rattling dewdrops down from above. A dollop of water landed on my nose, and I let it ride down and caught it with the tip of my tongue. Creatures scuttled about in the undergrowth, perhaps hunting for mice or voles, or wondering where they would hibernate this winter.

My ears rang with piercing silence, the silence of my own white noise judging me for the choices I'd made.

I'd done it for love. I did it all for love.

The house. She watched me now with her big, square, glass eyes, wondering what I'd do next as I scampered towards the woods. And then I saw a figure staring at me from inside, peering from the kitchen window: a black, willowy silhouette, still and wary.

It was Jen. I was almost sure.

I couldn't risk her scrutiny, questions, wondering why I was outside so early. I was not dressed for a hike. An oversight on my part; I should've planned ahead.

I made my way back immediately, falling over myself as I stumbled to my room, praying Jen, like the house, had not slipped inside my mind with telepathic powers. Because clever people can do that sometimes. They can hear what you're thinking. Beautiful, cool Jen. The three of them like a triptych in a modern museum. Their value priceless, their presence unfaltering.

They might be onto me.

CHAPTER EIGHTEEN

Paralyzed with wavering vacillation about what to do next, I scurried back to my room and ran a hot bath. I had nicked my calves on broken sticks outside, and a thorn had poked its way into the hard flesh of my right heel. My ankle throbbed. Had I twisted it again? I doused the bath water with orange blossom oil and submerged myself, wishing I could soothe away my predicament the way I would now soothe away my wound.

After a good ten minutes of soaking myself, I dug at my foot with some tweezers and finally eased the culprit out. A thorn. Just a little black dot, that's all it was. Amazing how such a tiny thing could throb so badly, impinge your freedom, make you limp. Just like my situation now. A little secret holding me ransom, forcing me to be its guardian.

Making me paranoid with every new whisper, every new look.

I observed the view—nearly every room in this house was witness to the great spread of heaving ocean, with its folding sky above—the sky, clouds and water-mass one big block of never-ending blues and grays: patterns within patterns. Shapes upon shapes.

I needed no art in this house. I lived inside a moving painting.

I heard movement above me. Breakfast. Talking. The triplets getting ready for work. Jen would no doubt be wearing some beautiful floaty dress. As a receptionist at her expensive hotel, she needed to look the part. And Kate would be dressed in hiking gear. I heard her footsteps clad in her work boots—heavier than

Jen's but sprightlier than Dan's—make their way to the driveway. Dan's hurried pacing next. The thud-thud across the living room floor. The front door clunked shut. The roar of his car's engine, the crunch of gravel, the squeal of tires. Both were gone. I then remembered it was Jen's day off.

She and I would be alone.

I sensed her presence. Light as a ballerina. Heavy as a judge.

It was only a matter of time before she'd figure me out.

Jen found me in the bathroom. I hadn't bothered closing the door because it hadn't crossed my mind that anyone would barge their way in. But of *course* Jen would barge her way in; how could I have overlooked her tenacious and curiosity-killed-the-cat personality?

"We need to talk," she said. She stood at the doorway. Wearing my bathrobe with confidence: teal blue silk, shimmering like cool flowing water. It reached her fine, delicate ankles, so delicate they looked as if they could be snapped in two.

"You're wearing my dressing gown," I pointed out.

"Oh, I'm sorry, I'll take it off if it bugs you. Just thought you looked so pretty in it. I love sharing clothing with best friends, don't you?"

Jen didn't even care that I was naked. Stood there, quite happily. I didn't know whether to be flattered ("best friends") or ashamed. I covered my breasts with crossed arms and wished I'd used bubble bath and not just oil. I loved that dressing gown. Juan had bought it for me in Paris. Along with some sexy silk underwear. But with my head groggy from lack of sleep, I wasn't in the mood to admonish Jen for wearing my robe.

"I would've brought you a cup of tea, but we've run out," Jen said, tucking a tendril of glossy hair behind one ear. In the light, her hair shone like spun gold.

"Run out of *tea*?"

"You've gotten us hooked on it."

For a second my blood bubbled. "How DARE you lot be so greedy with my tea!" I yelled, shaking. They had no idea how to make tea. I'd seen them heap in not teaspoons, but tablespoons of loose tea, piled high. And then dump the wet leaves into the garbage and start over again once they'd finished a pot. The art of adding boiling water hadn't occurred to them, despite my showing them how it should be done. My last lot of tea was from Harrods, and Fortnum & Mason, another gift from Juan, my special stock wiped out. Even the Lapsang Souchong, which they had scoffed at because of its smokiness, must have all been consumed. My hands were trembling.

"I'm so sorry, but, hey, calm down, it's just *tea*. I can get you more."

I sucked in a breath and counted to ten to combat my temper. Jen was right, it was just tea. I was being mean and chintzy. Being an only child sometimes made me forget to share. They were still kids. I should be delighted they had taken to my country's national drink.

Lighten up.

"You know what?" she said cheerily. "Way better than tea, I'll bring you some of your champagne."

My eyes lit up. I could taste the soft, rose-hued bubbles on my tongue already. The sweet, fresh, zesty fruits. "But it's the squawk of dawn, Jen."

"So?"

"I haven't had a drink for weeks," I fibbed. "I'm trying to give up, I'm trying to—"

"Just one little glass of Mumm won't hurt. You need to wind down. You've been working too hard lately at Mr. Donner's. *Relax.* Now lie back, just chill out. I'll be back in a jiffy." The triplets loved teasing me with my silly expressions and clichés.

Jen left the bathroom before I could protest further. I peeked from half-mast eyes to catch the sight of my blue robe shimmering as she glided out of the room. Jen had read my mind. Had sensed how nervous I was after my stint in the garden. I had thought about pouring myself a glass anyway—the taste, the relief, the sheer bliss of it—and Jen knew. Of course Jen knew.

She floated back to the bathroom and set the champagne glass and bottle at the side of the tub. It was like a Roman bath, practically, oval in shape, edged with Italian glass mosaics all around, which served as a ledge for magazines, drinks, even a laptop. Sometimes I'd spend hours catching up with work or reading. Jen poured me out a glass, and I took it from her, the pink bubbles fizzing with a beautiful hiss. Juan knew I loved pink champagne, especially Mumm, and had ordered it specially. Lucky. I wanted to just take a sip, but downed the glass almost in one go, like lemonade on a boiling hot day. So refreshing. My tongue rested on the myriad flavors like a weary head on a pillow.

Jen poured me another. I felt ashamed but couldn't resist. This was all wrong: me naked in the tub, drinking at seven in the morning, and Jen, practically a teenager, administering me my "drug of choice."

Wrong, wrong, *wrong*.

I swilled the bubbles around my mouth and gulped the next lot down. "It tastes delicious," I said, letting out a gasp of satisfaction. The lemony-rose tang danced on my taste buds. "You don't want any?" I said this out of politeness. That bottle had my name on it; I knew I'd down the lot.

"No, sweetie, I'm good," she said. Jen made to leave, but before exiting, leaned languidly against the doorway. "We kind of need to talk," she said, her deep tone a far cry from the "back-in-a-jiffy" voice five minutes earlier.

Adrenaline spiked through my solar plexus. The reality of the situation came rushing back. What had Jen seen? My mouth puckered at the thought of what I'd buried; my heart vaulted.

I took another gulp from my glass. "Oh yes?" I said, trying to sound unfazed. "What about?"

"You've been acting kinda weird lately. Spending time on your own. Why didn't you join us this morning for breakfast?"

I made my mind up I wouldn't deny being in the garden. I *knew* she'd seen me. "Because you were in a rush. And I was cold outside in the garden, in my bare feet. Came in for a hot bath."

"What were you doing outside so early?"

I splashed some water on my face. "It's my house, Jen."

"You keep saying that. And reminding Kate it's your car yet you never even use it and she's busting her ass for you. Shopping, driving you around. We get hurt feelings, you know."

I pressed my clammy hands to my eyes.

"Don't you want us here? Maybe you'd prefer it if we weren't around at all." Jen's pretty mouth pouted and she stared at the floor.

The quiet words are the ones that stab the hardest. The cold jab of them sank in. The idea of getting rid of them after the whispers had crossed my mind, true, but now she was suggesting leaving herself, the notion of being alone again was abhorrent. The looming silence. No banter. None of their music playing, or Kate's clompy footsteps. Nothing to distract me from my loss of Juan. Christmas was coming up soon. "No! No, I love you being here, Jen." The whispers, I decided, had been in my head. Perhaps I had dreamt them, the way I had dreamt about Juan and the blotting paper. Choppy sleep patterns, mixed with even the mildest tranquilizer, can do that to you—distort your mind, make fantasies and dreams seem so three-dimensional. Even a regular dream can spin you way off-kilter.

"We can leave, you know," she offered, "if you're uncomfortable having us around. My friend Janice said I can sleep on her couch."

I shook my head in a decisive "no" and looked down at my nibbled, ripped cuticles. The shape of her words smothered me with rising panic. I'd be a sitting duck for the drone operator without Dan here to protect me. It wasn't just a coincidence that drone hadn't come back, surely? Not to mention the isolation. I'd feel like a widow once more. A sad, lonely, grieving widow.

"If you don't feel like sharing," she continued in a somber voice, "if you'd prefer to go back to the way you were before. Before you met us… we'd totally understand. No hard feelings."

Reality clipped like a pair of shears. "No, please, Jen. I do *not* want you to leave."

"Then please be more honest with us. Trust us. Share yourself more. Open up."

"Share what? I thought I *was* sharing."

"Sure, you've shared a *little*. You made a big effort at the beginning, but now you're holding out. The way you hold back… your feelings, it hurts."

I absorbed her words and hurt tone. "Okay, I'll make a note of that," I said, and poured myself a fresh glass.

"Our mom is *dying*. You're all we have right now. We need stability. Being strong all the time for someone is tough for us. We need a little love. You're our rock. You're everything to us right now."

It was true. I'd only been thinking of myself. "But you have each other," I said, my pulse racing with relief—relief that she wasn't repeating the whisper-talk I thought I'd heard the other night. The dreaded words, "Dig deep," the threat that they were onto me. A fumbled joy tugged at my heartstrings to know they even cared. That they needed me.

"We're just kids still," she went on in a soft voice. "Even Dan. He acts so brave, but he's just a boy inside. Do you know how much this means to us? To have you include us, take us in and share your life with us? You've been like a parent. Don't hold out on us now."

"I'll try. I'm just—"

"Your husband, you mean? You're still sad?" Jen's quick green eyes held mine for a beat. I looked away awkwardly and turned the tap to hot. Water gushed into the tub.

"Yes, I'm still sad," I murmured through the tumbling splashes.

Jen changed her weight from one leg to the other and adjusted her (my) silk dressing gown. "He died in a car crash, right?"

I blinked at her. "Look, I really don't want to discuss this right now." I was glad the churning water drowned out my voice. A lump gathered in my throat.

"Okay." But then she asked, "How many years were you married?"

"Ten." *Give or take.* I wasn't about to tell Jen the nitty-gritty truth.

"Happy years? You had a good marriage? You wanted kids?"

"Jen, I don't care to visit that place right now, it's all so…" I couldn't finish my sentence. My vision blurred with tears—champagne tears or real tears, I wasn't even sure—and before I could gain any control over myself my naked body began convulsing with sobs. I began thinking of my miscarriage with Juan, the whole IVF fiasco, the knowledge that I'd never have children.

"You tried for a family?" Jen persisted.

It all poured out in a torrent. "I suffered a miscarriage. I was forced to go under general anesthesia and have a D&C the day after they did an ultrasound and found our baby had no heartbeat and was dead in my womb. I was heartbroken. We tried for a baby again, but I didn't get pregnant a second time."

Jen laid her hand on my sweaty forehead. "You poor, poor thing." Her voice was soft and caring, which made me cry all the more.

Tears were streaming down my face. "I was so d-desperate for a child. My mum was begging me for a grandson. My gynecologist suggested IVF, and I was, you know, thrilled at the idea, but when I put it to Juan, a look of absolute fury flickered in his eyes, and he said, '*IVF?* Are you *kidding* me?' I realized his pride was more important to him than starting a family. He was convinced we could get pregnant without it."

"Men can be pigs," Jen said. "Excuse me, but that was real selfish of him."

"When I told my gynecologist how opposed Juan was to IVF, she told me, 'Well, you don't have much choice. From the results of his semen analysis, you've either got to do IVF or your husband needs a vasectomy reversal. It's a miracle you got pregnant the first time—one chance in a million—not likely to happen again.' And I said to her, 'But he hasn't *had* a vasectomy.' And she said, 'With that low sperm count, I can assure you he has—believe it or not, some men hide it from their partners.' So you see, Jen, I felt totally betrayed by him all round."

"No shit."

"I guess I must've erased that conversation with the gynecologist from my mind. She was young, fresh out of residency. I decided she must be an ignoramus. I never did bring up that discussion with Juan. You know, talking about his low sperm count with a stranger, even if she was a doctor, especially knowing how opposed he was to IVF to begin with. I couldn't have risked it."

"Couldn't've risked what?" Jen asked.

"Couldn't have risked losing him."

There was a throb of silence then she said, "I can see how you felt betrayed by him. I hate to say this, but d'you think he was cheating on you? Like, in love with another woman?"

I flinched at her words but didn't reply. Just went on crying, sobbing my heart inside out. Exposed and nude, I felt more vulnerable, more broken than ever.

Jen bent down and kissed my forehead. My shimmering blue robe, sumptuous on her long willowy frame, grazed my cheek. "There, there, don't cry. It's *okay*. Everything'll be okay. I'm here." She took a sponge and squirted it with some lavender bodywash. "We all need each other, we're family, right? You, me, Dan, Kate. We're all working our asses off so we can go visit our mom, but meanwhile we need you to get us through this, so be strong for us. You're our mom number two!" She smiled and mustered up a small laugh. "Forget your past and whatever Juan did. You've got *us* now."

"I'm so… sorry," I heaved.

"It's *okay*. Let it all out. Just let it all… *out*." She laid her free hand on my forehead and pushed back my hair from my sweaty brow.

I closed my eyes. "I'm sorry, I feel such an idiot."

Lathering up the sponge till it was foamy, she laid it gently on my back, her slender wrists making circular movements on my skin. I bent forward, crouching in a semi fetal position, hiding my breasts. The intimacy was awkward. But it felt soporifically soothing—I hadn't been aware of how tight my muscles were—as Jen rubbed me all over, taking care to let the sponge creep up my spine, the nape of my neck, and along each shoulder, one by one. I could feel the knots loosen. It hit me that nobody had done this for me since I was a little girl. Not since my mother had bathed me. It made me blub all the more. I gulped great mouthfuls of air and made a strange baying sound that seemed as if it came from somewhere else, not my own lungs.

Jen was the grown-up. I was the child. We had shifted roles.

Everything was out of kilter.

CHAPTER NINETEEN

Before I knew it I had polished off the whole bottle of Mumm. It tasted so delicious, so easy, like an old friend settling down for a long chat. The familiar buzz and honeyed sweetness—sweet, but not too sweet—was a welcome guest.

The bathroom felt like a boudoir. Under-floor, radiant heating. A chaise longue. A coffee table piled full of magazines. And, of course, the floor to ceiling picture windows, looking out to the ocean. Sometimes I could spot gray whales in the wintertime, on their way to their calving waters in Mexico. And on a moonless night, phosphorescence like sparkling diamonds.

This view was magical.

One in ten million houses were this special.

I'd been soaking in the tub for two hours. But it was still only nine o'clock. I jolted to attention as Jen re-entered the room, a trail of marijuana billowing behind her.

"You smoke weed?" I asked her. I had never allowed smoking in the house. I wanted to tell her smoking was forbidden, but it was like the pot calling the kettle black, considering I'd downed that bottle of Mumm. The champagne haze had completely taken hold of me, from the tips of my toes all the way up to my scalp. I was plastered. Hardly setting a good example of propriety.

"I indulge now and then," Jen said. "I thought I'd keep you company, but I see you've drunk the lot. 'Birds of a feather flock together' like you say. Want a hit?"

"No. God no. I've got to go to work later." The words trilled a little on my tongue. I wasn't due at Mr. Donner's until three o'clock. Still, it would take me a while to ride this out and freshen up. A couple of liters of water would do the trick. No big deal, it wasn't like I'd drunk a load of whiskey or anything. I'd be able to function perfectly.

"I canceled for you," Jen told me casually.

"What? Jen! You can't go canceling my work! Mr. Donner's expecting me!"

"Not anymore."

"How did you even have his number?"

"It was in your phone."

I remembered I had deactivated the password as I kept forgetting it.

Note to self: put new, easy-to-remember passwords on everything.

"Jen! You can't do things like that. There are barriers." But it didn't come out like that. I heard the lisp in my voice… barrierrzz. I had meant to say "boundaries," but boundaries and barriers were all rolled into one confusing mix. My excitement caused me to slip violently backwards in the sheeny bathwater, submerging me as I slithered around and spluttered up the oily, orange-blossomed water. When I came up for air I saw my toes and fingertips were shriveled little prunes. How had this happened? How had I allowed Jen—practically a teenager—to hang out with me in my bathroom smoking weed, while I was *naked* in the bathtub, and boozing? Black and white had been blurred into a hazy gray. It was shameful.

Get a grip!

"You call him right back, and you tell Mr. Donner that I will be there at three o'clock sharp. I cannot believe you did this!"

"I'm sorry, but I didn't like seeing you so stressed out, so sad. Thought you needed a break. Anyway, he seemed relieved. Happy to have the day off. Said he'd go to Pebble Beach and play golf."

"That's my *income* you're meddling with! I have a reputation to think of. That's my *job*, which I happen to take extremely seriously!"

Jen pouted. "Don't be mad at me. I felt like hanging out, is all. Wanted to put a smile on your face."

I had no answer. Should I be flattered? Furious? This job was my lifeline. No kids, husband dead. At least my job gave me a sense of self-worth. But then, how would Jen, at her age and with her limited life experience, know how I felt? How my career and doing well academically had been the one thing I could rely on, the one thing that had never let me down?

Jen took another drag of her fat, badly rolled joint. Sitting at the dressing table, she dabbed some of my expensive French perfume behind her ears, and in the crook of her slender wrists, all with the joint still in her hand, as if it were the most natural thing in the world. I suspected this was more than just a "now and then" vice and bet the others smoked too. She languidly stretched herself up like a yawning lioness, and I sighed, but she had no intention of leaving. No, she simply sprawled herself on the chaise longue and picked up December's *Vogue*.

"I tried modeling once," she said dreamily, tapping her finger on a glossy Gucci ad. "But I didn't like it. It's shitty work, you know. They make you schlep around with your book, all over the city. Which is really dumb, because they don't even care what you look like in the flesh. I suffered New York for one long, hot summer. It was so *boring*. And humiliating, actually. I didn't have the look they were after anyway."

"*You*, humiliated? I can't imagine."

"Yeah, there were girls taller and prettier than me, it made me feel small. Haven't you ever felt that way? Like everyone else is more special than you?"

"Of course."

"When?"

"Well, I had a terrible time at school."

"Really? Why?"

I hesitated then slurred, "I was born with a birth defect that affected me horribly."

"No way! Like one of those strawberry birthmarks?"

"Six fingers." *Oops, I didn't mean to share that with anyone. Too late.*

Jen's jaw dropped. "No way!"

"It's more common than you might think. It's called 'finger hexadactyly.' They also call it radial or preaxial polydactyly." I heard my tongue try and roll around the words "preaxial" and "polydactyly." Was I really so drunk?

"Sounds like a dinosaur or something."

"That's just how I felt as a child, like a freaking dinosaur. 'Freaky Fingers.' 'Edward Scissorhands,'" I lisped.

Jen laughed and threw her head back. She looked like her mom in that photo they showed me. "I don't know, it's kind of cool to have six fingers. You could have, like, played guitar extra fast or something. Or done card tricks."

"True, but I didn't have that kind of bravado."

"So how come your parents didn't take you to a surgeon to get finger number six removed?"

"They did, but not till I was thirteen. As it was well formed and healthy the doctors advised them that there was no reason I should have it removed, unless for psychological or aesthetic reasons. They warned my parents I might get teased at school. Ha! That was the understatement of the year. Spiteful children don't have much empathy for disabilities, do they?"

"Jeez, why did it take your parents so long? Pretty cruel, huh?"

I thought of my father's roaring temper, my mother's snappy voice. I remember feeling at the time it was all my fault. "I guess they'd never read *Lord of the Flies*. I used to lurk in the playground, in corners and shadows, to avoid the bullies. Society was less politically correct about handicaps back then. Nobody came to my rescue, not even the teachers. Eventually, though, I found ways of dealing with the bullies."

"Dude, school must've been harsh. Speaking of your mom, she called on the landline yesterday. I pretended to be the cleaner."

"Why didn't you tell me she'd called, Jen? I don't want you lot interfering with my calls, you've all got your own phones!" Secretly I was glad she had lied to Mum. So far, I hadn't told her about the triplets. I didn't dare. My mother would be horrified to know I had "strangers" I'd "picked up" on my walks, living with me.

"Sorree. I was curious. Wanted to know what your mom sounded like. I told her you were out."

"You shouldn't take liberties in someone else's house, Jen."

She didn't reply. I waited for her to get up and leave, but she carried on casually thumbing through *Vogue*. My pulse was thrumming with agitation.

"Jen, really, I need to get out of this tub and get dressed."

"Go ahead, get drezzzzed," she copycatted. "I'm not stopping you."

"Stop it! I know I've had too much to drink, but I'm going to snap myself out of it. Get myself together and, whatever you say, I'll call Mr. Donner back and at least give him the option of working with me today. You had no right to—"

"Just chill. Like I said, he'd rather play golf." She rolled onto her stomach. "You were up to something this morning, weren't you?"

Her sudden question zapped me like an electric shock. The bath was getting cold, and I didn't want to stand up in full naked view so I added more hot water. Pretended I hadn't heard her.

"You were sneaking around in the bushes, going somewhere secretly. Don't dee-ny it!" She made a singsong of the word "deny." This was a game to her. She was treating me like her playmate.

I needed to take my power back. "That's enough, young lady. You get *out* of this room and give me some privacy. You'll have to leave this house if you can't learn to *respect* me!"

Jen leapt up suddenly and tossed her long blond hair, glancing at me over her fine chiseled shoulder. "Soreee, I was just kidding! All I wanted to do was hang out and make you feel better. Remind me not to give you any more alcohol if you're going to *hate* me so much." She stomped out of the bathroom. At least, "stomping" as much as her delicate bare feet would allow.

The room rang in silence. My harsh words ricocheted back at me like a punishment. My hand twitched in a spasm, taking me way back to that person I did not want to be: the friendless loner.

Two minutes later I already missed Jen's presence. Her boundary-pushing was her way of feeling close to me, of being my buddy. I reminded myself that this was the way young adults behaved in all homes. *All* families. Everyone complained how youngsters had a sense of entitlement these days. Some of my friends' children acted like spoiled brats. Still lived at home, many well into their twenties—even thirties—without jobs, and without contributing anything at all to the household. Their mothers even did their laundry and cooked all their meals. At least the triplets pulled their weight. In fact, I was the lazy one by comparison. They were doing everything for me.

I'd let myself slide.

I'd let myself lose control.

CHAPTER TWENTY

I got dressed, selecting a pair of stretchy black slacks and a cream silk blouse. I gathered my dull brown hair into less than a fist's worth—because sadly, the mane I hankered after lived only in my imagination—and smoothed on a sheen of something that promised body and shine, and scraped my paltry locks into a high ponytail. I grabbed a bottle of mineral water from where my wine lived—in the special fridge—and glugged down the whole liter without stopping.

There! Under control. The thud of a distant headache, like thunder threatening to roll in from afar, lurked in my temples, but I nipped it in the bud with a couple of migraine tablets, downing them with another full glass of water.

All new again.

I was now mentally prepared to call Mr. Donner. Fill my stomach with something nutritious to soak up all that champagne, something like porridge with dollops of local honey, sprinkled with raisins, and healthy slices of organic apples from Joe Flynn's farm, courtesy of the triplets' fabulous shopping habits.

I'd give Jen a real bollocking. Show her who was boss in my own house.

I purposefully marched up the stairs, my posture arrow-straight and indomitable. But then I heard a noise. Whispering again. Interspersed with tears and great gulps of air. I had sounded like that just a while earlier myself.

It was Jen. Talking on her phone. Sobbing.

"I shouldn't've… but, you know, I thought we were such good *friends*. I miss you, Mom, and I believed me and her really had a bond. I guess I ju-just don't understand… sorry? What did you say?"

Silence. Her mother was evidently giving her wise advice on the other end of the line. My heart pattered unevenly. Poor Jen. I'd trampled on her feelings. You could never underestimate the "bravado" of a female who was not yet a real woman but no longer a teenager. Caught in between a hard place—and not a rock, exactly—but the obstacle of her own self-doubt. Now aware she wasn't the cocky thing I had taken her to be, my stomach dipped with sympathy. At her age, I'd had my nose in my studies, my head immersed (in my free, non-study time) in a world outside my own: books. Mostly about true crime. That's what held my interest. Non-fiction books about serial killers and hot-headed, dysfunctional family members, perpetrators of domestic murders. I had hardly ever had conversations with people older than myself, apart from my parents, because my world seemed so dull by comparison to my book world, and apart from teachers at school, I didn't often have the occasion. I read and read and read. Originally, I had wanted to be a criminal lawyer, but my inhibitions put obstacles in my path. The idea of speaking in public, especially before a judge and jury, horrified me. They had given us exercises in law school so as to weed out the less confident ones, the ones cut from the wrong cloth to be barristers. They let us know in no uncertain terms what the stakes were, how you'd have to put yourself on the line and be as clever an actor as you were a mind. With an infallible memory, too. Since falling off a horse at the age of fourteen, I tended to get certain things mixed up: dates and so on. It was why I was so bad at remembering passwords and numbers. I had to send text messages to myself sometimes so I didn't forget. All my passwords were locked in my safe, but then I needed the code for the safe itself so I had it hidden in a faux "book" about opera. Then I freaked out that one of the triplets (or Mrs. Reed) might find it so I picked a password I'd never forget: a date nobody else would know about. I was useless with statistics, too. No, I hadn't stood a chance of making a good barrister. Not a chance. Still, my fascination with the criminal mind had never wavered.

Little did I know back then I'd have my very own crime scenario to deal with.

Jen continued the conversation with her mother, weeping quietly into the phone. "But I really thought we were… I shouldn't've expected so much. I just feel so *hurt* inside. I was beginning to… well… *love* her. That's it, we all love her so much! She's family now. She's smart and quirky and… I know it sounds crazy, but I feel so *vulnerable*. You know, Mom, dropping out of college and all, I need a grown-up to get me through this. Listen, Mom, I need to go, this call is costing me a fortune, the Internet's down so Skype's not working. I can't even pay for food right now, or gas. Things are so expensive, and we've been cooking her really special meals, you know, to say thank you. But… I'm really, really broke." They chatted on for a while before Jen said her goodbyes and finished the call.

They loved me? I was family? Guilty, I took my ear away from the door. It was true; the triplets had been cooking delicious meals for us all. Not frozen TV dinners heated up—the sort I had relied on—but real, hearty meals at the dining room table, with organic fruit and chicken, and things I'd never even tasted before, like quinoa from Bolivia. They had brought me into the bosom of family-hood, and I'd taken them for granted. I'd been so out of touch with reality. Me, the rich girl, cushioned by her husband's lucrative wheeling and dealing, in her gilded, modern, towering castle, like a sort of Rapunzel—yet without the prince and without the bounty of hair to go with it—my bank balance nice and healthy, letting virtual *children* cook for me, work for me for free. What had I been *thinking*? I'd been so selfish. Giving them money for groceries, yes, but clearly not enough! Jen was crying and in financial straits. What was *wrong* with me?

I'd been as insensitive as a concrete wall.

I hovered by Jen's bedroom door, not knowing what to do next. Playing mother, or a surrogate mother, was no picnic. The triplets were, what, seventeen years younger than I was? Not a big age difference for people in their thirties or forties, but a great divide for those in their twenties. I'd read sweet Jen all wrong from the start. She wasn't this tough, glamorous, "fuck-you" twenty-year-old, but still a child. How could I even imagine what she was going through with her mother? The triplets' mom was on her deathbed, by the sound of it, the disease devouring her every cell, and all I had thought about was myself. They loved me. I was all they had right now.

"Jen?" I said tentatively. "Jen?"

"Go ah—way," she blubbered, her words muffled by her pillow. She was face down on her bed, bawling.

"Jen, please. I'm so sorry. I didn't mean it. Please. Please, let's be friends."

"You don't wa-want me here, it's so *obvious*."

"I do, I love having you all here, I'm just not used to a house full of young adults, that's all. I love having you all to keep me company."

"Kate, yeah, you love *her* because she's 'infallible' and 'as strong as an ox.' And Dan, only 'cause you think he's *cute* and fixes everything."

I tiptoed over to the bed and laid my hand gently on her soft blond head. Had I unknowingly flirted with Dan?

"You're *all* cute," I assured her. "I'm fond of *all* of you, in equal but different ways."

"Fond? What does that even mean, 'fond?'"

"That I have fee—"

"I know what it means, it means *bullshit*. Don't you get it? Don't you get that we all feel so much *more* for you than just 'fond?' We *love* you!"

Her words stunned me. "I love you too," I said, caressing her hair, and I sort of meant it. As much as you can "love" people after only a month or so of knowing them.

I stayed like that for a while, gently stroking her head, whispering sweet soothing nothings. She calmed right down and dried her tears with her comforter.

"I've got an idea!" I said brightly. "Why don't you and I spend the day together? Why don't we go and have lunch, or do a little road trip somewhere? We could drive down the coast to Hearst Castle. Get out of the house, how about that?"

"You've been drinking, you can't drive."

I had already forgotten that. "Well *you* drive, then."

"I've been smoking a shitload of weed."

"Good point." I laughed. "We could do Uber?"

"How much money do you have to burn? Hearst Castle's miles away."

"You're right. Well, I could call a friend and get her to come along, too?" I thought of horsey, jolly Pippa. I didn't particularly want to see her, but I knew she'd say yes. Plus, I felt bad for being so cold with her at the restaurant and hadn't seen her in weeks; I needed to make it up to her. She made her own hours and could always take time off work. She could even write a piece about her day out. Sell it to some travel magazine. I wouldn't tell her who Jen was, that she and her siblings used to own my house. No, that would get Pippa all riled up and judgmental—looking out for my interest, of course—for my "own good"—and I wasn't in the mood to see concern plastered all over her long-jawed face. I'd tell her that the triplets were second cousins. I wouldn't get away with "nieces and nephew," because Pippa knew too much about my family. Second cousins sounded plausible. Even though

I wasn't even sure what, exactly, second cousins were. I'd brief Jen on my little white lie in case she put her foot in it.

Jen shrugged. "Sure, bring your friend."

My offer was two-fold. Yes, I wanted to spend some quality time with Jen, and just Jen, not the other two. Her jealousy—the competition she felt with Dan and Kate—surprised me, and she visibly needed extra attention. But I had a deeper reason for prizing her away from the house.

She needed to wipe this morning's shenanigans—me heading into the woods—clean from her mind.

CHAPTER TWENTY-ONE

The day was perfect for an outing. Every cloud swallowed by the great cobalt jaws of the sky, every last wisp of mist seared by the blazing sun. We had decided to go straight to Hearst Castle—a two-and-a-bit-hour drive—stopping off for lunch if we felt hungry, or leaving it until after the visit if we weren't.

Pippa was flattered to be invited, blissfully unaware of the reason why—that she was our chauffeur. I sat beside her in the passenger seat, Jen in the back. Pippa's brand-new car was a monstrous SUV, black tinted windows, fit for a president. The kind you never get to see in Europe because they won't fit down most streets. I assumed it was part of her divorce settlement.

I introduced Pippa and Jen, but it turned out they already knew each other from the hotel where Pippa sometimes had business lunches.

Oops.

"Darling, I thought you said you were cousins of some sort," Pippa said.

Jen beat me to it. "Yeah, we are," she said. "But the connection's so complicated, I won't even try to explain as you'll get so, like, lost with all the great aunts by marriage and uncles and shit."

"But I don't understand," Pippa went on, "because you live here. I mean, you're American."

"We have British blood," Jen lied.

I waited, both fascinated and wary to see where this would lead, nervous to intervene. I felt proud of Jen for taking on my tale with such gusto. She was a natural.

"*We?*" Pippa said.

Lying to a journalist perhaps hadn't been the smartest idea.

"Me and my siblings," Jen clarified.

"There are *more* of you?"

"Yeah, we're triplets."

"Good Lord, triplets? *Triplets?*" Pippa turned to me. "Darling, how come you didn't let me know all this captivating scoop? Triplets! How fascinating. Split sperm?"

"Nope," said Jen, "we're not identical, one of us is a boy. But we're a whole lot alike."

"So, what are the other two called?"

"Dan and Kate."

Too much information, I thought. *Nip this in the bud.*

"And why aren't they coming out with us today?"

Jen slid forward on the sumptuous leather seat. It squeaked embarrassingly. She giggled. "That wasn't me by the way, the seat farted, not me."

Pippa handed me my pink silk scarf, one I hadn't remembered losing. "You left this behind, darling, that day in Carmel. Left it on the back of the chair."

It was too hot for a scarf. I folded it neatly and laid it on the dashboard, so I wouldn't forget it again. "Thanks, Pippa, I had no idea."

"So, darling, where *are* they?" Pippa probed.

"They're at work."

"Oh, yes? What do they do?"

"Dan waits tables and Kate's a hiking guide."

"Where does Dan work? Maybe I've seen him."

"You have seen him," I said. "When we were at the corner café in Carmel. Remember? The handsome young waiter?"

"No, no, I don't remember him."

"Because you were too busy stealing my French fries," I reminded her. *Shut up with the questions, Pippa!*

Jen giggled again.

"So how old are you, anyway?" Pippa asked. "If you don't mind my being nosey. You look like you should be in college, not working at a reception desk."

I nudged Pippa's elbow and glared at her.

Pippa took both hands off the steering wheel, her palms raised in the air. "What? What did I *say?*"

"Not everyone can *afford* to go to college in America, you know, Pippa."

She placed her hands back on the wheel. "Sorry, that was tactless of me. Quite right. I'm sure your jobs are fabulous, and your hotel is a wonderful place to work."

I needed to veer her away from the triplet conversation. "So, tell us all about Hearst Castle. I bet being a journalist, you know a whole lot more than we do."

Pippa hung a sharp right at the end of my long, bumpy driveway and said, "You know the film *Citizen Kane* was inspired by the newspaper mogul Randolph Hearst? Many movie buffs and famous directors think it's the greatest film ever made. Orson Welles wasn't much older than you are now, Jen, when he directed it. Except they never used Hearst Castle to film it in the end."

"The last time I visited Hearst Castle I was, like, nine," Jen said, leaning forward. "Mom took us. We played hooky from school one day. It was so cool. All my friends were real jealous of us, that we had such a great mom who broke all the rules."

"I was going to ask you, Jen, darling. Where *are* your mum and dad?" Pippa said.

Uh, oh. I now realized I should've just told Pippa the truth. This was going to get complicated.

"Mom is… away," Jen said.

I turned around and caught Jen's eye. She looked like she was welling up.

"She's ill," I broke in. "Being treated for—" and then I mouthed the words to Pippa, "cancer."

"Oh, so sorry, you must miss her terribly," Pippa said in her bold, boomy voice.

Jen wiped away a tear. "I do, I think about her every day."

I waited for Pippa to grill Jen for details, but she didn't push it further. There was an awkward silence. Jen dabbed her face with the hem of her long flowery dress. Just awful. My heart went out to all three of the poor things.

Pippa opened her mouth to speak, but I pinched her elbow. "Pippa, I think that's enough. Jen's *crying*."

We rode along in silence for a good ten minutes.

"So what made you choose your husband?" Jen suddenly piped up, fully recovered, her bronzed bare feet resting in between the two of us, poking through to the front, on the elbow rest. Her question was directed at me. I was beginning to regret this whole outing. Bringing Pippa along had been my dumbest move of today—it even trumped my Mumm meltdown earlier.

"You're wearing your seat belt, I hope, Jen?" I said, glancing back. She was.

"What was it that attracted you," Jen pressed on, "about your husband?"

I ignored her question. I felt shameful for drunkenly sharing so many details about my marriage and private life earlier.

"Well, I'm divorced now," Pippa answered, thinking Jen was addressing the question to her. "And… good question. I ask myself that every day." She laughed, her lips wide, baring her wholesome white teeth: a set of genuine gnashers.

"I was referring to Juan," Jen let us know.

I'd been hoping Jen would steer away from the subject of Juan. Especially now. The last thing I needed was Pippa on my case. Besides, I didn't want to feel down. I'd cried enough for one day.

Jen wiggled her toes, still pointed in our direction, her heels poised on the armrest between Pippa and me. She sported a silver toe ring on her right foot. "You were a little younger than him, right? He must've been very cute."

"Very," Pippa answered for me. Which was the spot-on truth. "Eat your heart out George Clooney," she gushed. "George Clooney several movies back, I mean."

"Smart?" Jen asked.

I replied this time. "Extremely smart, that was until—" I stopped myself, regretful that I'd volunteered any information at all.

Jen nudged me with her foot. "Go on, tell me."

"You know, sometimes things aren't what they seem," I said.

"What do you mean?"

"Nothing."

"Oh, *please*. I hate that! That's *so* not fair! To let out an itty-bitty trickle of info and then, like, hold out on me with some enigmatic *bullshit*!"

"I'm used to being discreet. It's my job. Used to keeping secrets with clients," I said primly, "and used to keeping secrets of my own."

"What secrets?"

"If I told you, they wouldn't be secrets anymore, now, would they?"

Pippa laughed. "You're barking up the wrong tree, Jen. Lawyers never tell."

"Spill your secrets!" Jen demanded.

"No," I said.

"You're so *lame*!"

The "lame" word stung. It was just a silly expression, here in America—but after sharing my childhood secret with Jen about my six fingers, it struck a nerve. The past has a way of keeping you in chains even after you've cast them off.

Jen leaned forward and said, "Funny, I never asked you. Were you his first marriage or second?"

"First," I said. "But before me he had a string of girlfriends. He played the field for a long time but eventually got fed up and wanted to settle down."

"A bit of a 'ladykiller' then," Jen teased.

"You could say that." Where had the sweet, nurturing Jen gone? Was this all a game to her? Her machine-gun questions were making me feel twitchy, on the point of exploding. I counted to ten and took a deep breath.

"I don't get it. Why don't you ever go back to England?" Jen probed. "You must have a bunch of friends there. Must miss your friends and family. How come you never talk about them?"

I said nothing, a tad ashamed that not only did I not keep in touch with the few friends I had back home, but that I didn't even call the New York lot, mainly because they were Juan's friends, not mine. I hadn't felt the need for anyone else in my life but him. Juan had been my world.

A mistake. I'd put all my eggs in one basket.

As for my parents. Well, how could I begin to explain the unloving, staccato relationship we had?

I didn't want to reveal anything more to Jen, so I got out the road map—never did like the digital vibe of a GPS—and distracted Pippa and Jen with possibilities of where to have lunch, and whether to buy our Hearst Castle tickets online first or wait until we got there. The lack of cell phone reception closed down that idea anyway. Then we stopped for gas, and when Pippa went in to pay, I took the opportunity to talk to Jen alone. Something she had said earlier alarmed me.

I twisted my body so I was almost facing her, as she lounged in the back seat. "How did you know, Jen, that I was younger than Juan?"

Jen was still trying to google Hearst Castle on her phone. "What?" she said distractedly.

"A while back you seemed to know that my husband was a little older than me. How did you know that?"

Jen stopped what she was doing. "You're right, the reception really *is* crap around here." She laid her phone on the back of the plush leather seat. "I guessed because the pictures in your photo album show you looked really young."

"You've been snooping through my things?"

"Photo albums are up for grabs, aren't they? Kind of like Facebook photos."

"No, they're not 'up for grabs' unless someone invites you to look at them. I never gave you an invitation to rummage through—"

"They were in the library, not your bedroom."

"Okay, fair point," I conceded. I looked out of the car window to see how Pippa was getting on. She was still inside the garage, paying. "So why did you ask me earlier if Juan was handsome if you'd already seen pictures of him?"

"I wanted to hear you say it," she said.

"Jen, you must remember to always *ask* before you—you look at people's things. You're old enough to know better."

"They were just photos. Just wanted to get to know you better."

"That's nice, but those albums are personal, and speaking of which, you mustn't borrow my clothes in the future without asking first. All right?"

"Like your robe, you mean?"

"Like my robe, yes. Or anything else you might have your eye on. My closet is *private*, some of my things gifted from loved ones; I don't want you rummaging through it."

Jen pouted. "Isn't it fun to wear each other's clothing?"

"And, I noticed, someone has put all the glasses upside down in the kitchen cabinet, when I'm used to having them face up."

"What's the difference?"

"It's disconcerting to find things in your own house rearranged." I could feel my nerves on edge.

"Does it matter? The glasses are more stable upside down, right?"

"As a matter of fact, yes, I do happen to like the new system. However, it's not for you and your siblings to decide such things when you're guests." I instantly felt unwelcoming and neurotic. Bad move, reminding Jen that they were guests. "Forget it," I said, "never mind about the glasses, you're right, it really doesn't matter."

"I was only trying to be tidy. Trying to help out."

"I don't mean to be such a stickler, but it's just respectful and polite. If you've got good manners you'll get a lot further in this world. Good manners are free, they don't cost a penny." My mother's words had just sprouted from my lips, but I didn't want to take them back. I sat resolutely into the bucket of my seat and adjusted it back a little. We still had a way to go.

"So Juan died in a car crash, what, like, seven months ago, right?" Jen asked suddenly.

I flinched. "I told you I don't care to go there! I just want to have a nice day out, and I'd rather talk about *you*, anyway. How's your mum doing. Better?"

"No, she's not better. She's dying. She just doesn't want to admit it. She could even be dead, right this minute."

"Don't say that." I hated to think Jen had jinxed her mother by saying those words. "Jen, I've been thinking," I said, "running this over and over in my mind." I paused to make sure I'd be able to stand by what I was about to offer, and stick to my word. "I'd like to buy the three of you round trip airfares to Switzerland to go visit your mum for a week or two. I'll pay for your hotel—nothing too fancy—just a nice hotel nearby, and enough money for food and things. What hospital is she at?"

"It's like a sanatorium, not a regular hospital. Near Zurich."

"When we get home, I'll google it, and we can check out nearby hotels and look at airfares, how about that?"

"Nuh-uh."

"*Excuse* me?"

Pippa arrived back, laden with sodas and potato chips. I needed to put my conversation with Jen on hold.

"Bloody long queue," Pippa grumbled. "Took ages. Who wants Coke and who wants fizzy mineral water? I got two of each."

"Water, please," I said. "Coke's so sweet these days, I can't even drink it anymore."

Jen stretched her hands through to the front. "Water, please."

Despite myself, I felt pleased Jen and I had made the same choice, like two best friends. Silly. We set off again. I blinked at the road ahead. Seeing as we were all being so *cozy* with personal details of our lives, I let Pippa in on the offer I had just made Jen.

"That's bloody generous, darling!" Pippa exclaimed, swerving over the road as she struggled with her can of Coke. I snatched the can away from her, pulled the tab and handed it back. Pippa held it to her lips and slowed the car way down. A shiny red truck honked from behind us, and a furious man in a MAKE AMERICA GREAT AGAIN cap sped past, overtaking us, waving his fist. The booming, rumbling honk made a surge of adrenaline course through my body like a shot of some dangerous drug. Heart pounding. Pulse racing. I took a deep breath and glanced at Pippa, who was concentrating on the road again, one hand on the wheel, the other holding the can. Perhaps Jen or I could have done better in the driving skills department ourselves even "under the influence." I sucked in another breath to steady my nerves.

"Slow down, Pippa!"

"So, what do you say, Jen, to that incredibly brilliant and wonderful idea?" Pippa said, oblivious to the danger she had just subjected us to. "I think that's super generous."

"I say thank you very much for the awesome offer, *but*," Jen replied coolly, "I think I'll pass for now."

I looked back at her. She was staring ahead, squinting into the sun, the heel of her nude foot back up again, toe ring glinting in the sunlight. Neither the truck nor my offer had fazed her one bit.

"*Why*?" I said. "I thought you'd snap *up* this opportunity in a heartbeat! Thought you'd be *thrilled*." Then, realizing my tone was a little harsh, added gently, "You're scared of how your mum's going to look? That she won't be the same person you remember? Even if she's lost her hair and is frail and weak from chemo and radiation and stuff, she's your mum and she needs you right now."

Jen let out a sigh and planted her feet on the floor. "I'll think about it. And thank you, I really appreciate your kindness."

We drove along in silence, the ocean on our right, gleaming like a mirror. The sun hung high in the crystalline blue sky, heat pelting down on the black roof of the car. Pippa turned on the air conditioner. Just yesterday had been wet and cloudy, the mist blanketing most of Big Sur. The weather so changeable, you could never dress right and could be caught out any time. Everyone complained about the lack of spring and autumn, worldwide. From one extreme to the other. Anyone who was in denial about climate change was in cloud cuckoo land.

"Well," I said, after a full ten minutes, "I bet Kate and Dan will be thrilled at my offer."

Jen didn't reply.

Pippa shrugged her shoulders.

I didn't want to make a scene in front of Pippa. We needed a happy, carefree day out. Then I started toying with the possibility that Jen would rather be with me than her own mother. Possible? Not only was Jen an enigma to me, but I was an enigma to myself. What were my priorities? Being in control? Or being loved? Was I so much like family to Jen now that I was allowing her to blur boundaries?

There are two camps of people in this world: those that can control children, teenagers, puppies and dogs, and those that can't.

I was the latter.

And Jen knew it.

CHAPTER TWENTY-TWO

When we got home, Kate and Dan were waiting at the door, Kate's face pinched. I observed the wheels of Pippa's SUV crunch on the driveway like a big black tank as she powered off, waving. I had insisted on being chauffeur on the way home, after Pippa's dodgy driving. She declined my invitation to come in, saying she had to pick her sister and niece up from the airport.

Kate stood there glowering at us, arms crossed. Dan went inside, slamming the door behind him. I wished Pippa had stayed.

"They look pissed," Jen remarked with a little shrug. Did I detect a sort of Mona Lisa smile on her face? As if she had "one up" on them: a little secret she and I shared.

Our visit to Hearst Castle had gone beautifully. Touring through all the rooms—which overflowed with opulent art and furniture, in a hotchpotch of different periods in history—we were amazed at the amount of religious relics there were. Even lampshades made from illuminated manuscripts: pages that had been ripped out from priceless books, hand-bound painstakingly a few centuries before, and pored over by monks by candlelight. Sacrilegious! Our small party made it to the very top of the castle, into gilded rooms with views out to the ocean, glittering like a smooth lake, twenty miles away in the distance. We were told stories about the castle's legendary parties, attended by famous guests, such as Cary Grant, Charlie Chaplin, and Greta Garbo. Kate and Dan hadn't figured in our thoughts all day. I didn't revisit the subject of Jen's sick mum again, nor did Jen mention Juan.

Pippa indulged in scandalous gossip about movie stars. Being a journalist, she had all sorts of inside scoop, some of it probably myth, but it entertained Jen. Me too. We discussed future college plans for Jen, and Jen said she wanted to travel the world one day. She even suggested we could go together. Pippa told her about all the places she'd backpacked to when she was in her teens and early twenties. It turned out she had met Juan in Mexico during her gap year and when he was visiting his grandparents. I had forgotten that, the way they'd met. Although Juan's father was Mexican—a diplomat—his mother was a genuine WASPy New Yorker—a lawyer. Juan was born and bred in Manhattan and led a very privileged life spending his childhood in several countries because of his father's profession. Later, Juan went regularly to Mexico, especially on business. He was, of course, bilingual.

Jen waved to Pippa as she drove away. Jen looked radiant from her day out.

Kate stood by the front door, glaring at her sister. "Where have you been?"

"It's my fault," I offered quickly. "I should've called you. There was terrible phone reception at one point, and then we lost track of time."

"No," Kate said. "*Jen* should've called us. Dude, why didn't you call and let us know where you were? We were worried!"

In that second, it occurred to me that we were not family, and I'd been mistaken to imagine we were. Were they worried about us? About me? Of course not, it was Jen they had missed. Was my house just a hotel for Kate and Dan? Was I, the resident, a blip, a misfortune, a thorn?

No, of course not. I shook off my negative thoughts and focused on all the fun we'd had over the weeks, as a team. Jen and I had really bonded today. Apart from my meltdown in the bath with the champagne binge, this was the sort of day I had dreamed about spending with my daughter. The daughter I never had. Dan and Kate just felt left out, that was all. I'd need to spend quality time with them, too.

I had rebuked Jen today for bad manners but realized the relationship I had with the triplets was rare, despite my reservations. In today's world, children and young adults are becoming more and more alienated from their parents, even if sometimes it's the parents' fault. Members of families individually glue themselves to laptops or video games, and cute kitten posts on Facebook, despite the fact they may be in the same room as one another, communicating through inanimate objects, not directly.

These three were not like that, and I needed to lighten up about "boundaries" and work on developing a tighter relationship with the other two. I was not their mother or older sister, true. But I was their friend, and I needed to act like it. They had offered me so much of themselves. Scintillating conversation at the dinner table, enjoying all those lovely meals they'd cooked. Fun times. Games, larking around. Wonderful walks, chatting all the while.

I yearned to draw Dan and Kate closer to me.

Jen brushed past Kate and pushed the front door open. "Get a life, you guys," she drawled. Jen then clunked the door shut as if punctuating her hammering words.

The atmosphere inside was charged with mistrust. Or rather, a whiff of betrayal floated in the air… along with…

"Is anyone wearing perfume?" I asked, sniffing the house, my nose twitching like a rabbit. I laid my pink silk scarf on the back of a chair—the one I'd remembered to grab from Pippa's car and not leave behind this time.

Dan was doing a crossword from the Sunday paper, left over from the weekend. Another thing I'd got them all into as well as afternoon tea: the Sunday papers. He was purposefully ignoring us, in a sulk, didn't even ask where we'd been all day.

"Dan? Do you wear aftershave of any sort?"

"Nuh-uh," he said, his mouth puckered in distaste. "Gross."

"Kate?" I said. She didn't answer.

"Kate doesn't like perfume, do you?" Jen said. Jen still wore that happy smile. The "We're friends" smile. I felt warm inside. "Ignore my sister, she's just jealous that she didn't get to come today, too."

"I smell something," I persisted. "Do you smell it too? Jasmine? Is it jasmine I detect?"

"I don't smell anything," said Jen. "Maybe it's your own shampoo."

I let my hair out of its ponytail, shook my head and sniffed the air again. "No, not my shampoo. I could have sworn—"

"That's because you've been drinking," Kate said. Her frosty accusation was a poke to my gut. Unexpected. Out of nowhere. Or, perhaps, punishment for not being included in our outing. She must have seen the empty bottle of Mumm by the bath.

"Yes, I did have a drink today," I admitted. "And?"

"Your senses are dull when you drink," Dan piped up from his crossword. He smoothed the newspaper and added a letter. "Taste buds, olfactory senses… stultified." His vocabulary was becoming very sophisticated since he'd been doing crosswords. "And if you add sleeping pills to the mix? Even worse."

"Sleeping pills? Wherever did you get that idea?"

"It's none of our business, of course," he mumbled. "Sorry I brought it up."

"They're not prescription sleeping pills, you know, Dan. And I just take the odd one."

"Yeah, whatever," he replied, under his breath.

Kate took some apple juice from the fridge and poured herself a long tall glass, watching me all the while. As if admonishing me for drinking alcohol while *she* only drank healthy, wholesome apple juice. "If you want to drink, then drink," she said. "It's totally your choice."

I turned to Dan. "What's it to you anyway, even if I do have a drink every now and then?"

"We care, that's all."

I sneezed. "I smell something… different in this house! Something, I don't know, it's hard to describe. Sweet but also musky. Maybe woody, but mostly floral."

Kate smiled at me sweetly and swept past me. "You. Are. Imagining things." She fixed her eyes on my Thermos.

"Where are you going, Kate?"

"Outside, to look for Beanie."

"Beanie?"

"Didn't Jen tell you? We got a dog."

"What! You can't have a dog here, Kate. I'm allergic! You all knew that. I remember telling you."

"*Allergic*? No, you never told us. We thought you'd be happy. We got him for you. He's a rescue from a shelter. He's the cutest thing ever."

"You can't—we—this is the kind of thing we need to discuss first!" I shouted.

Kate's eyes filled with tears. "We thought you'd feel safer with a dog. We thought you loved animals!"

"I do. But I'm allergic."

"Well I guess we'll have to take him back," Dan said.

Jen jumped up and down with excitement. "Where is he? I want to meet him!"

I ignored her enthusiasm. This could not happen! "I love dogs but I can't live with them, I—"

Jen opened the front door and started yelling the dog's name.

Their blatant boundary breaking was so outrageous I didn't know what to say. Their sense of entitlement had gone from 0-60 in what seemed like seconds. How had I allowed this? Was I really such a pushover? "Wait! We need to discuss this over supper, this is something we have to talk about seriously," I bellowed.

But Kate, grabbing her jacket, replied, "No worries, I already made us dinner. All I have to do is heat it up. You'll like it. A recipe my mom used to make. She was a really great cook."

Jen glared at her, her eyes darts. "*Is* a really great cook, Kate," she said. "Is."

Was this a hint about what a crap job I was doing of feeding them properly? "Thank you, Kate," I said. "That's so thoughtful of you, I can't wait to taste your mum's lovely recipe. I'm sorry, but I am very—"

"Sad about not being able to keep Beanie? Me, too." Her head bowed, she made towards the door.

But Jen was grinning. "Let's go find Beanie. I'm so psyched! He's the cutie we saw in the photo?"

"No, that one was gone already."

I hoisted my hands on my hips. "You planned this?"

Kate looked up at me, her lashes wet. "We wanted to surprise you. Thought he'd be perfect for you. Picked him out specially for *you*."

"What kind of dog is he?" Jen said.

"A mutt—you'll see. Beanie? Beeeen-ie!"

The door clunked shut.

I ransacked every bathroom cabinet downstairs until I found what I was looking for: antihistamine pills to guard against runny eyes and nose, to protect me from animal dander. I had suffered for years, even without touching an animal, even if an animal had been in the room several days before.

I made my way back upstairs and felt a chill from the open front door, and the dog, a little terrier "Heinz 57" with wiry russet hair, elongated body, floppy ears, and a cheeky face, came bounding into the living room, jumping up with excitement on us and every piece of furniture in sight. His genuine and instant love for his surroundings, for Dan, and not least for me, made my heart melt, and I knew I didn't have the resolve to send the little thing back to the shelter or wherever they'd rescued him from.

Jen's snappy "Get a life" words were prophetic. They *had* just gone and got a life. And I felt horrible about this little thing being taken back to the shelter. This was what family life was all about, wasn't it? Going with the flow, accepting the unexpected? The sisters, I noticed—re-bonded by Beanie—were now the best of friends again, cozying up to each other like little kittens, their claws retracted, their paddy paws soft as silk.

CHAPTER TWENTY-THREE

Beanie slept on my bed that night, his trusting eyes laying his vulnerable little life in my hands. Lucky for him I was such a softy and my allergy meds seemed to work. And, the truth was, it had been my lifelong dream to own a dog, but I had never dared. My father had forbidden pets. Keeping Beanie was the ultimate F-you to Dad. It made me feel empowered.

But I couldn't deny that I began to have my doubts about the triplets, not so much because of their cheek of bringing Beanie into my life without discussing it first, but the way Jen had spurned my offer to go and visit her mother in Zurich—all expenses paid by me. It got me wondering.

Why?

A few days later, at breakfast, my question about Jen's reaction to the Zurich invitation was answered. I had a morning meeting with Mr. Donner, so I got up bright and early to face the day with enthusiasm. I was even making pancakes (from a mix, but still) for Dan and Kate. Beanie was wolfing down his breakfast and looking up every now and then as if to thank me. My meds were doing the trick. He was my dog now.

"We've been thinking about your offer to see our mom and would love to take you up on it," Dan began. "It's an awesome offer." He came over to me—I was standing at the fancy stove, mixing away—and hugged me, his piercing green eyes intense, his face somber. "Thank you."

Kate had her laptop open. She was sitting at the breakfast bar. "Look, come and check out the clinic where Mom's staying."

"Let me just get this on," I said, pouring the mixture into the pan and turning down the heat. "I don't want to burn these." I wanted to impress them with my pancake-making skills. "Where's Jen, by the way?"

"Sleeping," Dan said. "Look, I know Jen was a little weird the other day about going to see Mom."

"Yes, I was surprised by that."

"She's freaked out about flying," Kate explained. "It's like a phobia, not just a silly fear. She's even been to see a hypnotist about it."

"Oh, I see." I poked at the edges of the pancake with a spatula, without a clue what I was doing. Beanie had finished breakfast and was hoping for a treat.

"She has nightmares and shit." Dan glugged down some juice. "About flying."

"But she told me she spent a summer in New York, when she tried modeling," I told them. "How did she get there?"

Dan shot a look at Kate then said, "She did a drive-away, you know, when you drive someone's car cross-country? That's how she got to the East Coast without flying."

"I see. That explains it."

"Jen feels kind of embarrassed, felt ashamed the other day that you were offering her this awesome opportunity to go to Zurich, and she blew you off—sounded so ungrateful."

"She's been tossing and turning all night," Kate added, "trying to come up with a solution. She so wants to visit Mom, but the anxiety is killing her. Killing Jen," she clarified.

I wanted to stress to them the fact that this might be their last chance to see their mum before she died, but that might make them lose hope. I shared with Dan the story I had told Kate about being locked in a cupboard at school. I wasn't looking for sympathy, but I wanted them to know I identified with having a phobia. Was Jen's fear of flying really as bad as my panic of small spaces?

"It's one of the reasons I like living here so much," I said. "I need open spaces."

"You've never thought of living somewhere else?" Dan asked.

"No, never," I replied, trying to read his expression. "This house is perfect, all open and light the way it is. And the setting. I never feel closed in or *pinched*, you know what I mean? America's perfect for me. Big huge skies. In Britain, it's all so pinched and small, and gray and gloomy, clouds closing in on you, pressing down on you. I mean, here, even if it's misty or gray it never lasts very long before you get another bright blue sky. Ugh! Just thinking about the gray oppressive skies in England makes me remember how miserable I was living there. When I came to the States, I knew I'd found home. Even in New York, you get a lot of blue sky, even in winter."

"Wow," Kate said. "That's a really ace argument for staying here!"

"Crap!—the pancakes. I hope you don't mind them a little overcooked." I dug them out of the pan and piled them onto a plate. So much for playing mummy today. I found some maple syrup in the cupboard, from Massachusetts—a gift from a client—and set it on the table with the rather burnt, sad, dog-eared pancakes. Kate poured out orange juice for us all. Beanie sat watching us rapturously. After breakfast, I'd take him out for a brisk walk before going to work. The antihistamine tablets were working better than I'd imagined.

"The coffee'll be ready in a sec," Kate said.

"Anyway," Dan continued, "Jen will just have to stay behind if she can't deal. But me and Kate would be psyched to go and see Mom and take you up on your offer."

"Great," I said, "we can go online later and search for flights and hotels."

"Bummer is," Kate said, her voice guarded, her face scrunched, "is that…" She didn't finish her sentence.

"What?" I drenched my dry pancake with syrup and took a tentative bite.

"Hematological problems."

"Which means?"

"Blood clots."

"Oh." I wanted to spit out my mouthful of pancake, it was disgusting. "Don't eat this by the way, it really isn't… blood clots?"

"DVT. Deep vein thrombosis."

"At *your* age? Kate, are you sure?"

"Yeah, I can't fly for any length of time. I mean, in coach, that is. Because it's dangerous for me… unless I'm stretched out. Unless my legs are totally stretched out, you know, horizontal?"

I could see where this was heading. "What about those compression stockings you can buy?"

"I tried once, they don't work."

"They say if you do lots of exercises, drink plenty of water, and make sure you get an aisle seat so you can get up and move around every so often, or even an emergency exit seat so you can stretch—"

"Tried that too. The only thing that works is if I'm horizontal, trust me. It's not worth the risk for me to develop a pulmonary embolism. They upgraded me once and then it was fine, problem solved, like, instantly."

"Business class will cost a *fortune*, Kate. Not even *I* fly business class, not even for work—well, unless the client's paying. Two business class tickets to Europe… well, that wasn't the budget I had in mind at *all*."

Dan laid his hand on Kate's arm. "Mom will understand… if you can't come." Neither he nor Kate had touched their pancakes—taking my warning to heart. Beanie looked up at me expectant, his "Poor me" gaze wrenching at my conscience.

I slipped Beanie a little pancake and turned to Kate. "Is this condition at your age normal? Maybe you should see another doctor," I suggested.

"I'm on the pill. Oral contraception can sometimes be the cause."

"Oh," I said. "I hadn't thought of that." I wondered if Kate, like Dan, had a string of friends with benefits. She hadn't mentioned anyone in particular. "You want cereal instead?" I offered. There was no way I'd fall for this moral blackmail. "Look, please understand I want to help, but there are limits."

"It's not a myth," Dan said, the pupils in his eyes dilated with concern. "Do you know that more than two hundred thousand Americans suffer from pulmonary embolism every year? Over a third *die*. The incidents are higher than breast cancer and AIDS combined."

I looked down at my plate. What was I meant to do? I dropped the subject.

After a rather silent breakfast (toast and cereal), Kate and Dan went to their bedrooms to get ready for work. Kate's laptop was sitting there, the lid half-mast. I stood over it, wavering for a second, dithering with indecision but then opened it up. Thought I'd take a peep at her mum's clinic she'd asked me to check out earlier. But it wasn't there. So I clicked on browser history. They'd snooped around enough into my life; now it was my turn.

This is what I saw:

Italy. Rome. Florence. The statue of David. Flights between Zurich and various Italian destinations on EasyJet and Volotea airlines. Train schedules. Best pizza in Italy. Best gelato. Naples. The Cinque Terre.

It seemed to me that this trip to see their ill mother… was actually a fun little vacation opportunity, funded by yours truly. The question was: why did Jen not want to go too? Because I wasn't buying for one second her flying phobia.

What other pretty little lies had they cooked up?

CHAPTER TWENTY-FOUR

Later, when Dan and Kate were at work, and I was confident Jen was still sound asleep, I launched into some online research. First, the "sanatorium" (Jen's word of choice) their mum was supposedly staying at near Zurich. Who even used words like that these days? It sounded like a throwback from tuberculosis times, a century ago, when people went to Switzerland to be locked up and cured, "to take the fresh air."

There were several "Klinics," though, in and around Zurich. One was a sort of "quack" place—not that I'm against alternative medicine—but when someone has stage four cancer, a colonic irrigation, suction massages, and injections of mistletoe (really?) are unlikely to do the trick.

I found another one, the photos showing bedrooms fit for a five-star hotel: a potted orchid in the foreground, a delicious breakfast laid on a silver tray, the interior design worthy of Philippe Starck. Beyond expensive, no doubt. This place did everything. Like when you go to a restaurant and the menu goes on for five pages. No prices. This hospital offered state-of-the-art treatments, and nursing in every single specialty imaginable. Births, oncology, venous surgery, dermatology, coloproctology... the "ology" list went on and on.

Then there was the University Hospital, the first in the world that offered TrueBeam technology to treat cancer, whatever that was. In fact, the number of places where the triplets' mother could be undergoing treatment was longer than my arm. I began to doubt my previous suspicions. Zurich really was a center for cancer treatment.

The triplets were not fibbing. At least not about this.

I backtracked on my suspicions. They were not much older than teenagers. They were under horrible pressure. Of *course* they wanted to take a break from all this and whip over to Italy and eat the best gelato in the world while they had the chance. It was normal. They might not get another opportunity to visit Europe for years—maybe never. I was being jaded. Suspicious. Uncharitable. Yet, still, something niggled at me. *Why* didn't they want to spend more time with their mom? Then I remembered Kate mentioning how Lee had shut Dan in the laundry room for "time-out." And I thought of my own mother/daughter relationship. Maybe that explained it.

"What are you doing?" It was Jen.

I nearly jumped right out of my skin.

She stretched her arms and yawned. "I overslept. Been so jittery lately." She leaned down and patted Beanie's head. "Hey, sweetie." Then she said to me, "Did he go out already?"

"Good morning, Jen. Yes, he's done all his business. Just checking out hospitals in Zurich. You can show me which one your mum's staying at. Kate and Dan told me about your flying phobia, by the way."

"Sometimes I dream I'm flying, just me, you know, not in an airplane. And it's fine. I'm happy and free. But stick me in a plane and I freak out."

"Why didn't you explain this to me when you rejected my offer the other day? I would've understood better."

"I guess I felt dumb."

I poured her some juice and handed her the glass. "But surely if it means visiting your *mum*? Maybe for the last—" I stopped myself. "What kind of cancer does she have?" I couldn't resist testing her.

"It's spread everywhere now. Started as breast cancer, then went into the lymph nodes and then the lung." Jen slumped down on the kitchen stool and plunked her elbows on the breakfast bar.

"I'm so sorry, that's awful," I said, my memory swearing they had told me it was lung cancer from the start.

I asked Jen the name of the clinic in Zurich, to see if I recognized it. I did. It was the five-star hotel one. Guilt tumbled in my solar plexus anew; Jen had been telling the truth, after all. Or not? I was like a yoyo, back and forth between suspicion and self-remorse. Didn't know what to believe, how to feel.

"Is it true about Kate's blood clots?" I asked.

"Kind of."

"*Kind* of?"

Jen shrugged. "You should ask her."

"I did. It just seems strange to me that two out of three of you are not taking me up on my offer of a lifetime. I hate to say this, but if your mum—bless her—doesn't make it, you may really, really regret this."

"What did Kate say?"

"Oh, some story about how she, basically, in so many words, can only fly business or first class because of a list of complicated medical problems."

Jen adjusted her nighty, floaty and diaphanous. "I need to tell you something," she said, her head cupped in her hands, elbows still planted on the table.

Then silence.

"Please, you can tell me anything. Anything at all, I won't judge, I promise, but I do want the truth."

She lifted her wide green eyes and, batting her lashes, said, "We've been lying to you all along."

CHAPTER TWENTY-FIVE

I observed Jen, the palms of her hands covering her entire face. I wondered what was going through her head. Regret? A sort of amused satisfaction for having caught me out with whatever latest fib they'd whipped up? Did they even care for me one *whit*? Or was all this just a game to them? Something to amuse themselves? And what, I asked myself, was the lie? Perhaps there were several. Were the triplets even who they said they were?

Wow, I'd been blind. So keen for their company, so eager for that feeling of family nucleus and not living all alone, that I hadn't verified anything. Hadn't got them to show me their ID cards, or passports. I couldn't even be sure about their age!

"What have you been lying to me about?" I asked her, my tone frosty.

She looked up at me again, her dark lashes wet with emotion. "Please don't hate us."

"Hating you is something that would be extremely hard for me. You'd have to do something really, *really* bad. What's the lie?"

Jen weighed up her options; I could see the little cogs ticking. Probably making up a new lie to cover the first. Whatever the first was.

"Tell me, Jen, I won't bite."

"They'll be mad at me."

"I knew something was amiss, anyway. It was just a matter of time before I wised up."

"Our mom?"

"She's not in Zurich?" I guessed.

Jen raked her hand through her waterfall of hair. "She *is* in Zurich. But not in the way you think."

"She doesn't have cancer and isn't at a clinic?" I guessed again.

Jen bit her lip and blinked, forcing plump tears to spill from her evergreen eyes. "Our mom is… she's dead already."

Was this a new lie? The truth? How was I meant to react? "Jen, I'm so sorry for your loss."

"She's buried there, in a cemetery."

I was taking no chances this time, regardless of how sad this might be. "What's the name of the cemetery?"

"Fluntern Cemetery, it's where James Joyce is buried too." She didn't miss a beat. Her gaze was steady. It seemed like she was telling the truth this time.

"Why didn't you just *tell* me? From the beginning?"

"Because… I… I… don't know. We got caught up in our lie. We didn't want you to hate us."

I knew about that one. Getting tangled in your own fibs. "But I would've been just as sympathetic—more so—knowing your mum had passed away." I laid my hand gently on her shoulder. "When did she die?"

"Eight months ago. Around the same time when you came along and bought the house."

"So what you said about your mum selling the house to pay for her treatment was another—" I searched for the right word, that didn't sound too accusing—"*embellishment* of the facts."

"Not really. It just happened a whole lot sooner. We had to sell 'cause of Mom's shitstorm of debts that then became *our* debts even before she actually passed away. We had no choice," she said, her mouth twisting with bitterness. Even with her twisty lips in this grimace, Jen's vulnerability still shone through. She was an orphan. They all were. Whatever reservations I'd had about their behavior, my heart bled anew. Poor things.

"There was no life insurance?"

"Nope, not a cent. My mom wasn't very together about that kind of stuff. We were backed up against a wall, without a choice. Had to sell."

"So it was you lot who sold my husband the house, then? Not your mother?"

Jen looked down. "The agent handled the sale."

"You were all at college and had to drop out, to pay off the medical bills?"

She rocked back and forth on her stool, shoulders rounded in defeat. "We were never at college. We're still only nineteen."

My heart thumped wildly with both sympathy and fury. Another lie I'd fallen for, hook, line, and sinker. I steadied her rocking or she'd go tumbling to the floor. Why hadn't the triplets simply told me the truth from the start? Such intricately woven lies, smoother and more detailed than a Persian rug! Lies hard to keep up with, even for them. Was it Kate who'd said she and Dan studied chemistry? Jen, musicology? They'd given themselves very fancy credentials.

"So you needed a bed?" I said.

"We needed a *home*. And you think it gave us pleasure to stretch the truth that way? I *wish* she was having treatment and still alive—at least that would give us some hope—but the fact is she's already gone."

"I'm so sorry about your mum," I repeated. "But I can't deny I feel gutted that you didn't come clean with me from the beginning. I'm your *friend*. I want to help. I'm extremely hurt."

Jen looked at me through her wet lashes. "But *you* lied too! About Juan being alive when we first met you. And you lied to us about being pregnant. Maybe you're hiding other stuff from us too?"

I said nothing.

"Please forgive us. *Please*?" She started crying again.

I exhaled a deep breath I'd unconsciously been holding in. "Any normal person would kick you straight out. You know that, don't you, Jen?"

"I kn-know," she stuttered through her tears. "But you're all we ha-have. We love living with you. I'm s-sorry. Please forgive us." The tears were real and rolled down her unblemished cheek. "You're our family now," she told me.

I said nothing for a beat. What was I going to do? Chuck them out of the only home they'd ever known, their mother dead? I'd been agonizing incessantly about the pros and cons of living alone, and for my own selfish reasons I'd been keeping them here. Jen was right; we were like family. Lies and all. And that's what families do; they stand by each other through thick and thin, stick with each other even when they're disappointed, even when someone has let them down. Families give each other second chances, and third and fourth chances, even when they're furious with one another.

"I'll give you *one* more chance," I conceded. "But any more monkey business and that's it. Understood?"

Jen's back straightened. "We can stay?"

"You can still stay," I said. "For now. But don't push your luck."

Jen's lips twitched into a grateful smile. "Even after all this?"

I held her hand. It was clammy and soft. "Jen, we all make mistakes, we all tell white lies."

"But this was—"

"You were protecting yourselves," I broke in. God knows I knew all about that.

"Yeah," she said, "we were."

I thought of all Jen's fabulously realistic phone conversations. "Talking to your mum all those times? It seemed so genuine," I said.

She looked down at her nails then gnawed the cuticles, before saying, finger in her mouth, "Yeah, I know. Talking to her comes so naturally. I have conversations with my mom on a regular basis. In my head. Out loud. I miss her sooo much."

"I bet," I said.

I grabbed an unopened bottle of champagne from the fridge. There was no way I was going to play by the rules anymore—play the grown-up. Their games were too screwed up, even by my standards. From now on, if I wanted a drink, I'd have one.

"I'm so sorry if I hurt your feelings," Jen murmured. "I was feeling dishonest. I didn't want you paying for a fake trip to Italy." She didn't want to look me in the eye, her knees now drawn up to her chest, as she still fidgeted on the stool. Regarding her again more closely—yes, she did look nineteen. I'd been so gullible. Such a bumbling, gullible fool. They were teenagers without guidance. They needed an adult to straighten them out.

"Look," I said, "this is all a bit overwhelming. You've hit me with humdinger news about your mum already being dead, that you're only nineteen… you *are* nineteen, I hope? You'd better not be under eighteen. I mean, if you're all still minors—children in the eyes of the law—I could get in trouble." Jen breezily smoking that joint came to mind. Good Lord, I could even be arrested or had for kidnap!

"Don't worry, we are nineteen."

Trusting the triplets would be a huge leap of faith now. I wished I'd paid more attention when Juan bought the house. Although I had verified with the real estate agent and Mrs. Reed that the triplets existed, I had never looked at their IDs, never double-checked.

"Wait a minute," I said. "This house. Did it *really* belong to your family? Or is that another total fabrication? Because, Jen, I don't even know who you lot *are*! I'd like to see your passports, actually. That would make me feel much more at ease. I mean, not because I don't believe you, or that I mistrust you—although I have to admit you've been pretty shady with me, concocting your elaborate backstory—but if something happened, anyone could get run over by a bus, any time, any day!" I used Mr. Donner's favorite expression. Something clicked: every time Mrs. Reed had come to clean, the triplets hadn't been home. I needed concrete verification.

"I'll show you my I.D., sure," Jen said easily. "I'm sorry, we've been totally out of line. I can understand why you'd never want to give us another chance."

"I didn't say that. I didn't say I wouldn't give you another chance. I think everyone deserves another chance. Well, almost anyone. I just need you to be straight with me from now on. All of you."

"Straight as a dice. As a die," Jen said with finality.

CHAPTER TWENTY-SIX

A week later, the triplets hadn't gone anywhere, least of all to Napoli to eat the best pizza and gelato in the world. Things carried on as normal. Better than normal, apart from my bouts of depression about Juan and my sleep-deprived, sweaty nights. The triplets behaved impeccably and were being more attentive and sweet than ever, helping around the house, doing the shopping, cooking lovely meals, and always cleaning up after themselves. They were on their best behavior.

On the days I wasn't at Mr. Donner's and when the triplets were at work, the house fell silent without their banter. Staring at the view—the ocean a shimmering blanket of blues and afternoon golds—I felt loneliness creeping into me, crawling along my flesh, giving me a taste of how it would feel if they weren't living here. The chill of it made the hairs on my skin rise. I imagined myself alone again, encased in the lonely womb of Cliffside for good. No more fun dinners. No more of Dan's pontifications about science and physics. The girls' wide smiles and Jen's cheekiness a memory. And something else was battering at the threshold of my mind: the anonymous warnings had stopped the moment I became friends with them. I could swear their presence was keeping me safe.

I was glad I had let them stay on.

Later in the day, as I was cleaning up in Jen's room, I found a photo album she had made. Pictures of all of us. At the beach. Laughing. Playing charades. She had carefully drawn hearts and flowers in the margins. I started humming the song she had written for me, "Pretty Brit Widow."

Pretty Brit Widow,
We've grown so close
Pretty Brit Widow
In our Big Sur house

These three were my family. So they had pushed boundaries a bit. Made up a story to protect themselves. Was that so terrible? Didn't all young adults see what they could get away with? Wasn't that what all relationships were about? The balance of power, ebbing and shifting?

It was in my interest to give them a second chance. I needed them as much as they needed me. The house was running so smoothly, the windows sparkled. I had light in my life. I no longer felt that heavy, solo weight on my shoulders. I didn't *want* to go back to the way things were before I had met them, whatever my niggling inner voice was saying.

We all carried on with our jobs and hung out in the evenings (when Dan and Jen weren't doing evening shifts), and acted like any regular family. Dog included. They showed me their passports, which I scanned for good measure and even sent to my lawyer for safekeeping (yes, even lawyers have lawyers), and I checked their photos with the real estate agent I'd been in touch with. I sent her the scans, and she confirmed they were the very same people she'd met when she first came to view the house and had agreed to put it on the market. For some reason, I didn't completely trust Mrs. Reed's confirmation about the triplets' identity. That woman, with her sharp face and pointy chin, gave me the heebie-jeebies.

With the lies behind us, I pursued my new goal: getting them to retake their SATs and apply for university. It was crazy that these highly intelligent individuals were doing jobs that anyone could do. They needed an education, all three of them, and I was prepared to pay for their tuition fees. I had in mind bold plans. The triplets were clever enough to get into any top university. For the first time in my life, I felt like a real parent.

But I was still suffering from sweaty nights and bad dreams. Then I succumbed to temptation. Things took a turn for the worse.

It was Dan's day off. And mine too. We went for a walk, hiked down to the beach, little Beanie in tow. On the way up, Dan—his hands stinging like crazy—realized he'd touched poison ivy at some point on the walk. The leaves should have turned golden and fallen by now, but with the bizarre way seasons had begun to mix themselves up—bees collecting pollen in December, buds being tricked it was springtime—Dan had mistakenly grappled with the wrong foliage.

"Let me have a look," I said. He was wringing his hands together, jumping around like a banshee.

"Fuck, this hurts like hell," he yelled out. He was about to shove his fingers into his mouth.

"Don't touch your face or lips!" I bellowed. "Or it'll be *agony* everywhere. Look, just run home and douse yourself with soap and water. Do *not* touch any part of your body. I can't remember what you're meant to do with poison ivy, but we can look it up online, or I can run you to the pharmacy if we don't have the right stuff. Check in Kate's bathroom, that's where the medicine cabinet is. I'll follow you, but you're faster than me, so dash right home."

He raced ahead, and with Beanie still choosing to stay by my side, I plodded back through the pines, weary for some reason. I'd had a little white wine binge the night before. It was Jen's fault. She had pilfered a bottle of Blanc de Blanc they'd been raving about at her hotel. A new, local winery that was winning awards. It started off as an innocent wine tasting, Jen and Dan joining in, although they spat theirs out. Before I knew it I'd polished off the whole bottle, pretty much solo. But still, one bottle of wine? It didn't make sense I was feeling this bad.

I trudged up the hill, my feet heavy, my head a block, Beanie a little way ahead. He was turning out to be my dog after all. Perhaps because I was the one who fed him daily—he knew where his bread and butter lay. I rubbed my aching eyes. I should have stuck to good old Mumm (no surprises), not unknown wine. My temples throbbed heavy behind my dull eyes. We had work to do, SAT tests to practice—I had no time for hangovers. I leaned on a redwood, still a long way from the house, bent over, and let a rush of vomit spill from deep inside me. My eyes lingered halfway between closed and fluttering. A bitter and metallic taste puckered inside my cheeks, and I let loose another flow of bile-like, watery sick.

One step, two steps, one, two. I thudded towards Cliffside, wondering how this hangover had taken so long to develop. Then my attention was stopped, and I realized where I was: by *the* redwood tree. I recognized it: taller than the Statue of Liberty, with its gnarly wart-like burl on the base of its trunk. I stared at the spot that had taken an age to dig. Seven months ago. May. The ground hard and dry, but just moist enough, thanks to the fog-drip and sandstone soil. Seven whole agonizing months ago.

Strangely Lee, too, had passed away not long before that.

I looked over my shoulder and up at the house in the distance. All still. Just the salty breeze and the last of the sun. Twilight dancing with the shadows of the trees. And me. Just me. The girl with eleven fingers, despite the fact I now had ten.

I turned my left hand over just to assure myself. Sometimes that sixth finger's nerves paid me a little visit. Especially at night. I still wore my wedding band and my stunning Tiffany diamond engagement ring, which had cost Juan a small fortune. I rarely took it off except to clean it now and then. I was terrified of losing it. Not just because of its value but because of Juan's message engraved inside: "*Yes, you.*" It was a secret joke between us, inspired by the movie *Gilda*, with Rita Hayworth. Juan and I quoted lines from classic movies to each other all the time. I wished I'd had Gilda's confidence, her luscious mane of hair, and that "Me?" was just how I'd felt: Juan was going to marry a girl like *me*? Really?

So he engraved his answer back:

"Yes, you."

Some things were irreplaceable. My ring. Cliffside.

Juan.

Beanie trotted on ahead. I thought of Juan and how it was his fault I had become so nervy and jumpy. His pig-headed greed forcing me to do something so out of character for me, something I could never have imagined carrying through. But I didn't have the option at the time, did I?

The site was untouched. The earth smooth, and camouflaged with its surroundings: shrubs and cones and leaves covering the spot very nicely.

Nobody would have any idea what was buried deep beneath.

CHAPTER TWENTY-SEVEN

"What are you doing?" It was Dan. He'd been watching me, my gaze fixed on *that* spot. Staring at me from behind a pine tree, reaching into my guilty thoughts, for sure. Beanie barked as if demanding the same question.

I spun round, my heart lodged in my stomach, my pulse shot with adrenaline racing a thousand miles an hour.

"Dan! Oh my God, thank heavens you're here. And Beanie—I didn't know where he was. What a fright! I just saw a rattlesnake. It was—it got into coil mode, but when you called my name it got scared by the noise and slithered off!"

"Are you sure?" Dan's eyes were suspicious slits.

"Yes! It was right there!" I waved my arms vaguely. I didn't want to draw attention to the site. "It disappeared really fast when it heard you." I staggered towards Dan uneasily, trembling from my close call. What had I been thinking? Lurking and hovering around so close to the *last place on earth* I wanted him to discover.

"Rattlesnakes usually hibernate," Dan said.

"I know, but with the weather as crazy as it is, the winters so warm and climate change, there's been a surge of confused rattlesnakes! It frightened the life out of me!"

Dan held my gaze, unbelieving.

"The rain hasn't helped either," I went on. "With all that tall green grass around, it encourages more rodents, which means more rattlesnakes."

"Let's get out of here, it's getting dark," Dan warned. "What the hell were you doing taking so long? I was worried about you."

"I'm really low on energy. I've been trudging up that hill for what seems like hours. How's your poison ivy?"

He turned his hands over; both the palms and the backs did not look in the slightest bit red.

"False alarm," he said. "Maybe a spider bit me or something. I guess I just freaked out. You know, once bitten twice shy?" He enunciated his last sentence as if it had a double meaning, his eyebrows disappearing behind his flop of hair.

I stole a glance at him—we locked eyes for a nanosecond. What was he *saying*? Was that an allusion to the phantom rattlesnake, or some cryptic warning? My paranoia whooshed through me like a seventh wave. What did the triplets know? Had they been playing me all this time? I regretted trusting them. I should have followed my instincts and got rid of them. I hung my head, afraid I'd vomit again.

"I got poison ivy all over me once, as a child," Dan explained. "Never had so much pain in my life. But then I thought about it. It's December, there's no poison ivy around right now."

The penny dropped. He'd been spying on me all along. Poison ivy, my foot. It was a ruse. They'd fooled me too many times already, these canny triplets.

Just because you love certain people, it doesn't mean that they shouldn't be axed out of your life. And that's exactly what I was going to do. Axe them out.

Tomorrow. First thing in the morning. This time I meant business.

CHAPTER TWENTY-EIGHT

"Man, she's such a liar." It was Dan's voice I heard first.

"Yup, she twists the truth all right." Kate.

The whispers again. Fading in. Fading out. Carried by the wind. I had taken to leaving the kitchen window and the sliding doors to my bedroom open, ever since I'd first heard them talking.

I lay in my bed, in a stupor. The migraine worse than before. Or was it flu? My weak ankle throbbed like crazy. Had I twisted it again? How? Sweat was spiking every part of my body. My ears clamored in my thrumming head. Jen had fetched me a hot chamomile tea, earlier, and a cool wet washcloth that she'd draped over my brow. I could barely breathe I felt so bad. My fingers groped for my migraine pills beside my bed and I downed a couple to numb the pain.

"There *was* no accident. There is no proof of an *accident*!" Dan again. His voice flew in on a breeze. It pained me to think we'd become so close. This perfect family situation—the family that had become mine, these three young adults who had felt like my very own children—would all soon become dust to me. Ashes to ashes, dust to dust.

Tears pooled in my eyes.

My head hammered.

I groaned in my bed. Covered my eyes with the comforter. How could a hangover be this bad? There was a bottle of champagne by my bed, and a glass. *Hair of the dog*—I'd feel better soon. I managed to sit halfway up and pour myself some.

"She said he crashed near Ragged Point, and how she 'lost' him."
More conversation.

"Yeah, true, now I think about it she's never mentioned…"
Kate's voice, now, but someone's cough blocking out the rest of
the sentence.

I drained the glass. Maybe I could sleep this thing off? I cradled
my two hundred pound head in my trembling hands. I felt as if
it had been in a vice and my brains would explode any second.

Kate's voice pattered on, "I bumped into Pippa the other day.
Asked her about the details of the crash. She changed the subject,
pronto. Don't you think she would *know*, being a journalist, of
all the nitty-gritty details? Not to mention the two women being
old friends."

"She's a sociopath. A taker and a user. An alcoholic too." Dan.
His words falling on a gentle whisper yet stabbing me in the heart.
"We have two choices," he said.

"One choice, Dan," Jen corrected, her voice fired with emotion.
"It's *a* choice, not 'two choices.' When you have a choice, you
already have A CHOICE between two things."

That's right, Jen, you tell him. I smiled to myself, amused that
my mother had passed her grammar pet peeves via me onto Jen
and that Jen, in her way, was sticking up for me. New clustering
thoughts swirled and simmered. I lost the next few patches of
conversation. My body, as if out of itself, spun on a penny. I felt
like a London taxi doing a U-turn. Surreal images popped into
my head, mixing with the stark reality of what I was hearing.

"So what do we do? Call the cops?" Dan again. "Demand
them to reopen the investigation, say we suspect something?"

The *investigation*? I felt another wave of nausea wash over my
floppy doll body.

"Are you *crazy*?" Kate said. "That's the dumbest idea ever, asshat!
The last thing we want is to attract attention to ourselves, it could
screw up everything. And it wouldn't help us get it back, would

it? Like we agreed, we need to take stuff into our own hands. *We can deal with her. We'll take control.* This weekend? When we all have the day off? We'll go down there and see what the hell…" The sentence slipped away.

"Yeah, I want to know what the fuck happened," Dan agreed.

"Me too." Jen's words eddied in my milky brain.

"The body must be somewhere. And my guess is? It sure as hell isn't at the bottom of Ragged Point."

Their sentences spun together like cotton candy turned to a sticky, sickly mess. I had to get out there! Dig it up before they did. Shit! This weekend? What day was it?

I tried to heave myself out of bed but was pinned down by some invisible force, dull and heavy like an opiate. I couldn't move, not even wiggle my toes.

"But you know what? I kind of feel bad."

"Jen! How can you feel bad when…" Kate's words turned hazy. A gust of wind stole them clean away.

"Because I've grown to love her," Jen said. "Even after what she did."

Birds of a feather flock together.
Birds of a feather flock together.
Birds of a fea…

That's when the fever took hold of me and robbed my thoughts. Like a cleaver.

If only I'd put two and two together.

But I was too out of it to see sense.

CHAPTER TWENTY-NINE

Awake, my brain lived in a deep freeze. But asleep, in my dreams, it thawed. Slowly defrosting… dripping into coherent memories.

Two weeks before Juan's accident:

I am beginning to see the light. Not all of it, but a sliver, like when you spy through a keyhole, squinting one eye shut, and a gust of air blows into your iris. Then, because you can't resist, you peer through again. You see a fleeting glimpse, a flash, a flash of something dangerous, or terrible, or too sexy to repeat, but you can't stay for long because someone might catch you and shame you.

I know all about shame.

That sliver of light was revealed to me today. I should have suspected something all along. Whatever did Juan see in a girl like me? Well, he picked the wrong girl. I am the wrong material. The bullies at school knew it. And Juan should've known it too.

It was past midnight when he came home. Like an eager child, I waited up for him, anticipating the crunch of tires on the driveway, the familiar smell when he walked through the front door. The woody aroma that gusted with him from the outside, of the surrounding woods, the ocean, the musk of his neck. I swear I could smell it all, even from where I was in the bedroom.

He poked his head round the door. Spoke to the bed, where I lay, because it was so dark he couldn't make me out, nor I him. Whispered, "Honey, are you awake?"

My heart picked up a beat. I groaned. He would know exactly the meaning of that groan, he'd be able to read the tone of it, its velvet desperation. He shook off his shoes and took a step towards the bathroom, but I stopped him with my voice. "Juan," I said, my pulse racing with desire. He'd been away for a week.

"I'm going to take a shower first," he said.

"No, please don't rub the you off yourself," I begged. It *was* a beg, he would have heard the plea of my voice.

He blew me a kiss from across the room. "Shower," he said. "Trust me, babe, I need one."

"No!" There was another whiff, a whiff of something alien to me mixed with his own Juan scent. Sweet. Not cloying or cheap, but definitely, possibly definitely—I just couldn't be sure.

Female?

I wanted to get up out of bed. Race across the room and embrace him. Inhale the telltale story of him, right then and there. But I didn't. Instead, I lay petrified between the sheets like a jagged stone. I dared not invite any more doubt into my already suspicious mind. I heard the shower's spray, his hands slapping on the soap, the same hands scrubbing himself clean, his long fingers massaging the scalp that carried his crown of thick black hair. I had in my mind's eye the white lather on his head frothing down his taut muscles, the water running its course like a waterfall over rocks, his pectorals hard, his mouth catching the water, the same mouth that may have run itself over the nape of another neck, a neck scented with something that smelt of… jasmine, was it?

Tomorrow I'll sniff his suit, look through his pockets.

No, stop! *I have to stop myself right there. Because whatever he's done…*

I don't want to know.

CHAPTER THIRTY

My eyes were squeezed shut, but I could feel Jen leaning over me, her long hair like soft feathers on my sweaty cheek. "I've brought you more champagne," she whispered.

Jen steadied my shaky body as I maneuvered myself up. My ankle still seared with pain. How? Why? I'd been so careful not to twist it again, yet every time I woke up it felt more painful than ever. Jen lodged a pillow behind my back and handed me an opened bottle of Mumm. I vaguely remembered the triplets discussing me while I was half asleep. But I couldn't muster up any details of the conversation.

"Pass me my migraine pills," I said. "I feel like shit." My sight was hazy, and I couldn't focus. The room felt small and airless; they must have closed the blinds to my view outside, but with my eyes so heavy I didn't have the energy to look around me or even ask for a doctor. I wondered if I had meningitis or some kind of virus, I felt so bad. But too weak to even care, I glugged down some water and what was left of the champagne and swallowed another pill, eager to get back to my Juan dreams.

Jen took my ankle in her hands. "It looks bruised, shall I get some ice?"

I yawned and turned on my side. "Leave me, I just want to sleep."

Jen took the pillow from behind my head. "You get some rest then. It's for your own safety and ours," she murmured, and I slumped back beneath the covers and slipped back to my memories, a month or so before the accident.

Juan came home today from one of his long weekends away. I'd been mulling something over and over in my head, and I wanted the answer.

"Darling, why, when you're away, do your charge cards and credit cards have no movement on them?" I was at the kitchen sink, doing the washing-up but quickly took off the ugly, bright blue gloves. My mother's voice told me to. Always warned me, it did, to hide my evidence. "Don't let your husband see you with the Hoover, darling." That voice often danced in my head at unexpected moments. Sometimes when I was in the middle of a business meeting with a client, or at the gym—places my mother had no right to be: "Be a cook in the kitchen, a maid in the living room and a… well, you know…" She never got to the "whore in the bedroom" part. These sorts of words were never actually spoken out loud. My mother was too proper for that. She believed in a Stepford Wife type of marriage.

"What do you mean?" Juan had that face on again. The "What—who, me?" face that told me he was lying. The pupils slightly dilated, the neck pulled back into itself—just a touch—as if to say, "How dare you, don't you *trust* me?"

But I did dare. I did dare ask. And no, I didn't trust him. How could I? That handsome face and physique *demanded* women's attention. Juan didn't have to do a thing. Just smile his disarming smile, just be himself. He didn't even have to flirt.

I said it again. "It's as if you don't spend any money at all when you're away. What about clients' dinners? Taxis, hotels? There's never any record of any spending. How come you don't use your corporate card?"

"A lot of the tabs are picked up by the clients. Or I pay cash, as you well know."

"Most people pay for everything by card, even chewing gum. People of our generation, anyway." My parents did still believe in cash. (If you don't have it, don't spend it.)

"Honey, you're welcome to go through my expenses with a fine-tooth comb, but please don't read anything into the fact I like to pay cash."

Juan was like Michael Corleone not wanting his wife to ask him about his "business." Although Juan's method was less direct. He never actually told me to keep out of his business. He just skirted things with a laugh, or, "It's so boring, honey, you don't want to know." Had I been more confident of myself, less in love, I would have tackled him about his evasiveness. But each day was like a gift wrapped in gold, and like a little girl who's just been given a birthday present and is terrified to let anyone touch it, in case the giver might change his mind and take it away from her, I couldn't risk it. I had always felt that Juan was mine only by a hair's breadth, and I didn't want to jinx my luck by letting him see how consumed with jealousy I was.

But I had my suspicions about what my husband was up to. My guess was he didn't want to rub it in my face. Wanted to be discreet about his affair. Hotel bills and restaurants would be a dead giveaway showing up on a credit card statement. Especially romantic places. Better to pay in cash. No paper trail. No questions. No drama. My pulse pounded at the thought of him being unfaithful. There was no proof, whatsoever, just my wandering mind. If I said something, he'd deny it. He wouldn't want to hurt my feelings. He believed in marriage. He was Catholic. But like many men, I guessed, he had double standards.

I wondered who she was.

Then again, perhaps it was safer I didn't know.

Safer for her.

CHAPTER THIRTY-ONE

I woke up in a start, panting. The room felt unbearably hot and stifling, as if I were encased in a box. I lunged sideways to turn on my bedside light, but it wasn't there. In a panic, I hauled my achy body out of bed—but even that felt different. I was on a mattress on the floor! Where the hell was I? I stumbled around the room in the dark and felt myself smash into an alien piece of furniture. The shooting pain in my ankle made me remember I could hardly walk.

Then everything fell into place. I was in the *laundry room*! I had collided into the washing machine. I walked my fingers around the walls until they fell upon the light switch. I flicked it on then made straight for the door. It was locked fast. They'd found the key in one of the tins? Of course they had. I supported my lollopy head with cupped hands and surveyed the room. My double mattress took up most of the space.

The triplets had brought me down here without my waking up. Set up this bed for me, with my usual comforter. Knowing about my claustrophobia, they had castigated me with the worst possible punishment.

How had I been oblivious to all this? How had I not woken up? Why were they doing this to me? What did they or didn't they know?

Fine, I thought. *Take a deep breath. Calm down.* There was a landline down here. I grabbed the phone. Nothing. The line dead. I searched the room for my cell phone, or anything to link me to the outside world. Clean laundry everywhere, but nothing of any use for my present predicament. I pummeled on the door and screamed for someone to let me out, but the chilling silence from above warned me I was quite alone. Cliffside sounded empty, and all I could hear was my own blood ringing in my ears, and my intake of breath, and the gasp of air I let out from my lungs filling the eerie silence.

A Spanish expression Juan had taught me popped into my mind: *Más solo que la una*, or in my case, being a woman, *Más sola que la una*. Lonelier than number one. I pictured myself as the digit number one on a big ticking clock, the minute hands going round and round and me, as ONE, just sitting there, the big hand never moving, the clock set at one o'clock forever more. *Más sola que la una*. What if they left me in here to rot? Nobody would ever guess I was down here.

There was a window up high, but no more than a horizontal slit, enough to let some fresh air into the room, but there was no way I could squeeze myself through it. Maybe a tiny ten-year-old could fit their head through, but I didn't stand a chance. Panic slammed in my chest, the walls closing in on me, my knees buckling. I collapsed back on the bed. I was woozy still from my sleeping pills. I felt so feeble. Judging from the light, it was dusk. I prayed my captors would be home from work soon and they'd pity me and set me free. Was this some kind of warped joke?

Then I remembered Jen's words:

"It's for your own safety and *ours*."

What did that mean? Had I done something crazy? Why were they doing this to me? Defeated, and with a heavy drowsiness cloaking me once more, I succumbed to sleep and slipped back again to a territory just as harrowing. A week before Juan's death.

*

The proof I had so dreaded came to me without my even having to look for it. I discovered a note in Juan's pocket—well, not a note exactly, but a bar napkin, and scribbled on it, in black, was:

I am done with you, please stop trying to contact me
I cannot give you what you want. Keep away from me.

It was in a suit Juan hadn't worn for ages. There were also some sticks of old chewing gum, the wrappers all glued together. My discovery must have come several months later.

The note was a stab to my heart. Definitely a woman's hand.

I remembered once seeing Princess Diana's handwriting—a thank you card to a hat maker of hers, whom I had a chance meeting with when my mother wanted to splurge on a hat for a society wedding. The milliner had framed the card. The writing was similar to this note: girlish, curvy, and bold. Fun. The idea that Juan was chasing some "fun" woman, to this extent—and that she was rejecting him in such a final way—made me feel as if I'd drunk bleach. She was done with *him*? With *Juan*? Where did she get off being so arrogant? He was obviously pursuing this woman—no—worse, she was *done* with him, which meant they'd *had* something, and now it was all over. But he was being insistent… *please stop trying to contact me.*

Jealousy—neon, lime green envy, the poisonous kind that seeps into your veins—roiled in my guts at the thought of *my husband* chasing another woman, and her having the gall to reject him. Reject Juan? Was she *crazy*?

Of course I was glad she wasn't interested.

But who the hell *was* this goddess, though, who could go around rejecting a man like Juan? *I cannot give you what you want.*

He *wanted* her. Wanted more of what he couldn't have.

It made me puke.

CHAPTER THIRTY-TWO

I don't know how many hours I lay on the mattress in the laundry room. I do remember hobbling to the sink to pee and frantically gulping down tap water, because I didn't find any bottles of water by the bed. To quench my thirst I had polished off all the champagne in sight, and once back in bed again, I stayed there. I didn't have the energy to drag myself back to the sink. I felt like hell. At some point, I must have put on a freshly laundered T-shirt of Dan's, a bird with the word *Liberty* emblazoned on the front, an irony not lost on me, even in my foggy state.

I'd been a fool not to get rid of them when I had the chance. With my dodgy ankle and locked in here, I was hardly in the position to call the shots now. My wits were my only tools left to me. Three to one. They held all the power. And if my mother, Pippa or Mr. Donner called, who knew what lies the triplets might feed them about my absence? All I could think about was how gullible I'd been plopping myself right into the triplets' honeyed trap. The freak with six fingers wanting to be part of the gang. Why hadn't I learned my lesson from childhood? Popular people will only be your friend:

    a. If you are cooler than they are.
    b. If you're wealthy and they think your riches could rub off
       on them.
    c. If you have something of value to offer.

I wasn't cool or wealthy at school, so I had offered up what I could: my intellectual services, letting the bullies copy my homework. Becoming their "friend." My protection mechanism so they wouldn't taunt and tease me.

History had repeated itself with the triplets. I felt such a sucker, such an idiot.

If only they'd release me from this claustrophobic solace! Screaming and pounding the door had done nothing to help me. At one point, I did hear a car coming down the driveway. Voices. Pippa? I heaved myself up to the slit of the window and yelled out, but nobody heard me and then the car drove off. Like the lump I had become, I must have crashed back down on the mattress and slithered back into my memories, which were now mixed with a medley of fantasies and dreams, thickened with fever. Sweat dripped from my body, the sheets soaked with illusions and hallucinations. The comforter tossed one minute, then coveted for warmth the next.

Ice. Sweat. Ice. Fire.

I drifted out of my being. In my dream, I got up, stumbled to the garden shed, where I found a spade. And staggered into the undergrowth, dragging the spade behind me like a corpse. The moon, a thin crescent and no more, barely lit my way—chilly, with only a smattering of spangled stars to guide me, instinct my only chaperone. I found the spot and dug all night. An owl observed me, its eyes round and keen as if he understood, and then he spoke, his hoot letting me know I'd done what I had to do to protect myself. "Things are not what they seem," he said. He flew off, the movement of his wings more silent than the still air.

Where had I heard an owl say that before? And then I remembered I had it wrong:

"The *owls* are not what they seem." I spoke the words from *Twin Peaks*, out loud, repeating them over and over, remembering my three-dimensional dream. These words made more sense than anything so far.

I lay in bed for days. At least, it seemed that way.

It was Jen who finally woke me. Leaning into me, her breath close to mine, the back of her hand soft on my puffy, putty-like cheek.

"She's finally awake," Jen whispered. I fluttered open an eye. Dan, Kate, all on the edge of my bed, and I could feel the weight of Beanie curled up asleep by my feet.

"You've been sick," Jen let me know. She handed me a glass of water. The water was coolish, but not too cold, the way they knew I liked it. Icy water is a killer on the teeth. You can take the girl out of Britain but you can't take Britain out of the girl. No ice. Marmite. Crisps. Fish & chips. Heinz baked beans. Tea and milk. These were my homesick, feverish thoughts as I gulped the water down without stopping.

"You were humming a tune in your sleep," Jen said.

I rubbed my eyes.

She scrutinized me with her stare. "'Teddy Bear's Picnic.'"

I looked blank.

Jen sang:

"If you go down to the woods today
You're sure of a big surprise."

My pulse picked up speed at the little song. *Have they dug it up, found the spot in the woods?* I'd snap in two, unravel, disintegrate. I couldn't keep myself together. I willed myself to stay calm, not let her know I was fazed. Pretended to ignore her words and concentrated on gulping down all the water I could without vomiting. I must have been dangerously dehydrated.

I tried to haul myself out of bed. "Why have you locked me up?"

Dan rested his leonine gaze on me. His muscular arms reminded me how strong his body was compared to my weedy little frame. He looked tough. Uncompromising. My left ankle still throbbed like a beating heart. "Are you over your little episode now?" he said with a sneer.

"My little *episode*?" I yelled. "You lot locked me up!" I turned my aching neck around to take in my claustrophobic surroundings. But I was back in my real bedroom. Had I imagined being in the laundry room all along? I drew in a grateful breath, my thoughts picking at the details of the last few days. Outside, it was getting late, the sunset a menacing purple, edged in black, the rain slamming at the great glass walls, thunder rumbling. To see a view again, and not just blank white walls, made my vision smart. I remembered the owl, but my dream was so far off in the distance, I couldn't catch it back.

"Do you feel better now?" Jen asked.

Brushing damp locks of hair from where they were sticking to my chapped lips, I rasped, "Why did you lock me in the laundry room?"

Dan let out a "You're crazy" chuckle. Then Kate said, "We would never do such a thing. You were having bad dreams, you imagined it."

I needed backup. I'd send Pippa an SOS, call the cops. "Where's my phone?"

Nobody answered.

"Where's my fucking phone?"

Kate shrugged a shoulder. "Who knows? And even if we could find it, nobody's phone is working anyway right now. The storm. No landline. Cells are down. Internet's down."

Jen brushed her hand across my dripping brow. "Do you think you could manage a little dinner?"

"I'm just thirsty," I croaked. "I'd kill for a Coke." They looked at each other knowingly, their faces dead serious. My choice of words echoed in my ears. "I don't know how I got so sick. How I hurt my ankle."

"Alcohol poisoning," Kate told me, her tone very matter-of-fact. "You were out of control, no wonder you hurt yourself. We were so *worried* about you."

"What? From one silly bottle of white wine? Not even a whole bottle! And you'd got it from your hotel, Jen, you said it was a fancy label, that people had been raving about what great quality it was. And the champagne, that was just a 'hair of the dog,' a needed pick-me-up to help with recovery, not the cause itself!"

Jen widened her pretty green eyes. "Don't you remember anything?"

Kate said, "You downed a half bottle of vodka, too, and then one whole bottle of champagne straight after. Not counting the one by your bed."

"No. No. I never—almost never—not since my student days—mix my drinks. Vodka? No, where would I have got vodka from?"

"In the freezer. It was right there. Right there, in the freezer. You don't remember? We all played Scrabble that evening, and you won with the word OWL. Dan made a fire and we sat by the wood burner. And then we tried to play charades, but by this point you were so drunk you blacked out, so Dan carried you to bed."

"No. *No.* It's not true!"

"And we were super worried and wanted to call a doctor, but knew one might not come because of all the rain—the highway's real dangerous right now—so we called your friend Pippa, and she told us that this is typical behavior, that you often go on binges and then black out and can't remember stuff the next day, that you even get reckless and violent sometimes—for us to watch out—and we shouldn't worry and that you'd be fine. So we just let you sleep and checked on you every so often to make sure you didn't choke on your own vomit or anything."

I sat up. My head spun with the sudden movement. They were lying about Pippa saying that. Unless… "Pippa was here, wasn't she?"

"No," Kate said.

"But I heard her voice, her car."

"Nope, you're imagining it," Dan snapped.

"No," I whispered. "No!" Were they right, had I been imagining things? Had I been violent? My head hammered on with my own white noise, the buzz of paranoia about what I had or hadn't done and everything that could go wrong. Everything that was already wrong.

"And then there've been these weird anonymous calls," Kate added. "Someone who's hung up every time one of us answered the landline. And now the landline's down 'cause of the weather." I remembered the dead phone in the laundry room.

"Can someone give me my cell phone, please?" I hauled myself out of bed but tumbled straight back. I was one big, aching mass of bruised flesh and bone.

Nobody spoke. Jen glided out of the room, and Dan followed. Kate remained sitting on my bed. "Speaking of phones, maybe you can explain the anonymous calls," she said. "Someone breathing and then hanging up when they hear it isn't your voice. Anyway, they won't be calling again. Last night's lightning strikes have made us totally incommunicado."

The triplets' whispery conversation popped up in my mind like a vicious Punch & Judy show. Punch, punching me. Judy kicking. *We can deal with her. We'll take control. This weekend? When we all have the day off? We'll go down there and see—*

"Where's my cell phone?" I yelled again. "You've taken my phone away from me? Look, you three need to get OUT of my house! This has gone far enough!"

Kate raised her eyebrows in a "Tut tut, you're such a fool" way. She pointed a varnished black nail at me and said, "Now you know that's *never* gonna happen. Calm down, little lady."

"How DARE you!" But the words chafed in my raw throat. I ran the options through my head. It was true; there was no way they'd leave this house without a fight. They might be no more than teenagers, but there were three of them against one skinny, weak, frazzled me. I could barely even walk. And Dan was buffed up. "Look, I'll sort out a really nice apartment for you. I'll pay for six months' rent up front."

Kate laughed again and held my clammy hand. "Why would we want to live in some strange apartment when we can be here with you, in our own home? Our tax returns get sent to this address, we're registered to vote at this address, we get our mail here. This is the only home we know and love."

I swallowed, taking in the ugly truth of her words. Kicking them out legally would be no easy feat. They'd cleverly established their rights.

"Besides, you need looking after," Kate continued, her voice sugary. "Look what a state you're in. You can't even walk, there's no way you'd be able to drive your car. You know how hard it is to use the clutch on your cranky old Land Rover's stick shift, even on a good day. With your twisted ankle? Forget it. We do your shopping. We cook for you. You need us. Just chill. We're *not* your enemy, you gotta—"

"Please just give me my bloody cell phone! *Please,* Kate!" I spat out.

"My guess is?" Kate went on. "Someone wants to talk to you, and only you and that's why he or she kept calling. Know who it could be?" She sounded like a police officer in a TV show. I wondered if they'd been digging in the rain. The way Dan had looked at me when I was by the burial site was as if he could read my mind. They might have honed in on the spot, maybe even found what was buried.

"I think I'm going to be sick again." I lurched to the bathroom, got down on my knees and held my head over the toilet. Nothing, just watery bile. And the throaty retch of knowing my face was so close to the loo, clean though it was. Suspiciously clean. It sparkled with a lemony sheen. Had Mrs. Reed come while I was out cold, plastered to the bed? She always did such a thorough job and often came when I was at work. Yet… didn't she normally do the washing on a Friday? If so, why hadn't she come to my rescue? Did she know I was locked up? Was she in on it too? No, that thought was ridiculous. More bile flowed from my bitter mouth.

I staggered back into the room. "I'll give you money," I cajoled. "Just tell me how much you want. But I need you to get your own place. This is not working out."

She let out a giggle as if what I said was the most absurd idea in the world, but her eyes were hard as pebbles. "Don't. Be. Silly. You're not thinking straight. You can hardly walk. You need us right now."

"Then take me to the hospital! I need a doctor to look at my ankle."

"None of us are going anywhere right now. The weather's too crazy."

I heaved myself up and hobbled to my wardrobe. I was so puny I could hardly even open the cupboard door, hardly stand up. Visions of smashing the triplets over their heads with my reading lamp evaporated as my shaky hand fumbled with a coat hanger. I tried in vain to pull out a dress. I couldn't even do that. Couldn't even hold on to a piece of clothing, I was trembling so hard. The dress fell in a ripple to the floor. I stabbed the coat hanger in Kate's direction. "Get out of my house! Don't you get it? I don't want you here anymore! Leave! Or—"

"Or what? You'll call the cops? I hate to break it to you, but your phone has totally vanished. Like I said, the landline's dead. And our cell phones aren't working with this crazy weather. You can't drive your car. In fact, none of us should drive anywhere at the moment. It's too dangerous till things let up. Chill out, dude. Get some rest. And we ain't goin' nowhere. You needed to accept that fact, like yesterday."

Jen ambled back into the room with a Dr Pepper. She snapped the ring and handed me the can. "Drink this, it'll give you energy."

I took the soda and glugged it down. "Where's my laptop?" I demanded, letting out a burp.

"It won't do you any good. Everything's completely down 'cause of the lightning and thunder. No Internet. Our cell phones aren't working either."

My heart went free-fall, spiraling in despair. I was their prisoner. I collapsed back on the bed. "My ankle hurts like crazy," I moaned. "I don't even remember falling over."

Jen gently took my leg and cupped my tender ankle in her hands. "This hurt?"

"Yes."

"It's swollen. And bruised. You'll be okay, just give it time. You see how you can't be left alone? What would you do without us?"

I clawed the soda can with both hands so I didn't drop it. Trembling. Five fingers apiece.

"Who was that anonymous caller?" Kate demanded.

"How on earth do I know? Maybe my mother? I need to call my poor mum, she'll be worried."

"If it was her calling, why would she hang up?"

"She's impatient. It would bug her I wasn't answering, and I never let her know you lot were moving in. She must've been confused. She calls every weekend." The second I'd said those words about Mum not knowing they lived here, I regretted it.

Kate crossed her arms. "The calls were from yesterday, too. And the day before. We could even hear breathing."

"Mr. Donner? He must be wondering why I haven't showed up for work."

"Nope. We called him. Let him know you were sick."

"Mrs. Reed?"

"We called her, too. Told her to take some time off."

My heart sank. They had alienated me. "Pippa, maybe?" I said hopefully.

"Pippa's on a long vacation. She called to let you know."

Bullshit. Tears welled in my eyes. I was all alone, at their mercy. I downed the last drops of Dr Pepper, the fizz burning my nostrils and the back of my sandpaper throat, but my thirst was unquenchable. "Just a cold caller selling something, I guess."

If Kate was lying, she deserved an Oscar. Maybe the drone operator was back.

CHAPTER THIRTY-THREE

The have-I-left-the-iron-on doubt—when you know you haven't left the iron on—made me question myself. Had I gone on a bender? Got so drunk I'd passed out? Had nightmares about being locked in the laundry room? No! The triplets were gaslighting me! Trying to make me doubt my own sanity.

I wasn't crazy. They were lying. But why? Did they have a reason for locking me up? Did they know something they weren't letting on? Hearing their footsteps outside my room, I kept waiting for one of them to come in and confront me. I rewound Dan's words: *The body must be somewhere. And my guess is? It isn't at the bottom of Ragged Point.* If only I had gone with my first instincts and got rid of them when I'd had the bloody chance! Now it was too late. My only possibility was to summon outside help. Rain slashed the windows. I longed to go down to the site, to see if the triplets had found anything. Limp my way along the coast and then hitchhike to safety. Get away from them. Damn, why hadn't I bought a gun? It was true what they said about my Land Rover. I couldn't drive the thing in the condition I was in; my ankle felt like a matchstick that could snap any moment.

Jen slipped in silently to my room, with a tray. Soup and dry toast. I needed to eat. Get my strength back so I could get the hell out of here.

"Jen. I need you to tell me the truth about what happened. Please."

"Like we said. You went on, like, a wild drinking binge, mixing vodka and wine. You were totally out of control, a danger to yourself. Maybe even us."

"A danger? So you're admitting you shut me up then?"

"No! You're imagining things. What happened was that you were prowling around for more champagne and snuck downstairs to the drinks fridge. Somehow you ended up in the laundry room."

Was it possible? The laundry room was right by the fridge. But I knew my way around this house blindfold. Even if I had been that drunk, I would've found the champagne. "But I was shut in there, Jen. The door was locked."

"We did find you in there, sprawled out on the floor, but there's no way anyone locked the door on you. There's no key in the lock! You want to check? You're imagining stuff, sweetie. You passed out, is all." Her voice was soft. Her honey hair and gentle eyes told me she was an angel, but I knew what lurked beneath.

"Why was my mattress there then? My comforter?"

She laid her pretty hand on mine. "You're imagining things. You had alcohol poisoning real bad."

My mind was doing somersaults. I'd been there for days, hadn't I? No wonder I'd lost so much weight and my ribs were sticking out. I can't have eaten a thing. Jen blew on a spoonful of soup and aimed it at my mouth. I opened up, swallowed it down and remembered how starving I was. My stomach gurgled with recognition. Food at last.

I pressed my fingers on my eyes. The cool of them felt good. "My head hurts like hell still. Would you bring me my migraine pills, Jen? And my antihistamine meds. They're in the bathroom cabinet. Oh, and I need my reading glasses too."

"Sure." Jen left the room and came back with my Beanie pills and a glass of water. While she had her back to me, I double-checked the label on the vial to make sure they were the same pills I normally took: Benadryl. They were. But my hands were

194   Arianne Richmonde

too weak to turn the childproof cap. I wanted to ransack the house for a laptop, my phone, car keys, anything to connect me to civilization, but I could barely muster up a breath, let alone enough energy to go rampaging around the house.

Jen sat on the bed and laid her hand on my sweaty brow. "I couldn't find your glasses anywhere," she said, opening the bottle and popping out a couple of pills.

I took the Benadryl and chased them down with some water. "Another reason I need my phone. So I can use the torch to find things. Even if there's no connection, I still want my bloody phone!"

"I swear on my mom's life, we hunted for it everywhere and can't find it."

"Maybe I dropped it outside on my walk. When it stops raining, I'll go and take a look."

Jen's smile was candy-sweet. "Nuh-uh. You're not going outside. You're not going anywhere, sweetie. You're not well enough, you'll catch pneumonia in your state. And just in case you get any crazy ideas about leaving, Dan made sure all the doors and windows in the house are locked. For your own safety."

I clamped my eyes at her. "Jen, why are you doing this to me?"

"What? We just want you to get better. You've been a danger to yourself. We just want to protect you from harm."

"I want to go out!"

She giggled. "You're not going. Any. Where. You might hurt yourself. Play nice, now."

What did they know? What had they found? *For your own safety and ours.*

I sat up and tried to crawl my way out of bed. I felt like a beetle at the end of the season, on my way out—one squish and my life would be extinguished, a splotch on the floor. Jen pushed me back down. Her little finger was stronger than my whole body. "Then take me to see a doctor, for my ankle," I pleaded.

"There's nothing any doctor can do that we can't do for you ourselves. I'll get some ice for it. RICE. You know that one? Rest. Ice. Compression. Elevation. I'll fix you up. I'll play nursie."

She left the room. I shoveled myself out of bed again and hobbled to the sliding doors. Locked. I remembered what Kate had told me about these doors. Not even an angry Dan with a hammer had managed to make a crack. Earthquake-proof, no doubt. I checked the landline again. Dead. I plopped back down on the bed like a two-ton pile of rubble. I'd never felt so powerless.

Despite my fragile state, I needed to get the hell out of the house. Via the garage? While Jen and Dan were upstairs in the kitchen, and Kate was having a shower, I hobbled to the garage (or rather, crawled). But when I pressed the button for the automatic door, it didn't budge. Locked. But the tin of spare keys would still be here, hidden in the toolbox. I rummaged around and found the tin, along with a spare set of my Land Rover keys. I grabbed a small hammer for good measure and hopped out on one foot as fast as I could, back to the laundry room. I hid everything in a pillowcase, which I lodged behind the washing machine. Just in case the triplets locked me in there again. I collapsed, slumped over the dryer, panting from the effort, my ankle puffed like a blowfish. Then I remembered there was a spare front door key at the back of a kitchen drawer under a pile of linen napkins (I hoped) and realized I should bring the pillowcase with me and drag myself upstairs to the kitchen, escape Cliffside while I could, get the—

"What are you doing in here?" It was Kate, her dark hair slick and wet from her shower, but dressed for work.

"Just looking for some fresh sheets."

"Get back to your room. I'll bring them to you."

"No, Kate. This is my freaking house! How dare you boss me around!"

She clinched me by the wrist. I flailed my arms around and tried to punch her in the chest so she'd back off, but my knuckles met nothing but air and I ended up crashing into the wall.

Kate flew upon me, yanked me by the arm, her fingers pinching my bare flesh. "You are out of control, little lady!"

I wrenched myself away from Kate's claw-like grasp and made a run (a limp) for it again, but she seized me by my pajamas, eyes flashing with rage. Clamping me by my wrist again, she twisted my arm behind my back.

"Let go!" I yowled. "That hurts!"

Jen appeared like magic. She had that ability to float on air and conjure herself up from nowhere. "Kate, stop! Go easy. Let's take her back to her room. She'll injure herself."

"Let me go!" I wailed. "Please! I'll give you all the money you need and you can get your own apartment! A house, even. I'll rent you a whole house, whatever you want."

Kate tightened her grip. "We'll have to lock her in her room. We have no choice."

"Please!" I begged.

She pressed her big, muddy hiking boot on my bare toes. "What would you prefer? Your lovely bedroom with a drop-dead view and beautiful bathroom? Or the claustrophobic laundry room?"

I was about to choose the laundry room, now I had my Land Rover keys here and a way to escape, but Jen said, "No, Kate, that's cruel." Then to me, "Play nice. It's for your safety and ours, we'll take you to your room."

"Just leave me here," I pleaded. "Leave me where I am, I don't even care anymore!"

Jen laid a gentle hand on my shoulder. "We'll take you to your room so you can rest up, till you're all better, okay, sweetie?"

I bucked and struggled, screaming at them to leave me here alone, but they insisted. The two of them were powerhouses versus my frail, feathery body. Kate dragged me back to my bedroom. I was defeated.

At least for now.

CHAPTER THIRTY-FOUR

I heard them arguing in hissy whispers, outside my bedroom door, about which one of them should be in charge of the key. They decided to leave it in the lock.

The first thing I did, as soon as they were all asleep that night, was to jimmy the key out of the keyhole with a wire coat hanger. I managed. It dropped to the ground, and I spent hours attempting to fish it back from under the thin crack at the bottom of the door. No joy; it had fallen too wide. I tried this on several occasions over the following days until the triplets wised up.

Time chugged past like a freight train, slow and heavy, but too fast for me to jump onto. I felt weak, almost numb, no will or energy to do anything, and more depressed than ever about Juan. I was locked in my bedroom twenty-four seven, my only solace the view, the stock of books in my e-reader, and the TV.

I attacked the triplets on several occasions. Or at least tried to. But they always came in twos, usually Dan and Kate, so I caused minimal damage. After lunging at Kate one time with my bedside lamp, they removed all heavy objects from the room. The lamp, the flower vase, and anything glass. No bottles to smash over their heads. Not even a chair. They had searched my bedroom from top to bottom, under the mattress, behind books, in between magazines, under rugs. It was a good thing I hadn't hidden my car keys here. These triplets were smart and had thought of everything. I screamed and yelled—I lunged at Dan, too, left him with a tiger's scratch on his arm. He just laughed at me. Flipped me over his shoulder as if I were no more bothersome than a little girl having a tantrum.

But they didn't take me back to the laundry room as I hoped they would. They just kept me locked up in my bedroom.

Helpless.

Another week went by—was it a week? My sense of time was fuzzy. Christmas must have come and gone. No landline. No cell phone. No laptop. Nothing but the deluge of rain and the triplets' silence, except when they brought me my meals and filled up my Thermos. I had stopped eating pretty much immediately, didn't trust the food they were giving me. I stopped taking my allergy meds, stopped my painkillers, the Mumm, but then I felt worse than ever and too weak to even think straight, and Beanie's visits being my only solace, I needed to take my meds. My instinct for survival was too strong, so soon I began eating again, although since my spate of illness—the monster hangover that I still didn't believe was from mixing vodka with wine—I had very little appetite. I had a nasty virus? Anything was possible. The triplets refused to take me to a doctor and told me I was being a hypochondriac.

Had they found what was buried in the woods? I needed to know why they had locked me up and what they knew, but every time I asked what the hell was going on they were silent. Even talkative Jen, whose expressions told me she felt sorry for me, yet she wouldn't go against her siblings and actively *help*. How had they wooed me so convincingly in the first place? By being indispensable? By luring me into the "family" bosom? They had sensed my weak spot. Honed in on my loneliness. How blind I'd been.

The hands on the *más sola que la una* clock inside my brain ticked torturously. Each morning, around breakfast time, before they set off for work, I expected the conversation to turn when they popped in to give me my breakfast. They were always cordial but dispassionate. The fun-loving triplets were a thing of the past. Every time I asked to be let out, they ignored me, or smiled, or laughed. I told them I had a fever (I did) and needed a doctor. My ankle still rendered me pretty incapacitated. But nothing I said budged them. I plotted and schemed. I'd smash them over the head with something—what?—I'd make my escape. But I was weak, muddled, their coltish legs too nimble, their brains too quick. They didn't miss a beat.

I cried, screamed, begged, bribed. All to deaf ears. Nothing would convince them to set me free. So I decided to try a different tactic. I told them I wanted to have a chat. I had to find out what their plan was. What did they want from me? See if I could entice them in some way, try bribing them again. Everything had a price, didn't it?

Jen billowed into my room, flushed from a long hot bath. Followed by Kate and, lastly, Dan with a tray of food. I didn't feel like eating. The only solace was little Beanie. He jumped on my bed and I gave him a huge squeeze. At least *he* loved me. I had to take extra allergy pills, but it was worth it for his company.

The triplets behaved as if everything were completely normal. I felt sick with anticipation of how I would broach the conversation.

"How's work?" I asked Dan, trying to warm him up. Lately he'd been behaving as if I were a dull piece of old brown furniture. There's nothing more painful than being ignored, nothing more soul destroying. *Scream at me, yell, tell me I'm a jerk, but don't just pretend I'm not here!*

The hard patter of rain rapped at the windows.

Dan, cupping a mug of coffee, not even looking at me, said in a monotone: "Work? It's like I'm on automatic pilot. I mean, it's not as if I give a shit, it's just a stopgap till I figure out my next move."

Next move… under the circumstances that sounded beyond ominous.

"Customers tipping well?" I said.

"Always."

"They give terrible tips in England, you know." I gave a pathetic little laugh as if to apologize for the country I no longer belonged to. "A lot of the time they add twelve percent to the bill as a matter of course, because customers might not pony up otherwise. They're pretty darn stingy too when it comes to tips, not like here where you get twenty percent. I mean, bartenders getting tips in Europe? Not a chance. I remember when I first came here people looked at me like I was chopped liver. It took me a while to understand why. Because I had no idea I was meant to tip a bartender!" My voice sounded so leaden and monotonous. The anticipation was eating away at me. "Anyway," I continued, "I bet you'll sail into Harvard or Princeton. Maybe even MIT. Or if you don't want to go so far away, there are some great universities right here in California."

"We'll see." He was staring at the view, the mug of coffee still in his hand. Contemplative, marking time. My stomach twisted in fear.

I carried on, trying to keep my voice chirpy and light. "You've got the brains, Dan, let's see if luck plays a part too. That's what I say. It's fifty percent determination and hard work, twenty-five percent skill and ability, and at least… at *least*, twenty-five percent luck."

"Luck's something I've been down on recently," he mumbled, still not looking at me.

"Luck?" I said. "You don't feel lucky? I could change that. Just tell me exactly what it is you want."

But he turned abruptly, suddenly catching my gaze like a fish on a hook. "We do need to have a little chat," he said. "You're right."

I felt my lips tremble into a small smile. You could hear it in the breath I exhaled, measure its molecules in the air dancing between us. Finally, finally we'd deal with this. I'd find out once and for all if they knew anything and what exactly they wanted from me. But I heard myself say, "About what?"

"About your husband," Dan said.

That very same relief quickly morphed into a heart-jammering dread.

"You might want a drink," Dan suggested. "I realize the subject is very, very sensitive." He left the room with purpose. Kate stood like a bouncer against the door. Jen's gaze followed me, her eyes wide. The look on her face was sympathetic, almost apologetic. Dan came back with a bottle of Mumm, popped the cork and filled up my Thermos to the brim. "Let's not pretend anymore," he said, giving me one of his winks and white, flashy smiles. Dan's charm was almost like a separate being, with a separate soul. Disarming. He was like a professional actor. The very same smile filled his pockets every day with generous tips from desperate women. Women like me. But his false charm meant nothing to me now.

Up until now I had stopped the Mumm. I was trying to stay alert. But I didn't want to make waves, so I gulped down the champagne. My mouth felt dry. The truth was, the bubbles were deliciously welcome.

Lifting my eyes to Dan's sickeningly handsome face—because it did now make me sick—I said, "What exactly do you want to talk about?"

"Can't you guess?" Did I detect a trace of a smirk edging up the corners of his lips?

I opened my mouth to speak but instead raised the Thermos to my mouth and swallowed another gulp. My heart scampered all over the place, my mind pacing up and down, scanning the galaxy of possibilities of what could happen next.

Dan looked at his sisters then said, "This accident that you say happened? That involved your husband."

"That I 'say' happened? What, you think I *invent*ed it? You can read about it in the news!"

"Oh, we know there was an 'accident,' but what *kind* of accident, that's the million-dollar question." His choice of words held more weight than he realized.

"What the hell are you getting at?" I said. The stench of fear made it hard to breathe.

"It's funny," he continued, "because we found out that Juan Trujillo may not have definitively died in that accident. No body was ever found. The California Highway Patrol even searched with dogs."

"That means nothing," I retorted. "Juan's car *flew* off that cliff! It exploded on impact. It's no wonder they found nothing. Everyone was perfectly satisfied with the circumstantial evidence, even the insurance company."

"Handy," Kate joined in, "that you benefited so nicely from Juan Trujillo's life insurance policy. With him being such a high earner. That was a shitload of money they paid out. Enough to pay off all the federal estate tax for Cliffside and a shitload more into the bargain."

My pulse skipped a beat. "How do you know how much insurance was paid out?" Had they been snooping through my files? Most of my paperwork was locked, but the hiding place for the key was an old tea tin in the kitchen. "How do you know about the life insurance payment, Kate?"

"Just a good guess," she said, her face a little flushed. "Him being a lawyer and all."

"Anyway, everyone knows what happened," I said, "that Juan was driving to the airport and en route he swerved on that nasty bend near Ragged Point—there are skid marks still on the road, all this time later. Everyone knows how treacherous that highway is, particularly there. It's not the first time a car has ended up on those rocks below."

"But nobody *saw* the actual crash," Kate went on. "At least, not till the car had already been in flames for a while. Car debris was found, yet no body parts."

"What are you insinuating?"

"We've been thinking that maybe, just maybe, he didn't die that way," Dan said. His mouth slid into a knowing smile.

"It just seems weird," Kate added, "that they never found the actual body, not even teeth and stuff. Maybe he was murdered beforehand. Maybe his body's buried somewhere… nowhere near the crash. And the car accident was, like, faked. There was a lapse of time, right, from when he went missing to the discovery of the car?"

"Look," I said. "Is this some kind of joke to torment me? Talking like this about my—my husband's… *body* parts? To taunt me with this? You think there could be a survivor of a crash like that? A car exploding on *impact*?"

"We were just wondering if it was possible," Jen added, "that he was never in the car in the first place. That maybe it was, like, parked… maybe the car—it was a vintage Mustang, right?—that the handbrake was off, maybe someone rolled it over the edge of the cliff without him in it. That he died… elsewhere. That the killer used that as a cover-up, that—"

"That's insane! Why are you making me revisit this horrible—I can't believe you're all bringing this—look, I'd rather not talk about this, please." Tears threatened, and I encouraged them to spill down my cheeks by squeezing my eyes. Maybe waterworks would make them more sympathetic towards me. Now, at least, I knew why they were locking me up. They thought I'd murdered my husband. This was insane!

"It's just strange," Kate went on. "Strange they never found more than a man's watch and a burnt shoe."

"A shoe and watch I identified as his. I gave him that Rolex for our tenth anniversary present. It was engraved on the back with

Juan's initials, and a personal message. The shoes were one of a kind. Bespoke. He had them made by a cobbler in London. The same cobbler who hand-makes shoes for Sean Connery. There *are* no other shoes like that! As I said, unique. Proof it was Juan! The investigation was closed. I can't believe you're bringing this up when it's a solved case!"

"Yeah, handy, that. No human body parts, just items, which the murderer could have thrown in with the debris. Classic. Seen it in a million cop shows on TV."

"Look, nobody else found anything fishy so why should you? Why are you delving into my private—?"

"Private?" Jen said. "You think we aren't interested in your *family*? Your husband? The man who took this house from us?"

The way she said "family" startled me. It sank home that not even Jen had ever considered me family. It had all been my gullibility and self-made fantasy that had propelled me into this heinous situation.

Jen pulled out her phone from her pocket (so there was a connection, after all), and scrolling through it, read out, "Authorities had planned to search the site for the body on Wednesday, the day of the accident, but rain and the treacherous terrain were slowing efforts, according to Lola Cipriani, a spokeswoman for the San Luis Obispo County Sheriff's Department, who said, 'It's very difficult for crews to rappel down to that dangerous location.'"

I felt bile rising in my stomach. "Anyway, what's this to you? Why are you suddenly so fixated on my husband?" I drew a sharp breath. I wondered what, exactly, they wanted from me. To blackmail me? Had they found what was buried? Or was it just Cliffside itself they were after? That's all they had ever cared about. They didn't care about money; they just wanted Cliffside.

I tried to remain calm. "You're getting yourselves worked up over something that none of us can control," I said under my breath. "What happened, happened. My husband is dead, and the way you all speak of him like he was some thief who stole your house, I wonder why you would care one iota about his death anyway."

"Oh, we don't give a shit about *him*," Dan said, "but we do live with *you*, and trusted you. It would be nice to know who we have in our house."

Our house.

*Pretty Brit Widow in **our** Big Sur house.*

I wanted to remind them it was *my* house, they were here because of my generosity, and that they were in no way obliged to stay. Especially if they considered me a murderess, which was what they seemed to be driving at. Were they worried they might be next on the list? Obviously. Powerless. I eyed up Jen's phone, plotting and scheming about how I could get my hands on it. If I could just get her on her own, she might cave in.

Why, oh why, hadn't I got rid of them then, when I had the chance? I felt furious with myself. Dad was right, I was a "brainless fool." But all I said was, "What else did you find out? I'd love to know actually. If there's a puzzle to solve, we could work together." All was not lost. If I could somehow get them on my side without revealing too much, I might be able to turn the situation around. Gain my freedom and get the hell out of here.

Dan slowly moved over to the window and stared at the view. "What 'else?' You mean there's more?" Clever bastard, Dan was. He'd make a good lawyer.

I crossed my hands—clammy and cold as dead fish—neatly on my lap, lacing my fingers together, almost in prayer. "This is ridiculous. You're holding me a prisoner in my own house when I haven't done anything!"

Dan stood, hands clasped behind his back. He had a habit of speaking to the ocean view when something was bothering him. And I had been bothering him a lot lately. "Okay, we'll let you know what we believe, based on what we've found out so far."

I was exhausted. Talk about beating around the bush. "Good," I sighed, "just let it out. Tell me what else you think you know about me, apart from being the femme fatale in *The Postman Always Rings Twice*." I waited for the punchline. The great reveal. Like a game of chess in my head, I set the scene for all the possible outcomes—not least how I'd languish in jail, or worse, have to escape the aftermath, the ones who'd come after me in revenge.

Nobody said anything. The triplets just studied my reaction. A triangle of shared emotions that made up this trio. Kate glared at me with a wintry gaze that suddenly seemed to me the true makeup of her face. Her cheekbones looked more prominent, her pupils darker—her hardness was staggering. Jen sat there, eyes green as a meadow, widened and expectant, hopeful, maybe, that I'd redeem myself by confessing all and then we could be friends again. I couldn't work these three out. Did they know something or didn't they? Unless they were tricking me into confession, it looked as if they had zero evidence of anything. Had they broken into the safe?

"I thought perhaps you'd found some kind of evidence," I ventured, treading as lightly as I could.

Dan laughed. "What do you mean, 'some kind of evidence?'"

"After all these accusations, I thought you were going to say you'd *found* something," I insisted. "Something crucial. Something that would shed light on the whole story. Something not already in the newspapers."

"Found something?" Jen asked.

"What *is* the whole story?" Dan spat out, turning on the heel of his boots so he was facing me.

But I couldn't tell him the whole story or I'd probably end up dead.

CHAPTER THIRTY-FIVE

Over the next few days, because of Dan, Kate, and Jen stirring trouble with their big wooden spoon, half of me expected the cops to show up at my door any second, but at the same time I knew the triplets didn't want to burn their bridges. Cliffside was their home, and any trouble would jeopardize that. Anyway, they had no proof of anything, or they would have let me know. It could have all worked out. If they'd ever given a damn. We had lied to one another—well, I had never *lied* but omitted information. Little white lies, maybe, about being pregnant or whatever, but not *black* lies.

The paranoia of what would happen next—the aftermath of what could unfold if the truth were revealed—hung on my every thought, trickled into every vein of my brain. I couldn't concentrate on anything. It was like a ticking time bomb waiting to blow up in my face. Half of me wanted it to all be over. I was tempted to tell them my secret. But it was just too risky.

I watched the weather and news on TV. Last year's fires and drought—followed by all the recent rain—had caused sudden mudslides rendering several parts of Highway One impassable. Rain, rain, and more rain, flowing in torrents down to the ocean.

I imagined it washing away the burial site, revealing everything, leaving it naked and exposed. What would happen next? I envisioned myself with a team of lawyers, trying to explain it all away. "I did it for love," I'd tell them. That was the good scenario. The bad? I didn't even dare entertain.

I stared out the window at the obscured view. Cliffside seemed to be weeping. Torrents of rain smashed against the glass, gushing down through her gutters and out to sea. Juan's death was pounding down on me, more than ever. I reflected on my precarious situation, yet again, the possibilities and consequences spinning round and round in my head.

Even if the triplets did let me out, by all accounts, and from what I gathered from the news on TV, getting anywhere fast would be near impossible. Because of the geography of the surrounding territory, Highway One was the only route out, unless you had a helicopter. Serpenting above the ocean and sandwiched in between the road and the ocean, as Cliffside was, the only means of escape were steep trackless hills bordering my estate, now flowing with oozing mud, rendered useless. Even with my Land Rover. I don't know why the roads closing in on me was something I had never imagined happening, because now that it was upon us, it seemed so obvious. We residents were living in some of the most expensive real estate in the world, yet my neighbors were also virtual prisoners in their homes, even without the doors and windows locked.

Nobody could drive south past Big Sur anymore. The roads were shut off. Pfeiffer Canyon Bridge was threatening to collapse and was too dangerous to cross with a vehicle. Everything revolved in and around the house, even for the triplets, now. The highway, due north, was still open, but treacherous. The three braved it out nonetheless. For groceries or whatever they needed. And to work.

But Jen could no longer drive to her hotel. She had to take the car to Pfeiffer Canyon Bridge, park, hike, then get a lift from someone on the other side. The result was that she ended up staying for long periods at the hotel without coming home. My plan of getting her alone and appealing to her better side stymied.

If I thought I felt isolated before, it was even scarier now. A giant landslide cutting Big Sur off from the south, since the imminent collapse of the bridge, had really changed things and was dominating the news. Children going to school had to be dropped off on one side of the bridge and picked up on the other. Kate, being a guide, was getting more work than ever helping people find their way, even carry their groceries. Old trails were being used again, simply to get from A to B. The fancy hotels had become even more exclusive: guests were being flown in by helicopter from Monterey. It made me appreciate how vulnerable we all were, living on a precarious coastline that had fallen victim to fires and drought, and now this relentless flash flooding. Everyone was trapped. However much money they had.

Mother Nature wielding her power.

Even with so much danger out there, nothing compared to the fear I felt locked up here. I had to get out but was running out of ideas. I feigned an epilepsy attack one time, pretending I'd suffered as a child in hope someone would take me to the hospital or call 911. I dribbled and foamed at the mouth. It turned out that Dan was the only one home and didn't give a damn—left me on my bed, legs kicking in spasms, eyes rolling. Either he knew I was lying or genuinely wished me dead. I was being locked up for reasons other than the triplets' paranoia about me being a murderer. If they were so suspicious of me why hadn't they called the police?

No, they had other, more sinister plans for me.

I *had* to get back into the laundry room, however claustrophobic. It was a risk; they may have already discovered my pillowcase there, but it was the last glimmer of chance I had left. If the spare front door key was still at the back of the kitchen drawer under that pile of linen napkins (which I knew the triplets never used), I'd be a free woman.

Jen, whenever home, was the only one of them who was still friendly to me, not that her "friendship" was worth much, but still, it gave me hope. She brought me a box of chocolates she'd pilfered from her hotel, whispering to me in a hiss not to let the others know about her gift. Inside the box, she'd stashed my reading glasses. A kind gesture, but too little too late. Funny how I'd once thought that Kate was the loyal one. You never know who people are, do you? Jen, despite her pouts and demands and bolshie behavior, seemed like she cared, just a little. Or were her efforts some kind of good cop/bad cop trick? I didn't even need my glasses anymore. No phone to look at, and I could enlarge the print on my e-reader. My glasses were useless to me now.

The chocolates were a nice thought though. Nobody had gifted me chocolates since Juan. He was so generous at birthdays and Christmas: fancy chocolates galore, huge bouquets of flowers, and always jewelry. Juan was great like that—surprising me with presents, making me feel like a million dollars… well, he *tried* to make me feel like a million dollars. It wasn't his fault that I was so unsure of myself and still felt like a freak inside. I closed my eyes, wishing him back, savoring the day he proposed to me. Or at least, proposed that we got engaged.

Well. Sort of.

After dating him for several years, I began to badger him about getting a ring on my finger—I felt "less than," felt insecure. Wanted to know, like any normal woman, where our relationship was heading.

"Is that what's bothering you, honey, that you don't have an actual wedding ring?" he asked one morning as I was knotting his tie. He always dressed elegantly. Italian suits, Turnbull & Asser shirts, handmade shoes. I'd polish those sleek shoes; it gave me great satisfaction to do that.

"Well, yes. We've been together for four years now. I want to know what this relationship means to you," I said, with a spike of bravery. "Where it's going."

"Okay, I'll get you a wedding band."

My face lit up for a second, but my smile then dropped. "People usually get engaged first." I couldn't deny I felt a tad hurt that he was "relenting" to marry me, that it wasn't his own free will.

"You'll get that too. An engagement ring. We can kill two birds with one stone. Go shopping today, if you like."

Kill two birds with one stone? "I don't understand," I said, my heart dipping with disappointment.

"You want rings, I'll get you rings. You like Tiffany, right?"

"You make me sound so grabby, Juan. It's not just about the rings. It's—I want to know we belong to each other." I'd dreaded this conversation and hoped it would never get to this point: me begging him to marry me. I had dreamed of a white wedding. The big dress, the posy of flowers, bridesmaids. It dawned on me that expecting more than a registry wedding was absurd, or any nuptials at all. Girls like me didn't get men like Juan. Looking a gift horse in the mouth was risky.

He took my hand away from his tie then kissed it. "You know what, sweetheart? What you're suggesting is a good idea, actually. Rings are a good idea."

"Rings usually go hand in hand with a wedding though." The word "wedding" came out as barely a whisper.

"Can't do that," he said, throwing down my hand.

The moment had come, I thought. The moment when he'd dump me for good. I should have kept my trap shut. *Too pushy!* But I ventured, "Why not?"

"It's complicated."

I could feel a lump gather in my throat. "Is there someone else?"

"Babe, I do not have a relationship with another woman."

"That's what Clinton said, or something along those lines."

He winked at me. "Look, you have to believe you're the only woman I have a loving relationship with. Apart from my mother."

"*Loving relationship.*" What did that mean? Was he sleeping with someone else?

"Then why can't we get married?" I asked, tears welling.

He regarded me for a long while as if weighing up various possibilities, before saying, "Fiscal reasons. Like I said, it's complicated. Trust me, it's better this way. We'll get rings, hell, you can even change your name to mine. For the world at large, and my parents, you'll be my wife. We can even throw an engagement party, if you like. But let's just not tie the knot legally, okay?"

I nodded. A tear slid down my face. Pathetically, it was a tear of gratitude. I'd be his "wife."

Even if only make believe.

CHAPTER THIRTY-SIX

A spike of rage about Juan—and the triplets' malevolence—coursed through me as I wallowed in the bathtub, planning my escape. In their "sweep-outs" they had overlooked my makeup bag. Pretty Brit Widow was going to strike. I'd sharpen an eyebrow pencil to a vicious point. When Jen and Dan had left for work, I'd attack Kate while she brought me my breakfast. Go for the jugular. Whatever it took to get out of here.

In for a penny, in for a pound.

Reminiscing about Juan and the mess he got me into, I lay slumped in my bath, admiring my engagement ring. One thing, at least, I could still appreciate. It twinkled in the pinkish dawn light that shone through the colossal windows of my big glass house.

The square, yellow diamond solitaire shimmered majestically. Set on a simple platinum band, it glinted at me in recognition, a witness to everything we'd been through together. So elegant, cut so it sparkled in a thousand directions. A ring I had picked out from an advertisement in *Vogue*, never dreaming Juan would actually buy it for me, hence the message, *Yes, you,* engraved inside the band. The diamond was originally antique, the jeweler at Tiffany had informed me, so it had to be made specially. So expensive, it didn't even have a price tag. I remembered the thrill of unraveling the bow of the thick, silky white ribbon from the trademark Tiffany box. Just the box alone had got my heart racing with anticipation let alone the ring itself.

As I twirled it around now, my sixth, invisible finger twitched on the edge of my knuckle, the muscle memory still there, the scar almost invisible. The surgeon had done an amazing job. I turned the ring over carefully, rejoicing in the smoothness of the platinum on my skin. I had lost weight. It was worryingly loose.

All that glitters is not gold. This was never truer than this moment. The platinum glinted white. I held my hand up to the light and waved it this way and that, thrilled with my happy five-fingered hand and its special treasure of a ring to call its own. The diamond made prisms of light reflect on the ceiling, and dance around the room like tiny mirrors, in a kaleidoscope of colors. I rejoiced again at my ring finger that belonged to a hand of five digits, not six. The hand that my husband had kissed. He *had* to be in love with me, or why would he have spent so much? This Tiffany ring was worth a fortune.

Doubts about his loyalty melted away like butter on toast, or ice cream on a sunny day, drenching me with a renewed sweetened bliss. The man of my dreams bought me the ring of my dreams.

I lay back in the warmth of the water and focused on the view beyond. The ocean was kicking up white horses everywhere, and the sky was a crystal pink shot with bolts of silver. Infused with a sense of tranquility, I nodded off into a deep, REM sleep, flitting through the past.

Ice creams on a sunny day, holidays, the sun, the seaside and…

Tulum. We had arrived by private yacht. Our first vacation together, years ago, when Tulum was still a secret—sand as white as refined sugar, the sea a shimmering turquoise. I spotted the ancient Mayan ruins in the distance.

Juan was massaging sunscreen onto my shoulders then trailed his fingers into the nook of my neck. I shivered with desire. "Someone might see," I said, embarrassed. Just one touch from him and my body gave itself away.

"I told the crew to take the day off, we're all alone." He turned me around to face him, and cupping my face with his large hands said, "I'm all yours, honey. This is the way it's going to be from now on. Just you and me, no third parties. Nobody's going to spoil our happiness, I promise."

At the time I wondered what he was talking about. It was only later I understood exactly what he meant.

More memories swirled in my head. My dreams wandered back to Juan, before the accident.

Back to the bold, feminine note.

> *I am done with you, please stop trying to contact me*
> *I cannot give you what you want. Keep away from me.*

Juan was having an affair. Of course I wanted to know with whom, but I also knew that if I found out for sure, I would be devastated. I needed to weigh up the pros and cons thoroughly before I tasted the apple. Because once I took a bite, the knowledge would become part of me, and I'd never be able to look back.

Knowing I wasn't enough for him tore at me, but confronting him wasn't an option. It would give him an excuse to leave me. And who knew? This woman might well be playing games. *Treat 'em mean, keep 'em keen.* He'd want her all the more because of her attitude. I'd have to wait it out, bide my time, nibble the crumbs that came my way.

I couldn't risk losing him.

Just a few days after I found the note, Juan proposed to me. For real, this time.

Keeping my mouth shut had paid off.

"Babe, I've been thinking," he said, one evening. "It's time you and I tied the knot. You've—we've waited long enough."

"Marriage? Legal marriage?" I asked, my whole body aflame with excitement.

"We're going to Vegas today. Pack your things."

"I've got nothing to wear."

"Who cares? Wear jeans, if you like. The main thing is we'll make this legal. Man and wife, till death do us part."

"*Really?*"

"Really. Come on. Let's get this show on the road. We need to leave in half an hour."

"You're sure you want to tie the knot?"

"Are you crazy, second guessing me? Don't you see how happy you make me? My life was empty before I met you, honey. Marrying you is all I ever wanted, believe me. It has just taken a while to get there."

That was three weeks before he bought Cliffside. After we moved in, the feeling was priceless. The feeling of partnership, of ownership.

Cliffside was mine, too.

CHAPTER THIRTY-SEVEN

Dawn crept into morning, light gradually spilled into the bathroom, but Cliffside was silent. Nobody was up yet.

Then I heard footsteps. Two pairs of clunking feet. Dan and Kate. Not the right moment for my eyebrow pencil attack. My eyelids fluttered half-mast as they unlocked the door. The bath water had turned cold. I must have been asleep, dreaming about Juan. I shivered. I'd feign sleep. Garner my energy for later. They strode into the room. Dan not caring I was naked in the tub.

"She's so strung out," he whispered.

Kate clomped over to the bath. I could feel her breath on my clammy wet skin. She sang "With A Little Help From My Friends," bursting into a fit of breathy giggles every time she hit the word "high."

What were they saying? I kept my eyes squeezed shut.

"Should we lift her out of the tub?"

Dan cleared his throat. "If she drowns, she drowns."

I heard them march off, the key turn in my bedroom lock. Silence.

I sprang up, spluttering, but crashed back down, icy water spilling over the sides of the bath. My bruised ankle had given way, golden-green like a rotten apple. I slowly levered myself out of the tub, careful not to slip, mustering up all my strength just to stay standing. Clutching a towel, I caught a glimpse of myself in the mirror and nearly screamed. My eyes were hollow, my hair stringy and matted. I looked like something out of a zombie movie. "Strung out," Dan had said.

I rummaged frantically through the box of chocolates Jen had given me, picked out my reading glasses and scuttled to my bedroom. Grappling the canisters of pills with tremulous hands, I double-checked the labels: a tub of extra-strength headache pills for my migraines, Excedrin Migraine, and the vial of antihistamines, basic over-the-counter Benadryl.

But the pills themselves?

I tried to prize open the caps, my weak fingers fumbling. The caps swiveled round and round. Finally I got them off with my teeth. I let the meds spill onto the table.

No wonder the triplets had hidden my reading glasses from me. So I couldn't see the tiny stamp on the pills.

I inspected them now. I knew the Excedrin had an "E" etched on each pill, as in the past I had sometimes cut them in half. No E. And the pink and white Benadryl capsules? They appeared to be legit, but when I examined closer, they looked like they had been tampered with, the join not perfect. I pulled one apart. Too easily. I shook out the white powdery content. Benadryl? Or something else? The reality of what a halfwit I'd been came crashing down on me. I'd been in so much pain from that phantom "hangover" of supposedly mixing vodka and wine, I'd been guzzling down pills like Smarties. Opiates the triplets had got their hands on? Stuff they'd bought online then crushed up and placed into the capsules? You could buy any old shit online these days without a prescription. I wracked my brains, back to when I had started feeling out of sorts. It was even before the supposed drink binge, wasn't it? The sweaty nights, the weird dreams?

Were the triplets right? Was I really that "strung out?" "High?" No wonder my head was so fuzzy all the time and I'd felt like death warmed up when I'd stopped taking everything for that brief period. They had half convinced me I had alcohol poisoning.

Then I wondered if I had flu or caught a virus. Then I blamed it on myself for mixing alcohol with antihistamine meds—everyone knew there could be side effects, but this? *Pill-tampering?*

They *wanted* me out of it, they wanted me drunk. Being locked up wasn't enough for them. How long had this been going on? From the first day I sprained my ankle? I remembered Kate's concern: "You should take an aspirin or some kind of anti-inflammatory for that." And Beanie, too. Planned from the start so I'd take the meds. "We thought he'd be perfect for you. Picked him out specially for you."

I looked in the mirror at the pale ghostly figure before me, the woman I hardly recognized. I told her, "We will get out of here, I swear. We will beat this, I promise."

CHAPTER THIRTY-EIGHT

"Wake up, it's dinner."

I opened an eye and saw a hazy version of Jen leaning over me, her long blond hair spilling over her shoulder, tumbling onto my face. As my vision cleared, she became three-dimensional. I had resisted. Hadn't swallowed one single pill, and my body was screaming at me because of it. "How long have I been asleep?" I asked groggily. I was curled into a fetal position, sweat soaking the comforter. I felt like an army had marched over me. Jen sashayed off, out of focus.

Kate came into view. "You're always asleep when we get home," she snapped. "Your bedroom's a mess, you know, you could have cleaned up a little." She poked me with her elbow. "Seriously, haul your lazy ass out of bed. Make an effort, clean the scum off your bath, you lazy slob. If you don't get up now, you won't sleep tonight." She stomped out the door in her big black hiking boots, leaving me there: the lump on the bed who had done nothing all day other than will myself not to take any pills, will myself not to drink any Mumm.

A wave of shame flushed over me, hot through my torso. Shame that I'd been such a dunce not to put two and two together about the Trojan horse meds. I thought about the science programs Dan had got me into. How our bodies are as intricate to a cell as the universe is to us, and how each of my cells was flushed with humiliation and disgrace. And how opiates—or whatever they'd given me—were flowing through my veins and would be for several more days, until I could get them out of my system.

I heaved myself up, feeling like I weighed four hundred pounds, even though the mirror told me I was leaf-thin. My head was still muzzy and thick, the withdrawal pains unbearable, my brain a block of concrete. I flicked my gaze down to my left hand to check my ring was still there. If I focused on this one thing I could block out the pain. I gazed at the yellow diamond, glinting, not from natural light now, because it was almost dark outside, but from the overhead lights in the room. The middle of my ring looked like a doorway with a thousand corridors, like the golden Palace of Versailles. A serene little smile tipped up the corners of my mouth as I thought about Juan. My engagement ring felt like it was all I had in the world right now.

"What. What are you smiling at?" It was Dan. His aura was gray. I'd taken to seeing people's auras lately, or imagined I could. He strode into my room and set a tray of dinner down. There was a banana. Lucky. I needed the potassium. I'd force myself to eat it, although I felt like vomiting.

"Hi, Dan," I mumbled. "How was work?"

He gave me a crushing look, his eyes flinty and hard.

Kate was back, standing by the doorway, guarding it. "Has Beanie been here with you today?" They'd bring Beanie in to visit me. I had supposed they were being thoughtful (yeah, right) but now I understood why they encouraged me to hang out with Beanie—so I'd take more medication.

"I thought Beanie went with you, Kate, on your hike?"

"I told you my boss doesn't *want* Beanie to come along. Jesus! You mean you've been sleeping all day and don't even care or notice where Beanie is?" Kate shot Dan a look and rolled her eyes.

I looked at her, incredulous. "You all locked me in here! I have no *say* where Beanie is or what his movements are!"

"She's a hot mess. Just look at her." *She.* Kate gave me another withering glare, before she left the room and slammed the door, yelling Beanie's name as she went.

I sat on my bed, hardly moving a muscle. I needed all my energy just to ride out this cold turkey. Sweat was pouring down my face, trickling into my eyes. My legs were so weak I had to crawl my way to the bathroom when I needed to pee. I had the runs, too.

Dan smiled. A tiny smirk that once I would have found charming but now turned my stomach. "You're one fucked-up bitch," he said. "You're pathetic, you know that? You actually make me laugh you're so fucking strung out."

"Would you bring me some more Mumm, Dan?" I slurred in reply. "I'd kill for a drink," I lied.

"Sure, why not?" He winked at me, and his lopsided grin made me wonder for the first time if he was actually the devil's righthand man.

CHAPTER THIRTY-NINE

"Take your meds," Kate instructed, handing me my Mumm-filled Thermos and a handful of "Beanie" pills. I was tucked up in bed. They always came to bid me goodnight. Now I knew why.

"Did you find Beanie?" I asked.

"He's fine. The vet told us what to do. We gave him some milk and he's wide awake, happy as a lark, to use one of your clichéd expressions. Pop these babies in your mouth."

I pushed her hand away. "What happened to him?"

"He ate something he wasn't meant to eat."

"Oh, no! What?" *One of my pills?*

"Nothing you need to know about. Take your meds."

"I'm fine, Kate, really, I don't have a runny nose," I garbled, making myself sound drunk. Not hard; I felt like death. The last thing I'd do was let them know I knew. I hadn't lost hope.

"Take your goddamn meds!"

"Really, Kate. I feel okay." I had planned, earlier, to replace the contents of the pills with face powder from my makeup bag, before I realized they had taken all my makeup away, eyebrow pencil included.

"Swallow these *down*." She crammed the pills into my mouth. "Take a swig and swallow."

Dan stood in the doorway. Extra backup. "Do as she says," he ordered.

I reluctantly took a sip from my Thermos.

Kate's hand smothered my mouth. She laid her finger on my Adam's apple to check the pill was going down the hatch. "Night, night, sleep tight," she said in a faux sweet voice.

The second they were out of my room I stuck my fingers down my throat and vomited up the pills and champagne. I poured the Mumm down the sink, tears streaming down my face as I did so and topped up my Thermos with tap water. God, I craved alcohol. It took every ounce of willpower, because I'd never felt so bad in my whole life. I needed to glug down as much water as I could before I died from dehydration. I tried to swallow, but I could hardly find my throat. It was so parched and raw—rough as unused sandpaper. I felt as if I'd been bashed with a baseball bat, my head spinning, blood-red stars flashing behind my eyes. As well as my jaw and ankle, other pains were emanating from within, deep inside my muscles. My skull was like a withered walnut shell, my brain the nut rattling inside.

Everything about me was wrong. I crawled back to bed.

Later, I could hear voices from my room. The sound floated through the cracked-open skylight in the bathroom (way too small to crawl through even if I'd had a ladder). The girls were in the Jacuzzi. Their voices traveled in waves, sometimes clear, sometimes a mutter. They splashed and chatted as I lay in the dark. Earlier I had been dripping with sweat. Now I clutched my comforter around me like a cloak, teeth chattering.

I was frazzled, but I forced myself out of bed, crawled along the floor and craned my head up towards the skylight, hoping to catch their talk. The crash of the surf rose up from the cliffs, and I heard a coyote somewhere in the distance. But as for the voices? Silence. Had the girls gone to bed? But then I heard a laugh and another splash.

My ears perked up like a dog's.

"We can only blame ourselves," Kate was saying, her words faint. But then there was a crash of a wave from the shore, so the next sentence, spoken by Jen, was inaudible.

"But you're right, it's backfiring on us now." Kate again. A splash. But not a fun splash. Her tone of voice was heavy and serious. "Look what happened tonight. We need to regroup. Perhaps our plan wasn't so smart after all."

"Maybe we need to drop it. We've got a good thing going, so why spoil it." Jen talking.

"No way, we can't give up now."

"If it ain't broke, don't fix it."

"Another of her little sayings, funny how many we've picked up."

Dan's voice now. "She loves talking in ready-made expressions, proverbs and clichés, have you noticed? Endless clichés."

"Yep, she does. Look before you leap, she loves that one."

"What about a stitch in time saves nine?"

"Putting all your eggs in one basket, jeez, so corny. Where does she get this stuff from?"

"The pot calling the kettle black, what does that even mean?"

"It means don't be a hypocrite."

"The writing's on the wall." Kate cackled. "The writing sure *is* on the wall but she's too strung out to do anything about it."

Dan laughed. "She has such a limited imagination of her own. Has to use these dumb sayings."

"Clichés can be as true as the truth." Jen now speaking. "Jack Kerouac said something to that effect. He lived round here."

"Duh, I know that."

"This never happened."

"He said that too?"

"Something like that. *This never happened.* It can be our mantra. Nobody must ever know. Our secret to the grave."

"I feel badly for her, you know." Jen.

"Why, because she's so fucked up?"

"She's like a child. And she still trusts us. Can't we go back to the way things were?"

Another seventh wave, smashing over the next thirty seconds of conversation. The voices melded into one; I could hardly even detect who was saying what. My head was still hammering, the pain in my stomach and arms and legs vying for my attention, but I snapped my concentration back to the conversation.

"We don't know that for sure."

What do they "not know for sure?"

"Shit, it's cold when you're not in the water. Fuck, I need to get back inside." Jen.

"Did you notice how she's been gloating over her engagement ring lately?"

"That ring must be worth a fucking fortune."

"And how she's dressing like a six-year-old? She even had her hair in pigtails the other day."

"Kind of sad. I feel badly for her. You guys didn't have to smash her ankle so hard." Jen speaking.

I wanted to vomit but swallowed my bile back down. They'd done a full-out *Misery* on me? Then blamed it on me and my "drinking binge?"

"Don't feel sorry for her, Jen. Remember what we came for. Remember why we're here."

"Gotta keep our focus clear." Kate. "I'm going inside, I'm freezing my butt off out here."

I rewound the triplets' sentences over and over in my tangled thoughts, trying to straighten out the knots:

"Remember why we're here," and, "Our plan wasn't so smart, after all."

They had a plan, all right, and that plan *had been yours truly, all along.*

CHAPTER FORTY

A sharp laugh awoke me. Voices wafting through the door. The triplets were just outside my room, talking in whispers, peering in on me. I still hadn't succumbed to one single pill. I felt like a bulldozer had run over my head and body.

"This is getting expensive. And not so easy anymore now that Mom's stash has run out. We're up to, like, how many a day now?"

"A lot, dude."

"I told you, we need to make it real. A daily habit or nobody will believe it. Then, after we get her to sign… you know, she'll get a little too… dependent. More Americans OD on prescription drugs than even illegal drugs. Last count? Forty-six people a day go down."

"I don't like this, you know I don't." Jen.

"You want our house back or not?"

"We were all doing so well as a family."

"Jen, she is not our fucking family, she's an imposter, when will you register that? And don't hog the joint, dude, hand it over."

"An eye for an eye." Was that's Kate's voice? I heard her take a long deep drag and wheeze out a giggle.

Beanie snored soporifically by my feet. The blood in my head pounded. They wanted me dead. With the door open, all I could think about was bolting. But I needed to be smart. Three against one in my state? I'd be toast.

"Look, I know it's not… right, but at the same time, we'll put her out of her misery. Like putting an animal down. It's a mercy killing, not—"

"It's murder, Dan."

"Fine, if you want to see it that way, go ahead. She's unhappy. Lonely, pathetic, hasn't got kids—"

"She thinks of *us* as her kids. Remember all those adoption pamphlets we found in her closet? She never got to have her own. I feel badly, you guys. This has gone too far."

Their footsteps paced into the room. Marijuana smoke billowed after them. I squeezed my eyes shut, feigning sleep. They were moving stuff around, no doubt searching through my things.

"Jen, Dan, you won't believe this. Look! Her photo albums." The sound of thick pages. Fingers thumbing through.

"Wow, she was kind of beautiful."

"Still is. I mean, if you actually *look* at her, like now when she's out of it. It's the whole 'I'm a nobody thing' she's got going that makes her the way she is, the way she fiddles with her fingers. But feature for feature? She's pretty cool looking."

"Look, guys, she looks like a model in this photo—must've been a while ago."

"What *is* this? A modeling portfolio?"

"I don't think so. Looks like a boyfriend did this or something. Maybe Juan Trujillo himself. The photos aren't professional."

"What's *with* her then? Why's she so insecure about herself?"

"Maybe she got beaten as a child. Who knows."

"We got the shit kicked out of us nearly every day, and we're okay." A laugh. Dan's laugh. Then they all got uncontrollable giggles. I could hear how high they were. Good. Maybe I'd get a chance to escape.

"Like she's apologizing for herself when she doesn't need to."

"Some people are just born that way. Like when I went to the rescue center and picked out Beanie? He was part of a pack of unwanted puppies, all from the same litter. Cute little mutts. Some were friendly and came up to you, others cowered in a corner. Yet they were all in the same team, all with the same life experiences, same shit. Some of the puppies had taken the abandonment personally, others had obviously forgotten."

Another wheezy laugh. "Is that, like, a reference to us?"

"What do you mean?"

"Like we're the pack of puppies?"

"Some of us took the abandonment personally, is that what you're saying?"

"This is so fucked up."

"What is?"

"Us. Doing this. For what? A *house*? Since when did bricks and mortar mean—"

"Stone and glass, Jen."

"It's an expression, dummy."

"It's just a way of evening things out. Equilibrium, it's called."

"Well I don't like it."

I peeked through the slit of one eye. They were still crouched around my photo album, passing the joint around. Could I make a run for it? No. Too risky. I needed one of them to slip up. I flopped my head back and did the dribbling, tongue-lolling technique—anything to make them believe I was beyond hope. It wasn't far from how I really felt as the withdrawals were so acute. Now I knew why. They'd given me medication prescribed for a stage four cancer victim: their poor mum. The triplets continued to turn the pages of the photo album. I remembered the day Juan took those pictures. I was so embarrassed and shy.

"*Please*," I had protested, "I'm so unphotogenic."

"I don't believe it," Juan said.

"I promise. I am, really, truly."

He held the camera in my face and clicked over and over again. "You're beautiful, actually. Quite beautiful. You have an unusual face."

"Unusual is a code word for weird," I said, and laughed.

Six fingers.

Sextasaurus. She's a sextasaurus but she'll never have any sex because she's a freak.

The bullies. I'd catch the words floating down the school corridors in little hisses and shushes.

I never did let on to Juan about that sixth finger. I didn't want to blot my copybook. Blot my copybook, where did I get that expression from? My dad? Blot. The blotting paper in my dream?

I still couldn't get over it. Couldn't get over the fact that a man like Juan, all sexy and cool, would want an outsider like me.

"You're beautiful," he told me, as the camera clicked, over and over. "And smart, too. And exotic."

I laughed. "Me? Exotic? You must be joking."

"And funny. You make me laugh, babe. My funny little valentine. Take your hand away from your face, let me see those fabulous eyes of yours. Look up. Look into the camera lens. You look gorgeous, babe." *Click. Click.*

"'Me?'" I said, tossing my hair and doing my best Rita Hayworth impersonation from *Gilda*. I giggled, embarrassed. I could never accept a compliment, mostly because I couldn't believe it was true. *Sextasaurus.*

Juan chatted on. "I remember when you first walked into my office and you handed me your resumé. Straight As, top of your class, glowing references. Brains as well as beauty. An English rose. *In all the towns, in all the world, she walks into mine.* I knew right then I wanted you. Look into the lens, babe. Part your lips. Beautiful." *Click.* "I love you, honey."

"So what are we going to do with her?" Kate said, wrenching me away from my precious memory.

I let a guttural snore escape my throat and clucked my tongue.

"She's so out of it, man."

"Are you sure she isn't going to drown in her own vomit or something?"

"If she does, she does." Dan. *Tough words.*

"Yeah, but we need her to sign first. Better, get her to write the whole thing out in her own handwriting."

"Witnesses?"

"Won't be a problem. We only need two 'disinterested parties.' I can drum up a couple of potheads... they won't know what they're signing and won't even care."

I swallowed hard. I hoped they couldn't hear the violent thump of my heart. *Stay calm. Stay focused.*

"Do we have enough supply?" Dan was humming The Rolling Stones' "Mother's Little Helper" tune.

"Let her sleep it off, and we'll give her more in the morning." Kate.

"Man, I've got the munchies," Dan said, striding out of the room. "Who wants a sandwich?"

Kate clunked out after him. "Wait up! I'll do 'em or you'll scoff all the mayo."

The light went dim—I could feel it through my closed lids. A rustle of the bedclothes. Breath on my ear. Someone holding my hand, stroking my fingers. "I feel so bad for you. I feel like... like I've made a pact with the devil or something. It's so wrong! I can't let them do this to you," Jen said, crying. "They want to... put you to sleep. Like a sick dog! They never told me this was the deal! It's not okay. No way is this okay." She shook me and tried to make me sit up. I let some drool edge out of the corners of my mouth again, spill in bubbles down my chin. I didn't trust her. She wiped my face with the sheet. "Fuck! Oh, fuck! How did I get myself into this fucking shit! I've got to get you out of here." Jen left the room.

Without locking me in.

CHAPTER FORTY-ONE

Fearful yet fearless and fueled only by adrenaline, I crawled in my pajamas, out of my bedroom, on my hands and knees. I had made it look like I was still in bed by plumping up pillows under my comforter. Would the triplets fall for that old trick? At least it would buy me some time.

The corridor was dark, thank God. The key was tied on a string, looped around my bedroom door handle and in the keyhole. I shakily stood up, locked it and prayed the triplets would be too stoned to check on me before going to bed. Too weak to even stand, and feeling a slamming head-rush, I got back on all fours. I'd make my way to the laundry room and grab my car keys, then bide my time. If they caught me, I'd tell them I was heading for the drinks fridge. I'd play drunk. Hopefully, the last place they'd suspect to find me would be that claustrophobic room, which they knew I hated. Once I was sure they were all asleep, I'd sneak upstairs to the kitchen, find the spare front door key and drive away in my car.

If I didn't escape tonight, I'd be dead.

I *had* to get out of this house.

Sweat plastered my hair to my forehead; I picked hair away from my eyes, my fingers shaking, bare and thin. I took a double take at my left hand. Bare fingers? My engagement ring was gone! Jen? Kate? My heart told me to go back and look for it in my bedroom, but my head screamed at me to keep going. My *life* was at stake. I fantasized again about that handgun I'd deliberated so much over, and I knew that if I made it out of here, I would never again be that needy, trusting person I was before.

I had changed as a human being.

The TV droned above me loudly, interspersed by cackles from Dan and Kate at whatever they were watching. *They must all still be high, stuffing their faces.* I continued my silent crawl, each inch forward feeling like an eternity. I couldn't make a sound.

Heart hammering, I dragged my way inside the laundry room, claustrophobic panic surging through me, but then I found the pillowcase and the contents inside, tucked behind the washing machine, and my pulse beat steadily again. I checked everything was there: the jar of keys, my Land Rover key and the hammer. I quietly lodged the pillowcase back in its hiding place, just in case anyone discovered me. I had left the door ajar.

All I could do was wait. Wait until the house was silent. Wait until they had gone to bed. Then I'd escape.

I thought about the money buried in our woods. Just sitting there, inciting me, all this time, with paranoia and fear.

Eight million dollars.

CHAPTER FORTY-TWO

I felt like an undertaker that day we buried the money. You'd think having eight million dollars in your backyard would be a dream come true, the biggest thrill of your life, but being guardian to that type of booty does nothing but sail you off to a desert island—which may seem beautiful and exciting at first—until your nerves are shipwrecked on a bed of dry, scalding sand. Too hot to touch. And then paranoia breaks into your brain like a fever, and you end up alone.

Más sola que la una.

Not to mention the guilt attached to it, which ate at my conscience, daily.

It was a bright sunny day in May, that day, not a cloud in sight, a white-hot blaze searing high in an azure sky. I heard Juan's car roll down the driveway, The Police blaring out from the speakers—he was playing our song. He'd returned from the airport after a business trip, and I grinned, knowing we'd make passionate love. He burst into the house and tore off his Armani jacket, tossing it on the living room floor. He didn't even say hello. Obviously something was awry, because he'd usually hang up his suits with care.

"Help me get this goddam tie off!" he roared, grappling at the noose around his neck. "Get this fucker *off*, it's strangling me!"

"Don't panic," I told him calmly. "Just stay still."

He took in a deep breath. "I've missed you, honey, I need you to calm me down."

His words zapped straight between my legs. When Juan was in a state he needed sex to relax him. My own body readied itself right then, my skin tingled, my breasts ached with longing. Juan and I had a mutual, symbiotic relationship, almost as if we were feeding off each other. I had looked forward to him coming home all week, thought of nothing else.

I freed him from his tie and then took off my sweater and slipped out of my skirt, brushing my lips against his, waiting for him to say, *Up against the wall, babe,* or *Bend over.*

But he shook his head and pushed me away. "Honey, I don't have time for that now." This was a first. Juan always had time for it.

"What's wrong?" I said, panic spiking my veins. That note came to mind. The reminder that Juan was having an affair. He'd been with her today, they'd had breakfast together. Made love. And now he saw me with indifference, even disgust. I felt a tear slide down my cheek.

"Just, just—not now," he said. "I need to do something important, but I don't want you involved. Something—" He broke off from his sentence, his mind turning.

"What is it?"

"Nothing," he said sharply. "Trust me, you don't want to know." His eyes shifted around the living room. We had only been at Cliffside a couple of weeks. I still couldn't get used to the luxury of this place, the fact that this was our home.

"What's going on?" I asked, my voice shaky. It would all flood out now. His confession. I'd find out about that woman, the woman who wanted nothing to do with him, the one who begged him to leave her alone. That note on the napkin was a woman's handwriting, I was positive of that. Juan had finally won her over with his persuasive Juanish ways. She'd been unable to resist him. They were in love. Jealousy consumed every molecule of my body at the thought of him touching another woman.

"What is it?" I whispered. I put my clothes back on and made my way out the door, to his car. If there were any telltale signs, he'd be sure to keep them there. In the glove compartment maybe.

"Where are you going?" he yelled at me.

"Nowhere," I said. "And don't shout at me."

"It's for your own peace of mind, babe, please, please see reason."

I marched to his shiny white Range Rover and went to open the door, but it was locked. He never usually locked his car and always kept the keys in the ignition. He was guilty of something. I peered through the windows. The seats were down flat to make space in the back. There were loads of black bags inside. He rushed up beside me.

"Honey, would you mind fixing me breakfast? I'm starving."

"What are those?" I asked, pointing at all the stuff in the back.

"Nothing. Please, babe, let's go inside. You know what? Forget breakfast, let's go to bed. *Bed.* He suggested this to get me off the scent, to defuse the situation. Then he came out with some romantic line from *Casablanca.* Typical Juan behavior.

We made love after that, but I could tell how distracted Juan was, his mind off in another direction. He'd led me to the bedroom to appease me, bide his time.

Day drew into evening, evening shaded into night. Juan's darting, shifty eyes confirmed to me that he had something to hide. I pretended to fall asleep, pretended I hadn't noticed anything. At around midnight, he slipped out of bed and sneaked outside into the dark. After a couple of minutes, I opened the sliding door and waited silently outside our bedroom. I heard him rootle around in the garden shed then walk up to the driveway. I heard his car door open. By the time he was loading up the wheelbarrow, I appeared like a phantom, catching him red-handed. He couldn't deny it now. There he was, those black bags piled high in the wheelbarrow.

I stood there, hands on my hips like a schoolmarm. "Whatever you're doing, Juan, you're obviously up to no good." That was the understatement of the year.

I thought he'd be angry, but he let out a laugh. "Busted."

"I deserve an explanation."

His smile now erased, he bowed his head in shame. "I can explain. But I really didn't plan to get you involved in this, honey."

"I'm already involved," I said. "I have a right to know what goes on under my own roof." Those words felt good to say. Under California law, now that we were officially married and I was his real wife, we were fifty/fifty all the way. But fifty/fifty also meant taking on the bad with the good. And this was looking really bad.

"It won't be under this roof, honey, don't worry."

"Where are you going with all that then?"

"To the woods."

"Our woods?" I asked. "In our backyard?" We owned four acres, much of it wooded.

He nodded.

"What's inside those bags?"

"It's not a dead body if that's what you're thinking." He laughed.

"No, I wasn't thinking that, but now you mention it…"

Juan had a temper that could flare up every so often if someone pushed the wrong buttons. He rarely lost it with me though. I had a knack of keeping him calm, defusing any possible blow-ups before they happened.

I stepped closer so my breath was on his face. "I have a right to know what the hell you think you're doing. I take it it's something illegal? Something you don't want anyone to discover?" Paperwork, I thought, could be shredded. Maybe ledgers with his dodgy transactions?

He looked hard into my eyes but said nothing. "We have picks and shovels, right? I couldn't find them in the garage."

Then I imagined the worst-case scenario—bits of rotting body—and realized, right then, I'd do anything for Juan. Cover up for him. Help him dig. I'd be his partner in crime, without question. That's how in love with him I was.

"There's a whole lot of stuff in the shed," I said. "Come on, tell me, what is it we need to bury?" *We.* I was in it up to my neck now.

He was silent for a beat as if he were weighing up his options, then finally he said, "Eight million dollars."

For some reason this didn't shock me. Up until this moment, I'd pretended I'd had no idea about my husband's shenanigans. I'd closed my eyes and ears to it. But nobody comes by eight million dollars in cash just from hard work. All that traveling he'd been doing, back and forth, all over the globe. He'd refused to divulge any details, "for your own protection," he'd always said. And I never asked. Knowing would make me guilty by association. But I could read between the lines. The real estate deals he'd been negotiating for his "VIP client" must have been money laundering on a very high level. Or a very low level, depending on how you looked at it. Juan had unwittingly got mixed up with some vicious, unsavory characters, and I was pretty positive he was working for a man who was working for a man who was working for some sort of money laundering operation, or organized crime syndicate, even a drug cartel. The writing was on the wall, but I had blocked it all out.

It finally made sense, the puzzle pieces slotting into position: Juan's insistence upon paying with cash for everything. He rarely used a credit card. He'd bought this expensive house. The ring. He had cash coming out of his ears.

"What are you mixed up in?" I demanded.

"Nothing you need to know about, babe. But trust me, I earned this money. It's mine. And I didn't hurt anyone. Don't worry, I'll smooth things out."

I'd pulled the wool over my eyes for long enough. "It's drug money, isn't it?"

Juan shook his head in denial. "This money itself? No, it's clean."

"Bullshit, Juan, please don't lie to me."

"Look, this is real estate money."

"Maybe, but it's laundered money, isn't it?"

The sheepish look in his eyes told me I was right.

"I hope to God it's not money that originated from drug deals," I snapped. "People getting killed. Children. Families destroyed. Blood money. All-out war. I've seen *Narcos*. I know how vicious it gets. Or mafia. I read somewhere the Russian mafia are everywhere, even in America."

"Honey, your imagination's running away with you."

I said nothing, just stared at his face in the moonlight. How could I believe him?

He squeezed my hand. "Babe, I didn't plan it this way. When I earned this, trust me, I had no fucking idea who my client worked for. I'm as good as innocent."

"Take the money back," I said.

"Impossible. If I do that, I'm a dead man. You think I want to draw attention to myself?"

"A dead man? Great, that's just great. And it proves to me how dirty this money is. Give it to charity."

"Ditto, babe. Any financial transactions of mine need to stay under the radar. And not even charities accept chunks of cash anymore."

"But if I have to keep this secret—"

"Trust me, it's fine."

"But what if they come after us?"

"They won't. My client knew who I was, but all transactions were made under different names. Nobody'll trace it back to me."

"Why didn't you tell me about this? Why did you hide this from me? *Ever hear of the word 'trust'*?"

He sighed, a low guttural moan. "I'm sorry, but I didn't want you to get involved. The less you know the better. It is what it is now. If anything does happen to me, at least you know it was all worth it."

Blood rushed to my ears. "You must be joking, Juan. Nothing's worth—"

"Never, ever, tell anyone about this stash, however much you might trust someone. And don't get tempted to touch it. Especially if I'm away. That's my department. Promise?"

I nodded. I didn't insist on asking more. I didn't need to. Juan was neck-deep in some very dodgy state of affairs, and it was too late to turn the clock back. All I could do was help, despite my reluctance. He was my husband, what could I do?

"Promise?" he repeated.

"I promise," I muttered.

"And if anything were to happen to me—"

"Please don't *say* that!"

"Nothing'll happen, babe. I swear. But *if* anything does, let at least three years go by before you touch it, understand?"

I felt sick. Tears leaked from my eyes. "Did anyone follow you here?"

"Hell, no. Don't worry, it'll be fine. Still, honey, I want you to promise me. I want to hear you say it. 'I won't touch the money for at least three years, no matter what.'"

"I won't touch the money for at least three years," I repeated, my voice hitching on a sob. "No matter what."

Juan often left his phone behind on purpose, especially when he took a flight somewhere to do a big deal. He was the one who had alerted me to spyware and how having your phone on you was as good as a GPS tracker. Or how they could listen to conversations, even with it switched off or in airplane mode. For that reason, he often used prepaid "burner" flip-phones and made me swear to never talk about private matters near my cell phone, unless it was wrapped in aluminum foil and in the fridge. He told me to never hook the house up to any kind of smart surveillance system. No Siri. No Alexa. No Google Home. No video cameras that could be hacked into from a third party and used against us. He didn't even want the house alarm hooked up to the police.

"You can never be too paranoid," Juan warned me.

You had to watch it with credit cards, too. Your last movements so easily traced. Any stranger could be watching from a distance. Waiting. Spying. So many things were falling into place, now making sense. Except the *I am done with you* note from that woman. That still remained an enigma. I wouldn't bring it up now though.

One step at a time.

He'd stashed the money in several divers' waterproof dry-bags, the type you can put expensive cameras in and still go underwater. At first Juan did all the lifting, all the digging. He didn't want me to touch the bags, but I ended up helping him. If this hadn't been possible blood money I would've felt a sort of thrill from tip to toe, knowing Juan was trusting me like this, letting me be his partner in crime. But I felt disgusted. Implicated. Guilty as hell. If any death was related to this money—which I suspected it most definitely was—it was cursed, even if Juan had earned it in earnest.

It was only later that I allowed myself to feel anger. My own husband had put my life in danger, involving me in something I never should have known about. Not giving me a choice. Like back in school, I was being made to break the rules. Except, no… I wasn't being "made" to do anything. And I did have a choice. I had free will, didn't I? I had let myself be manipulated.

I'd told myself I was doing it for love. And I was.

"It's just temporary," Juan assured me as he wiped the sweat from his brow with his gardening glove, making his hands loom larger than usual. "Till I get this lot invested, a year or two from now. We can buy a villa in Tuscany, or Lake Como, how about that? It's easier to pay black in Europe."

The hole was now dug. It had taken hours: hacking between the fused but paradoxically shallow redwood roots, intertwining with neighboring trees in a network that held each other up—the tallest species of tree on the planet, around since the time of dinosaurs.

I was exhausted, both emotionally and physically. Who knew how heavy money could be? The moon, perfectly full and round—the ring around it like a halo—glimmered. A witness to our deed.

We chucked a couple of the bags into the burial site. "What if we're never able to find the money again?" I asked Juan. "What if we forget where we buried it?"

"I've marked the co-ordinates down, honey, don't worry. We can put them in the wall safe tonight. Too risky to store on any phone."

"Why don't we set up a hidden camera so we know if someone gets too close?"

"Bad idea. There's too much counter-surveillance equipment and bug detectors that can track cameras," he whispered. "The last thing we want to do is draw attention to the site. Tomorrow we'll come back and hide our tracks, smooth it all down and cover the earth with leaves and cones, smooth out the wheelbarrow marks. For tonight, I'm going to tie a string round this redwood. Mark the spot until the co-ordinates are written down and in the safe."

He'd thought of everything. We each took an end of string and encircled the great tree, our bodies meeting in a bump, our fingers fumbling together in the moonlit dark. The girth was enormous—a good fifteen feet around. I tied the knot around the tree's soft, furrowed and fluted bark. "Tying the knot" took on a whole new meaning to our marriage. I thought of the tree's Latin name, *Sequoia sempervirens*, meaning everlasting, and hoped it was a good omen for our union. This redwood was our protector.

Or so I had hoped.

But this was two days before Juan flew off that cliff in a race to get to the airport.

If anything happens to me.

It was as if he knew. Had these people killed him? I wondered that all the time.

At first, I had been tempted. Tempted, after Juan's death, to go to the authorities and let them know the full story. But then I raked through the consequences. At best, I would be seen as an accomplice to a crime or done in for tax evasion, which could get me into even more trouble, and then they'd take Cliffside away from me. Because let's face it, no innocent person has eight million dollars buried in their backyard. And at worst, word would get out, and Juan's VIP client's client would hunt me down.

Still, even keeping my secret, that buried money might as well have been a corpse for all the worry and paranoia it caused me.

I hadn't wagered the guilt would weigh me down so heavily. That blood-money guilt festered inside my gut like toxic, scarlet fungus slowly poisoning me. I'd made a choice. And I had protected that choice. And if Juan was worth killing, wouldn't I be next? The drone flying over, the text. The note with the roses. Everything had me fearing for my life. But never so much as now, the triplets being the biggest threat of all. The irony of it. The irony that having them live with me had made me feel safer!

The sound of footsteps snapped me away from my thoughts. Dan and Kate. They'd switched off the TV. Fear surged through me anew, that they'd swoop into my bedroom and find me gone.

"I'm so out of it, man, I'm hitting the hay." Dan.

"Better check she's still asleep," Kate said.

"You do it, dude, I'm beat." Dan slammed the door to his bedroom. Kate's heavy tread clunked its way along the corridor. In my mind's eye I had her switch on the light, rip the bedclothes away and scream blue murder when she found the pillows stuffed in the shape of my torso. Silence. I crouched in my corner by the washing machine, praying for mercy, for my freedom. The minutes ticked by; at least it felt like minutes. Then I heard a key turn and the door click open. A beat of silence, except my own blood pounding in my ears. Then the key turned again. Kate locking "me" in. She stomped off to her room. The door clicked closed. But Jen? Where was she? She tended to move about the house barefoot. Was she in her room, asleep? I didn't trust her, despite her small efforts to show herself less of a monster than the other two.

I didn't dare move. Not yet. My head hammered to the beat of my heart. How long until they all fell asleep? My instinct told me to wait. Stay calm. Don't rush. I couldn't blow my only opportunity.

The door creaked. Terror squeezed me by the throat as the door inched open, but then I heard the tap, tap of Beanie's little paws, his claws clicking on the tiles. He sniffed me out immediately.

I pulled him close. "Ssh." His ears cocked and he was off again. Jen wandering around the house? She was a bit of a night owl, Jen was.

I waited. Thirsty and dizzy from dehydration, but too scared to even take a swig of water from the sink in case I made a noise. I heard Jen talking softly. To whom? Beanie? On the phone? Finally, I heard the click of her bedroom door closing.

I counted to a hundred.

Time to leave.

I padded on my silent journey, barefoot along the corridor, then up the stairs to the front door. The key. I doubled back towards the kitchen. Beanie rustled about in his basket, alerted, and followed me, ears cocked with curiosity, but thank God he didn't bark. I fumbled around in the dark until I found the napkin drawer. I fished out the key and shuffled barefoot to the front door, with one hand holding my pounding head. I turned the key gently, terrified it wouldn't work, that the triplets might have changed the lock. But it did work. Beanie darted out the door ahead of me. I closed it as silently as I could. Locked it again, wincing with every tiny sound.

Outside, I squinted through the darkness until my eyes adjusted. I was wearing nothing but my pajamas, so the cold braced me.

I have to escape from my own home.

My Land Rover was like a beacon. The interior light was on. For a second I thought I saw Kate sitting in the front seat, and I froze, but it was just the headrest. The car door wasn't locked, and Beanie leapt over the driver seat into the back, his tail wagging and barks piercing the crisp dawn atmosphere.

"Shut up, Beanie," I hissed, my fingers fumbling in the pillow-case. I drew out the car keys and stabbed them into the ignition, missing a few times because of my shaky hand. But something halted me, catching my attention. On the passenger seat, I spotted my signature written at least ten times all over a piece of paper. Beanie was jumping around excitedly on top of it. Next to it was another paper. A copy of the will I had prepared for Mr. Donner on my company letterhead. They were using it as a template:

I hereby revoke, annul and cancel all wills and codicils previously made by me, either jointly or severally…

I felt sick. Kate had been practicing my handwriting. The forgery of my signature was good. Really good.

They had obviously bypassed the need for me to write my own will. No! They'd do it *themselves*. That's what they'd been up to while I was locked up: sifting through my old letters, or anything with my signature on it. Rifling through my work files.

I turned the key and started the ignition, put the car into first gear, but the car groaned. The battery was all but dead. I tried again. Nothing. I cursed, tears welling in my eyes. I seized the forged will for evidence, crammed it into the elastic of my pajama waistband. Beanie let out a shrill bark, wondering why we weren't going on an excursion. I had to make a split-second choice. The beach? Or the highway?

I'd have to take my chance and hitchhike, if I was lucky enough to even make it to the road.

CHAPTER FORTY-THREE

I opened the car door as quietly as I could and scrambled out, my feet landing on muddy gravel. The rain had started again in earnest. Beanie vaulted out after me, and I willed him not to bark, pressing a finger on my lips. He didn't. He followed me as I hobbled towards the gate, adrenaline overriding the pain in my ankle. I buzzed the gate open and the creaking and clanking was as loud in my ears as a Manhattan garbage truck. Dan and Kate would hear. They'd catch me before I made it up the driveway. I hurled myself through the gap, Beanie at my heels, rain slamming my face, pelting down on my chest. My steps were ploddy and deliberate, moving more slowly than I wished, despite my racing heart. I began to pick up pace, even with the pain of gravel digging into my bare feet, even with the searing ache of my bad ankle. Beanie scarpered on ahead, a bark of excitement escaping him, and a rush of nausea rose up inside me knowing it was a matter of minutes before one of the triplets would pop up like a Jack-in-the-box and haul me back to my bedroom, or worse, the laundry room. This time they'd lock me up for good.

The sharp gravel pummeled the soles of my bare feet, but I scurried with all my strength, swinging my arms to give me momentum to get me up the hill, the rain and wind roaring in my ears, a dull throb at the base of my skull.

I tripped on a stick and crashed on my knee but forced myself to scramble back up and keep going, wincing with the shooting pain in my ankle as I flung one leg in front of the other. Blood trickled down my calf, and the insides of my legs threatened to collapse to jelly, splat-splot on the driveway, but I willed myself on. *Stay alive*, I repeated over and over. *Stay alive. Core of steel.* I turned my head as I ran and saw with relief that the gate had closed on itself and Beanie was still following me—not that having a dog would help me now, no, he'd be a hindrance. But the knowledge I was not completely alone in this world gave me extra strength.

I didn't have time to reflect on the madness of the last couple of months, only that I'd be dead if I didn't keep going. *Breathe. Run. Breathe. Faster. Faster. Get to the main road. Run. Come on. Faster. One foot ahead. Keep going. Faster. Come on, you can do it. Stay alive. Stay alive. Please. Please let me live. Faster.*

A hawk flew across my path, its great wings missing my nose by inches. The shock of it gave me an adrenaline surge that I welcomed, propelling me up the hill. I needed to make it to the camouflage of the woods, but I had another hundred yards of driveway to go yet where the terrain wasn't so rocky. I gulped air, my lungs raw with oxygen. *Faster. Go. GO! Keep running.* Behind me, I heard the roar of an engine. Car tires spinning on the gravel. I let out a yelp of fear and pushed one leg forward, pain searing at my knee, my feet now numb with smashes and cuts as the blood and rain washed over my right leg.

Keep going. Faster. Faster.

I still had a chance.

Or so I thought. With the sound of a car behind me—Dan? Kate?—I veered off the driveway and took a shortcut up through the woods to Highway One, so I wouldn't get mowed down. The driver, my pursuer, was closing in on me fast. I was off the track but now faced an even steeper climb, a sheer face of slippery mud and rocks interspersed with pines. I heard the car screech to a halt, the door slam, and I knew Kate or Dan would be upon me any second, their hiking skills a hundredfold better than mine.

Turning my head for a split second, I saw Kate, her great hiking boots trampling through the undergrowth, her dark shine of a bob swinging, her mouth set in a hard, determined line. I groaned in terror, weighing up my options and quickly doubled back to the driveway again.

"Why are you resisting?" she yelled at me through the rain. "Come back to the house, we haven't done anything."

Kate continued yelling after me, nearer now, closing in on me fast. I scrambled like a hunted animal towards the brow of the hill. I clawed myself up, up, my hands breaking my fall as I stumbled along. I felt the forged will slip down my legs, out through my pajamas, but I didn't have a spare second to save it. My palms were bleeding. Turning a corner now, I briefly lost Kate and could see Highway One up ahead like an oasis in a desert. So close yet so far, Kate's thud of boots a hair's breadth behind me. Beanie darted ahead, and I had a new worry now, that he would charge in front of a vehicle and get run over. But I didn't hear any cars or trucks. What if there'd been another landslide between here and Carmel? The road would be completely closed off.

I'd be done for.

Up, up. Please. Faster. Please.

But as I reached the top, Dan's big black pickup came thundering down the driveway. How did I miss that? Had it doubled back on itself? Dan was the driver? My bedraggled rain-swept hair was flying in my mouth, rainwater blocking my view. I screamed at the top of my lungs, the fear of being sandwiched to death by these two ruthless triplets. Kate was still running just behind me. I could hear her measured breaths.

I lost my footing and collapsed on myself, a useless spent heap of a victim crumpled on the driveway. "Leave me alone!" I gave out a cry somewhere between a shriek and a gasp.

My last pathetic beg for help.

CHAPTER FORTY-FOUR

"Get in the car!" a voice ordered.

"No," I panted, focusing my gaze on my bleeding feet, my limbs a rag doll's. "No!"

"Can you get up?" The car door opened, two trousered legs planted themselves on the ground.

But they didn't belong to Dan. Or Kate.

My eyes took in a pair of red Gucci flats. I looked up. "Pippa?"

"What the hell's going on? I thought you were away, darling, in England. The triplets told me they were housesitting and you'd gone to visit your parents. But then I got this frantic call from Jen, begging me to come and get you. I came as soon as I could. But a tree was down, blocking the road." Pippa leaned over and helped me to my feet, but my knees buckled again, and I tumbled back down in a lump.

"I was never in England. They locked me up. Kate and Dan want to kill me," I rasped, my throat so sore I could hardly get the words out.

"What do you mean?" Pippa's voice was gentle.

I looked around me, but Kate was nowhere to be seen. Beanie continued barking.

"Let's get you in the car, darling," Pippa said. "I'm taking you home with me. Good Lord, look at your legs, you're bleeding. In your pajamas, no shoes? What happened?" She hoisted me up, and I collapsed on her strong shoulders, my gratitude flashing white stars at the back of my eyes.

"It's a long story," I croaked.

She eased me into her car and put the seat almost flat. The warmth of the heated leather instantly calmed me, but it also made me aware of my body. An agonizing mass of pain.

"Sleep," Pippa soothed, "just lie back. Here, have some water, darling, you look like you need it." I gripped the bottle of Evian and glugged down as much as I could. A rush of migraine flooded the back of my eyes.

"Where's Beanie?" I gasped.

"Right here at your feet. Soaked and muddy. Thanks, Beanie, for messing up my brand-new car, I'd just had it detailed at that valet place in Carmel."

I let out a groan of relief, lolled my floppy head back on the headrest. "I thought you were Dan. The black car."

"His old beaten-up thing? I take that as a huge insult."

"I couldn't see for all the rain—"

"The weather's gone mad, hasn't it?" Pippa started the engine and put the car into drive. In my side passenger mirror, I caught a glimpse of Kate staring after us, longingly.

Her golden goose was fleeing the nest.

I collapsed into sleep, Beanie's head resting on my bashed-up feet.

CHAPTER FORTY-FIVE

The next week or so was a haze of agony and bone-aching limbs, sleepless, endless nights, and demons bashing at my brain. I was withdrawing from the pills, and it was a roller-coaster ride through a flaming inferno. But I was resolute about Pippa not taking me to the doctor, to not let me persuade her however much I begged. I knew what would happen; any doctor, even if it was to wean me off the medication, would prescribe me more of the same, or worse, something else equally addictive, and the cycle would begin all over again. I wouldn't have the willpower. At first, I'd feel fabulous. Confident. On top of the world. Then the same old dependency would rise up like a merciless sphinx and eat me whole. I would *not* be its victim anymore. I had things to live for: a career, a beautiful home.

At least… I did.

Now I needed to re-evaluate my life.

Pain was my new middle name. Pippa acted as nurse, administering me vitamins, Tylenol, liters of mineral water, bowls of chicken soup, bananas for potassium, Imodium to stop the runs, and hot bath after hot bath of Epsom salts to sweat out the poisons. My head felt like it belonged to a giant. My stomach a vomiting, retching gargoyle. I hoped my liver was okay.

I had lost track of time, but at least a week must have gone by.

Pippa laid a wet washcloth on my forehead. "You've got to hold on in there, darling. In a couple of weeks, you'll be your old self again. Then you can start going to AA or NA meetings. Maybe a trip to England would be a good idea. When you're better you can work on getting those nasty people out of your house."

I mulled all this over in my scrambled-egg mind as I lay in bed, in Pippa's lovely spare bedroom, my eyes focused on the red and green parrots darting about on her pretty French wallpaper. It was only now, away from Cliffside, away from the nightmare of the triplets, and clean for the first time in ages—without mood changers flowing through my veins—that I could be objective.

"Your old self," Pippa had said. What or who *was* my old self? I didn't even know anymore. In any case, I didn't *want* my old self back. I wanted a new self. Someone strong. A person who could hold her own against bullies, against people parading as friends, who, in the end, always wanted something from me. Against men who knew what was best for me, the "protectors" of my world. Every time I had trusted someone, a man, in particular, he had shown me he had his own selfish agenda. My father, my husband. Like the wedges of cash and Juan's dodgy dealings with his VIP client, I had blocked my ears and eyes to it.

Hear no evil, see no evil.

I could only blame myself.

From now on I'd be in control of my own destiny. I would not be a victim anymore.

CHAPTER FORTY-SIX

Pippa had gone shopping for the day. Humming tunes all morning, she was obviously thrilled to get out of the house. Looking after me all this time must have made her feel like a prisoner in her own home.

I knew all about that one.

As relieved as I was to feel better, all I could think about was Kate and Dan and what evil new plan they were hatching. I bet they guessed I was here at Pippa's. Maybe Jen had admitted to calling Pippa, to come and rescue me. I kept waiting for the doorbell to ring—they'd have means of finding out where she lived. Beanie was here, and I expected them to demand him back. The door was firmly locked, but every time I heard the wind rustle a tree branch, or a car drive by, my heart hammered. Each time I made up my mind to call the police, a voice inside me told me to deal with the triplets on my own terms.

I'd been here a week.

Not a word. Their silence scared me.

I'd been dissecting possibilities of what to do with them, over and over in my mind. I felt so much stronger and had put on a little weight, and my eyes were clear, the black circles almost gone, the withdrawals a thing of the past.

I was ready. I didn't just want them out of my house.

I wanted to even the score.

But how, exactly, still eluded me. Call the police and let them escort me to Cliffside and kick the triplets out? A possibility.

Although what would I tell the authorities? That I'd allowed three wayward youngsters to stay at my house full-time, trusted them with my credit card, lent them my car, let them move in, hook, line, and sinker, and now I was unhappy about it? The authorities would want specifics. Had I been physically threatened? Not that I could prove. It would be their word against mine, even with my bashed-up ankle. Had they stolen from me? Not technically. Had they destroyed any of my property? No. The opposite, they'd helped me fix things. Where was my proof? The sodden piece of paper with my forged will would have disintegrated on Cliffside's driveway in the rain. The Trojan pills flushed down the toilet, no doubt. The triplets would tell them how they'd been looking after me, cooking for me, doing my shopping. Abseiling from dangerous heights, uninsured, to clean my windows. Working for free, in fact. If I told the police the story about them locking me up, I had no proof whatsoever. And if Pippa acted as my witness, the truth about my dependence on drugs and alcohol would be blown open—it would look even worse. In the eyes of the law, Cliffside was the triplets' residence. I'd need to give them thirty days' notice. Any law enforcement officer would say it was a civil matter, and they couldn't get involved.

They were no fools. They had established themselves at Cliffside as permanent tenants, despite the fact they had no lease. Kate's words ricocheted in my mind: "This is our *home*. Our tax returns get sent to this address, we're registered to vote at this address, we get our mail here." Smart. They had established legal rights. Getting them to leave was not something I could do overnight. Not via the legal route, anyway.

A person did not have to be listed on a formal lease to gain protection under tenancy laws. Worse, the triplets could even gain protection by having established residency at Cliffside. They had no other home. They were orphans. Even if I'd offered to *buy* them an apartment, I knew they'd never budge.

As I ran my lawyerish thoughts through the legal process, a chill sliced along the ridges of my backbone like a razor blade. Getting them out quickly would be impossible. When a home-owner wishes to remove a guest, but that person can no longer be considered a "transient guest," formal eviction procedures have to be followed. Law enforcement personnel would only be able to remove transient guests from a dwelling by force. The triplets were not transient; they had been at Cliffside for months and would be able to prove it. Even moving in a pet showed permanent residency. Beanie's papers were registered at Cliffside!

The eviction process would be a hassle. First, I'd need to serve them Notice to Quit. Next, I'd have to serve up Summons and Complaints. They'd have to appear in court. No chance. Next would come a motion for judgment for failure to appear, and an endorsed copy of the Notice to Quit with the court clerk. The court would then enter a judgment against the tenants and issue an order to vacate. The triplets would dress themselves up as the perfect victims, and knowing how Dan's mind worked, they'd list airtight arguments for staying. Next would come the trial. But, still, the triplets would stand their ground. And all through this, they'd continue living in my house.

Just thinking of this exhausted me. It would take forever, not to mention the stress. Hell, I could even imagine them filing a personal injury lawsuit and suing me for emotional distress—by letting them live in their childhood home and then mercilessly kicking them out.

I wanted my life back. My house, my car. The triplets sat like young royals on thrones in *my* castle. They had all the power.

Meanwhile, there was the added problem of the buried money. What was I meant to do?

Maybe, with all their snooping around, they'd even found it by now.

CHAPTER FORTY-SEVEN

With Pippa still out shopping, I wandered downstairs to the kitchen, and Beanie eagerly followed me. He needed to go out. That was something Pippa had been taking care of all this time. She'd walked and fed him. Had showed herself to be a real friend.

My heart drummed against my ribs at the thought of opening the back door, let alone going outside with the dog. Kate or Dan could be lurking behind a bush and come out and grab me. But if I simply let Beanie out without a lead, he might run off. Pippa's house was set back from the road but wasn't wild like Cliffside. The road was pretty close, her driveway short.

Pulse-pounding decisions.

Beanie whimpered and spurred me into action. I was done with them ruling my life. I clipped on the leash Pippa had kindly bought him, which was hanging on a coat rail, and, leaving the kitchen door ajar and checking the latch to make sure I wouldn't lock myself out, I braced myself for a little walk in Pippa's garden. Beanie lifted his leg immediately on a nearby rosebush. The second he had finished, I pulled him back inside. I locked the door behind me again.

Not knowing what to do next, not even what to *think* next, I picked up the phone and dialed a number I knew by heart.

My poor mother hadn't heard from me in weeks. I owed her a call.

"Mum," I said, eyes misting, throat lumping. My mother and I had little in common, and she'd hardly treated me with kid gloves when I was growing up, but she was still my mum. I cradled the phone between my shoulder and ear and filled the kettle. Perhaps a cup of tea would help me think straight.

"Darling, I've been worried silly about you."

"I'm sorry," I said.

"Why did you change your number without telling me?"

"I didn't, Mum."

"Every time I called, they told me it was the wrong number!"

"Who did you speak to?"

"Whom, darling, whom. I spoke to different people every time I rang. Sometimes a young man, other times his wife, sometimes the daughter. And your mobile number always goes to voicemail. I left so many messages. I've been watching the Big Sur floods and landslides on the news and was beside myself with worry, although I knew you must be all right."

I swallowed hard. "I'm so sorry, Mum. So sorry I didn't call, I was really sick with flu."

"Anyway, I did call the police and they promised they'd send someone from Highway Patrol to pay you a visit."

I almost laughed. There was no way, with bridges collapsing and trees falling down with these wild floods the police would have time to venture all the way down my driveway and check on little old me. They had more important stuff to do.

"That was sweet of you, Mum, but you needn't have worried. I'm staying with my friend Pippa till the bad weather gets better. I'm closer to civilization here. It's safer."

"Well you should've let me *know* that, darling! Ahead of time. Selfish, stupid girl."

"I had a terrible flu, Mum, that's why I didn't call. Was out like a light, so sorry I was too ill to call."

"Not ill enough to waste your time on Facebook."

"What do you mean? Since when have you been using Facebook, Mum?"

"It's fun, I've reconnected with so many friends, made new ones. It's no good liking my posts, darling, sending stupid hearts and smiley faces without actually getting in touch."

"But I didn't—" I stopped myself, realizing that of course my phone wasn't "lost." The triplets had stolen it and were sending my mum bloody hearts and smiley faces! I almost wanted to laugh. I changed the subject. "Anyway, I'm thinking of selling the house or maybe renting it out." I plopped a teabag into a mug and waited for the kettle to boil.

She had her lecture voice on. "Well I'm glad you're getting away from that eyesore in the middle of nowhere. For once in your life making a sound decision."

I poured the hot water over the teabag and scoured Pippa's fridge for milk.

"Darling, are you still there?" she screeched.

"Yes, I'm here. Just making a cup of tea. How's Dad?"

"It would be nice if you came home and found out for yourself. You promised you'd come for Christmas and you never even called! That was extremely selfish and rude."

"I know, I'm *so* sorry, Mum, but I had horrendous flu and literally couldn't get out of bed. Maybe I could come for Easter?"

Silence.

I stirred my tea and imagined what my father's reaction would be if I came home. It's a satisfying thing when someone no longer has control over you, but when they don't even know who you are, which is what happened last time I visited, all you feel is pity. That storm of a man had become as helpless as a baby, his brain mashed potato. I didn't relish seeing him.

"Darling, are you still there?"

"Mum, I can hear Pippa's car, she's just got back, better go," I lied. "I'll call you again tomorrow, okay? Big kiss." I hung up. Telling my mother even a tenth of what was going on in my life would be laying all my troubles on her shoulders, and she already had enough to deal with. It would make her even more hysterical. Yes, I could go and visit her, right this minute, but that would mean the triplets had won. I had to go back to Cliffside and face them, sort out the mess I'd got myself into. But I'd need backup. Mr. Donner? No, too doddery and frail; I didn't want to drag the sweet old man into my drama. Sam the contractor? Good idea, he was tough; I'd try him.

Cradling the mug of tea, I shuffled in my borrowed slippers (Pippa's eleven-year-old niece's, who'd left them behind) from the kitchen to Pippa's cozy, pristine sitting room, mulling over what to say to Sam. I hadn't been exactly polite to him when he'd come over that time. The kid's slippers looked up at me goofily with two big crocodile eyes and open-jawed teeth as if asking me the same question. I needed to sit down and think this thing through clearly. Hatch a clever plan. Going to Cliffside on my own was out of the question.

Tick tock, tick tock. Eight million. I hated being its guardian, but now I was physically parted from it, I felt like a dog without its prize bone. The more I considered it, the crazier the whole thing was. What the hell had Juan been thinking? Why didn't he just put that money into an offshore account? Surely he could've done that without being traced? Who, in their right mind, *buries* money? And who in their right mind goes along with it? A woman so in love she couldn't think straight, apparently.

Pippa's sitting room was like a *Homes & Gardens* magazine. Thick toile de Jouy curtains set off her pretty picture windows, pooling on the lush cream carpet in luxurious swathes. Two sumptuous Conran sofas, a gilded Italian mirror above a brick fireplace, and bookshelves lining the walls. I collapsed into one of the squidgy sofas, my mind whirring. Beanie, wagging his tail, leapt up. His long sausagey body nestled between me and the comfy cushions, and he pressed his wet nose on my lap.

This place was light years away from Cliffside. My eyes ran along the walls decorated with botanical prints of English flowers

set in gold frames, and the coffee table books stashed in the
bookshelves. My gaze then landed on a set of photo albums. I
placed my mug gently on a coaster—careful not to spill tea—and
got up, propelled by curiosity. My own words rang in my ears, the
stern telling-off I'd given to Jen for snooping without permission.
Nevertheless, I pulled out a couple of the albums and sat back
down to browse.

The first album was filled with Pippa as a child. Horses and
ponies. Lots of them. Pippa winning rosettes for show jumping.
Pippa on vacation, on what looked like the Cornish coast, frolick-
ing and shivering in the cold sea, in a flowery swimsuit, tall and
gangly, grinning at the camera with her signature toothy smile.
I flicked mindlessly through, between sips of tea, and moved on
to album number two. This was more interesting. Pippa with
a backpack on her shoulders, in her early twenties. Thailand,
Vietnam. I turned the pages rapidly until I arrived at Mexico. And
there I saw Juan. Very young. Less handsome in his youth than he
was later. His face looked different. Familiar, yet so different. His
expression, as he gazed straight into the camera, made me feel like
I'd just seen him last week. I thumbed on towards the end, but as
I was about to lay the album on the sofa, a big card slipped out.
The kind of card Americans do for Christmas, with a family photo
stuck to the front. I was about to slide it back in when the smile
of the woman in the picture took the air from my lungs. I'd seen
that wide smile before. The head thrown back, the laughing eyes.
It was Lee, the triplets' mother! Three small children stared at the
lens. Two little girls and a chubby-faced boy. Jen, Kate, and Dan.
They couldn't have been more than six months old.

But what really knocked the wind out of me was the other figure
in the photo: Juan. Not smiling, but staring vacantly into the lens.

Blood drained from my limbs; my hands felt numb as I held
the card with my shaky fingers. A spasm from my invisible sixth
finger made me drop the card.

I picked it off the floor and opened it. The writing was unmistakable, the "I am done with you" writing:

Good luck with your new job, Pippa. We'll miss you.
Love, Lee, Juan, Danny, Katey, and Jenny. Xxx

Vomit and tea rose up from my esophagus. I swallowed it back down.

I could hardly breathe.

Juan? *My* Juan? In a cute family photo? Father of the triplets? No wonder Juan's face as a young man in the photos felt so familiar. He looked like Dan! That's why Dan and the girls had an old-soulish-have-known-you-in-another-lifetime feeling. Why I had been so attracted to them in the first place. Because they were Juan's *children*! How could I have been so blind? Now it made sense… why Juan refused to marry me all that time.

BECAUSE HE WAS ALREADY MARRIED TO LEE!

I pictured the napkin:

I am done with you, please stop trying to contact me
I cannot give you what you want. Keep away from me.

Was he still in love with her when she wrote that, all those years later? Had he been leading a double life the whole time? What, exactly, did it mean?

And Pippa? Where the hell did she fit into this cozy ménage? And Cliffside?

I looked closer at the photo, and my fear was confirmed. The stone walls of Cliffside, unmistakable, the backdrop to this family gathering held immortally on film, in this telltale picture that made me gag.

I heard Pippa's car roll into the driveway and sat on the sofa, dazed, too shocked to even cry. My whole adult life had been a lie.

My relationship with Juan a farce. I felt like a wife of a serial killer who'd had no idea. No idea, because she'd been such a numbskull.

The front door unlocked, and I stared into space, in a trance of disbelief.

"Hello?" It was Pippa, the betrayer, the liar, yelling up the stairwell. "Darling, I'm back. God, it's mayhem out there. Roads blocked. It's started raining again."

I didn't reply, just closed my eyes and wished my life away. I might as well have let the triplets kill me for all I cared now. Cliffside held a whole new meaning, a whole new feeling. Nothing mattered anymore. I could drink myself to death, and nobody would care. Except Beanie, perhaps. I scooped him up and folded him in my arms and let out a heaving, baying sob.

CHAPTER FORTY-EIGHT

"Darling, what ever's the matter?"

I looked up and saw Pippa standing there, perplexed. Her pained eyes caught the photo albums spread on the sofa. "Oh, dearie me, you saw the pictures of Juan and now you're feeling sad?"

I pulled out the family photo card and jerked it before her long-jawed face. "What. Is. This," I said between gritted teeth. "Why didn't you tell me, Pippa?" *Some friend.*

"Oh, God. Where on earth did you find that? I forgot I even had that old thing. Look, darling, I can explain."

"Really? You can 'explain' why you never told me that Juan was married to this woman Lee? I'm assuming he was married, at least… if not, he—he was father to the bloody TRIPLETS! I mean, it's true, isn't it? That he was their father?"

She looked at the floor. "Yes, it's true. I'm sorry, I should've told you sooner."

"Sooner?" I yelled. "You never told me at *all.*"

"I was going to, I swear, it's just I promised Juan and—"

"Juan is *dead*! I suppose you think the triplets gate-crashing into my life like that wasn't important. And you knew the connection all *along*?"

"I promised him I wouldn't tell. He made me swear. He was going to tell you himself, but the timing never seemed right and then—"

"Why didn't you tell me after—after he was gone? You could've *warned* me."

"Yes, well, look—" She didn't finish her sentence. What could she say? No excuse was good enough. She had betrayed me, and she knew it. A nasty thought flashed through my mind for a split second; was Pippa in cahoots with the triplets? *No, that wouldn't make sense, or she wouldn't have come to rescue me.*

"Was Juan still *seeing* Lee?" I demanded. "Still in love with her?"

"God, no! No, you've got the wrong impression."

"The wrong *impression*? There's evidence, Pippa, evidence, right here in my hands, of a happy family, and you were part of this—this—" My fury held me back from finishing what I couldn't even express in words, with this cacophony of emotions whirling in my head. Fury, loss, a hopeless feeling of betrayal, loneliness, shock. Suspicion.

I sat there crying, my shoulders rounded in a slump, Pippa silent, not knowing what to say. After an awkward hiatus, with nothing but my howling sobs, I let her know about the note on the napkin that matched Lee's writing. She winced and shook her head but didn't elaborate.

I could hardly think.

"What more are you not t-telling me, Pippa?" My words came out in chopped chokes. "You c-came with me and Jen to Hearst Castle that day, and all that time you and Jen *knew* each other?"

"Yes, I mean, no. Jen has no idea who I am. None of the triplets do."

"Don't lie!"

"I hadn't seen Jen since… well… practically since that photo was taken."

"But you were obviously Lee's friend, or she wouldn't have written you that card!"

"I was the triplets' nanny. Briefly, for just a few months. Juan got me the job. He couldn't cope, he—"

"Poor, poor diddums, Juan," I spat out sarcastically. "How awful for him not being able to cope with his DOUBLE LIFE!"

"You don't understand, this was long before he met you. He had left Lee and the triplets ages before you came along. He walked out of their lives when they were just babies."

"Well that makes me love my husband a whole lot more. That he had a beautiful family and then just walked out on them. And later took their home away. Bravo, Juan, what a great fucking guy you were. Like… that's meant to make it all okay? Meant to make me feel better?"

"You're upset, darling. I totally understand, but it wasn't like that. Not at all."

"Well please enlighten me to what it *was* like then, because right now—" I burst into tears again, my anger laced with disgust about the man I'd wasted over ten years with. A man whose every word I'd clung on to. All lies, all deceit. What a fool I'd been.

Beanie lay on my lap and pressed his nose against my beet-red face, licking away the tears in gentle lapping kisses. Pippa put her arm around me. I shook it off with a rough thrust of my shoulder.

"Look, Juan was tricked by Lee," she said. "He was miserable after less than a year of marriage. Stupidly, at the beginning of their relationship, he'd agreed to IVF. Then, when he realized their marriage was a disaster, he wanted a divorce. He contacted the fertility clinic telling them to destroy his sperm. Well, Lee—with her brilliant forgery of Juan's signature giving consent—managed to continue with the IVF treatment, without Juan's permission. She got pregnant. He was horrified. Kids with Lee was the last thing in the world he wanted. It was a total shock to him."

I gauged her expression to see if what she was telling me was true, then asked, "Why didn't they get divorced then? Why did he still stay if he was so unhappy after she'd lied to him?"

"She had him by the balls, excuse the rather apt expression. Under California law, she'd get half his money, Cliffside too, because she had three kids to raise, plus he'd have to pay her one hell of a lot of alimony."

"But you say he was tricked?"

"Yeah, well, Lee did such a good job forging his signature, there was no way his innocence would've held up in a court of law if they'd called in forgery experts. Juan had even paid a private handwriting expert himself, and the result was ambiguous. Nobody was willing to testify a hundred percent that it was fake. Juan even questioned *himself* it looked so like his own signature, and he'd already signed all sorts of documents before he backed out. The woman was really smart, really scheming. Juan threatened to sue the clinic, but again, it was going to be difficult to prove. And the last thing he wanted, by this point, was to spend years on a complicated lawsuit. Three small kids versus a reluctant, angry father? They'd be on the side of the woman with her babies, obviously. The damage was done, anyway, the triplets born. All he could do was make the best of it."

"Which was?"

"Juan and Lee made a deal. No monthly alimony, just a one-off payment to set her on her feet before going back to work. No divorce. No obligations for Juan to play father. And in return? Lee would get Cliffside to live in, free and clear until the triplets turned eighteen. Then she'd give the house back. They'd keep this secret from the children. She got what she wanted, which was to be a mother and live with her kids at Cliffside—so they'd have a good home—and Juan got his freedom."

"But couldn't Lee have kept the whole house, forever, it being the family residence as it was?" I said.

"Cliffside was always in Juan's name, even though she designed it. They weren't married when he purchased the land, and it was all his money. He paid for the house to be built, and I think they had a pre-nup, too. Even so, if they'd gone to court, in all likelihood they would've had to sell the house and split the money two ways."

"True," I said, trying to take all this in.

"Remember," Pippa said. "Lee had spent all her expertise and time designing it, so it was complicated. Yet, because she hadn't put up a cent, she might have lost it because of the pre-nup. She wasn't willing to risk that. From her twisted point of view, she was doing Juan a huge favor by offering him this deal. She could've taken him to the cleaners but chose not to. And he accepted, because he could have ended up with nothing if the courts went in Lee's favor. They cooked up this mutual deal where both could live at Cliffside at different points in their lives."

"That doesn't explain why he didn't insist upon getting a divorce."

"He just wanted out. A divorce would've wrapped them up in the courts for ages, dividing this and dividing that. You're a lawyer, you know how it goes. Especially in California. He wanted to be free, above all. I know, it's a bit ironic, but if you knew Lee, you'd understand."

"What about them? The triplets. Surely when they turned eighteen, they'd wonder why they were losing—" I stopped myself. Now it all made sense. Somehow, they must have got wind of what was happening. Must have discovered who their real father was, and knowing he had abandoned them had sent them off the rails. A deal robbing them of their heritage, their inheritance, of a house they'd lived in all their lives. Knowing they were unwanted by Juan, and their birth was a mistake (at least on his part), would have made them want to get even. They had certainly kept their discovery very quiet, though. Hadn't let on to me.

I took a sip of tea. It was tepid. "Pippa, when did the triplets find out about Juan?"

"I don't know if they ever did. I don't think they have any idea. You'd know better than I would. Did they mention him?"

I didn't reply. They had told me their father had died in the line of duty. Lee's clever lie, no doubt. Perhaps Juan's too. Lee must have got her hands on a forged dog tag and given it to

Dan as a memento. Maybe she even bought it online. There was a backstory there when it came to Cliffside. The triplets blamed me. Questions and answers ricocheted in my brain, trying to piece together the things they'd said—the whispers I'd heard.

"Why," I asked Pippa, "would Lee ever want to leave Cliffside, ever? I mean, how could Juan have trusted her to hand the house over when the triplets turned eighteen?"

"They drew up an airtight contract. Like I said, all he wanted was out. He had no desire to be a father to children he never wanted in the first place."

"Yes, but knowing what she was like, how could he trust her not to pull some clever number on him?" I held Pippa's gaze, but she looked away and stared at the floor. I sensed there was something else she wasn't telling me.

Silence. Pippa was deep in her own thoughts, standing there, staring into space.

Sinking further into the sofa, with my arms around Beanie and tears still spilling down my cheeks, I absorbed all this bizarre information. Accepting it was like trying to chew on glass.

"Why?" I pushed on. "I mean, I understand how upset Juan must've been, but still, he could've contributed to the triplets' upbringing, could have been part of their lives, even if just seeing them for the odd weekend, or for holidays. For better or worse, they were still his flesh and blood."

Pippa kicked off her shoes and finally sat down, shoulders curling over her chest, her knees up, feet up on the sofa, jiggling her toes back and forth in agitation. "Lee was a nightmare. A real bitch. Dealing with her was impossible. Trust me, I know, I worked for her. Asking a man to be father to one child he didn't ask for would be bad enough, but three? Can you imagine? Juan wanted a fresh start. Didn't want to be dragged down by Lee and her manipulative ways. She was devious and calculating. Violent too. He didn't want to deal with her on any level and would've had to if they'd shared the children. And if he'd dragged her through the courts, he could've lost everything. So he let her have Cliffside, gave her a chunk of money and called it quits, knowing that one day he'd get his beloved house back."

It was falling into place… *Watch me make an offer they can't refuse. I'll get you that house.*

If only I'd known the true price attached.

"Didn't he have any *empathy* for his children though? For how those kids would feel one day when they found out about him?"

"That was part of their contract too. The triplets would never know. They'd believe their father was… I can't remember what lie Lee cooked up."

"A war hero," I mumbled. A fresh bout of weeping put a stop to my onslaught of questions. I pinched myself to make sure this wasn't one of my pill-induced dreams; that I wasn't drunk, that this was really, truly happening. Pippa laid her arm around my shoulder again and gave it a squeeze.

I shook her off. "Get *off*, Pippa! You pretend to be my friend? You could have *told* me all this. The triplets nearly killed me!"

"Killed you? Come on, darling, that's an exaggeration, isn't it? I'm sure they—"

"They locked me up, Pippa! They were going to forge my will! It's their fault I got hooked on those pills."

"You have proof of this?"

"What the hell, Pippa! You saw my bruises!" I clenched my jaw to the point of pain and felt my fingernails dig into my palms. If Pippa doubted me, knowing the state I was in when she rescued me, I had no chance getting anyone else to believe me. "Forget it, if you don't—"

"Look! I tried to get you away from them, darling! I drove to your house, but they told me you were in England. You'd given them full reign of Cliffside, handed them money and credit cards, even allowed them to bring a dog into the house when you're allergic. Of course they took advantage. You *let* them. Honestly, darling, what did you ex*pect*?" Then she said more softly, "But you're right, you need to stay well away from them and get help from the authorities; they sound bloody dangerous."

Truth thudded in my ears. I *had* given them full reign of Cliffside. "They're malicious," I heaved, on a sob. "They want Cliffside back and will do anything to get it. Anything. Now it all makes sense."

"I should've warned you, I'm so sorry."

"You *knew*? You *knew* they had a plan?"

"Of course not. But I guessed something wasn't right. And they are their mother's children, after all. Bad blood. But you seemed so happy with them, there was only so much I could *do*. Besides, as I said, I made a promise to Juan."

"Why didn't he want me to know the truth?"

Of all the things I had found out, this was the most painful of all. Why, oh, why hadn't Juan confided in me? After the initial shock of discovering he was married and had triplets, I wouldn't have cared, it wouldn't have made any difference to how much I loved him. He hadn't trusted me. It now made our whole life together an empty shell.

"Why didn't he *tell* me, Pippa? *Why*?"

"I don't know. I asked him that myself, not that it was any of my business."

"And what did he say?" I was grasping at straws, my desperation a clamor in my heart. Still holding on to shreds of love.

"I think he just wanted a fresh start, didn't want to spoil what he had with you. Thought he could wipe his past away. And he did manage to do that, didn't he? I mean, the fact that none of his past caught up with him until now says a lot. He loved you. You were everything to him." Color drained from Pippa's face. The look in her eyes told me that she was still in love with Juan herself. Always had been, always would be. Saying those words aggrieved her as much as they surprised me.

"I never felt I was enough for him," I admitted. "Never felt special enough or pretty enough."

"You're mad, you know that? Don't you *see* how beautiful you are?" She laughed. "I mean, not a week ago, when I found you in a heap on your driveway in your pajamas, looking like a startled skeleton, but you're special, darling. Juan wouldn't have stayed with you all that time otherwise."

Pippa's words warmed me. I thought of how I had imagined Juan was having an affair all that time, and how wrong I'd been. The "Keep away from me" note on that napkin. It all fell into place now. He wanted Cliffside back, for his contract with Lee to be honored, and she was telling him to keep away from her, that she couldn't give him what he wanted. I let out a sigh of relief.

But I couldn't let him off the hook completely. Even if his vasectomy and aversion to IVF and having children now made sense, it didn't help my anger. I'd been tricked. Used. My chances of having children ripped away from me. He had put me off the idea of adoption too. Who *was* I anymore?

I turned my attention back to Pippa and the triplets. I had more questions on the tip of my tongue. "So all that stuff about the triplets' mother selling Cliffside to raise money for her cancer treatment was a load of rubbish? Or was that the partial truth?"

Pippa shifted her eyes away from me. She curled into a ball, hugging her knees. "I-I have no idea. I used to see her from time to time, at Whole Foods and out and about. But then she disappeared around the same time as Juan—please, darling, don't"—her lips quivered—"please don't hate me."

"I pretty much *do* hate you right now, Pippa. And I'm not your 'darling.' I've been lied to by everyone, I'm so—"

"Does my coming over to Cliffside"—she rose to her feet, her voice shrill—"to rescue you from the chaos you'd got yourself into, count for nothing? Does weaning you off those bloody pills, bathing you four times a day and nursing you, with a wet flannel on your brow, mean nothing? Nursing you through the sweats and chills of that miserable cold turkey? You think I enjoyed all that?"

"No, of course not. I'm really grateful. You saved my life," I muttered. "I'm sorry, but all this news is overwhelming." I sat there feeling small, as she towered over me, her hands shaking, her gaze drilling through me. She was right, without her I'd probably be dead by now—my new, fake will at the triplets' law firm, everyone scrabbling for a slice of their "inheritance." Whatever information Pippa had hidden, I'd need to remember that. She had rescued me from them and saved my life.

Did I even want to live at Cliffside anymore? Knowing Juan was part and parcel of the triplets' history tainted Cliffside's magic. The house was no longer his special gift to me, and how could I live there peacefully after all that had happened? Still, the idea that Dan, Kate, and Jen were swanning around *my* home, usurping *my* property made my cauldron fester and bubble. How dare they rob me of my only means of happiness? Rip me of my dignity, steal my trust, and then stamp all over it! We'd been so happy! I was content to share what was mine with them. But no, their greed—Kate's and Dan's especially—pushed away any possibility of communal happiness. Not only had they dissed me, dismissed me, they were planning to *kill* me!

This sick tale was unraveling like a dirty bandage, festering with old dried blood and germs. Lee had reneged on the deal she made with Juan, and that's why he suddenly married me. When Cliffside became half mine, she no longer had a stake in it. Legally, after the triplets turned eighteen, Lee wasn't able to claim them as dependents anymore—Juan was free and clear of any responsibility. I imagined him serving the divorce papers the second he was able to, and how under California law, even if she didn't finalize them with a signature, the courts would grant a default divorce, unless, of course, she had contested.

"Cup of tea, darling?" Pippa asked, cutting into my thoughts.

Pippa's offer jolted me back to when I was fourteen, in the hospital, after my riding accident. The first thing the nurse had asked me, after I came to was, "Cuppa tea, love?" As if tea was the perfect remedy for a concussion. As if tea could help me now.

I nodded. "By the way, did Lee contest the divorce?"

"Her signature was on the papers," Pippa said, a little smirk playing on her lips.

"You're saying Juan forged her signature?"

Tit for tat.

"I'm not saying anything. Earl Grey or PG Tips?"

"Earl Grey." I shifted Beanie off my lap and stood up. I was still in Pippa's niece's flowery pajamas and animal slippers. Apart from a new toothbrush she'd given me, I had nothing. No clothes. No car. She had helped me cancel all my credit cards, so the triplets couldn't go AWOL, but I hadn't dared to go out shopping with my new ones yet. I needed to lie low.

If Dan and Kate were capable of murdering me, they'd be capable of anything, even killing their own parents. If Lee was the monster Pippa described her to be, the second they turned eighteen they would've wanted their nasty mother out of the picture and inherit Cliffside after her death.

As for Lee herself? She never did have cancer, I bet. That little story was one big fat lie. Fluntern Cemetery in Zurich, my foot! A ruse by the triplets to get me to feel sorry for them, to open up my house, my heart to them… these poor, poor, homeless orphans. Now it all made sense. Thinking they would inherit Cliffside, they had murdered Lee. Had perhaps done the same to her as to me… playing nursie with her prescription until she got hooked. Maybe even locking her up in the laundry room. Then, expecting the house to fall into their laps, they got the shock of a lifetime when Juan showed up as owner. Their plan stymied, not to mention the double shock of finding out they had a flesh and blood father who had evaded them all their lives, robbing them of their inheritance, favoring his new wife over them. So they killed him out of revenge.

And that's why Juan and Lee had disappeared around the same time. The question was, how did the triplets pull it off?

CHAPTER FORTY-NINE

As Pippa made tea, minutiae of conversations clamored in my head, each detail screaming for attention. I rewound the one where Dan, Kate, and Jen were accusing me, in so many words, of murder. This was their ploy, their twisted technique: everything they were guilty of they boomeranged at me. I replayed Jen's words: *"Maybe it was, like, parked—it was a vintage Mustang, right?—maybe the handbrake was off, maybe it just rolled over the edge of the cliff."*

I'd reflected on that, the fact that Juan had driven to the airport in his prized 1969 Mustang convertible. He did like to take it for a spin in warm weather, but still, it seemed uncharacteristic. He hated parking it in public places, so why would he have risked it at the airport parking lot? I had a doctor's appointment that fateful day, wasn't home when he set off so never got the chance to ask. That night, I remember feeling hurt that he hadn't returned my calls, and I couldn't sleep, but after fretting till dawn I found his phone in the bathroom, under a towel. That mania he had of leaving it behind so as to not be traced.

It was ten days until the remnants of his car was discovered. Ten harrowing days of hell. The police did grill me about Juan's cell phone after his death, did find it suspicious that he had left it behind, but I guessed they verified my alibi and traced my credit card spending that day and realized I was innocent. Because they never bothered me again. When the insurance company contacted me, I was dumbfounded, had forgotten Juan even had life insurance. They too wanted to know why he didn't have his phone with him at the time of the accident, and all sorts of other personal questions. Obviously, I didn't let on, didn't tell them about Juan's paranoia. I just pretended he'd forgotten it.

But the Mustang haunted me. I never did understand why he'd chosen to drive it to the airport instead of taking his Range Rover.

Because, he obviously hadn't! Maybe the triplets had shoved him into the car—possibly drugged, or even already dead—and rolled the Mustang off the cliff at the carefully selected Ragged Point, knowing what a dangerous place it was, and where other drivers had met their fate in the past, assuming he'd never get found for months. It was a possibility. Since the body had never been discovered, maybe they had disposed of it elsewhere *then* pushed the car over the cliff?

If only I'd been home when Juan set off for the airport!

Juan had been going on about that upcoming meeting, telling me what a big deal it was. I wished now I could remember every scrap of conversation, every look, every smile, every last parting word. I still had a mental snapshot of him that day, winking at me and saying, "Take care of yourself, my English rose." We had made love early that morning; he was more passionate than ever, kissing every inch of me, his lips lingering on each of my fingers as he moved rhythmically inside me. "I love your pretty hands," he'd whispered. "Every quirky little curve of you, every funny little bone in your funny little valentine body." And then he called out my name, as I too gave him all of myself in that moment of symbiotic pleasure and release. The insatiable need we had for each other momentarily sated.

And then I drove off to Carmel for my appointment, already missing him, replaying the details in my head. His dark locks hanging over his brow, the sweat on his forehead, the sound of his desire for me. When I got home, the emptiness I felt in the space where his beloved Mustang had been haunted me, as if I knew right then something was very wrong.

Had the triplets arrived at Cliffside straight after I'd left for my doctor's appointment? And taken him by surprise? Maybe they pretended they wanted to rekindle a relationship with him. Isn't that what most biological children do when they track down a real parent, if they've been adopted or something? They would have arrived at the door, all smiles and charm, then Juan contrite, wishing he'd been a proper father to them the second he laid eyes on his gorgeous grown-up brood.

Doing something as premeditated as his murder would take a huge amount of skill and organization on the triplets' part, not to mention brute force. But Dan was strong. Worked out. Three against one, with the element of surprise working in their favor, Juan didn't stand a chance.

Forensics could trace all sorts of stuff these days. To make a car explode, to guarantee a person's death, you'd have to lace the car with gasoline, and there'd be a trail of evidence, surely? But there was an answer to that, too. Because of a spate of unusually bad weather the day Juan disappeared, and the days that followed, and that dangerous drop off the sheer cliff face, it wasn't until ten days later that the police were able to rappel all the way down there successfully, by which time the storm had washed away most of the debris. A helicopter had surveyed the car's wreckage, of course, but nobody had been able to examine anything.

The triplets had it all planned out. Knew exactly what they were doing. They *knew* how hard it would be for rescue teams to rappel down there.

The riddle was solved. They had murdered their parents.

And then they set their sights on me. An easy target. Husband dead, no children. Lonely.

A sucker who'd usurped their rights.

So they moved right in. Got even with me.

Easy as pie. Their charm winning me over.

Well not anymore.

CHAPTER FIFTY

Pippa laid a mug of tea on a coaster in front of me and took a slurp of hers. When I asked her if she believed Juan had crashed his car, her eyes glazed over and, before I could read anything into her odd expression (she was still in love with him, wasn't she?), her cell phone bleeped. A text. Her gaze slid over me then shifted uneasily around the room. "Excuse me, I just need to make a quick work call." The way she slithered out of the room, throwing a sly glance my way before she closed the door behind her, spoke volumes. In the time I'd been at her house, I knew it wasn't characteristic of her to conduct business calls in private. From what I'd seen, she loved showing off about work, loved sharing the scoop.

I got up from the sofa and padded to the door, turned the handle as noiselessly as I could, and strained my ears towards the corridor. She had gone into the kitchen. I could hear her muffled voice. I lifted my hair away from my ears.

"Thank God you called. I wasn't sure if you'd got my message. I've been waiting for your call for days."

Who was she talking to?

"Yup, she's here with me. Clean as a whistle. All new. What? No, she's fine. But there's something… look, she knows the whole story. No, not *that*… I didn't, I couldn't tell her. Please don't say that. Look, I was weak, I admit it. I just couldn't bring myself to. Don't be angry. Listen, instead of screaming at me about what I should've done, can't we just deal with the situation at hand?"

There was a long lull, and I thought Pippa had hung up, but then I heard her stifling a sob. Did I just hear her say "Dan?" My heart drummed with terror. So Pippa *was* in with the triplets? She'd been "weak," come and saved me, regretted it, and now had to deal with "the situation at hand?"

"I'm sorry, please understand the position you put me in, I—" Silence. And then, "I agree, too risky. What? I don't think so. I don't know if she'd fall for that."

Too right I won't bloody fall for that.

A pause. More hushed words being spoken on the other end of the line.

"Okay. Where shall we meet? I'll try my best."

Silence again, then the sound of Pippa scraping a chair and then talking again. This time it did sound like a work call.

I closed the door and raced back to the sofa, laying myself down horizontally. Pippa opened the door. I kept my eyes squeezed shut but after a beat looked up at her in a faux groggy haze. I moaned, "I'm not feeling so good, Pippa. Feel a bit queasy."

"Look, I need you to get dressed and come with me."

"Where?" I asked, curious as to what lie she was going to cook up.

"I've got to go out. Urgent work matter. It's about the bridge. Apparently it should've been upgraded years ago, and now everyone's up in arms. I need to get the piece written, pronto. Have to meet one of the structural engineers. I don't want to leave you alone in the house." Her words ran together, her voice tense, clipped. Irritated even. Her shifty eyes darted this way and that.

I laughed. "You expect me to believe that? You've left me alone before."

"Yes, but I've been thinking about the triplets, and I think you're right; they're too dangerous. That was a nasty bash they gave you. I want you to come with me."

"I'm not going anywhere, Pippa. I don't feel well. I'm staying right here."

"Please. *Please.* I can't tell you more but please trust me."

"No way am I going anywhere."

We went on like this for several minutes, me refusing to budge. "Go, Pippa. I'll be fine. Take care on the road—it looks like it's still pouring outside."

Finally Pippa left. When I heard her SUV purr out of earshot, and as soon as I was sure the coast was clear, I raided various wardrobes, found some sneakers of her niece's, and got dressed and ready. I picked up the landline and called Sam, the contractor, to ask him to meet me at Cliffside, but his voice message picked up saying he was on vacation.

I was about to dial 911, so I could arrange for an officer to meet me there, but then stopped myself. They would ask me, "What's your emergency?" and what could I say? My crazy, convoluted story about how the triplets, maybe aided by Pippa, were out to kill me? Where was the proof? They'd think me nuts. And with the problems on the highway right now, collapsing bridges, and God knows what other road emergencies, my story would be at the bottom of their agenda.

There was only one choice I had left. To deal with this on my own. And with any luck, and if my memory served me well, it wasn't just Pippa's spare car that was going to save my hide. There was her gun, too.

CHAPTER FIFTY-ONE

My heart thrumming wildly with nerves and trepidation, I sat in Pippa's Toyota, the car still in park, Beanie woofing at me, excited to go on an outing. I had the triplets in my mind's eye and almost laughed about their gall. They had the nerve to accuse *me* of murder? How dare they! A spike of fury jabbed at me, spurring me on, needling me to take action, reminding me of how I'd been treated, how they'd killed my husband. Ruined my life.

I dug my hand into the glove compartment, adrenaline surging through me as I felt the cold metal with my fingertips, the textured handle. I curled my fingers around the pistol to test my grip.

Pippa's handgun was neat and compact. She had probably forgotten all about it, or she would've transferred it over to her new car. I had remembered our conversation, how she kept it here, too nervous to bring it into the house.

I took it out from its hiding place and stroked its chilly contours, ran my eyes along its masculine backbone. I clenched the handle again. It molded to my hand as if it had been designed especially for me. I felt its weight.

A frisson of excitement and terror.

A chill of a premonition.

I drove off carefully, the car's wheels sloshing through the rain. Because of Pfeiffer Canyon Bridge being closed there was only so far Pippa could go south on Highway One. Either she had gone to meet the triplets at Cliffside or somewhere nearby. I assumed she'd gone to the house.

Rain slashed at the car windows and even with the wipers on the fastest mode, I could hardly see through the windshield. I leaned forward in my seat, squinting at the road ahead. Yes, I was being reckless going to Cliffside, but I didn't care anymore. Something stronger than my own self-preservation was urging me forward: a sense of justice, a steely resolve, a force of empowerment, now I had a weapon. I knew nothing about guns, didn't even know how to check if it was loaded or not. I assumed it was, and I'd need to handle it carefully. My sum total experience was from watching cop shows and movies. Still, the pistol would do the trick even if it wasn't loaded, because the triplets would believe that it was. Bullies are cowards. And I was one angry human being right now. Kate and Dan weren't as tough as they thought!

The highway was awash with mud sliding off the soggy banks, which flanked the flooded road. I passed Bixby Bridge, my speed steady, eyes peeled, senses alert. Then a field on my right, the grass a lush, emerald green from all the relentless rain, the car tires sloshing and splattering as it sailed along the moody landscape, sodden clouds scudding through the hissing sky.

My plan ticked in my head. My eyes stared ahead in concentration. I'd force the triplets to leave, force them to get in their cars and promise to send on their belongings. They could go to a hotel. I'd pay. Bribe them with money. Hell, they could even take the eight million if they wanted. Good idea! I didn't even want that bloody money. All it had done was cause heartache. It was tainted, cursed. It disgusted me.

I'd get the house cleaned up, change all the locks, fix the fence, make Cliffside like Fort Knox again, then put it on the market. It didn't even matter if it didn't sell straight away. I was still a qualified lawyer, I could go back to work. I could change countries even, adopt a child as a single parent.

I could do anything. The architect of my own fate, my own future.

"You're strong," Juan had always said. "You have a core of steel."

"Yes, I'm strong," I told Juan, the universe, my heart.

Or maybe, no, damn them! I'd keep Cliffside. Go back to the retreat plan. Change the furniture, put my stamp on the place. Make it my own.

It was *my* house. And nobody could take it from me.

As these thoughts tumbled around in my head, the rain eased up a bit, and an unexpected slant of golden afternoon sunshine peeped through a purple cloud, its light a laser. A rainbow emerged. An arc of hope.

Cliffside is mine.

Suddenly, thunder rumbled, and, just a second later, forked lightning gashed white beneath the rainbow, slamming its electrical roots somewhere into the ocean. A bolt so fast I hardly caught it, but it wasn't my imagination. I pulled into my driveway, my renewed courage eclipsed by my thudding, fearful pulse. Turn back?

No, I hadn't come this far to cop out now.

I can do this. I am strong.

I halted the car, out of sight from the house, turning it around first so I could make a quick escape if need be. I wanted to check the lay of the land first. Wearing gray, as I was, it made me blend in with the sleety rain. I was dressed in a pale gray Burberry mac, too, courtesy of Pippa. I took the gun from the glove compartment and slipped it into the pocket of my raincoat. Beanie was jumping around in the back, excited to be home.

"No, Beanie, you're staying here. At least for now." I cracked the windows just enough to give him some fresh air.

Beanie had shown such allegiance to me, and my allergy to dander seemed to have melted away in the past week, without any antihistamines. Strange that. A little golden Labrador puppy my mother had bought me as a child popped into my archive of memories. I had forgotten about that sweet boy. He was returned two days later. My father, who had been away on a work trip, arrived home in a blaze of fury, instantly ignited the second he laid eyes on me with the soft blond puppy in my arms. I had not sneezed the whole time the dog had been with us. I did not have a runny nose, yet the puppy was unceremoniously snatched away from me and his new forever home and given back to the breeders. The reason? My supposed allergy.

I trod lightly as I pattered up to the house and through the open gate. Why wasn't it shut? It was unnervingly quiet. Neither Dan's car nor my Land Rover were parked in the driveway. The garage door, too, was open, a strange car I didn't recognize parked inside. Mrs. Reed had bought a red Mini Cooper? Racy was not her God-fearing style. It was a Friday, though. Her day to clean. I hadn't seen her for ages. The triplets had told her to leave, hadn't they? I didn't understand why Pippa hadn't arrived yet, assuming coming here had been her plan.

Just as I was contemplating my next move, I caught sight of a light going on in the house.

My right hand groped in the pocket of my raincoat, the pistol warmer now, the sweat of my shaky, naïve hand unfamiliar to its touch.

I was just about to march away, back to the safety of my car, when the front door suddenly swung open.

I blinked, fear shooting through, white-hot. Instant remorse at coming to Cliffside, all alone. For not making that call to 911.

"Well, hello! How fabulous to see you!" a strange voice called out.

Focusing my eyes through the rain, I saw Kate, but she'd dyed her hair blond. But no, it wasn't Kate, but an older Kate, a blond Kate who flung her head back when she laughed.

Standing at the door was the triplets' mother. Juan's ex-wife. Lee. It had to be. A woman I'd presumed murdered.

But alive. Very much alive. I opened my eyes wider. Drops of rain plopped down my cheek. I took a long hard stare. There was no mistaking it.

It was Lee.

CHAPTER FIFTY-TWO

I stood there, frozen to the spot. The space between us diminished to a thin line as Lee skipped closer. Long legs, long neck, an older Jen in motion. All this time, I'd had a cancer victim in my mind, a woman whose hair was falling out, strand by strand, a brave wisp of a dying mother, a soldier's widow, pale and sad. Then she had become a corpse, buried in a cemetery outside Zurich. Then a murder victim, killed by her own greedy children. A myth, a character in a Greek tragedy.

In all my imagined scenarios, I had not pictured what stood before me now: Lee, alive.

She was beautiful. As buoyant as her laugh in the photo that Kate once showed me. Almost as young as that picture, too. An ageless beauty.

She was wearing my yellow raincoat—the one I'd wear on my hikes down to the beach. She knotted her brow as she observed me, but then her lips parted again, and a wide grin cut into her pretty face. She had greeted me like an old friend, half a minute earlier, but I wondered if she had any idea who I was.

Of course she knew who I was.

Her green eyes shimmering with what seemed like a genuine welcome, she said, "Well, well, well, look who's here. So sorry you missed the children."

"Where are they?" I mustered, not managing a smile myself, my mouth pinched in shock.

"Come in, why don't you. I'm Lee. So nice to have a visitor in this monstrous weather. Come in from the rain." She was holding her arms around her torso, her hands tucked up under her elbows as if to warm her body from the cold. California girl.

"I'm—"

"I know who you are," she broke in. "How wonderful to finally meet you."

I released my clammy palm from the grip of the handgun and gingerly pulled it—empty and trembly—from my pocket. But we didn't shake hands. I just looked at her, dumbly.

My enemy. Or *not*? I imagined she'd have an explanation for this. Maybe an apology? She'd want to apologize for her children's psychopathic behavior, surely?

"Come inside," Lee said, with a warm smile. "Be careful, try not to bring too much mud into the house. Isn't this weather insane?" Her tone was so friendly, her eyes filled with apparent kindness. Not the ogre Pippa had described at all. But now I knew Pippa was an all-out liar, that didn't actually surprise me.

Every plan I'd had, every solution in my brain, was shot to smithereens.

What now?

I weighed up my options. Stay where I was or find out what the hell was going on? My curiosity and fear raised—like hackles on a dog's back—I fingered the gun in my pocket. It gave me courage. I plodded behind Lee into the house, *my* house.

I'd wait for an explanation. At least give her a chance.

Lee took off her yellow coat (my coat) and hung it up. A part of me wanted to turn right around and race back to the car, but curiosity pushed me forward. The living room was gleaming clean.

"Take off your coat," Lee said in a sweet voice, her hands on my shoulders, ready to help. It annoyed me she was welcoming me into my own house. I noticed she was playing with her fingers. Perhaps she was as nervous as I was.

I stepped back. "No thank you." I was about to add, "I won't stay long," but bit my tongue.

My house. My house. This is my house!

"Where are Dan, Kate, and Jen?" I asked, sidling close to the door.

"Out. Would you like a hot drink? Coffee, tea, hot chocolate?"

"No, thank you." I chewed my lip. My right hand wandered to my face. I blew on my sweaty palm to dry off the clammy moisture. It smelled metallic. I waited for her to clarify the situation, but she seemed to be waiting for *me* to explain myself. God, the nerve!

"Lee?"

"Yes?"

"What are you doing in my house?"

She laughed, her teeth a shiny set of pearls, her hair a golden crown. She was an exact mixture of Kate and Jen, with a little bit of Dan thrown in. "But this isn't your house! At least, not for long."

"Lee, Cliffside belongs to me, fair and square." I shoved my hand back into my right pocket, my fingertips resting on the metal. I took a step back.

"They'll be here soon," she warned.

"The triplets?" My voice was creaky.

"You'll find the top of the driveway blocked."

My stomach folded, my ears buzzed. I'd stumbled right into her snare.

"And Pippa?" I asked.

"Pippa got detained," Lee said. A supercilious smile twitched on her face. *So I was right, Pippa was in on it?*

My fingers curled around the gun. God forbid it should go off in my pocket. This woman could not claim she was resident here the way the triplets could. I could shoot her right now as a trespasser. Protecting my property. *I have the right to bear arms*!

Lee moved closer and took off the green sweater she was wearing. It was in that brisk movement that a whiff of something unmistakable floated towards me: the scent of jasmine. The smell

I was never able to place, the scent the triplets told me I'd been imagining. Lee had been coming and going all this time.

She'd been part of the equation from the beginning, the brain behind it all. The "real estate agent" who'd handled the sale of the house? Had that been Lee? Because we never had spoken, just been in touch by email. The email address that Lee, with her comings and goings, must have left on the back of that photo of Cliffside. How Lee must have had the last laugh when she confirmed the triplets' identity to me, after I'd scanned and sent their photos to her.

"My kids screwed up. The snowflake generation. Too soft, too sensitive, especially Jen. I had no choice but to step in," she said languidly, stretching her arms. "The drink binge plan didn't work, and then my fool kids were taking so long to get things wrapped up. Then Florence fucking Nightingale gate-crashed the party."

I stared at her, confused. Was Pippa on Lee's side or *not*?

"Poor pathetic Pippa," Lee went on. "She was over the moon when Juan and I broke up all those years ago, but then you came along and spoiled her chances—at least in her eyes. Keep your friends close, your enemies closer, I guess." Lee smirked. "Thank you for coming here today, by the way. It's made our lives so much easier."

A chill razored through my body. *The drink binge plan.* The way she said it so nonchalantly, as if attempted murder was the most natural thing in the world. "What are you planning?" I rasped.

She raised an eyebrow. "You'll just have to wait and find out."

In a panic, I grasped the door handle to make my exit. But I heard a car approaching. The triplets, no doubt. Or Pippa? I turned to face Lee again.

Gripping the gun, I drew it out from my pocket and aimed it at her, moving with slow, backward paces towards the stairs. I could escape from the lower ground floor. But even with the gun aimed at her chest, Lee just tossed her blond bob, unfazed. Her mouth curved into a sardonic little smile.

"I'm leaving now," I said, my voice reedier than I wished. "Just let me walk away in a nice easy manner or I'll call the police."

Lee snickered. Now she looked like Dan. A mocking Dan. Handsome and cold. Her stony green eyes held mine, unrelenting. But a twinkle spoke of a familiar touch of humor, the crease of crow's feet, mirthful. "Good luck, my dear. The landline's down."

I made a couple of wary steps backwards, not letting my eyes leave Lee's for a second. The landline was down, but Lee's cell might be working. It lay glinting on the kitchen island. Wait, no! It was *my* phone. My iPhone that had disappeared. The diamanté cover was unmistakable. I waved the gun at her. "That's my phone, Lee. Give it to me."

"Now why the hell would I do that?" She picked it up and cradled it close to her chest.

"Skid it across the floor. Quickly, or I'll shoot. I mean it."

"No you won't. You're a pathetic chicken-shit coward who's been a victim all her sorry-ass life. An eleven-fingered freak who doesn't have the guts to *call* the shots let alone *fire* a shot. Is that thing even loaded? I doubt it."

I fumbled with the gun, jabbing it in the direction of her heart.

She chuckled and went on, "You know, I always wondered what Juan saw in you. Now I get it. You're kind of funny. Kind of comic, if not unbelievably dumb. How you ever got to be an attorney, I'll never know." She made her way towards the kitchen, waving my phone, hips swaying with confidence.

"Stop moving, you bitch! Or I'll shoot."

Lee spun to face me, her gaze uneasy as she flicked her eyes at the door. "You killed Juan"—her voice shrill, it had lost its cool—"and now you want to kill *me*, is that it?"

I had her in my line of fire, gun loaded or not. The car outside squealed to a halt. The style of driving told me it was Dan. Maybe his sisters were with him.

One big, happy family. Out to kill me.

Arianne Richmonde

"It won't be long before we find Juan's body, you scheming whore!" Lee screeched, pointing her finger at me. "The body you buried on *my* land! Of course, none us give a damn the bastard's dead; you did us all a favor killing him off, but you could've at least—"

That's when I saw it on her finger. My engagement ring. She'd been hiding it up until that point, had twisted it backwards into her palm. Now it shone like a prism, glimmering dangerously. "It was you lot!" I yelled back. "*You* all murdered Juan, you and your unhinged triplets! And you stole my ring, you bitch. Give it back!" I was about to race downstairs, but heard a noise coming from there, too. I was blocked from above and below.

"Don't mind that banging noise," Lee said. "We had to lock Jen in the laundry room for a little time out. Make her see sense."

So Jen was on my side, after all? Or was this another set-up?

Lee cried out, "You think we don't *know* what you buried in the dell in the woods? You, skulking around by that big redwood whenever you got the chance? We have the GPS co-ordinates, you dumbass. 'Hidden' in the wall safe, written in your hand."

"Liar!" I screamed, panicked. *How did she know?*

She laughed and tossed her head. "The password to the safe was so damn easy to figure out."

"You're bluffing," I said.

"Baby Rupert's *date of birth*!" She cackled. "Your mommy just loves to share her pity party on Facebook, doesn't she?"

My stomach lurched. My mum probably had no idea about privacy settings on Facebook—no doubt her posts were public. Sharing personal information: Rupert's 40th "birthday," fuck! I could just imagine Mum wallowing in "I'm sorry for your loss" comments from friends and family, albeit thirty-nine years after the fact. The hearts and smiley face comments "I" had made on Mum's posts: was that *Lee*?

"My kids did start digging between the roots but must've been off by several feet, because they couldn't find anything. But we will. You, Mrs. Trujillo the Second, are a murderer. You thought you could get away with it, didn't you? All that juicy life insurance money on the back of my ex-husband! On the back of a house I built! On the backs of my children's inheritance, our blood, sweat, and tears! You thought you could swoop right in and take Cliffside away from us."

"*You're* the thief!" I screamed back, waving the pistol at her. "You and Juan had a *deal*! And, for your information, you know what's buried by that redwood? Not Juan, you idiot, but money. Eight million dollars! That's right! Take it, it's yours if you and your children just leave me alone and get the hell out of my life, you can have it!"

"You must think I was born yesterday. *Eight million dollars*," she shrieked, "is buried in your backyard?" She hooted with laughter. "I'm not that freaking gullible."

"See for yourself. It *is* next to that big redwood. You can *have* the bloody money," I yelled. "Take it. Just leave me in peace and let me go, and you can take all the money, every last filthy dollar."

"You're lying."

"Be my guest, Lee, find out for yourself." I was aware of the danger I was putting her in. I knew somebody might still be watching the house, and Juan had told me not to dig anything up for three years.

She waved her bony finger at me again. "This ring? It's collateral, honey. It stays on my finger until I find out if you're bullshitting me or not."

The sound of the doorbell cut out my cries. What? The *doorbell*? Had Lee locked the house? Didn't the triplets have a key?

We both stood there gawping at each other, stunned into silence. Lee looked as shocked and bewildered as I did.

She moved warily towards the door. I stepped back up to the top of the stairwell and craned my neck around to see, curiosity getting the better of me. She opened the door slowly.

It wasn't Dan, or his sisters. Nor even Pippa. It was a highway patrol officer in uniform, standing there, smiling.

"Mrs. Trujillo? I'm sorry to bother you, ma'am, but I had a call from your mother a couple days ago, from England? I promised her I'd check in on you. Excuse the delay but it's been crazy out there on the highway the last couple days."

I had never sprinted so fast in my life, stumbling over myself to get to the door, barging Lee out of the way, practically hurling myself at the officer.

"*I'm* Mrs. Trujillo!" I cried. "It was my mother who called. I'm coming right with you." I held the man's hand. Saved by the bell. Literally. All I could do was think about getting the hell away from Cliffside, away from this nest of vipers.

And now I'd revealed the whereabouts of the money I had a very strong feeling that some serious shit was about to hit the fan. And I sure didn't want to be around when it happened.

CHAPTER FIFTY-THREE

I gripped the officer by the elbow and slammed the door behind me. He tried to convince me to stay home with my "friend," that it was too dangerous on the highway, but I dashed past him and made a beeline for Pippa's Toyota. As I ran, his patrol vehicle crawled up alongside me, his window open as he tried to persuade me to stay here.

"Ma'am, what are you doing? The highway ain't safe. It's best to stay home right now. Who was that lady with you? She looks familiar. Hey, wait a minute, didn't she used to live here once? I remember now, she's the old owner of this house, she's real friendly, she's—"

"Dangerous," I cut in. "Believe me."

He laughed. "Not as dangerous as out here right now. You know how many accidents there've been, and trees down?"

Just as I was about to explain everything a call crackled in on his radio, and he picked up, distracted by something far more important than my sob story. I imagined he thought Lee and I were two bitchy ex-wives squabbling over the house or something. Great, that was all I needed.

Despite having cracked the windows, the Toyota was all steamed up by Beanie's breath, frantic and furious he was for being left behind, from entering his own house. He was leaping up and down, barking manically when he spotted me out of breath running towards the car. Adrenaline had given me extra strength, my heart beating with both terror and gratitude at my close shave with Lee. The gun lay hidden in my raincoat pocket. I knew it was illegal to carry a concealed weapon without a license. If the officer saw me with it, he could arrest me.

"I can't allow you to drive, ma'am," the officer shouted through his open window. "It's just too dangerous right now."

I turned to him and yelled back through the rain, "I'm not staying here! If you can take me to the sheriff's office or the police station, that would be great. I need your *help*! Isn't that why you're here? To help people?" I unlocked the car.

He hollered through the howling, slapping wind, "A call's just come in. A woman up ahead has a flat tire. The AAA are outta their minds right now. Can't deal with all the demand."

"Can I come with you?" I asked. "I just need to get my dog from my car, but can we come with you? I'll leave my car here."

He grimaced. "I don't know, ma'am. I'm still on duty. Got stuff to do. My day's not over yet. I can't put your life in danger by bringing you along with me. Rules are rules. Best you go back to the house. Stay warm and dry till this storm lets up."

Tears pooled in my eyes. "*Please*, it's more dangerous if I stay."

His half-arched eyebrow and flicker of a smile said, *You're wasting my time, ma'am.* Did he think I was making this up? He shook his head. "Much as I'd like to, it's against the rules. I could take you to a specific destination, a courtesy ride, after I deal with this flat tire, sure, but just having you ride around with me? Ma'am, we don't normally do that."

"You see this weather? You think *anything* about today's normal? *Please*," I begged. "If you don't take me with you, I'll drive myself."

He regarded me thoughtfully, weighing up his options. "Okay, but I'm going to have to pat you down first. You must keep in mind that being right-handed, my gun's in a holster on my right side and is in easy reach of anyone in the passenger seat. Just procedure, nothin' personal."

Blood rushed to my face, my scalp tingling with caught-in-the-cookie-jar-fear, as if he knew that the bulk in my pocket was a pistol. "No problem," I said. "Let me just quickly get my dog."

I got inside Pippa's Toyota, closing the door behind me. Beanie was jumping all over the place. The officer had his eyes peeled on me through his window. I couldn't put the gun back in the glove compartment without him seeing, so I bent over, laid the pistol gently on the floor, terrified it might go off, and grabbed Beanie so he didn't slip out the car and rush into the woods. I locked the Toyota again and piled myself and my dog into the patrol car. I was soaked, my hair drenched; globules of water and beads of sweat ran down my face. My pulse was galloping. I was a nervous wreck.

"Go ahead," I said, panting. "Search me all you like." I looked back to check if Lee was following us, but it was too rainy to see anything. His radio hissed and crackled incomprehensibly.

He eyed me up. God knows what a mess I looked. "Nah," he said. "You're clean. After this flat I need to make a stop near the River Inn. Folks reported a fallen tree. Then I'll take you to the sheriff's office."

I nodded, my arms clasped around Beanie. This dog was all I had in the world right now. "Let's get *out* of here," I said.

As we sped up the driveway, I looked back at Cliffside. I never thought I'd be glad to get away from that house, but it was sullied now. Just like my ring. Spoiled forever. Lee and her smirking, self-satisfied sneer filling up my beloved house with her bad aura, and knowing she'd been pulling the triplets' puppet strings all along was the last nail in the coffin for me.

At the top of the driveway, just as we swung a sharp right on Highway One, a fresh onslaught of rain lashing at the windshield, I saw Dan and Kate in the front seats of Dan's pickup. Their heads whipped round in our direction as Dan's car swerved into the driveway, his foot flat down on the pedal. I pictured Jen still banging on the laundry room door.

"Can you go any faster?" I pressed the officer. "I need to get away from here, *now*." I wondered about Pippa, where she had got to, and where my Land Rover was, and why Dan and Kate were in one car. Had Pippa gone to her meeting with the engineer, after all?

The officer squinted into his rearview mirror. "Somethin' bad happen back there, ma'am? You ran out of your house like a bat outta hell. And how come you need to speak to the sheriff?"

"Long story, but my life's in danger, and not because of the storm. My late husband's ex-wife is a psycho, and she and her kids are trying to take over my house. They tried to kill me."

He shook his head. "I see a lot of domestic violence," he said. "Sad but true. Glad to help in any way I can. Though I always took the lady to be very nice, very friendly."

"She's dangerous. Thanks for helping. You may have saved my life. As soon as you can get me to the police station, the better."

The officer opened his mouth to reply but something stopped him. His eyes grew large and round, his lip curled in disgust. The answer to my question about Pippa loomed into view.

"Jesus," the officer said. "D'you see what I see?"

Pippa's black SUV was up ahead, broken down on the side of the highway. At first it looked like a road-kill accident; blood was everywhere. A deer? But as we drew closer, I spotted her body, squished in two by her big tank of a car, her head out of sight, lodged under the vehicle, her legs ungainly splayed in a pool of fresh, vermillion blood. The back tire was deflated like an empty balloon. My stomach turned.

"Holy moly, close your eyes, ma'am. This is an accident you do *not* want to see. That poor lady was trying to change her freakin' tire. Oh, man, what a mess!"

I turned my head away from the gruesome scene. Dan, I thought. It had to be. Not only had they lured me into their trap, but Pippa too. A "liability" they needed to get rid of? They'd used her to help hatch their plan. But after she rescued me and screwed things up for them, they wanted her dead. She knew too much. Or was it revenge? *It could have been me that time Dan showed me how to change a tire.*

"This is no accident," I told the officer. "It's murder. I bet you anything you'll find a nail or something wedged into that tire." Pippa under her car's wheel made me retch. Whatever she'd done, she didn't deserve this. I began to recount my long story to the officer, but he wasn't really listening, too preoccupied with calling for help.

The hour that followed was a blur. Even now I can't remember the sequence. The rain had become so terrifying I feared the patrol car might get washed off the road completely. At some point I was alone with Beanie, while the officer—Bill, he said his name was—prowled around outside, waiting for help. But when I rolled the window down to peer out, I could see neither hide nor hair of him. Thunder roared. Spidery, luminescent veins of lightning crackled above, firing the sky up in a blaze of white, so loud they felt like explosions. Beanie and I stayed put in the car, me clutching on to him for dear life. Where could we go? Tears filled my vision. I couldn't see, and all I heard was the lashing of rain, pounding on the car's roof and intermittently the police radio, with urgent messages and promises to get to the scene ASAP. We couldn't leave, we had to wait for backup, for a tow truck to arrive and more officers. For the sheriff. An ambulance. For extra police to come and save the day, to take Dan and the others in for questioning. Outside the safety of the patrol car, I wasn't even sure what was going on. Before Bill had gone off, I had managed to blurt out most of my story. Whether he believed me or not, I wasn't sure. The calm look on his face was of skepticism, the twitch of a smirk, incredulity. As if Lee and I—two catty wives fighting over property—were just bickering, and it was a "domestic situation" best left alone. Lee had smiled at him so charmingly when he had buzzed on the door: a pretty, wide-eyed blonde who might fool any man.

I wanted to get the hell away from Cliffside, even from Big Sur, but my only option was to carry on sitting in the patrol car like a dumb target. I didn't even have that gun anymore. But then I remembered how I'd told Lee about the buried money, and I smiled. No wonder Dan was in such a rush to get back home. Lee would have phoned them on my cell. They'd be down in the woods, right this second, laden with picks and shovels, digging away by the redwood in the pouring rain, clawing at the earth on their hands and knees.

More voices clamored on the patrol radio, but when I leaned out the window—rain slamming into my ears and eyes—I couldn't see Bill anywhere. Had he walked back to Cliffside? From the information crunching through on his radio, the whole of Monterey County was suffering this flash flooding. With Beanie shaking from fear of the thunderstorm, and me shivering, the car was our only refuge. And then it all happened at once. Police sirens. The rumble of helicopters swooping in from above. Machine gun fire? I buzzed down the window again but even wilder torrents of rain flew in, so I had to zap it back up again. All the commotion was happening further down, towards the ocean, from the sound of what I supposed must be gunfire.

I buzzed down the window all the way this time, despite the water gushing inside. It was twilight, visibility almost nil with the rain.

That's when Beanie jumped out.

CHAPTER FIFTY-FOUR

I leapt out of the passenger seat, onto the road, but didn't dare look at the bloody devastation of Pippa beneath the car. Rivers of muddy water rushed towards me from the banks on the side of the highway, streaming down from the mountains. I belted my mackintosh and pulled up the collar, but within seconds I was drenched anyway, my feet squelching in my sneakers. Beanie had darted towards Cliffside and my heart clattered with dread of losing him for good. How would I find him in this turmoil? Another torrent flooded towards the road, washing with it a massive boulder in its wake, which smashed into Pippa's car nudging it several feet sideways and dislodging her body. Nowhere was safe, least of all the side of the road with mounds of wet mud clumping down the banks, flowing in brick-red estuaries and gushing waves.

I yelled out to Bill, my yodeling voice a whisper in the ruckus, but couldn't see him anywhere.

I bolted for my life.

I ran and ran and ran, away from the sluicing mud. Down, down, towards the ocean. Down towards Cliffside. I had no choice. Rain lashed at me like a whip; a wind I had never known in California before howled around my ears. I stumbled down ferny, sloshy banks; anything to escape the rivers of water surging at me, swirling around my feet like eddies in white water, splashing and splattering mud.

At the crest of Cliffside's driveway two patrol cars like tin cans after target practice lay in the middle of the lane, peppered with hundreds of bullet holes. Three officers, including Bill, lay dead in pools of their own blood, diluted now with the washing rain. Another roar above me. An engine this time. I ducked into the woods at the side of the driveway and, looking up, saw a huge helicopter overhead, and a man in black hanging halfway out, a machine gun firing at everything and anything. An explosion behind me and a lance of orange light, the smell of gasoline. Was that our patrol car I was just in going up in flames?

These didn't look like state or highway patrol helicopters, but something out of a blockbuster. Whoever it was meant serious business. Lee must have dug up the money and somehow these bastards had found out. *How?* A chill ran down my spine.

I kept myself hidden, out of sight, sometimes crawling like an animal on my hands and knees, and when I couldn't hear anything, I sprinted in quick bouts, as fast as I could. I'd hide somewhere later, but I had to keep going. An old, hundred-foot pine tree snapped like a toothpick, crashing only twenty feet away from me. This was a ferocious mudslide, a living entity, and I was caught in the middle of it. My best chance was to make it to the beach. I thanked God for my dull gray raincoat, and dull brown hair, and mud-splattered camouflage. I just prayed those bastards hadn't shot little Beanie.

I don't know how much time went by but soon it was nearly dusk. The helicopters had finally gone, and I could no longer hear any more man-made noises. No cries, no car engines, no shooting. Nothing. Still, the rain wouldn't let up.

I kept pushing my aching limbs through the woods towards the house. Stealthily, as fast as I could manage with my weak ankle. Beanie might head straight there. I'd find him, grab a leash from the hallway, and make my way down to the beach. Then I'd be able to scramble my way back out at Pfeiffer Beach and seek help.

Whatever had happened happened and was over. The fact that the helicopters had gone made me wonder if any living thing was left alive. I doubted anyone would be at the house. Would Lee have let Jen out of the laundry room? Lee and the triplets would all be down by the woods, by the redwood tree.

But then I heard Beanie bark, and I followed the sound. I was right, it was coming from the house. I passed by the Toyota and stopped. Miraculously, it was still in one piece, albeit sprayed with bullet holes. I opened the door and snatched the gun from the floor. Just in case I needed it. I still had no idea if it was loaded or not. It scared the shit out of me, so I held it out in front of me, terrified it might go off on its own in my coat pocket, with all my brusque movements and running.

The sun had set, and tigerish stripes in orange and cobalt blue patterned the horizon, peeping through the swathe of clouds, but quickly disappeared again under the heaving gray mass of the storm. Apart from the odd *woof* from Beanie, coming from inside the house, all I could hear was the slashing rain.

But then I heard a cry. A human cry. Someone in pain? Jen? My heart reached out. Against my better judgment, I entered the house. It too had been peppered with bullet holes, some of the glass shattered.

The door had been blasted open, and I stepped lightly into the hallway, but the squelching of my soaked feet and wet sneakers squeaking on the floor made it impossible for me to be soundless. Apart from that, Cliffside was eerily silent, the lights flickering on and off. I grabbed a leash for Beanie, hanging by the door, and pricked up my ears for any sound. I couldn't see or hear him. I stood stock-still. Had I imagined those cries? I tiptoed ahead, the gun still held out in front of me. I felt like a cop, or would have if I knew how to manage a firearm. Muffled sobs. I spun around and saw her: Jen bent over, crying in the kitchen, her pale blond hair flopped wet across her face, dampening her cries. Not locked in the laundry room, after all. I was standing in the same place where I'd had the showdown with Lee, near the top of the stairwell. A voice inside my head warned me what a fool I was. *Get out. Run towards the front door.*

I wanted to rush to help Jen, but instinct told me to wait. Was this another ruse? Were they using her as bait? "Jen?" I called across the room. "Are you okay?"

"They've killed them all," she bawled. "Who the *fuck* were those guys? What the fuck just happened?"

A dart of guilt jabbed at me. I'd done this. But I couldn't help feeling relief, too.

Thunder roared outside. A rumble so deep and raw, I felt the earth roll beneath my feet like a dragon surging from below the earth. Just as I took a step towards Jen, the whole house shook, the alarm sounded like a siren, the walls trembled, the great glass windows rattled in unison, shifting forwards, then backwards, then side to side. Backwards. Forwards… like a ship in a storm…

An earthquake. I hadn't imagined things could get worse.

I held on to the bannister but the stairway swayed and I lost my balance. The gun flew from my hand and clunked down each step. I lost my footing and fell after it, clinging to the bannister as it snapped in two, splintering like a cheap matchstick. I landed on my side with a thud, the ground buckling beneath me, the floor suddenly a small hill, rippling underneath: a living being like an undulating serpent. I tried to scramble to my feet. An excruciating pain seared through my right thigh as I limped ahead, not even seeing where I was going. The wall was coming in on me, golden stone crumbling like cake mixture, the white ceiling folding in like whipped cream. A smash, rubble tumbling around me in great chunks and slabs, just missing my head by inches.

A great cloud of dust choked the atmosphere. I tasted grit and sand, my gums and teeth clogged with filth. I spat and cleared my throat only to breathe in another cloud of filmy particles swirling in the thick white air. I shook my hair. Chunks of plaster landed on my shoulders, which were sore from my thumpy landing. I blinked away the dust congesting my vision, sticking my lashes together. I couldn't see a thing.

A piercing scream. Jen.

"Jen?" I shouted into the choked swirl of rubble.

Nothing.

I covered my eyes with my hands, my lungs wheezing from the haze of particles, debris flying and smashing, dangling and shredded from what was the ceiling only a minute ago. A piece of mattress poked through. A lamp shattered to smithereens.

I pulled the raincoat hood over my head and curved my nose down into my sweater to help myself breathe. There was another scream from somewhere above me. Kate?—at least I think it was her. The house creaked then tilted. The ground suddenly vertical, I tumbled like Alice through the rabbit hole and was in my bedroom on the ground floor, the great glass walls exploding as if a bomb had been detonated. The bathroom slid towards the ocean, part of the house falling in a great crack as loud as a firework.

In front of me, through the whirling clouds of dust, I could just make out a faint beam of light. I frantically crawled towards it. Sharp spikes of wall and upside down ceiling ripped into my hands and knees. Shards of broken floor tile stuck up like daggers. A TV spiraled across what was left of the room like a Frisbee.

Above me, I heard a great groan. It was Cliffside moaning in pain.

She was breaking apart.

More screams from above and then water flowing as if a dam had been released, mud whooshing through every crack, every orifice of the house. A river of oozing, russet mud, thick and red like blood gushing through arteries.

With only one eye open, my vision a blur, I kept crawling through the hole until I reached the light. I let out a gasp and filled my lungs with oxygen.

Fresh air, at last.

I eased and squeezed my body through the last part of the opening, glass slashing and ripping my coat, my mouth sucking at the clean air. I coughed and spluttered, my lungs thick with film. I had arrived at the terrace, where the hot tub was, and I stumbled towards the garden, falling over myself in a race to get away from the house before it caved on top of me. Before the deluge of flowing mud washed me over the cliff's edge.

Run. Run. You can do it.

"Core of steel," Juan's voice championed. That's what he used to tell me whenever I doubted myself. That I had a "core of steel." "You can do anything you put your mind to," he'd tell me. "You're my smart cookie, that's why I love you so much."

I heard a bark in the distance and followed the sound. Beanie. My guide.

My only friend in the world.

CHAPTER FIFTY-FIVE

It was only after I was well into the woods that I dared look back.

Just half of Cliffside remained. The red Mini Cooper hung like a limpet on the brink of the cliff, and Pippa's Toyota somersaulted like a dead leaf blowing in the wind towards the ocean. I heard a great explosion somewhere on the rocks below.

Cliffside was a crumpled heap of smashed glass and stone. Its lush mossy roof sat like a garish wig as estuaries of mud poured over her.

A hawk circled above.

I spun my benumbed head around toward the woods and focused back on my exodus. I had no choice but to continue towards the beach. Rivers of water gushed towards where I had been, just minutes earlier.

I passed the redwood and there lay Lee amongst the ferns, bespattered like a bright yellow star in my raincoat. My eye skimmed down to her hand, and I gasped in horror at what they'd done: hacked off her finger to a bloody stump, where my engagement ring had been just a few hours earlier. When they chopped off her finger, was it *me* they thought they'd found? *Revenge for the eight million.* I hoped they'd at least done it after they'd shot her, however vile she'd been. I turned my eyes away in disgust, saliva puckering my cheeks. I wanted to vomit. Dan lay near his mother, bullet holes like red paintball splotches in his back, the spade flung to one side.

All the money gone, the hole in the earth dark and gaping, swallowing up the twilight.

How did these vicious criminals *know*? How did they arrive so swiftly on the scene?

Then it dawned on me: my phone. My cell phone that Lee had stolen. If they'd had any suspicions about the money, they would have bugged it, hacked into it, would have listened in on conversations. They could do that, even when it was on airplane mode. Juan had warned me often enough how a phone acts as a GPS, a listening device. So that conversation with Lee when I told her about the buried money? All recorded. And my phone would have led them to Lee's exact position once she'd dug it up.

Karma's a bitch.

Beanie's distant bark snapped me back to attention, and I soldiered on, shock numbing every sense in my body, except my desire to survive, adrenaline spurring me forward.

The ocean's great breakers were getting louder as I slogged on through the dell of pines and redwoods, tripping as I scrambled with my limp, trying to keep myself on the path. I still couldn't see Beanie but heard his barks. I swallowed. My teeth like sandpaper, my throat barbed and dry as a cat's tongue.

I kept running.

I stopped for breath, my pulse thudding in my red-hot ears, but looked up and noticed water beginning to pour towards me in a cascade bringing with it rocks and earth. I turned my attention back to my escape, my hand clutching my rasping throat, wishing I had water to quench my thirst. As I ran with all my might, I tore off the ragged, ripped-up coat I was wearing and flung it to the ground. It was slowing me down like a parachute.

Run. Run. Run. The mudslide was a living entity, not stopping for breath.

I had now caught up with Beanie and followed him blindly. Rain lashing at my face. Feet stumbling. I could hardly see through my storm-whipped hair plastered to my face by debris. Beanie knew the way, his little legs taking us to safer ground. Down, down, towards the bay.

Oxygen whipped from my lungs and, exhausted, I finally reached the beach, where I hoped I could flee south then inland towards Pfeiffer Canyon Bridge.

I inspected my leg, which peeked through my torn, blood- and mud-soaked jeans, but I strangely didn't feel pain.

I sat on my favorite rock and caught back my breath, Beanie by my side. I took off each sneaker and emptied out glassfuls of muddy water, then put the soggy things back on, reluctantly. The waves rolled in, slamming the sand on every angry break. Hissing, frothing foam. Tides of mud, majestic redwoods, pines, and rocks, like Niagara Falls, tumbled in a steady wash over Cliffside, burying the place in a giant earthy tomb. I watched in horror, tears streaming down my face, as what was left of my house vanished before my eyes.

A new sound joined in the mayhem. More helicopters, but different from those before, dipped and spun above where Cliffside had been, shining beams of light onto the wreckage of this mudslide, which now covered the macabre deaths. The helicopters patrolled the sky, hovering over the landslide like wasps on honey. The aftermath well buried now, I wondered if anyone even realized what had gone down, had any idea what lay beneath? It was getting much darker, the sky covered in a thick layer of inky black rain clouds. Visibility really low.

Nobody had spotted me, the mud-splattered speck that I was.

But something told me I'd survive.

CHAPTER FIFTY-SIX

As soon as I mustered up enough strength I plodded ahead, hoping I could find my way out at Pfeiffer Canyon Bridge. Fortune was on my side; the tide was low, which meant if I was careful, I wouldn't get swept out to sea. The helicopters continued to circle, but nobody had seen me. A sudden gust of wind pushed away some dark clouds and lit up the sky a touch, but it was now well past dusk. Caked from head to foot in mud, the gray sweater I was wearing beneath melded me into the gray landscape. I was as good as invisible.

But out of the corner of my right eye, sliding into my peripheral vision, a helicopter swept in above the side of the beach, hovering there. A laser of light spiraled around me. I had finally been spotted. I froze in the glare of the beam, my vision blinded, but when the spotlight was off me, and in the blaze of after-image, I saw the helicopter was a different shape from the others now hovering above the wreckage. I held my breath. It dipped its nose and landed, still quite a distance from me, and a figure jumped out.

A figure I knew better than my own body.

I stared, mouth open in amazement. My heart floundered with disbelief. Surely it was the shock of surviving all this? The deaths, the earthquake, and seeing Cliffside disappear beneath the landslide? My eyes were playing tricks on me, weren't they? This was not real. How could it be?

The dark figure started walking towards me, feet kicking the sand as it moved closer. Each step a statement. Each step a moment closer to my finale. I stayed rooted to the spot, not taking my eyes off him. I wasn't imagining it. Or was I? But the shock I held in my eyes, and the leap of my heart, told me it could be just that.

Juan.

CHAPTER FIFTY-SEVEN

The next day I listened intently to the news on the radio, counting my blessings that I was alive.

"Six civilians and four highway patrol officers are thought to have perished along the Big Sur coastline in what is being described as the mother of all landslides that was partly activated after a 4.4 magnitude earthquake hit the coast on Friday. This massive landslide along California's iconic Highway One has buried the road under an impenetrable layer of rock and earth.

"With power cuts, faulty radio networks, and all evidence buried under the wash of mud, nobody knows for certain why so many officers had gathered together in the line of duty on Friday evening. Witnesses say they heard gunshots, but thunder and lightning, and loss of electricity at that time make it impossible to ascertain what really happened. Ongoing investigating is underway.

"Five million cubic yards of earth has buried not only the highway but the coast beneath it, taking in its wake a multi-million-dollar home named Cliffside. Ten people are said to be missing, presumed dead.

"The landslide has added thirteen acres of additional coastline and put Highway One under forty feet of dirt and rock, isolating Big Sur even more after the closure of Pfeiffer Canyon Bridge. This winter storm has caused an estimated two billion dollars in damage to state and local highways.

"The names of the Cliffside victims have not yet been confirmed but are assumed to be the residents of the house, their dog, and a visiting friend. The names of the four officers involved will be released shortly. Stay tuned for more updates."

EPILOGUE

Forgiving someone doesn't happen overnight. It's like a sports injury that will never go away completely, but you learn to live with it, and then one day, you realize you're not in pain anymore.

If only we could control our own hearts, cherry-pick each feeling, choose only the sensible best for ourselves, stamp out love whenever we know it hurts. But we don't get to govern how we feel, not deep down inside, anyway. All you can do is follow your heart, even if it leads you to your own blissful ruin.

We've been living on this island—somewhere in the Mediterranean—for over two years now. Being "dead" is surprisingly easy. And for Juan, being dead is a piece of cake. After all, he'd had a head start after he faked his own death in that car accident at Ragged Point.

He'd got himself into a real mess with that eight million, much of which he'd been saving as a gift for his three children, to buy them each a property when he took over Cliffside, to help them start their adult lives. He didn't want to leave them with nothing after they turned eighteen. But things had corkscrewed out of control with his VIP client, and after we buried it, Juan had to do a runner, "kill" himself to save his own skin. Something I had no idea about.

I was in the dark all along, a victim, not least of my own paranoia. I speak for myself as well as for Juan when I say we were both guilty of a crime, albeit indirectly. We all had a part to play in the events that unfolded, especially Pippa. Pippa was the one person Juan had let in on his secret. She had no idea about the money or whatever nasty crime syndicate Juan had inadvertently got mixed up with, but she did know Juan was in danger and had to hide. She was his confidante, and he had given her instructions to inform me that he was not dead, but very much alive, to let me know this after he had made his escape. He did this to protect me, he told me later, so I wouldn't talk him out of it or try to follow him.

But Pippa, of course, had kept me in the dark.

The drone spying on me? That was Juan controlling the drone from his computer, from his hiding place. The I'LL BE WATCHING YOU text? Juan had meant that as a friendly message, assuming Pippa had let me know he was still alive. At the time, it had freaked me out, thinking my life was at stake. But of course it was the lyrics from our song, "Every Breath You Take." Another clue I missed. How could Juan have imagined that his old friend Pippa had betrayed his trust? That his text would seem creepy and menacing? He thought it would offer me comfort.

The roses and the note? Also Juan. He had made an order via Interflora in Peru, where he was hiding. They screwed up the message when he dictated it by phone. Our favorite line from *Casablanca*—something Juan would say to me all the time—got transformed into a sinister threat.

Instead of "Here's looking at you," they'd put: HERE. LOOKING AT YOU, in scary capital letters separated with a period and worse, spaced on different lines. I should have worked that out, but my fear of being spied on had taken me over. Juan had supposed the message was a sure-fire way of me knowing it was him—a typical Juan message.

Strange how paranoia can take over and not let you see or think straight.

The Facebook banner that popped up on my laptop? Juan too. He was desperate by this point, because I was ignoring his messages. He'd got access to a friend's computer, someone who did Facebook ads regularly. That way it couldn't be traced back to him.

And the landline calls, Juan too, although the triplets had cut the connection, of course.

Juan lay in hiding in various countries in South America, perplexed as to why I hadn't responded, wondering why I hadn't reached out to him. Pippa had told him I wasn't answering her calls. Even insinuated I was dating again. Juan didn't dare come and see me directly. His VIP client's people had ears and eyes. Juan didn't want to put me in danger.

Then he ended up in jail in Guatemala. He had "borrowed" someone's identity card and this person happened to have a criminal record for shoplifting. Juan got arrested when they stopped him for speeding one time. ("The fucking irony of it," he joked later.) He couldn't reveal his true identity in case word got out, so he ended up doing four months' jail time. Hence his absence of contact.

Meanwhile, as well as the smiley faces and hearts to my mother, Lee had sent messages to Mr. Donner and pretty much all my American contacts telling them I was in England, to make sure nobody dropped by for a visit.

I never did ask Juan the details about the first six months he was on the run, because it didn't even matter anymore. He had to keep his distance from me, in case his pursuers got wind that he was, in fact, alive—that was the gist of it. He'd made a dog's dinner out of the whole thing, his life and mine. Something I won't forget. And for a while, I didn't forgive him either. I too did a disappearance act on *him*—volunteered at an orphanage in Costa Rica for a stint—while I decided what I wanted out of life. I needed time to think things through. And I knew a dose of his own medicine would do him good.

But forgive... you do forgive in the end, don't you? When you truly love someone?

I needed to forgive myself, too. The deaths that followed, especially Jen's. I always had a soft spot for that girl.

I was wrong about Pippa being in cahoots with Lee and the triplets. She genuinely wanted to help me, hence her rescue. I guess guilt had finally caught up with her. That sneaky call I eavesdropped on when I thought she was talking to Dan? It was *Juan* who was on the line, not Dan. Juan had already rented a helicopter by that point, had got wind that his enemies were sniffing around, and he feared for my life. He was planning to get me out of there and had been waiting for me at the other side of Pfeiffer Canyon Bridge. Lucky I didn't go, or I might have ended up under Pippa's car right alongside her, helping her change her tire.

When I didn't show up with Pippa, Juan was on his way to find me. With all the mayhem that ensued nobody spotted him circling Big Sur in his helicopter searching for me. He refused to lose hope and finally discovered me on the beach with Beanie.

Serendipity.

I've had time to reflect on Pippa's motivation for not telling me that Juan was alive. She must have been hoping that I'd let Juan go, move on, find a new man, and that she'd be his shoulder to cry on (however chipped), and they'd have some sort of friends-to-lovers happily ever after, with me out of the picture. She had suggested to me several times, as I remember, that I forget Juan, urging me to date someone new, sell Cliffside and move on.

Do I forgive Pippa? She saved my life, so I'll always be eternally grateful for that. Forgive and forget. You have to, don't you? If you want to move forward in life?

Juan has regrets. Of course he does, not least the secret he kept from me during our entire relationship, hiding his past, keeping his family under wraps. His excuse was that he was frightened of losing me if I found out the truth, losing his "funny little valentine," he told me, "the love of my life." I had never imagined

Juan could be insecure when it came to me. But I never shared with him the story of my sixth finger, so I do identify with that: pulling a veil over your own history.

As for Juan's supposed vasectomy, I was mistaken. It had never taken place. We're expecting a baby in May, three years to the day he sacrificed his beloved Mustang and Rolex to Ragged Point. I'm clean, of course. Haven't touched a drop of alcohol or any medication since Pippa saw me through that cold turkey.

My father passed away, and my mother met another man. On a cruise, apparently. I read about their engagement in *The Times*. She would have believed, like everyone else, that I was washed away with Cliffside, alongside the triplets, Pippa, and Lee, and all those poor, unsuspecting officers in the line of duty. It was on the news, the names of the deceased, mine included.

My mother's prediction had come true. I had no choice but to let Mum believe I'd lost my life in that earthquake and landslide. I couldn't contact her, or anyone I knew; it was too risky. By all accounts, she recovered from my death pretty quickly. She probably felt a little chuffed that she had warned me all along. *Told you so, you stupid, stupid girl.*

I didn't make Juan's life easy; he had to earn me back. Prove to me he was worthy of my trust. He bought an old stone farmhouse for me, surrounded by lemon groves, restored it, stone by stone, beam by beam, tile by tile, with his own hands. Taught himself on the job. The deeds, of course, are in my name. I accepted his gift of contrition, his peace offering. Because I knew what I wanted; for better, for worse, it was Juan Trujillo.

We lead a simple life now, Juan, Beanie and I, on our sunny island, with our new identities and new house. Juan had a healthy stash he'd stowed away with him when he faked his death. Real money, not tainted. Money he'd earned from before he'd unwittingly got involved laundering for his "VIP client." The rest of that money is in a bank account in my name alone. I will never lose control of my own destiny again, never allow myself to be the guardian of someone else's bad choices. I call the shots now. Literally. I've even learned to shoot a gun. Not that I'll ever need to, I hope, but I won't go through life unprepared again.

Did Juan's client and co believe Juan's "death?" Or ever suspect he was still alive? Who knows, and that's why we remain incognito.

I could have started anew, the way I had planned, adopted a child as a single mum. But when Juan picked me up in that helicopter and took me by the hand, I knew I was done for.

In that second, I learned something important.

Home is where the heart is.

A LETTER FROM ARIANNE

I'd like to say a big thank you, dear reader, for choosing to read *The Wife's House*, and I hope you enjoyed immersing yourself in the story. This book was a very emotional journey for me, both high and low. It started as a dream, when I woke up in my bed startled, after meeting the triplets by the ocean, telling me I was living in their house, and it ended with a different kind of dream when an editor at Bookouture, Helen Jenner, told me she had fallen in love with my book and wanted to publish it. However, along the way, my number one muse and assistant (my beautiful black Labrador, Ludo, who lay at my feet while I wrote) unexpectedly died, leaving me grieving and bereft and with terrible writer's block. This novel holds a part of him and a piece of my heart on every page. Thank you for sharing his journey, too.

If you would like to join a mailing list for alerts on my future novels, please sign up here. You can unsubscribe at any time, and your email address will never be shared.

www.bookouture.com/arianne-richmonde

If you enjoyed *The Wife's House*, I would be so grateful if you'd recommend it to your friends and family and, if you have a moment, leave a review, even if it's just a few lines. It's always wonderful to get readers' thoughts and feedback, and you would also be helping like-minded readers discover my work.

I love chatting with my readers, so please feel free to reach out. You can join me on my *Facebook page* or *Twitter*, or my *website*.

Thanks again for including *The Wife's House* in your library. There are so many fabulous books in the world, I feel honored you chose mine.

Arianne

AuthorArianneRichmonde

@a_richmonde

ariannerichmonde.com

@arianne_richmonde

ACKNOWLEDGEMENTS

Many friends and loved ones have been with me on this journey. From my husband—bringing me home-cooked meals when I was on a writing roll (making sure I never starved—thank you!)—to my team of trusted women, who have given me insight and encouragement from the very first draft.

My amazing editor and publisher, Helen Jenner, thank you from the bottom of my heart, for loving my writing and bringing *The Wife's House* to life. And to the rest of the Bookouture team for your seamless collaboration along every step of the way. It is a joy to work with such consummate professionals, Kim Nash, Noelle Holten, Alexandra Holmes, and Peta Nightingale, and all of you, who know how to make your authors shine. I am so proud to be part of the Bookouture family. Also, thanks to Jane Eastgate and Becca Allen for your eagle eyes.

Betty Kramer, thank you for always believing in me, from the time I turned up on your doorstep when I was nineteen years old and you gave me a home, to reading everything I've ever written, however jumbled. Lisa Cavender, you have bolstered me no end with your cheerleading, great observations, and your laugh that always puts me in a good mood.

Claire Owen, I am indebted to you for coming up with the perfect title, *The Wife's House*. Andrea Robinson, thank you so much for your spot-on and intuitive editorial notes. And Sarah Bedingfield, huge appreciation for your input and detailed edits that helped shape this novel.

Nelle L'Amour, thank you for being the best pen pal a girl could ever ask for—we've been on this crazy trip together. Zoje Stage, you gave me confidence to have faith in my work, thank you for being there.

And Alessandra Torre, your generosity and support mean so much. Sharon Tomas Sastre, you have been amazing, thank you.

Gratitude also to Nancy Sanders, for showing me around Big Sur and sharing some of its beautiful secrets—you inspired this book. Any inaccuracies or embellishments about the region, or liberties with time lines (particularly concerning the collapse of Pfeiffer Canyon Bridge) are my own and the result of a writer's active imagination and creative license.

Lisa Salvary, Cheryl Tenzen, and Paula Swisher, thanks, as always, for your fabulous notes and attention to detail, you are my rocks.

And Suzie Mackenzie, I am so grateful for your wise words and support.

Finally, a big shout out to my readers, new and old, and to all the bloggers who review and recommend my books. You have given me the best job ever.